From #1 *New York Times* bestselling author Nora Roberts comes the second novel in the unforgettable new trilogy of destiny and desire. This is Dana's journey. . . .

Even with all Dana had seen and done, with all she'd been a part of over the last four weeks, it was hard to believe she was stretched out in the backseat of her brother's car, heading back up the steep winding road to the great stone house of Warrior's Peak. And what waited for her there.

It wasn't storming, as it had been on her first trip to the Peak, after receiving that intriguing invitation for "cocktails and conversation" from Rowena and Pitte, an invitation that had gone out to only two other women. And she wasn't alone. And this time, she thought, she knew exactly what she was in for.

Idly, she opened the notebook she'd brought along and read the summary she'd written of the story she'd heard on her first visit to Warrior's Peak.

Each daughter, demi-goddess, has a specific talent or gift. One is art, or beauty, the other is knowledge or truth, the third is courage or valor. A spell is cast on the daughters. The daughters' souls are stolen, locked in a glass box, known as the Box of Souls, which can only be opened by three keys turned by human hands. If the quest is completed, the Box of Souls will be opened and The Daughters of Glass freed. And the three women would have a cool one million dollars each.

An interesting story, Dana mused, until you understood it wasn't a story but fact. Until you understood you were one of the three women who had the means to unlock the Box of Souls. Then it just got weird.

Turn the page for a complete list of titles by Nora Roberts and J. D. Robb from The Berkley Publishing Group . . .

Titles by Nora Roberts

The Chesapeake Bay Saga

SEA SWEPT
RISING TIDES
INNER HARBOR
CHESAPEAKE BLUE

The Dream Trilogy

DARING TO DREAM
HOLDING THE DREAM
FINDING THE DREAM

Titles written as J. D. Robb

NAKED IN DEATH
GLORY IN DEATH
IMMORTAL IN DEATH
RAPTURE IN DEATH
CEREMONY IN DEATH
VENGEANCE IN DEATH
HOLIDAY IN DEATH
CONSPIRACY IN DEATH
LOYALTY IN DEATH
WITNESS IN DEATH
JUDGMENT IN DEATH
BETRAYAL IN DEATH
SEDUCTION IN DEATH
REUNION IN DEATH
PURITY IN DEATH
PORTRAIT IN DEATH
IMITATION IN DEATH

SILENT NIGHT
(with Susan Plunkett, Dee Holmes, and Claire Cross)

OUT OF THIS WORLD
(with Laurell K. Hamilton, Susan Krinard, and Maggie Shayne)

Key of Knowledge

NORA ROBERTS

DOUBLEDAY LARGE PRINT HOME LIBRARY EDITION

JOVE BOOKS, NEW YORK

This Large Print Edition, prepared especially for Doubleday Large Print Home Library, contains the complete, unabridged text of the original Publisher's Edition.

KEY OF KNOWLEDGE

A Jove Book / published by arrangement with the author

PRINTING HISTORY
Jove edition / December 2003

Copyright © 2003 by Nora Roberts
Excerpt from *Key of Valor* copyright © 2003 by Nora Roberts
Cover design by Richard Hasselberger
Book design by Kristin del Rosario

For information address: The Berkley Publishing Group,
a division of Penguin Group (USA) Inc.,
375 Hudson Street, New York, New York 10014.

ISBN: 0-7394-4036-5

A JOVE BOOK®
Jove Books are published by The Berkley Publishing Group,
a division of Penguin Group (USA) Inc.,
375 Hudson Street, New York, New York 10014.
JOVE and the "J" design
are trademarks belonging to Penguin Group (USA) Inc.
PRINTED IN THE UNITED STATES OF AMERICA

This Large Print Book carries the
Seal of Approval of N.A.V.H.

For Ruth and Marianne,
who are that most precious of gifts—
friends

It takes two to speak the truth—
one to speak, and another to hear.

—THOREAU

Chapter One

Dana Steele considered herself a flexible, open-minded woman, with no less than her fair share of patience, tolerance, and humor.

A number of people might have disagreed with this self-portrait.

But what did they know?

In one month's time, her life had, through no fault of her own, taken a sharp turn off its course and into territory so strange and uncharted she couldn't explain the route or the reason even to herself.

But wasn't she going with the flow?

She'd taken it on the chin when Joan, the malicious library director, had promoted her own niece by marriage over other, more qualified, more dependable, more astute, and certainly more attractive candidates. She'd sucked it up, hadn't she, and done her job?

And when that completely undeserved promotion had caused a squeeze resulting in a certain more qualified employee's hours and paycheck being cut to the bone, had she pummeled the despicable Joan and the incessantly pert Sandi to bloody pulps?

No, she had not. Which in Dana's mind illustrated her exquisite restraint.

When her greedy bloodsucker of a landlord raised her rent to coincide with her pay cut, had she clamped her hands around his scrawny neck and squeezed until his beady eyes popped?

Again, she had demonstrated control of heroic proportions.

Those virtues might've been their own reward, but Dana enjoyed more tangible benefits.

Whoever had come up with that business about a door opening when a window closes hadn't known much about Celtic gods. Dana's door hadn't opened. It had been blown clean off its hinges.

Even with all she'd seen and done, with all she'd been a part of over the last four weeks, it was hard to believe that she was now stretched out in the backseat of her brother's car, once again heading up the steep, winding road to the great stone house of Warrior's Peak.

And what waited for her there.

It wasn't storming, as it had been on her first trip to the Peak after receiving that intriguing invitation for "cocktails and conversation" from Rowena and Pitte—an invitation that had gone out to only two other women. And she wasn't alone. And this time, she thought, she knew exactly what she was in for.

Idly, she opened the notebook she'd brought along and read the summary she'd written of the story she'd heard on her first visit to Warrior's Peak.

The young Celtic god who would be king falls for a human girl during his traditional sojourn in the mortal dimension. (Which I relate to spring break.) Young stud's parents indulge him, break the rules and allow him to bring the maid behind what's called either Curtain of Dreams or Curtain of Power, and into the realm of the gods.

This is cool with some of the gods, but pisses others off.

War, strife, politics, intrigue follow.

Young god becomes king, makes human wife queen. They have three daughters.

Each daughter—demigoddess—has a specific talent or gift. One is art, or beauty, the second is knowledge or truth, the third is courage or valor.

Sisters are close and happy and grow to young womanhood, tra-la-la, under the watchful eye of the female teacher and the male warrior guardian given the task by god-king.

Teacher and warrior fall in love, which blinds the eye enough that it isn't kept sharp on the daughters.

Meanwhile, bad guys are plotting away. They don't take to human or half-human types in their rarefied world, especially in positions of power. Dark forces go to work. A particularly evil-minded sorcerer (probably related to Library Joan) takes charge. A spell is cast on the daughters while teacher and warrior are starry-eyed. The daughters' souls are stolen, locked in a glass box, known as the Box of Souls, which can only be opened by three keys turned by human hands. Although the gods know where to find the keys, none of them can break the spell or free the souls.

Teacher and warrior are cast out, sent through the Curtain of Dreams into the mortal world. There, in each generation three human women are born who have the means to find the keys and end the curse. Teacher and warrior must find the women, and these women must be given the choice of accepting the quest or rejecting it.

Each, in turn, has one moon phase to find a key. If the first fails, game over. And not without penalty—each would lose an undisclosed year of her life. If she succeeds, the second woman takes up the quest, and so on. An annoyingly cryptic clue—the only help teacher and warrior are allowed to give the three lucky women—is revealed at the start of the four-week cycle.

If the quest is completed, the Box of Souls will be opened and the Daughters of Glass freed. And the three *women will each be awarded a cool one million dollars.*

A pretty story, Dana mused, until you understood it wasn't a story but fact. Until you understood you were one of the three women who had the means to unlock the Box of Souls.

Then it just got weird.

Add in some dark, powerful sorcerer god named Kane who really wanted you to fail and could make you see things that weren't there—and not see things that were—and the whole business took on a real edge.

But there were good parts too. That first night she'd met two women who had turned out to be really interesting people, and soon she felt as though she'd known them all her life. Well enough, Dana reminded herself, that the three of them were going into business together.

And one of them had turned out to be the love of her brother's life.

Malory Price, the organized soul with the artist's heart, not only had outwitted a sorcerer with a few thousand years under his belt but had found the key, opened the lock, and bagged the guy.

All in less than four weeks.

It was going to be hard for Dana and their pal Zoe to top that one.

Then again, Dana reminded herself, she and Zoe didn't have the distraction of romance to clog the works. And she didn't have a kid to worry about, as Zoe did.

Nope, Dana Steele was footloose and fancy-free, with nothing to pull her focus away from the prize.

If she was next at bat, Kane had better set for the long ball.

Not that she had anything against romance, she mused, letting the notebook close as she watched the blaze and blur of trees through the window. She liked men.

Well, most men. She'd even been in love with one, a million years ago. Of course, that had been a result of youthful stupidity. She was much wiser now.

Jordan Hawke might have come back to Pleasant Valley, temporarily, a few weeks ago, and he might have wheedled his way into being part of the quest. But he wasn't a part of Dana's world any longer.

In her world he didn't exist. Except when he was writhing in pain and agony from some horrible freak accident or a debilitating and disfiguring illness.

It was too bad that her brother, Flynn, had the bad taste to be his friend. But she could forgive Flynn for it, and even give him points for loyalty, since he and Jordan and Bradley Vane had been pals since childhood.

And somehow or other, both Jordan and Brad were connected to the quest. It was something she would have to tolerate for the duration.

She shifted as Flynn turned to drive through the open iron gates, angled her head so that she could look up at one of the two stone warriors that guarded the entrance to the house.

Big, handsome, and dangerous, Dana thought. She'd always liked men who were—even if they were sculptures.

She scooted up, but kept the long length of her legs on the seat—the only way for her to ride comfortably in the back of the car.

She was a tall woman with an amazon's build that would've suited that stone warrior. She combed her fingers through her long swing of brown hair. Since Zoe, the currently unemployed hairdresser and Dana's new best friend, had styled it and added highlights, it fell into that casual bell shape with little or no help from Dana. It saved her time in the morning, which she appreciated, as morning wasn't her best time of day. And the cut was flattering, which suited her vanity.

Her eyes, a deep, dark brown, locked on the elegant sprawl of black stone that was the house at Warrior's Peak. Part castle, part fortress, part fantasy, it spread over the rise, speared up into a sky as clear as black glass.

Lights shimmered against its many windows, and still, Dana imagined, there were so many secrets in the shadows.

She'd lived in the valley below for all the twenty-seven years of her life. And for all of them, the Peak had been a fascination. Its shape and shadow on the rise above her pretty little town had always struck her as something out of a faerie tale—and not the tidied-up, bloodless versions either.

She'd often wondered what it would be like to live there, to wander through all the rooms, to walk out on the parapet or gaze down from a tower. To live so high, in such magnificent solitude, with the majesty of the hills all around and the charm of the woods only steps beyond the door.

She stirred herself now, shifting around so her head was between Flynn's and Malory's.

They were so damn cute together, she thought. Flynn with his deceptively easygoing nature, Malory with her need for order. Flynn with his lazy green eyes, Malory with her bright, bold blue ones. There was Mal, with her stylish coordinated outfits, and Flynn, who was lucky if he could put his hands on a pair of matching socks.

Yes, Dana decided, they were perfect for one another.

She thought of Malory as her sister now, through circumstance and fate. And really, wasn't that how Flynn had become her brother all those years ago when her father and his mother had married and merged families?

When her dad had gotten sick, she'd leaned hard on Flynn. She supposed they'd leaned hard on each other more than once. When the doctors had recommended that her father move to a warmer climate, when Flynn's mother had shoved the responsibility of running the *Valley Dispatch* into Flynn's hands and he'd found himself the publisher of a small-town paper instead of living his dream of honing his reporting skills in New York.

When the boy she'd loved had left her.

When the woman he'd intended to marry had left him.

Yeah, they'd had each other—through thick and thin. And now, in their own ways, they each had Malory. It was a nice way to round things out.

"Well." Dana laid her hands on their shoulders. "Here we go again."

Malory turned, gave Dana a quick smile. "Nervous?"

"Not so much."

"It's either you or Zoe tonight. Do you want to be picked?"

Ignoring the little flutter in her stomach, Dana shrugged. "I just want to get going on it. I don't know why we have to go through all this ceremony. We already know what the deal is."

"Hey, free food," Flynn reminded her.

"There is that. Wonder if Zoe's here yet. We can dive into whatever our hosts, Rowena and Pitte, picked up in the land of milk and honey, then get this show on the road."

She climbed out the minute Flynn

stopped the car, then Dana stood with her hands on her hips, studying the house while the ancient man with a shock of white hair hurried up to take the keys.

"Maybe you're not nervous." Malory came to stand beside her, linked arms. "But I am."

"Why? You dunked your shot."

"It's still up to all of us." She looked up at the white flag with its key emblem that flew atop the tower.

"Just think positive." Dana drew in a long breath. "Ready?"

"If you are." Malory held out a hand for Flynn's.

They walked toward the huge entrance doors, which swung open at their approach.

Rowena stood in the flood of light, her hair a firestorm falling over the bodice of a sapphire velvet dress. Her lips were curved in welcome, her exotic green eyes bright with it.

Gems sparkled at her ears, her wrists, her fingers. On a long braided chain that hung nearly to her waist was a crystal as clear as water and as fat as a baby's fist.

"Welcome." Her voice was low and musical and seemed to hold hints of forests and caves where faeries might dwell. "I'm so pleased to see you." She held out her hands to Malory, then leaned forward and kissed both of her cheeks in turn. "You look wonderful, and well."

"So do you, always."

With a light laugh, Rowena reached for Dana's hand. "And you. Mmm, what a wonderful jacket." She skimmed her fingers along the sleeve of the butter-soft leather. But even as she spoke, she was looking beyond them and out the door. "You didn't bring Moe?"

"It didn't seem like quite the occasion for a big, clumsy dog," Flynn told her.

"It's always the occasion for Moe." Rowena rose on her toes to peck Flynn's cheek. "You must promise to bring him next time."

She slid her arm through Flynn's. "Come, we'll be comfortable in the parlor."

They crossed the great hall with its mosaic floor, moved through the wide arch to the spacious room glowing from the flames in the massive hearth and the light of dozens of white candles.

Pitte stood at the mantel, a glass of amber liquid in his hand. The warrior at the gate, Dana thought. He was tall, dark, dangerously handsome, with a muscular and ready build that his elegant black suit couldn't disguise.

It was easy to imagine him wearing light armor and carrying a sword. Or sitting astride a huge black horse and wearing a cape that billowed at the gallop.

He gave a slight and courtly bow as they entered.

Dana started to speak, then a movement caught the corner of her eye. The friendly smile vanished from her face, her brows beetled, and her eyes flashed pure annoyance.

"What's he doing here?"

"He," Jordan said dryly as he lifted a glass, "was invited."

"Of course." Smoothly, Rowena pressed a flute of champagne into Dana's hand. "Pitte and I are delighted to have all of you here tonight. Please, be at home. Malory, you must tell me how plans are progressing on your gallery."

With another flute of champagne and a gentle nudge, Rowena had Malory moving toward a chair. After one look at his sister's face, Flynn chose the better part of valor and followed them.

Refusing to retreat, Dana sipped her champagne and scowled at Jordan over the crystal rim of her glass. "Your part in this is finished."

"Maybe it is, maybe it isn't. Either way I get an invitation to dinner from a beautiful woman, especially if she happens to be a goddess, I accept. Nice threads," he commented and fingered the cuff of Dana's jacket.

"Hands off." She jerked her arm out of reach, then plucked a canapé from a tray. "And stay out of my way."

"I'm not in your way." His voice remained mild, and he took a lazy sip of his drink.

Even though Dana wore heeled boots, he had a couple of inches on her. Which was just one more reason to find him irritating. Like Pitte, he could have posed for one of the stone warriors. He was six-three, every inch of it well packed. His dark hair could've used a trim, but that slightly curly, slightly unkempt, slightly too long style suited the power of his face.

He was, always had been, lustily handsome, with blazing blue eyes under black brows, the long nose, the wide mouth, the strong bones combining in a look that could be charming or intimidating depending on his purpose.

Worse, Dana thought, he had an agile and clever mind inside that rock-hard skull. And an innate talent that had made him a wildly successful novelist before he'd hit thirty.

Once, she'd believed they would build a life side by side. But to her mind he'd chosen his fame and his fortune over her.

And in her heart she had never forgiven him for it.

"There are two more keys," he reminded her. "If finding them is important to you, you should be grateful for help. Whatever the source."

"I don't need your help. So feel free to head back to New York anytime."

"I'm going to see this through. Better get used to it."

She snorted, then popped another canapé. "What's in it for you?"

"You really want to know?"

She shrugged. "I couldn't care less. But I'd think even someone with your limited sensitivity would be aware that you bunking at Flynn's is putting a crimp in the works for the turtledoves there."

Jordan followed her direction, noted

Flynn sitting with Malory, and the way his friend absently played with the curling ends of her blond hair.

"I know how to keep out of their way, too. She's good for him," Jordan added.

Whatever else she could say about Jordan—and there was plenty—she couldn't deny that he loved Flynn. So she swallowed some of the bitterness, and washed the taste of it away with champagne.

"Yeah, she is. They're good for each other."

"She won't move in with him."

Dana blinked. "He asked her to move in? To live with him? And she said no?"

"Not exactly. But the lady has conditions."

"Which are?"

"Actual furniture in the living room and he has to redo the kitchen."

"No kidding?" The idea had Dana feeling both amused and sentimental at once. "That's our Mal. Before Flynn knows it, he'll be living in a real house instead of a building with doors and windows and packing boxes."

"He bought dishes. The kind you wash, not the kind you chuck in the trash."

The amusement peaked, bringing shallow dimples to her cheeks. "He did not."

"And knives and forks that aren't plastic."

"Oh, my God, stemware could be next."

"I'm afraid so."

She let out a roll of laughter, toasted to her brother's back. "Hook, line, and sinker."

"That's something I've missed," Jordan murmured. "That's the first time I've heard you laugh and mean it since I've been back."

She sobered instantly. "It didn't have anything to do with you."

"Don't I know it."

Before she could speak again, Zoe McCourt rushed into the room, steps ahead of Bradley Vane. She looked flustered, irritated, and embarrassed. Like a sexy wood sprite, Dana thought, who'd had a particularly bad day.

"I'm sorry. I'm so sorry I'm late."

She wore a short, clingy black dress with long, snug sleeves and an abbreviated hem that showcased her slim and sinuous curves. Her hair, black and glossy, was short and straight with a long fringe of bangs accenting long-lidded amber eyes.

Behind her, Brad looked like some golden faerie-tale prince in an Italian suit.

Seeing them together made Dana think what a stunning couple they made—if you didn't count the frustration emanating from Zoe, or the uncharacteristic stiffness in Brad's stance.

"Don't be silly." Rowena was already up and crossing to them. "You're not at all late."

"I am. My car. I had trouble with my car. They were supposed to fix it, but . . . Well, I'm very grateful Bradley was driving by and stopped."

She didn't sound grateful, Dana noted. She sounded pissed, with that hint of the West Virginia hills in her voice giving the temper a nice little edge.

Rowena made sympathetic noises as she led Zoe to a chair, served her champagne.

"I think I could've fixed it," Zoe muttered.

"That may be." With obvious gratitude, Bradley accepted a drink. "But you'd have ended up with grease all over your dress. Then you'd have needed to go home and change and you'd've been even later. It's hardly a slap in the face to accept a ride from someone you know who's going to exactly the same place at the same time."

"I said I was grateful," Zoe shot back, then took a deep breath. "I'm sorry," she said to the room in general. "It's been one of those days. And I'm nervous on top of it. I hope I haven't held anything up."

"Not at all." Rowena brushed a hand over her shoulder as a servant came to the archway and announced dinner. "There, you see? Right on time."

It wasn't every day you ate rack of lamb in a castle on a mountaintop in Pennsylvania. The fact that the dining room had twelve-foot ceilings, a trio of chandeliers sparkling with white and red crystal drops, and a ruby granite fireplace big enough to hold the population of Rhode Island certainly added to the perks.

The atmosphere should have been intimidating and formal, yet it was welcoming. Not the sort of place you'd chow down on pepperoni pizza, Dana reflected, but a nice ambience for sharing an exquisitely prepared meal with interesting people.

Conversation flowed—travel, books, business. It showed Dana the power of their hosts. It wasn't the norm for a librarian from a small valley town to sit around and break bread with a couple of Celtic gods, but Rowena and Pitte made it *seem* normal.

And what was to come, the next step in the quest, was a subject no one broached.

Because she was seated between Brad and Jordan, Dana angled herself toward Brad and spent as much of the meal as possible ignoring her other dinner partner.

"What did you do to make Zoe mad?"

Brad flicked a glance across the table. "Apparently, I breathed."

"Come on." Dana gave him a little elbow poke. "Zoe's not like that. What did you do? Did you hit on her?"

"I did not hit on her." Years of training kept his voice low, but the acid in it was still evident. "Maybe it annoyed her that I refused to muck around in her engine, and wouldn't let her muck around in it either, as we were both dressed for dinner and were already running late."

Dana's eyebrows rose. "Well, well. Seems she got your back up, too."

"I don't care to be called high-handed and bossy just because I point out the obvious."

Now she smiled, leaned over and pinched his cheek. "But, honey, you *are* high-handed and bossy. That's why I love you."

"Yeah, yeah, yeah." But his lips twitched. "Then how come we've never had wild and crazy sex?"

"I don't know. Let me get back to you on that." She speared another bite of lamb. "Guess you've been to a lot of snazzy dinners like this, in snazzy places like this."

"There is no other place like this."

It was easy for her to forget that her buddy Brad was Bradley Charles Vane IV, heir apparent to a lumber empire that had built one of the country's largest and most accessible home improvement and supply chains, HomeMakers.

But seeing how smoothly he slid into this sort of sophisticated atmosphere reminded her that he was a great deal more than just the hometown boy.

"Didn't your dad buy some big castle place in Scotland a few years back?"

"Manor house, Cornwall. And, yeah, it's pretty incredible. She's not eating much," he murmured and gave a little nod toward Zoe.

"She's just nervous. Me too," Dana added, then cut another bite of lamb. "But nothing kills my appetite." She heard Jordan laugh, and the deep male sound of it cruised along her skin. Deliberately, she ate the lamb. "Absolutely nothing."

She was spending most of her time ignoring him, and taking swipes with whatever time she had left over. That, Jordan thought, was Dana's usual pattern when it came to him.

He should be used to it.

So the fact that it bothered him so much was his problem. Just as finding a way to make them friends again was his mission.

They'd once been friends. And a great deal more. The fact that they weren't now was his fault, and he would take the rap for it. But just how long was a man supposed to pay for ending a relationship? Wasn't there a statute of limitations?

She looked incredible, he decided as they gathered back in the parlor for coffee and brandy. But then, he'd always liked her looks, even when she'd been a kid, too tall for her age and with that pudge of baby fat still in her cheeks.

There was no baby fat in evidence now. Anywhere. Just curves, a lot of gorgeous curves.

She'd done something to her hair, he realized, some girl thing that added mysterious light to that dense brown. It made her eyes seem darker, deeper. God, how many times had he felt himself drowning in those rich chocolate eyes?

Hadn't he been entitled to come up for air?

In any case, he'd meant what he'd said to her before. He was back now, and she was just going to have to get used to it. Just as she would have to get used to the fact that he was part of this tangle she'd gotten herself into.

She was going to have to deal with him. And it would be his pleasure to make sure she had to deal with him as often as possible.

Rowena rose. There was something in the movement, in the look of her, that tickled something at the edge of Jordan's memory. Then she stepped forward, smiled, and the moment passed.

"If you're ready, we should begin. I think it's more suitable if we continue this in the other parlor."

"I'm ready." Dana got to her feet, then looked at Zoe. "You?"

"Yeah." Though she paled a bit, Zoe

clasped hands with Dana. "The first time, all I could think was don't let me be first. Now I just don't know."

"Me either."

They moved down the great hall to the next parlor. It didn't help to brace himself, Jordan knew. The portrait swamped him, as it had the first time he'd seen it.

The colors, the sheer brilliance of them, the joy and beauty of subject and execution. And the shock of seeing Dana's body, Dana's face—Dana's eyes looking back at him from the canvas.

The Daughters of Glass.

They had names, and he knew them now. Niniane, Venora, Kyna. But when he looked at the portrait, he saw them, thought of them as Dana, Malory, and Zoe.

The world around them was a glory of sunlight and flowers.

Malory, dressed in a gown of lapis blue, with her rich gold curls spilling nearly to her waist, held a lap harp. Zoe stood, slim and straight in her shimmering green dress, a puppy in her arms, a sword at her hip. Dana, her dark eyes lit with laughter, was gowned in fiery red. She was seated and held a scroll and quill.

They were a unit in that moment of time, in that jewel-bright world behind the Curtain of Dreams. But it was only a moment, and even then the end was lurking.

In the deep green of the forest, the shadow of a man. On the silver tiles, the sinuous glide of a snake.

Far in the background, under the graceful branches of a tree, lovers embraced. Teacher and guard, too wrapped up in each other to sense the danger to their charges.

And cannily, cleverly hidden in the painting, the three keys. One in the shape of a bird that winged its way through the impossibly blue sky, another reflecting in the water of the fountain behind the daughters, and the third secreted among the branches of the forest.

He knew Rowena had painted it from memory—and that her memory was long.

And he knew from what Malory had discovered and experienced, that moments after this slice of time, the souls of the daughters had been stolen and locked away in a box of glass.

Pitte lifted a carved box, opened the lid. "Inside are two disks, one with the emblem of the key. Whoever chooses the scribed disk is charged to find the second key."

"Like last time, okay?" Zoe gave Dana's hand a hard squeeze. "We look together."

"Okay." Dana took a slow breath as Mallory stepped up, laid a hand on her shoulder, then Zoe's. "Want to go first?"

"Gosh. I guess." Closing her eyes, Zoe reached into the box, closed her hand over a disk.

With her eyes open and on the portrait, Dana took the one that remained.

Then each held her disk out.

"Well." Zoe stared at her disk, at Dana's. "Looks like I'm running the anchor lap."

Dana ran her thumb over the key carved in her disk. It was a small thing, that key, a straight bar with a spiral design on one end. It looked simple, but she'd seen the real thing—she'd seen the first key in Mallory's hand, burning with gold, and knew it wasn't simple at all.

"Okay, I'm up." She wanted to sit, but locked her shaky knees instead. Four weeks, she thought. She had four weeks from new moon to new moon to do if not the impossible at least the fantastic.

"I get a clue, right?"

"You do." Rowena took up a sheet of parchment and read:

"You know the past and seek the future. What was, what is, what will be are woven into the tapestry of all life. With beauty there is blight, with knowledge, ignorance, and with valor there is cowardice. One is lessened without its opposite.

"To know the key, the mind must recognize the heart, and the heart celebrate the mind. Find your truth in his lies, and what is real within the fantasy.

"Where one goddess walks, another waits, and dreams are only memories yet to come."

Dana picked up a snifter of brandy, drank deep to untie the knots in her belly. "Piece of cake," she said.

Chapter Two

"McDonald's introduced the Big Mac in 1968." Dana swiveled lazily in her chair at the library's resource desk. "Yes, Mr. Hertz, I'm positive. The Big Mac went system-wide in '68, not '69, so you've had a year more of the secret sauce than you thought. Looks like Mr. Foy got you on this one, huh?" She laughed, shook her head. "Better luck tomorrow."

She hung up the phone and crossed the Hertz/Foy daily bet off her list, then meticulously noted today's winner on the tally sheet she kept.

Mr. Hertz had nipped Mr. Foy at the end of last month's round, which netted him lunch at the Main Street Diner on Mr. Foy's tab. Though for the year, she noted, Foy was two points up, so he had the edge on bagging dinner *and* drinks at the Mountain View Inn, the coveted annual prize.

This month, they were neck and neck, so it was still anybody's game. It was her task to officially announce the winner each month, and then, with a great deal more ceremony, the trivia champ at year's end.

The two had kept their little contest going for nearly twenty years. She'd been part of it, or had felt like part of it, since she'd started her job at the Pleasant Valley Library with her college degree still crisp in her hand.

The daily ritual was something she would miss when she turned in her resignation.

Then Sandi breezed by with her bouncy blond ponytail and permanent beauty-contestant smile, and Dana thought there were certain things she would definitely not miss.

The fact was, she should have given her two weeks' notice already. Her hours at the library were down to a stingy twenty-five a week. But that time could be put to good use elsewhere.

She'd be opening her bookstore, her part of Indulgence, the communal business she was starting with Zoe and Malory, in just a couple of months. Not only did she have to finish organizing and decorating her space in the building they'd bought, but she had to deal with ordering stock.

She'd applied for all the necessary licenses, had already combed through publishers' catalogues, fantasized about her sidelines. She would serve tea in the afternoon, wine in the evening. Eventually she would hold elegant little events. Readings, signings, appearances.

It was something she'd always wanted to do but had never really believed she could accomplish.

She supposed Rowena and Pitte had made it possible. Not only because of the twenty-five thousand in cold, hard cash they'd given her and the others as an incentive to agree to the quest, but also by putting her together with Malory and Zoe.

Each of them had been at a crossroads of sorts the first night they'd met at Warrior's Peak. And they'd made the turn, chosen the path to follow together.

It wasn't nearly as scary thinking of starting her own business when she had two friends—two partners—doing the same thing.

Then there was the key. Of course, she couldn't forget the key. It had taken Malory nearly all of the four weeks allowed to find the first. And it hadn't been all fun and games. Far from it.

Still, they knew more now, more about what they were up against, more about what was at stake. That had to be an advantage for this round.

Unless you considered that knowing where the keys came from, what they did, and who didn't want them found had absolutely nothing to do with finding one.

She sat back, closed her eyes, and pondered the clue Rowena had given her. It had to do with the past, the present, and the future.

Big help.

Knowledge, naturally. Lies and truths. Heart and mind.

Where one goddess walks.

There'd been a goddess, a singing goddess, in Malory's clue. And Malory—the art lover who'd dreamed of being an artist—had found her key in a painting.

If the other two followed the same theme,

logic dictated that she, the book lover, might find hers in or around books.

"Catching up on your sleep, Dana?"

Dana's eyes snapped open, stared directly into Joan's disapproving ones. "No. Concentrating."

"If you've nothing better to do, you can help Marilyn in the stacks."

Dana pasted a sunny smile on her face. "I'd be happy to. Should I ask Sandi to take over the resource desk?"

"You don't seem overrun with questions and requests."

And you don't seem overrun with paperwork and administrative duties, Dana thought, since you've got so much time to crawl up my butt. "I've just completed one involving private enterprise and capitalism. But if you'd rather I—"

"Excuse me." A woman stopped at the desk, with her hand on the arm of a boy of about twelve. The grip made Dana think of the way Flynn held Moe's leash. With the hope that she could keep him under control and the certain knowledge that he would bolt at the first opportunity.

"I wonder if you could help us. My son has a paper due . . . *tomorrow,*" she added with heated emphasis that had the boy hunching his shoulders. "On the Continental Congress. Can you tell us which books might be the most helpful at this stage of the game?"

"Of course." Like a chameleon, Joan's cold fish of a face warmed into smiles. "I'd be happy to show you several sources in our U.S. history section."

"Excuse me." Unable to help herself, Dana tapped the sulky boy on the shoulder. "Seventh grade? Mrs. Janesburg, U.S. history?"

His already pouty bottom lip drooped even further. "Yeah."

"I know just what she looks for. You put in a couple of solid hours on this, you can ace it."

"Really?" The mother laid a hand on Dana's, gripped it like a lifeline. "That would be a miracle."

"I had Mrs. Janesburg for U.S. and world history." Dana winked at the boy. "I've got her number."

"I'll leave you in Ms. Steele's capable hands." Though her smile remained in place, Joan spoke through gritted teeth.

Dana leaned forward, spoke to the boy in

a conspiratorial whisper. "She still get teary-eyed when she teaches Patrick Henry's 'Give me liberty' spiel?"

He brightened up considerably. "Yeah. She had to stop and blow her nose."

"Some things never change. Okay, here's what you need."

Fifteen minutes later, while her son checked out his books with his brand-new library card, the mother stopped back by Dana's desk. "I just wanted to thank you again. I'm Joanne Reardon, and you've just saved my firstborn's life."

"Oh, Mrs. Janesburg's tough, but she wouldn't have killed him."

"No. I would have. You got Matt excited about doing this paper, if for no other reason than making him think he'd be pulling one over on his teacher."

"Whatever works."

"My sentiments exactly. Anyway, I appreciate it. You're wonderful at your job."

"Thanks. Good luck."

She *was* wonderful at her job, Dana concurred. Goddamn it, she was. The evil Joan and her toothy niece were going to be sorry when they didn't have Dana Steele to kick around anymore.

                    *   *   *

At the end of her shift she tidied her area, gathered up a few books she'd checked out, then hefted her briefcase. Another thing she would miss, Dana thought, was this end-of-the-day routine. The putting everything in order, taking a last look around the stacks, the tables, the sweet little cathedral to books before the walk home.

She would also miss being just a short, pleasant walk from work to her apartment. It was only one of the reasons she had refused to move in with Flynn when he'd bought his house.

She could still walk to Indulgence, she reminded herself. If she felt like a two-mile hike. Since that was unlikely to happen, she decided she should appreciate what she had now, while she still had it.

She liked the predictability of her habitual route home, the things she saw season by season, year by year. Now, with fall in full swing, the streets were full of golden lights that streamed through the blaze of trees. And the surrounding mountains rose up like some fabulous tapestry woven by the gods.

She could hear kids, freed from school and not yet locked into the homework hour, shouting as they raced around the little park between the library and her apartment building. The air was just brisk enough to carry along that spicy scent from the bed of mums planted outside the town hall.

The big round clock on the square announced it was 4:05.

She struggled against a wave of resentment when she remembered that, pre-Joan, it would have read 6:35 on her way home.

Screw it. Just appreciate the extra time, the lovely walk on a sunny afternoon.

Pumpkins on the porches, goblins hanging from branches though it was weeks before Halloween. Small towns, she mused, prized their holidays. The days were getting shorter, cooler, but were still warm enough, still long enough to bask in.

The Valley was at its best in autumn, she decided. As close to picture-perfect as Anywhere, America, could get.

"Hey, Stretch. Carry those for you?"

Her pretty bubble of contentment burst. Before she could snarl, Jordan snatched the load of books away, tucked them under his own arm.

"Give me those."

"I've got them. Terrific afternoon, huh? Nothing like the Valley in October."

She *hated* that his words mirrored the ones that had played through her mind. "I thought the name of the tune was 'Autumn in New York.' "

"And it's a good one." He tipped up the books to read the spines. She had one on Celtic lore, one on yoga, and the latest Stephen King novel.

"Yoga?"

It was like him, just exactly like him, to home in on the one thing that she found moderately embarrassing. "So?"

"Nothing. Just can't see you assuming the dragonfly position or whatever." He narrowed his eyes, and something appealingly wicked moved into the blue. "On second thought . . ."

"Haven't you got anything better to do than skulking around the library waiting to accost and annoy me?"

"I wasn't skulking, and hauling your books isn't accosting." He matched his stride to hers with the ease of long familiarity. "It's not the first time I've walked you home."

"Somehow I've managed to find my way without you the last several years."

"You've managed a lot of things. How's your dad doing?"

She bit back a vicious remark because she knew, for all his many flaws, that Jordan asked the question out of a sincere concern. Joe Steele and Jordan Hawke had gotten on like white on rice.

"He's good. He's doing good. The move to Arizona was what he needed. He and Liz have a nice place, a nice life. He's taken up baking."

"Baking? Like cakes? Joe bakes cakes?"

"And scones and fancy bread." She couldn't stop the smile. The thought of her father, big, macho Joe, in an apron whipping up cake batter got her every time. "I get a care package every couple of months. First few contributions made excellent doorstops, but in the last year or so he's found his rhythm. He makes good stuff."

"Give him my best next time you talk to him."

She shrugged. She didn't intend to mention Jordan Hawke's name, unless it was in a curse. "End of the road," she said when they reached the door of her apartment building.

"I want to come in."

"Not in this or any other lifetime." She reached for the books, he swung them out of reach. "Cut it out, Jordan. We're not ten."

"We have things to talk about."

"No, we don't."

"Yes, we do. And stop making me feel like I'm ten." He hissed out a breath, prayed for patience. "Look, Dana, we've got a history. Let's deal with it like grown-ups."

Damn if he would so much as hint that she was being immature. The pinhead. "Okay, here's how we'll deal with it. Give me my books and go away."

"Did you listen to what Rowena said last night?" There was an edge in the tone now, one that warned her a good, sweaty argument was brewing. "Did you pay any attention? Your past, present, and future. I'm part of your past. I'm part of this."

"In my past is just where you're going to stay. I wasted two years of my life on you. But that's done. Can't you stand it, Jordan? Can't your enormous ego handle the fact that I got over you? Way over you."

"This isn't about my ego, Dana." He

handed her back her books. "But it sure as hell seems to be about yours. You know where to find me when you're ready."

"I don't want to find you," she murmured when he strode away.

Damn it, it wasn't like him to walk away from a fight. She'd seen the temper on his face, heard it in his voice. Since when had he yanked the snarling beast back and hauled it off?

She had been primed for the argument, and now she had nowhere to vent her spleen. That was very, very nasty.

Inside her apartment, she dumped her books on the table and headed straight for the Ben and Jerry's. Soon she was soothing her ruffled feathers with a pint of cookie dough straight out of the carton.

"Bastard. Sneaky bastard, getting me all riled up and skulking off. These calories are his fault."

She licked the spoon, dug for more. "But, damn, they're really good."

Refreshed, she changed into sweats, brewed a pot of coffee, then settled into her favorite chair with the new book on Celtic lore.

She couldn't count the number of books

on the subject she'd read in the last month. But then again, to Dana, reading was every bit as pleasurable as Ben and Jerry's and as essential to life as the next breath of air.

She surrounded herself with books at work and at home. Her living space was a testament to her first and abiding love, with shelves jammed with books, tables crowded with them. She saw them not only as knowledge, entertainment, comfort, even sanity, but as a kind of artful decoration.

To the casual eye, the books that streamed and flowed over shelves in nooks, on tabletops, might look like a haphazard, even disordered, jumble. But the librarian in Dana insisted on a system.

She could, on her whim or on request, put her hand on any title in any room in the apartment.

She couldn't live without books, without the stories, the information, the worlds that lived inside them. Even now, with the task ahead of her and the clock already ticking, she fell into the words on the pages in her hands, and into the lives, the loves, the wars, the petty grievances of the gods.

Absorbed, she jumped at the knock on

her door. Blinking, she came back to reality, noted that the sun had set while she'd been visiting with Dagda, Epona, and Lug.

Book in hand, she went to answer, then lifted her eyebrows at Malory. "What's up?"

"I thought I'd swing by and see what you were up to before I headed home. I've spent the day talking to some local artists and craftspeople. I think I've got a good start on pieces for my gallery."

"Cool. Got any food on you? I'm starved."

"A tin of Altoids and half a roll of Life Savers."

"That's not going to work," Dana decided. "I'm going to forage. You hungry?"

"No, go ahead. Any brilliant ideas? Anything you want Zoe and me to do?" Malory asked as she followed Dana into the kitchen.

"I don't know how brilliant. Spaghetti! Hot damn." Dana came out of the refrigerator with a bowl of leftover pasta. "You want?"

"Nope."

"Got some Cabernet to go with it."

"That I'll have. One glass." At home in Dana's kitchen, Malory got out wineglasses. "What's the idea, brilliant or not?"

"Books. You know, the whole knowledge thing. And the past, present, future. If we're talking about mine, it's all about the books." She dug out a fork and began to eat the pasta straight out of the bowl. "The trick is which book, or what kind of book."

"Don't you want to heat that up?"

"What?" Baffled, Dana looked down at the spaghetti in the bowl. "Why?"

"No reason." Malory handed Dana a glass of wine, then took her own and wandered out to sit at the table. "A book or books makes sense, at least in part. And it gives you a path to take. But . . ."

She scanned Dana's apartment. "What you yourself personally own would take weeks to get through. Then there's what everyone else in the Valley owns, the library, the bookstore at the mall, and so on."

"And the fact that even if I'm right, it doesn't mean the key's literally in a book. Could be figuratively. Or it could mean something in a book points the way to the key." Dana shrugged and shoveled in more cold spaghetti. "I said it fell short of brilliant."

"It's a good starting point. Past, present,

future." Malory pursed her lips. "Covers a lot of ground."

"Historical, contemporary, futuristic. And that's just novels."

"What if it's more personal?" Malory leaned forward, kept her attention on Dana's face. "It was with me. My path to the key included Flynn, my feelings for him— and my feelings about myself, where I would end up, where I wanted to go. The experiences I had—we can't call them dreams—were very personal."

"And scary." Briefly, Dana laid a hand over Malory's. "I know. But you got through it. So will I. Maybe it is personal. A book that has some specific and personal meaning for me."

Thoughtfully she scanned the room as she picked up her fork again. "That's something else that covers a lot of ground."

"I was thinking of something else. I was thinking of Jordan."

"I don't see how he's in the mix. Look," she continued even as Malory opened her mouth, "he was part of the first round, sure. The paintings by Rowena that both he and Brad bought. He came back to town with that painting because Flynn asked him to.

That played into it, although his part should have ended with your quest. And his connection to Flynn, which connected him to you."

"And you, Dana."

She twirled her fork in the pasta, but her enthusiasm for it was waning. "Not anymore."

Recognizing the stubborn look, Malory nodded. "Okay. How about the first book you ever read? The first that grabbed you and made you a reader."

"I don't think the magic key to the Box of Souls is going to be found in *Green Eggs and Ham.*" Smirking, Dana lifted her glass. "But I'll give it a look."

"What about your first grown-up book?"

"Obviously the steely wit and keen satire of Sam I Am escaped you." She grinned, but drummed her fingers, thinking. "Anyway, I don't remember a first. It was always books with me. I don't remember not reading."

She studied her wine a moment, then took a quick gulp. "He dumped me. I moved on."

Back to Jordan, Malory thought and nodded. "All right."

"That doesn't mean I don't hate him with a rare and beautiful passion, but it doesn't drive my life. I've only seen him a handful of times in the past seven years." She shrugged, but it came across as a hesitant jerk. "I've got my life, he's got his, and they no longer intersect. He just happens to be buds with Flynn."

"Did you love him?"

"Yeah. Big time. Bastard."

"I'm sorry."

"Hey, it happens." She had to remind herself of that. It wasn't life or death, it didn't send her falling headlong into a vale of tears. If a heart couldn't be broken, it wasn't a heart to begin with.

"We were friends. When my dad married Flynn's mom, Flynn and I hit it off. Good thing, I guess. Flynn had Jordan and Brad—they were like one body with three heads half the time. So I got them, too."

You've still got them, Malory nearly said, but managed to keep silent.

"Jordan and I were friends, and we both really dug reading, so that was another click. Then we got older, and things changed. You want another hit of this?" she asked, holding up her empty glass.

"No."

"Well, I'm having one." Dana rose, got the bottle from the kitchen. "He went off to college. He got a partial scholarship to Penn State, and both he and his mom worked like dogs to put together the rest of the tuition and expense money. His mom, well, she was just terrific. Zoe sort of reminds me of her."

"Really?"

"Not in the looks department, though Mrs. Hawke was really pretty, but she was taller, and willowy—made you think of a dancer."

"She was young when she died."

"Yeah, only in her forties." It still brought a little pang to her heart. "It was horrible what she went through, what Jordan went through. At the end, we were all practically camped out at the hospital, and even then . . ."

She gave herself a hard shake, blew out a breath. "That's not where I was going. I meant Zoe reminds me of how Mrs. Hawke was. It's that good-mother vibe Zoe has. The kind of woman who knows what to do and how to do it and doesn't whine about getting it done, and still manages to love it and the kid. She and Jordan were tight, the way Zoe and Simon are. It was just the two of them. His father wasn't in the picture, not as far back as I can remember, anyway."

"That must've been difficult for him."

"It would've been, I think, if his mother hadn't been who she was. She'd grab a bat and join in a pickup softball game as quickly as she would whip up some cookie batter. She filled the gaps."

"You loved her too," Malory realized.

"I did. We all did."

Dana sat down, sipped at her second glass of wine. "So anyway, the Hawke goes off to college, gets two part-time jobs up there to help pay his expenses. We didn't see much of him the first year. He came back for summers, worked at Tony's Garage. He's a pretty decent mechanic. Palled around with Flynn and Brad when he had the chance. Four years later, he's got his degree. He did a year and a half postgrad and was already getting some short stories published. Then he came home."

She let out a long breath. "Holy Jesus, we took one look at each other, and it was like bombs exploding. I thought, What the hell is this? This is my buddy Jordan. I'm not supposed to want to sink my teeth into my good buddy Jordan."

She laughed, drank. "Later on, he told me he'd had the same sort of reaction. Whoa, hold on, this is Flynn's little sister. Hands off. So we danced around those bombs and each other for a couple of months. We were either bitchy with each other or very, very polite."

"And then?" Malory prompted when Dana fell silent.

"Then one night he dropped by to see Flynn, but Flynn was out on a date. And my parents weren't home. I picked a fight with him. I had to do *something* with all that heat. The next thing you know the two of us are rolling around on the living room rug. We couldn't get enough of each other. I've never had that before or since, that . . . desperation. It was incredible.

"Imagine our chagrin when the smoke cleared and the two of us were naked on Liz and Joe's pretty Oriental carpet."

"How did you handle it?"

"Well, as I recall we lay there like the dead for a minute, then just stared at each other. A couple of survivors of a very intense war.

Then we laughed our butts off and went at each other again."

She lifted her glass in a mock toast. "So. We started dating, belatedly. Jordan and Dana, Dana and Jordan. It got to be like one word, whichever way you said it."

Oh, God, she missed that, she realized. Missed that very intimate link. "Nobody ever made me laugh the way he could make me laugh. And he's the only man in my life who's ever made me cry. So, yeah, Christ, yes, I loved that son of a bitch."

"What happened?"

"Little things, huge things. His mother died. God, nothing's ever been as, well, monstrous as that. Even when my dad got sick, it wasn't as bad. Ovarian cancer, and they found it too late. The operations, the treatments, the prayers, nothing worked. She just kept slipping away. Having some-one die is hard," she said softly. "Watching them die by inches is impossible."

"I can't imagine it." Malory's eyes filled with tears. "I've never lost anyone."

"I don't remember losing my mother; I was too young. But I remember every day of losing Mrs. Hawke. Maybe it broke something in Jordan. I don't know—he wouldn't let me know. After she died, he sold their little house, all the furniture, just about every damn thing. And he cut me loose and moved to New York to get rich and famous."

"It wasn't as cut and dried as that," Malory commented.

"Maybe not. But it felt like it. He said he had to go. That he needed something, and it wasn't here. If he was going to write—and he had to write—he had to do it his way. He had to get out of the Valley. So that's what he did, like the two years we were together was just a little interlude in his life."

She downed the rest of the wine in her glass. "So fuck him, and the bestsellers he rode in on."

"You may not want to hear this, at least not now. But part of the solution might be to resolve this with him."

"Resolve what?"

"Dana." Malory laid both of her hands on Dana's. "You're still in love with him."

Her hands jerked. "I am not. I made a life for myself. I've had lovers. I have a career—which, okay, is in the toilet right now, but I've got a phoenix about to rise from the ashes in the bookstore."

She stopped, hearing the way her words tumbled out. "No more wine for me if I mix metaphors that pitifully. Jordan Hawke's old news," she said more calmly. "Just because he was the first man I loved doesn't mean he has to be the last. I'd rather poke my eye with a burning stick than give him the satisfaction."

"I know." Malory laughed a little, gave Dana's hands a squeeze before she released them. "That's how I know you're still in love with him. That, and what I just saw on your face, heard in your voice when you took me through what you had together."

It was appalling. How had she looked? How had she sounded? "So the wine made me sentimental. It doesn't mean—"

"It means whatever it means," Malory said briskly. "It's something you're going to have to think about, Dana, something you're going to have to weigh carefully if you really mean to do this thing. Because one way or the other, he's part of your life, and he's part of this."

"I don't want him to be," Dana managed. "But if he is, I'll deal with it. There's too much at stake for me to wimp out before I even get started."

"That's the spirit. I've got to get home."

She rose, then ran a comforting hand over Dana's hair. "Whatever you're feeling or thinking, you can tell me. And Zoe. And if there's something you need to say, if you just need someone to be here when you have nothing to say, all you have to do is call."

Dana nodded, waited until Malory was at the door. "Mal? It was like having a hole punched in my heart when he left. One hole ought to be enough for anybody's lifetime."

"You'd think. I'll see you tomorrow."

Chapter Three

The odds of finding a magic key tucked in one of the thousands of books at the Pleasant Valley Library were long and daunting. But that didn't mean she couldn't look.

In any case, she liked being in the stacks, surrounded by books. She could, if she let her mind open to it, hear the words murmuring from them. All those voices from people who lived in worlds both fantastic and ordinary. She could, simply by slipping a book off the shelf, slide right into one of those worlds and become anyone who lived inside it.

Magic keys and soul-sucking sorcerers, Dana thought. Incredible as they might be, they paled for her against the power of words on a page.

But she wasn't here to play, she reminded herself as she began dutifully tidying the stacks while keeping an eye on the resource desk a few feet away. This was an experiment. Maybe she would put her fingers on a book and *feel* something—a tingle, a hint of heat.

Who knew?

But she worked her way through the mythology stacks without experiencing any tingles.

Undaunted, she wandered to the section of books on ancient civilizations. The past, she told herself. The Daughters of Glass had sprung from the ancients. Well, who hadn't?

She worked diligently for a time, reordering books that had been misplaced. She knew better, really she did, than to actually open the volume on ancient Britain, but it was suddenly in her hand, and there was this section on stone circles that swept her onto windy moors at moonrise.

Druids and chanting, balefires and the hum that was the breath of gods.

"Oh, gee, Dana. I didn't know you were off today."

With her teeth going to auto-grind, Dana shifted her gaze from the book in her hand to Sandi's overly cheerful face. "I'm not off. I'm working the stacks."

"Really?" The big blue eyes widened. Long golden lashes fluttered. "It looked like you were reading. I thought maybe you were on your own time, doing more research. You've been doing a lot of research lately, haven't you? Finally starting on your doctorate?"

With a bad-tempered little shove, Dana put the book back in place. Wouldn't it be fun? she thought, to get the big silver scissors out of the drawer in her desk and whack off that detestable bouncing ponytail?

She'd just bet that would wipe that bright, toothy grin off Sandi's face.

"You got the promotion, the pay raise, so what's your problem, Sandi?"

"Problem? I don't have a problem. We all know the policy about reading on the clock. So I'm sure it just *looked* like you were reading instead of manning the desk."

"The desk is covered." And when enough

was enough, Dana thought, you finished it. "You spend a lot of your time worrying about what I'm doing, slinking around in the stacks behind me, eavesdropping when I'm speaking with a patron."

Sandi's perky smile turned into a perky sneer. "I certainly do not eavesdrop."

"Bullshit," Dana said in a quiet, pleasant tone that had Sandi's dollbaby eyes going bright with shock. "You've been stepping on my heels for weeks. You got the promotion, I got the cut. But you're not my supervisor, you're not my boss. So you can kiss my ass."

Though it wasn't quite as rewarding as hacking off the ponytail might have been, it felt fabulous to just walk away, leaving Sandi sputtering.

She settled back at the desk and assisted two patrons with such good cheer and good fellowship that both left beaming. When she answered the phone, she all but sang out, "Pleasant Valley Library. Reference Desk. May I help you? Hey, Mr. Foy. You're up, huh. Ah, uh-huh. Good one." She chuckled as she scribbled down today's trivia question. "It'll take me a minute. I'll call you back."

She danced off to find the right book, flipped through it briefly in the stacks, then carried it back to the desk to make the return call.

"Got it." She trailed down the page with her finger. "The Arctic tern migrates the farthest annually. Up to twenty thousand miles—wow—between the Arctic and Antarctic. Makes you wonder what's in its birdy brain, doesn't it?"

She shifted the phone as she caught sight of Sandi marching, like a damn drum majorette, toward the desk. "Nope, sorry, Mr. Foy, no complete set of American Tourister luggage for you today. The Arctic tern nips out the long-tailed jaeger by a couple thousand miles annually. Better luck next time. Talk to you tomorrow."

She hung up, folded her hands, then lifted her eyebrows at Sandi. "Something I can do for you?"

"Joan wants to see you upstairs." Thrusting her chin in the air, Sandi looked down her tiny, perfect nose. "Immediately."

"Sure." Dana tucked her hair behind her ear as she studied Sandi. "I bet you only had one friend in elementary school, and she was just as obnoxious as you are." She slid off the stool.

Speaking of elementary school, Dana thought as she crossed the main floor, started up the stairs to administration, she herself felt as if she'd just gotten hauled into the principal's office. A lowering sensation for a grown woman. And one, she decided, she was sick of experiencing.

Outside Joan's door, Dana took a deep breath, squared her shoulders. She might feel like a guilty six-year-old, but she wasn't going to look like one.

She knocked, briskly, then opened the door without waiting for a response. "You wanted to see me?"

At her desk, Joan leaned back. Her salt-and-pepper hair was pulled into a no-nonsense bun that, oddly enough, flattered her.

She wore a dark vest over a white blouse that was primly buttoned to her throat. The material hung flat, with barely a ripple to indicate there were breasts beneath it.

Rimless half-glasses dangled from a gold chain around her neck. Dana knew her shoes would be low-heeled and sturdy and as no-nonsense as the hairstyle.

She looked, Dana decided, scrawny and dull—and the very image of the cliché that kept children out of libraries in droves.

Since Joan's mouth was already set in disapproval, Dana didn't expect the meeting to be a cheerful one.

"Shut the door, please. It appears, Dana, that you continue to have difficulty adjusting to the new policies and protocol I've implemented here."

"So, Sandi raced right up to tattle that I was actually reading a book. Of all the horrors to commit in a public library."

"Your combative attitude is only one of the problems we have to deal with."

"I'm not going to stand here and defend myself for skimming a couple pages of a book while I was working in the stacks. Part of my function is to be informed about books, not just to point the patrons toward an area and wish them Godspeed. I do my job, Joan, and my evaluations from the previous director were never less than exemplary."

"I'm not the previous director."

"Damn straight. Less than six weeks after you took over, you cut my, and two other long-term employees', hours and paychecks nearly in half. And your niece gets a promotion and a raise."

"I was hired to pull this institution out of financial decline, and that's what I'm doing. I'm not required to explain my administrative decisions to you."

"No, you don't have to. I get it. You don't like me, I don't like you. But I don't have to like everyone I work with or for. I can still do my job."

"It's your job to follow the rules." Joan flipped open a file. "Not to make and receive personal phone calls. Not to use library equipment for personal business. Not to spend twenty minutes gossiping with a patron while your duties are neglected."

"Hold it." Baffled rage spewed into her throat like a geyser. "Just hold it one minute. What's she doing, making daily reports on me?"

Joan flipped the file shut. "You think too much of yourself."

"Oh, I see. Not just on me. She's your personal mole, burrowing around the place digging up infractions."

Oh, yes, Dana thought, when enough was enough you definitely finished it. "Maybe the budget here has had its ups and downs, but this was always a friendly place, familial. Now it's just a drag run by the gestapo commandant and her personal weasel. So I'll do us both a favor. I quit. I've got a week's sick leave and a week's vacation coming. We'll just consider that my two weeks' notice."

"Very well. You can have your resignation on my desk by the end of your shift."

"Screw that. This is my resignation." She took a deep breath. "I'm smarter than you are, and I'm younger, stronger, and better-looking. The regular patrons know and like me—most of them don't know you, and the ones who've gotten to know you don't like you. Those are some of the reasons you've been on my ass since you took over. I'm out of here, Joan, but I'm walking out of my own accord. I lay odds that you'll be on your way out before much longer, too—only you'll be booted out by the board."

"If you expect any sort of reference or referral—"

Dana stopped at the door. "Joan, Joan, do you want to end our relationship with me telling you what you can do with your reference?"

Her anger carried her straight down to

the employee lounge, where she gathered her jacket and a handful of personal belongings. She didn't stop to speak to any of her coworkers. If she didn't get out, and get out fast, she feared she would either burst into hysterical sobs or punch her fist through the wall.

Either option would give Joan too much power.

So she walked out without a backward glance. And kept walking. She refused to let herself think that this was the last time she would make this trip from work to home. It wasn't the end of her life; it was just a corner turned.

When she felt the angry tears stinging her eyes, she dug out her sunglasses. She wasn't about to humiliate herself by crying on the damn sidewalk.

But her breath was hitching by the time she reached her apartment door. She fumbled out her keys, stumbled inside, then simply sank down on the floor.

"Oh, God, oh, God, what have I done?"

She'd cut her ties. She had no job. And it would be weeks before she could reasonably open the bookstore. And why did she think she could run a bookstore? Knowing and loving books didn't make her a merchant. She'd never worked in retail in her life, and suddenly she was going to run a retail business?

She'd thought she was prepared for the step. Now, faced with stark reality, Dana realized she wasn't even close to prepared.

Panicked, she leaped up, all but fell onto the phone. "Zoe? Zoe . . . I just—I've got to . . . Christ. Can you meet me at the place, the house?"

"Okay. Dana, what's wrong? What's the matter?"

"I just—I quit my job. I think I'm having an anxiety attack. I need . . . Can you get the keys? Can you get Malory and meet me there?"

"All right, honey. Take a deep breath. Come on, suck one in. Breathe easy. That's it. Twenty minutes. We'll be there in twenty minutes."

"Thanks. Okay, thanks. Zoe—"

"You just keep breathing. Want me to swing by and get you?"

"No." She rubbed the temper tears away. "No, I'll meet you."

"Twenty minutes," Zoe repeated and rang off.

*   *   *

She was calmer, at least on the surface, when she pulled into the double drive in front of the pretty frame house she'd bought with her friends. In a matter of weeks, they'd be signing papers at settlement. Then they would begin, well, whatever it was that they were going to begin.

It was Zoe and Malory who had the big ideas as far as ambience, color schemes, paints, and posies. They'd already had their heads together over paint chips for the color of the porch, the entrance hall. And she knew Zoe had been scouring flea markets and yard sales for the trash that she miraculously turned into treasure.

It wasn't that she didn't have ideas herself. She did.

She could envision in general how her section of the main floor would look when it had been transformed into a little bookstore/café. Comfortable and cozy. Maybe some good sink-into-me chairs, a few tables.

But she couldn't see the details. What should the chairs look like? What kind of tables should she use?

And there were dozens of other things she hadn't considered when she'd jumped into that dream of having her own bookstore. Just as, she was forced to admit, there were things she hadn't considered when she'd, basically, told Joan to stuff it.

Impulse, pride, and temper, she thought with a sigh. A dangerous combination. Now she was going to have to live with the results of surrendering to it.

She stepped out of the car. Her stomach was still jumpy, so she rubbed a hand over it as she studied the house.

It was a good place. It was important to remember that. She'd liked it the minute she'd stepped inside the door with Zoe. Even the downright terrifying experience they'd had inside it—courtesy of their nemesis, Kane—barely a week before, when Malory had found her key, didn't spoil the *feel* of the place.

She'd never owned a house, or any other property. She should concentrate on the very adult sensation of owning a third of an actual building, and the land it stood on. She wasn't afraid of the responsibility—it was good to know that. She wasn't afraid of work, mental or physical.

But she was, she realized, very afraid of failing.

She walked to the porch, sat on the step, and indulged in a good wallow.

She was too mired in it to do more than sit there when Malory pulled up with Zoe in the passenger seat. Malory angled her head as she climbed out.

"Crappy day, huh?"

"Don't come much crappier. Thanks for coming. Really."

"We did better than that." She gestured toward Zoe, and the white bakery box Zoe carried.

Overcome, Dana sniffed. "Is it chocolate?"

"We're girls, aren't we?" Sitting beside her, Zoe gave her a hard, one-armed hug, then opened the box. "Chocolate éclairs. A big fat one for each of us."

This time, it was sentimental tears threatening to fall. "You guys are the best."

"Take a few bites, wait for the kick, then tell us about it." Malory sat on the other side, handed out napkins.

Dana soothed herself with chocolate, pastry, and cream, and the story tumbled out between bites.

"She wanted me to quit." Scowling, she flicked her tongue at the corner of her mouth and licked off a bit of Bavarian cream. "It was some visceral animosity going on between us the minute we laid eyes on each other. Like, I dunno, maybe we were mortal enemies in a past life. Or, Jesus, married or something. It's not just that she ran the library like it was boot camp—that's bad enough—but she had it in for me, personally. And so did her little yappy dog, Sandi."

"I know it's tough, Dana. Boy, do I." Malory rubbed a sympathetic hand over Dana's shoulder. "But you were planning to resign in a few weeks anyway."

"I know, I know. But I wanted to sort of ease out. Cop the little going-away party with the staff, so it all ended on a high note. And the fact is, even with the pay cut, the salary did come in handy. More than. I could've used the extra paychecks before I walked."

"Telling her to cram it should be worth the paychecks. She's a bitch and we hate her," Zoe said loyally. "And when Indulgence is up and running, and the bookstore's the talk of the Valley, she'll stew in her own en-vious juices."

Considering, Dana pursed her lips. "That's a good one. I just panicked, I guess. I've always worked in a library. High school library, college library, then this one. And it suddenly hit me that that's done, and I'm going to be the owner of a retail business."

She rubbed her damp hands on her knees. "I don't even know how to work a cash register."

"I'll teach you," Zoe promised. "We're in this together."

"I don't want to mess it up. I don't want to mess up the key deal either. It's just that all this hit me at once."

Malory offered Dana the last third of her éclair. "Have a little more sugar. Then we'll go in and start making some serious plans."

"I've got two hours before I have to be home," Zoe told her. "When we picked up the keys, I asked the real estate agent. She said we could start on some of the basic cosmetic work if we want to risk the time and money. We could paint the porch, say, unless we're worried the deal won't go through."

Dana polished off the éclair. "Okay.

Okay," she said with more enthusiasm. "Let's go in and look at paint chips."

After some debate, they settled on a deep ocean blue. The color, they agreed, would make the house stand out among its neighbors and would add a touch of class.

Since they were in the mode, they headed back to the kitchen to talk about decor and space.

"Nothing too country," Zoe decided as she tapped her fingers on her hips. "We want it comfortable and homey, but, well, indulgent, right? So it shouldn't be sleek or anything, but it shouldn't be homespun either."

"Your upscale country kitchen." Nodding, Malory turned in a circle, trying to envision it. "Maybe that minty green for the walls. Nice, friendly color. A creamy white for the cabinets. Dana, you'll be using this space the most."

"That's okay, keep going." She waved them on. "You guys are better at this than I am."

"Well, what if we had the counters done in rose? Not pink, but stronger, then we punch things up with art. That would flow in from the gallery section. Then we'd set up some of the sidelines Zoe's talked about having up in the salon. The aromatherapy products, candles. And we do something like Dana's got in the kitchen in her apartment."

"We fill it with junk food?"

Malory glanced at Dana and laughed. "No. Books. We do like a baker's rack or kitchen étagère over there, and we put out books and some of the craft pieces from my gallery, some of the products from the salon. Fancy hand creams and soaps. It unifies this communal space."

"That's good." Dana let out a breath. "It's starting to feel good again."

"It's going to be great." Zoe slid an arm around Dana's waist. "You could have those tins and stuff of fancy teas and coffees on the counter."

"Maybe we could put in a table," Dana considered. "One of those little round ones, with a couple of chairs. Okay. Let's write down the paints we've got so far, see if we can decide on any others. I'll head out to HomeMakers and pick it all up."

"I think paint's going on sale next week," Zoe put in.

"Oh, yeah?" Dana's dimples flashed. "Well, I happen to have an in at HomeMakers. I'll call Brad and get us a discount today."

It helped to have a focus, a goal. Even if it was only several gallons of paint.

If, Dana thought, the library and her life there were now her past, weren't Indulgence and the building of it her present? As far as the future went, how the hell was she supposed to know? But she intended to think about it and try to find a connection to the location of the key.

It hadn't been difficult to wheedle a thirty percent discount out of Brad. As Dana wandered the wide aisles of the cavernous HomeMakers, she considered what else she might be able to pick up while she had her old friend's go-ahead.

Paintbrushes, of course, and rollers. Or maybe they should try out one of those paint sprayers. She studied one, crouching down to ponder the workings of it.

How hard could it be? And it would certainly be faster and less labor-intensive than slopping it on the old-fashioned way.

"Unless you're thinking about becoming a house painter, that one's a little much for you."

Jordan Hawke, she thought as a muscle in her jaw twitched. And she'd thought the day couldn't get any crappier. "So, Brad took pity on you and gave you a job?" she said without looking up. "Are you going to get to wear one of the blue denim shirts with the little house on the breast pocket?"

"I was in his office when you called kissing up to him for a price break. He asked me to come down and give you a hand because he got caught by a phone call before he could come himself."

Her hackles rose. "I don't need help to buy paint."

"You do if you're seriously considering buying that sprayer."

"I was just looking." Her mouth moved into a pout as she poked a finger at the machine. "Besides, what do you know about it?"

"Enough to know if I say too much more about it, you'll buy it just to spite me."

"That's tempting, but I'll resist," she shot back.

He reached down, cupped a hand under her elbow to lift her to her feet. "Seems like you've had enough to deal with for one day. Heard you quit your job."

There was sympathy in his eyes. Not the smug and sticky kind, but a quiet understanding that soothed. "What, does Sandi report to you too?"

"Sorry, that name's not on my list." He gave her arm a careless little rub, an old gesture that both of them remembered as soon as he did it. And both of them took a half-step back. "Word travels, Stretch. You know how it is in the Valley."

"Yeah, I know how it is. I'm surprised you remember."

"I remember a lot of things. One of them is how much you loved working there."

"I don't want you to be nice to me." She turned away to stare hard at the paint sprayer. "It's screwing up my mood."

Because he knew she would work through it better if she was angry or occupied, he nodded. "Okay. Why don't I help you take advantage of your friend-of-the-owner discount? It's always fun to scalp

Brad. Then you can verbally abuse me. That always cheers you up."

"Yeah, it does." She frowned a little, bumped the sprayer with the toe of her shoe. "This thing doesn't look so tough."

"Let me show you some of your other options."

"Why aren't you back at Flynn's hacking out a stale plot with cardboard characters?"

"There, see, you're feeling better already."

"Have to admit."

"What we have here is an automatic paint roller system," he began, steering her toward the machine Brad had recommended to him. "It's small, user-friendly, and efficient."

"How do you know?"

"Because when Brad told me to show you this one he used those specific adjectives. Personally, I've only painted a room the old-fashioned way, and that's been . . ." He trailed off. "A long time ago."

She remembered. He'd painted his mother's bedroom when she was in the hospital the first time. Dana had helped him, cutting around the trim, keeping his spirits up. They'd painted the walls a soft, warm blue so that the room would be fresh and peaceful.

And less than three months later she was dead.

"She loved it," Dana said gently. "She loved that you did that for her."

"Yeah." As the memory was painful on too many levels, he flipped the topic back. "Well, Brad's got a list here of handy products and tools to make your home improvement project more enjoyable."

"Okay, let's clean him out."

She had to admit that it added to the fun and interest of the expedition to have him along. And it was easy, a little too easy, to remember why they'd once been friends, once been lovers.

They had a way of slipping into a rhythm, of understanding short-speak and expressions that came from a lifetime of knowing each other every bit as much as from the two years of physical intimacy they'd shared.

"This is the color?" Jordan rubbed his chin as he studied her list. "Island? What kind of color is Island?"

"Greeny blue. Sort of." She handed over the paint chip. "See? What's wrong with it?"

"I didn't say anything was wrong with it. It's just not something that makes me think bookstore."

"It's not just a bookstore, it's . . . Damn it." She held the sample up, she held it down. She crossed her eyes and still couldn't envision it on the walls of her space. "Malory picked it out. I was going to go with this off-white, and she and Zoe jumped all over me."

"White always works."

She hissed out a breath. "See, they said I was thinking like a man. Men won't pick color. They're scared of color."

"We are not."

"What color's your living room in New York?"

He shot her a bland look. "That's entirely beside the point."

"I don't think so. I don't know why, but I don't think so. I'm going with this sort of greeny blue. It's just paint. It's not a lifetime commitment. And she said I should think Bryce Canyon and Spaghetti for accents."

"Brown and yellow? Honey, that's got to be ugly."

"No, the canyon deal's sort of deep rose. A kind of pinky, browny red—"

"Pinky, browny red," he repeated, grinning. "Very descriptive."

"Shut up. And the other's sort of cream." She fanned out the samples Zoe and Mallory had marked. "Hell, I don't know. I think I'm a little scared of color myself."

"You're sure as hell not a man."

"Thank God for that. Mal's going with this deal called Honeycomb. Zoe's is called Begonia, which I don't get because begonias are pink or white, and this is more like purple."

She pressed her fingers just over her right eye. "I think all this color's making my head hurt. Anyway, Zoe's already figured the square footage and the gallons per. Where's my list?"

He handed it back to her. "Brad was wondering why Zoe didn't come with you."

"Hmm? Oh, she had to get home to Simon." She studied the list, began to calculate, then glanced up. "Why?"

"What?"

"Why was he wondering?"

"Why do you think?" He looked over her shoulder at the list, surprised when she turned it over and he saw that it continued on the back of the sheet.

"Jesus, you're going to need a flatbed. Then Brad took a trip back to high school and asked me to ask you if Zoe had said anything about him."

"No, she didn't, but I'd be happy to pass her a note for him in study hall tomorrow."

"I'll let him know."

They loaded up the paint, the supplies, the equipment. Dana blessed Brad at checkout when even with the discount the total made her gulp. But it wasn't until she was outside that she realized the real dilemma.

"How the hell am I going to fit all this in my car?"

"You're not. We're going to fit it into your car and mine."

"Why didn't you say something about me buying more than I could handle when I was loading up in there?"

"Because you were having fun. Where do you want to store all this stuff?"

"Jeez." Baffled with herself, she scooped a hand through her hair. "I didn't think about it. I got caught up."

And, he thought, it had been a pleasure to watch her get caught up—and forget she hated him.

"I can't store all this at my place, and I didn't think to see if we could keep the keys and store it at the building. What the hell am I going to do with it?"

"Flynn's got plenty of room at his place."

"Yeah." She sighed. "Yeah, he does. I guess that's the way it'll have to be. He can't get pissed, because Malory will just bat her eyelashes and turn him into putty."

They divvied up, loaded up. The drive back to Flynn's gave her time to wonder how they'd managed to be in each other's company for the best part of an hour without a fight.

He hadn't been a jerk, which, she decided, was a rare thing.

And, she was forced to admit, she hadn't been one either. Equally rare when Jordan was involved.

Maybe, just maybe, they could manage to coexist, even cooperate, for the short term. If, as everyone else insisted, he was part of the quest, she needed him around.

Added to that, he had a good brain and a fluid imagination. He could be more than an annoyance through this. He could be an actual asset.

When they arrived at Flynn's, she had to

concede that it helped to have a man around who was willing to play pack mule with a dozen gallons of paint and the supplies that went with it.

"Dining room," she said, straining a little under the load she carried. "He never uses it."

"He's going to." Jordan wound his way through the house, veered off into the dining room. "Malory has major plans."

"She always does. She makes him happy."

"No question about that." He headed back out for the next load. "Lily put some serious holes in his ego," he added, referring to Flynn's ex-fiancée.

"It wasn't just his ego." She pulled out a bag loaded with extra paint rollers, brushes, shiny metal pans. "She hurt him. When somebody dumps you and runs off, it hurts."

"Best thing that could've happened to him."

"That isn't the issue." She could feel the resentment, the hurt, the anger starting to brew in her belly. Struggling to ignore it, she hauled out more cans. "The issue is pain, betrayal, and loss."

He said nothing as they carried the rest of the supplies to the dining room. Nothing until they set them down, and he turned to face her. "I didn't dump you."

She could actually feel the hair on the back of her neck rise. "Not every statement I make involves you."

"I had to go," he continued. "You had to stay. You were still in college, for Christ's sake."

"That didn't stop you from getting me into bed."

"No, it didn't. Nothing could have. I had a hunger for you, Dana. There were times I felt like I'd starve to death if I couldn't get a bite of you."

She stepped back, gave him an up-and-down study. "Looks like you've been eating well enough the last few years."

"Doesn't mean I stopped thinking about you. You meant something to me."

"Oh, go to hell." It didn't explode out of her, but was said flatly, which gave it more power. "*Meant* something to you? A god-damn pair of shoes can mean something to you. I loved you."

If she'd delivered a bare-knuckled punch to his face, he'd have been no less shocked. "You . . . you never said that. You never once said the L word to me."

"Because you were supposed to say it first. The guy's supposed to say it first."

"Hold on just a minute. Is that a rule?" Panic was trickling down the back of his throat like acid. "Where's it written down?"

"It just *is,* you stupid jerk. I loved you, and I'd have waited, or I'd've gone with you. But you just said, Listen, Stretch, I'm pulling up stakes and going to New York. It's been fun, see you around."

"That's not true, Dana. It wasn't like that."

"Close enough. Nobody's ever hurt me like that. You'll never get the chance to do it again—and you know what, Hawke? I'd've made a man out of you."

She turned on her heel and walked out.

Chapter Four

Being alone was something Jordan did very well, under most circumstances. When he was working, thinking about working, thinking about *not* working, he liked to fold himself into the isolation of his SoHo loft.

Then, the life, the noise, the movement and color on the street outside his windows were a kind of film he could watch or ignore depending on his mood.

He liked seeing it all through the glass, more, very often more, than he liked being a part of it.

New York had saved him, in a very real way. It had forced him to survive, to become, to live like a man—not someone's son, someone's friend, another student, but a man who had only himself to rely on. It had pushed and prodded him with its impatient and sharp fingers, reminding him on a daily basis during that jittery first year that it didn't really give a goddamn whether he sank or swam.

He'd learned to swim.

He'd learned to appreciate the noise, the action, the press of humanity.

He liked its selfishness and its generosity and its propensity for flipping the bird to the rest of the world.

And the more he'd learned, the more he'd observed and adjusted, the more he'd realized that at the core he was just a small-town boy.

He would forever be grateful to New York.

When work was upon him, he could drop into that world. Not the one outside his window, but the one inside his own head. Then it wasn't like a film at all, but more like life than life itself for however many hours it gripped him.

He'd learned the difference between those worlds, had come to appreciate the subtleties and scopes of them in a way he knew he might never have done if he hadn't stripped away the safety nets of the old and thrown himself headlong into the new.

Writing had never become routine for him, but remained a constant surprise. He was always surprised at how much fun it was, once it all got moving. And never failed to be surprised at how bloody hard it was. It was like having an intense, frustrating love affair with a capricious, gorgeous, and often mean-spirited woman.

He loved every moment of it.

Writing had carried him through the worst of his grief when he'd lost his mother. It had given him direction, purpose, and enough aggravation to pull himself out of the mire.

It had given him joy and bitterness, and great personal satisfaction. Beyond that, it had provided him with a kind of financial security he'd never known or really expected to know.

Anyone who said money didn't matter had never had to count the coins that fell between the cushions of the couch.

He was alone now, with the afterburn of Dana's words still singeing the air. He couldn't enjoy the solitude, couldn't fold himself into it or into his work.

A man was never so lonely, he thought, as when he was surrounded by the past.

There was no point in going out for a walk. Too many people who knew him would stop and speak, have questions, make comments. He couldn't lose himself in the Valley as he could in New York.

Which was one of the reasons he'd bolted when and how he had. And one of the reasons he'd come back.

So, he would go for a drive, get away from the echoes still bouncing off the walls.

I loved you.

Jesus! Jesus, how could he not have known? Had he been that clueless—or had she been that self-contained?

He walked out and climbed into his Thunderbird, gunned the engine. He felt like speed. A long, fast ride to no particular destination.

He punched in the CD player, cranked it up. He didn't care what pumped out, as long as it was loud. Clapton's blistering guitar rode with him out of town.

He had known he'd hurt Dana all those years ago. But he'd assumed the nip had been to her ego, exactly where he thought he'd aimed. He'd known he pissed her off—

she made that crystal-clear—but he assumed that was pride.

If he had known she loved him, he'd have found a way to break things off more gently.

Wouldn't he?

Christ, he hoped so. They'd been friends. Even when they had been consumed with and by each other, they'd been friends. He would never deliberately wound a friend.

He'd been no good for her, that's what it came down to. He'd been no good for anybody at that time in his life. She was better off that he had ended it.

He headed for the mountains and began the steep, twisty climb.

But she'd loved him. There was little to nothing he could do about that now. He wasn't at all sure there was anything he could have done at the time. He wasn't ready for the Big Love then. He wouldn't have known how to define it, what to think about it.

Hell, he hadn't been able to think at all when it came to Dana. After one look at her when he'd come home from college, every single thought of her had shot straight to his glands.

It had terrified him.

He could smile over that now. His initial shock at his own reaction to her, his over-whelming guilt that he was fantasizing about the sister of his closest friend.

He'd been horrified, and fascinated, and ultimately obsessed.

Tall, curvy, sharp-tongued Dana Steele, with her big, full bodied laugh, her questing mind, her punch-first temper.

Everything about her had pulled at him.

Damn if it still didn't.

When he'd seen her again on this trip back, when she yanked open the door of Flynn's house and stood there snarling at him, the sheer *want* for her had blown straight through him.

Just as her sheer dislike for him had all but taken off his head.

If they could work their way around to be-ing friends again, to finding that connection, that affection that had always been be-tween them, maybe they could work their way forward to something more.

To what, he couldn't say. But he wanted Dana back in his life.

And, there was no point in denying it, he wanted her back in his bed.

They'd made progress toward friendship

during that shopping stint. They'd been easy with each other for a while, as if the years between hadn't happened.

But, of course, they had. And as soon as he and Dana had remembered those years, the progress had taken an abrupt turn and stomped away in a huff.

So now he had a mission, Jordan decided. He had to find a way to win her back. Friend and lover—in whatever order suited them both best.

The search for the key had, among other things, given him an opening. He intended to use it.

When he realized that he'd driven to Warrior's Peak, he stopped, pulled to the side of the road.

He remembered climbing that high stone wall as a teenager with Brad and Flynn. They had camped in the woods, with a hijacked six-pack that none of them was old enough to drink.

The Peak was untenanted then, a big, fanciful, spooky place. The perfect place to fascinate a trio of boys with a couple of beers in them.

A high, full moon, he recalled as he climbed out of the car. A black-glass sky and just enough wind, just a hint of wind, to stir the leaves and whisper.

He could see it all now, as clearly as he'd seen it then. Maybe more clearly, he thought, amused at himself. He was older, and stone-cold sober, and he had—admittedly—added a few flourishes to the memory.

He liked to think of the scene with a layer of fog drifting over the ground, and a moon so round and white it looked carved into the glass of the sky. Stars sharp as the points of darts. The low, haunting call of an owl, and the rustle of night prey in the high grass. In the distance, with an echo that rolled through the night, the baying of a dog.

He'd added those beats when he used that house and that night in his first major book.

But for *Phantom Watch* there'd been one element of that night he hadn't had to imagine. Because it had happened. Because he'd seen it.

Even now, as a man past thirty with none of the naïveté of the boy left in him, he believed it.

She'd walked along the parapet, under

the hard, white moon, sliding in and out of shadows like a ghost, with her hair flying, her cape—surely it had been a cape—billowing.

She'd owned the night. He'd thought that then and he thought it now. She had *been* the night.

She'd looked at him, Jordan remembered as he wandered to the iron gates, as he stared through them at the great stone house on the rise. He hadn't been able to see her face, but he'd known she looked down, straight into his eyes.

He'd felt the punch of it, the power, like a blow meant to awaken rather than to harm.

His mind had sizzled from it, and nothing—not the beer, not his youth, not even the shock—had been able to dull the thrill.

She'd looked at him, Jordan remembered again as he scanned the parapet. And she'd *known* him.

Flynn and Brad hadn't seen her. By the time his mind had clicked back into gear and he shouted them over, she was gone.

It had spooked them, of course. Deliciously. The way sightings of ghosts and fanciful creatures are meant to.

Though years later, when he wrote of her,

he made her a ghost, he'd known then—he knew now—that she was as alive as he.

"Whoever you were," he murmured, "you helped me make my mark. So, thanks."

He stood there, hands in his pockets, peering through the bars. The house was part of his past, and oddly, he'd considered making it part of his future. He'd been toying with calling to see if it was available just days before Flynn had contacted him about the portrait of the young Arthur of Britain. He'd bought that painting on impulse five years ago at the gallery where Malory used to work, though he hadn't met her then. Not only had it been a major element of Malory's quest, but they'd discovered the painting, along with *The Daughters of Glass* and one Brad had bought separately had all been painted by Rowena, Jordan thought, centuries ago.

New York, his present, had served its purpose for him. He'd been ready for a change. Ready to come home. Then Flynn had made it so very easy.

It gave him the opportunity to come back, test the waters, and his feelings. He'd known, this time he'd known, as soon as he saw the majestic run of the Appalachians, that he wanted them back.

This time—surprise—he was back to stay.

He wanted those hills. The riot of them in fall, the lush green of them in summer. He wanted to stand and see them frozen in white, so still and regal, or hazed with the tender touch of spring.

He wanted the Valley, with its tidy streets and tourists. The familiarity of faces that had known him since his youth, the smell of backyard barbecues and the snippets of local gossip.

He wanted his friends, the comfort and the joy of them. Pizza out of the box, a beer on the porch, old jokes that no one laughed at the same way a childhood friend did.

And he still wanted that damn house, Jordan realized with a slow, dawning smile. He wanted it now every bit as much as he had when he was a sixteen-year-old dreamer with whole worlds yet to be explored.

So, he would bide his time there—he was cagier than he'd been at sixteen. And he would find out what Rowena and Pitte planned to do with the place when they moved on.

To wherever they moved on.

So, maybe the house was both his past and his future.

He ran bits of Rowena's clue through his head. He was part of Dana's past, and like it or not, he was part of her present. Very probably he would be part—one way or another—of her future.

So what did he, and the Peak, have to do with her quest for the key?

And wasn't it incredibly self-serving to assume that he had anything to do with it.

"Maybe," he said quietly to himself. "But right at the moment, I don't see a damn thing wrong with that."

With one last look at the house, he turned and walked back to his car. He would go back to Flynn's and spend some time thinking it through, working out the angles.

Then he would present them to Dana, whether she wanted to hear them or not.

Bradley Vane had some plans and plots of his own. Zoe was a puzzlement to him. Prickly and argumentative one minute, scrupulously polite the next. He would knock, and the door to her would crack open. He could detect glimmers of humor and sweetness, then the door would slam shut in his face with a blast of cold air.

He'd never had a woman take an aversion to him on sight. It was especially galling that the first one who did happened to be the one he was so outrageously attracted to.

He hadn't been able to get her face out of his mind for three years, since he'd first seen *After the Spell,* the painting he'd bought—the second one Rowena had painted of the Daughters of Glass.

Zoe's face on the goddess who slept, three thousand years, in a coffin of glass.

However ridiculous it was, Brad had fallen in love at first sight with the woman in the portrait.

The woman in reality was a much tougher nut.

But Vanes were known for their tenacity. And their determination to win.

If she'd come into the store that afternoon, he could and would have rearranged his schedule and taken her through. It would've given him the opportunity to spend some time with her, while keeping it all practical and friendly.

Of course, you'd think that when her car broke down and he happened by and offered her a lift, *that* interlude would have been practical and friendly.

Instead she'd gotten her back up because he pointed out the flaws in her plan to try to fix the car while wearing a dinner dress, and he, understandably, had refused to mess with the engine himself.

He'd offered to call a mechanic for her, hadn't he? Brad thought, getting riled up again at the memory. He'd stood there debating with her for ten minutes, thus ensuring that whatever she did they would both be late to the Peak.

And when she grudgingly accepted the ride finally, she spent every minute of it in an ice-cold funk.

He was absolutely crazy about her.

"Sick," he muttered as he turned the corner to her street. "You're a sick man, Vane."

Her little house sat tidily back from the road on a neat stamp of lawn. She'd planted fall flowers along the sunny left side. The house itself was a cheerful yellow with bright white trim. A boy's red bike lay on its side in the front yard, reminding him that she had a son he'd yet to catch sight of.

Brad pulled his new Mercedes behind her decade-old hatchback.

He walked back to the cargo area and hauled out the gift he hoped would turn the tide in his favor.

He carted it to the front door, then caught himself running a nervous hand through his hair.

Women never made him nervous.

Annoyed with himself, he knocked briskly.

It was the boy who opened it, and for the second time in his life, Brad found himself dazzled by a face. He looked like his mother—dark hair, tawny eyes, pretty, pointed features. The dark hair was mussed, the eyes cool with suspicion, but neither detracted a whit from the exotic good looks.

Brad had enough young cousins, as-sorted nieces and nephews, to be able to peg the kid at around eight or nine. Give him another ten years, Brad thought, and this one would have to beat the coeds off with a stick.

"Simon, right?" Brad offered an I'm-harmless-you-can-trust-me grin. "I'm Brad Vane, a friend of your mom's." Sort of. "She around?"

"Yeah, she's around." Though the boy gave Brad a very quick up-and-down glance, Brad had the certain sensation he'd been studied carefully and thoroughly, and the jury was still out. "You gotta wait out there, 'cause I'm not allowed to let anybody in if I don't know who they are."

"No problem."

The door shut in his face. Like mother, like son, Brad thought, then heard the boy shout.

"Mom! There's this guy at the door. He looks like a lawyer or something."

"Oh, Jesus," Brad mumbled and cast his eyes to heaven.

Moments later the door opened again. Zoe's expression changed from puzzlement to surprise to mild irritation in three distinct stages.

"Oh. It's you. Um . . . is there something I can do for you?"

You could let me nibble my way up your neck to the back of your ear for a start, Brad thought, but kept his easy smile in place. "Dana was in the store this afternoon, picking up some supplies."

"Yes. I know." She tucked a dishcloth in the waistband of her jeans, let the tail hang down her hip. "Did she forget something?"

"Not exactly. I just thought you might be able to use this." He lifted the gift he'd leaned against the side of the house, then had the pleasure of seeing her blink in surprise an instant before she laughed.

Really laughed. He loved the sound of it, the way it danced over her face, into her eyes.

"You brought me a stepladder?"

"An essential tool for any home or business improvement project."

"Yes, it is. I have one." Obviously realizing how ungracious that sounded, she flushed and hurried on. "But it's . . . old. And we can certainly use another. It was really thoughtful of you."

"We of HomeMakers appreciate your business. Where would you like me to put this?"

"Oh, well." She glanced behind her, then seemed to sigh. "Why don't you just bring it in here? I'll figure that out later." She stepped back, bumped into the boy who was hovering at her back.

"Simon, this is Mr. Vane. He's an old friend of Flynn's."

"He said he was a friend of yours."

"Working on that." Brad carried the step-ladder into the house. "Hi, Simon. How's it going?"

"It's going okay. How come you're wearing a suit if you're carrying ladders around?"

"Simon."

"Good question." Brad ignored Zoe and concentrated on the boy. "I had a couple of meetings earlier today. Suits are more intimidating."

"Wearing them sucks. Mom made me wear one to Aunt Joleen's wedding last year. With a tie. Bogus."

"Thanks for that fashion report." Zoe hooked an arm around Simon's throat and made him grin.

Then they both grinned, at each other, and Brad's eyes were dazzled.

"Homework?"

"Done. Video game time."

"Twenty minutes."

"Forty-five."

"Thirty."

"Sweet!" He wriggled free, then bolted across the room to the TV.

Now that her hands were no longer full of boy, Zoe didn't know what to do with them. She laid one on the ladder. "It's a really nice stepladder. The fiberglass ones are so light and easy to work with."

"Quality with value—HomeMakers' by-words."

The sounds of a ballpark abruptly filled the tiny living room behind her. "It's his favorite," Zoe managed. "He'd rather play baseball—virtual or in real life—than breathe." She cleared her throat, wondered what the hell she was supposed to do next. "Ah . . . can I get you something to drink?"

"Sure. Whatever's handy."

"Okay." Damn it. "Just, um, have a seat. I'll be back in a minute."

What to do with Bradley Vane? she asked herself as she hurried back to the kitchen. In her house. Plunked down in his expensive shoes in her living room. An hour before dinner.

She stopped herself, pressed her hands to her eyes. It was okay, it was perfectly all right. He'd done something very considerate, and she would reciprocate by bringing him something to drink, having a few minutes of conversation.

She never knew what she was supposed to say to him. She didn't *understand* men like him. The kind of man who came from serious money. Who'd done things and had things and gone places to get more.

And he made her so stupidly nervous and defensive.

Should she take him a glass of wine? No, no, he was driving, and she didn't have any really good wine anyway. Coffee? Tea?

Christ.

At her wits' end, she opened the refrigerator. She had juice, she had milk.

Here, Bradley Charles Vane IV, of the really rich and important Pennsylvania Vanes, have a nice glass of cow juice, then be on your way.

She blew out a breath, then dug a bottle of ginger ale out of a cupboard. She took out her nicest glass, checked for water spots, then filled it with ice. She added the ginger ale, careful to keep it a safe half inch below the rim.

She tugged at the hem of the sweatshirt she'd tossed on over jeans, looked down resignedly at the thick gray socks she wore in lieu of shoes, and hoped she didn't smell of the brass cleaner she'd been using to attack the tarnish on an umbrella stand she'd picked up at the flea market.

Suit or no suit, she thought as she squared her shoulders, she wouldn't be intimidated in her own home. She would take him his drink, speak politely, hopefully briefly, then show him out.

No doubt he had more exciting things to do than sit in her living room drinking ginger ale and watching a nine-year-old play video baseball.

She carried the glass down the hall, then stopped and stared.

Bradley Charles Vane IV wasn't watching Simon play. He was, to her amazement, sitting on the floor in his gorgeous suit, playing with her son.

"Two strikes, baby. You are doomed." With a cackle, Simon wiggled his butt and prepared for the next pitch.

"Dream on, kid. See my man on third? He's about to score."

She stepped farther into the room, but neither of them noticed her as the ball whistled toward the plate and the bat cracked against virtual cowhide.

"He's got it, he's got it, he's got it," Simon said in a kind of whispered chant. "Yeah, yeah, *shagged* that sucker."

"And the runner tags," Brad said. "Watch him fly, heading for home. Here comes the throw . . . and he slides, and . . ."

Safe! the home base ump decreed.

"Oh, yeah." Brad gave Simon a quick elbow nudge. "One to zip, pal."

"Not bad. For an old guy." Simon chuckled. "Now prepare to be humiliated."

"Excuse me. I brought you some ginger ale."

"Time out." Brad twisted around to smile up at her. "Thanks. Do you mind if we play out the inning?"

"No. Of course not." She set the glass on the coffee table, and wondered what she should do now. "I'll just be back in the kitchen. I need to start dinner."

When his eyes stayed so direct and easy on hers, she heard—with some horror—the words tumbling out of her mouth. "You're welcome to stay. It's just chicken."

"That'd be great."

He swiveled back around to resume the game.

Mental note, Brad thought: Forget the roses and champagne. Home improvement supplies are the key to this particular lady's lock.

While Zoe was standing in her kitchen wondering how the hell she was going to turn her humble chicken into something worthy of a more sophisticated palate, Dana was soothing her ego with takeout pizza.

She hadn't meant to tell him. Ever. Why give him one more thing to smirk at her about?

But he hadn't smirked, she admitted, washing down the pizza with cold beer. In fact, he'd looked as though she'd put a bullet dead center of his forehead.

Neither could she claim he'd looked pleased or puffed up about the knowledge that she'd been in love with him.

The fact of it was, he'd looked shocked, then sorry.

Oh, God, maybe that was worse.

She sulked over the pizza. Though she had her evening book open on the table beside her, she hadn't read a single word. She was just going to have to deal with this, she told herself.

She couldn't afford to obsess about Jordan. Not only because she had other things that should occupy her time and her thoughts, but it just wasn't healthy.

Since it was clear he was going to hang around for several weeks, and there was no avoiding him unless she avoided Flynn and Brad, they would be seeing each other regularly.

And if she accepted all that had happened in the last month, all she'd learned, she was going to have to accept that Jordan had been meant to come back. He was a part of it all.

And damn it, he could be useful.

He had a good brain, one that picked up on and filed away details.

It was one of the skills that made him such a strong writer. Oh, she hated to admit that one. She hoped her tongue would fall out before she spoke those words to him.

But he had such talent.

He'd chosen that talent over her, and that still hurt. But if he could help her find the key, she would have to put that hurt away. At least temporarily.

She could always kick his ass later.

Mollified, she ate some more pizza. Tomorrow she would get a fresh start. She had the whole day, the whole week, the whole month to do whatever she felt needed to be done. There'd be no need to set the alarm, dress for work.

She could spend the whole day in her pajamas if she wanted to, digging into her research, outlining a plan, surfing the Net for more data.

She would contact Zoe and Malory and set up another summit meeting. They worked well together.

Maybe they'd start to work on the building. Physical labor could spark mental acuity.

The first key had been hidden, in a manner of speaking, in the building they were buying. Of course, Malory had had to paint the key into existence before she could retrieve it from the painting.

Maybe the second, or at least the link to the second, was in the house as well.

In any case, it was a plan. Something solid to get her teeth into.

She shoved the pizza aside and rose to phone Malory first. With plans to meet for a full day's painting set, she phoned Zoe.

"Hey. It's Dana. Just got off the phone with Mal. We're going to start the great transformation at the house tomorrow. Nine o'clock. Malory voted for eight, but there's no way in hell I'm getting up that early when I'm not drawing an actual paycheck."

"Nine's fine. Dana." Her voice dropped to a hissing whisper. "Bradley's here."

"Oh. Okay, I'll let you go, then. See—"

"No, no. What am I supposed to do with him?"

"Gee, Zoe, I don't know. What do you want to do with him?"

"Nothing." Her voice went up a notch before lowering again. "I don't know how this happened. He's out in the living room playing video baseball with Simon, in a suit."

"Simon's wearing a suit?" Dana tucked her tongue in her cheek. "Boy, things're pretty formal at your house."

"Stop it." But she laughed a little. "*He's* wearing a suit. Bradley. He came to the door with a stepladder, and before I knew—"

"With a what? What for? To clean out

your gutters? That was not a euphemism, by the way. But, come to think of it, it'd be a pretty good one."

"He gave it—the stepladder—to me—to us—" she corrected quickly. "For the painting and stuff. He thought we could use it."

"That was nice of him. He's a nice guy."

"That's not the point! What am I supposed to do with this chicken?"

"Brad brought you a chicken?"

"No." There was helpless, hooting laughter over the line. "Why would anyone bring me a chicken?"

"I was just wondering the same thing."

"I have chicken breasts defrosted, for dinner. What am I going to do with them now?"

"I'd try cooking them. Jeez, Zoe, relax. It's just Brad. Throw the chicken in a pan, rustle up some rice or potatoes, whatever, add something green and toss it on a plate. He's not fussy."

"Don't tell me he's not fussy." She went back to the hissing whisper. "We don't do *cordon bleu* in this house. I don't even know for sure what *cordon bleu* means. He's wearing an Audemars Piguet. Do you think I don't know what an Audemars Piguet is?"

It was fascinating, really, Dana decided, to realize her old friend Brad turned a sensible woman like Zoe into a raving lunatic. "Okay, I'll bite. What is an Audemars Piguet and is it really sexy?"

"It's a watch. A watch that costs more than my house. Or damn near. Never mind." There was a long, long sigh. "I'm making myself crazy, and it's just stupid."

"I can't argue with you about that."

"I'll see you tomorrow."

Shaking her head, Dana hung up. Now she had one more thing to look forward to in the morning. And that was hearing all about how Zoe and Brad handled a chicken dinner.

But for now, she was switching gears. She was going to try out her tub book and a long, hot, soaking bath.

Chapter Five

She decided to make the bath an event. The first pure luxury of unemployment. Might as well celebrate it, Dana told herself, as cry over it.

She went for mango for that tropical sensation, and dumped a generous amount of the scented bubble bath under the running water. She lit candles, then decided a bottle of beer didn't quite measure up to the rest of the ambience.

Already naked, she headed into the kitchen, poured the beer into a glass.

Back in the bath, she anchored her hair on top of her head, then, for the hell of it, slopped on some of the hydrating facial cream Zoe had talked her into.

It couldn't hurt.

Realizing she was missing an important element, she went out to flip through her CDs, found an old Jimmy Buffett. Time to go to the islands, she decided, and with Jimmy already nibbling on sponge cake, she sank with a long sigh into the hot, fragrant water.

For the first five minutes she simply basked, let the hot water, the scents, the absolute bliss do their work.

A big white ball bearing Joan's irritated face bounced down a long incline, slapping into rocks, picking up grit. The face took on a shocked expression as it rolled straight off the edge of a cliff.

A bouncy blond ponytail followed it. Tension oozed away, drop by drop.

"Bye-bye," Dana murmured, well satisfied.

She roused herself to rinse away the facial cream with a washcloth, and reminded herself to put on some moisturizer when she got out of the tub.

She frowned at her toes, turned her head this way and that. Maybe it was time for a pedicure, ending it with some sassy, liberat-

ing color suitable for the recently unemployed and the soon-to-be entrepreneur.

It was coming in damn handy having a
stylist for a friend and business partner.

Ready for stage two, she decided, and
picked up her book from the edge of the
tub. With a sip of beer, the turn of a page,
Dana slipped into the story.

The tropical setting, the romance and intrigue, perfectly suited her needs. She
drifted along with the words, began to see
the deep blue shine of the water, the sugar-
white sparkle of the sand. She felt the
warm, moist air flutter over her skin and
smelled the sea, the heat, the strong perfume of the lilies potted on the wide ve-
randa.

She stepped off sunbaked wood and
onto sunbaked sand. Gulls cried as they
wheeled overhead, and the sound of them
echoing was a kind of chant.

She felt the powdery grit of the sand under her bare feet, and the teasing way her
thin silk wrap fluttered around her legs.

She walked to the water, then along its
edge, basking in the beauty of the solitude.

She could go wherever she wanted, or
nowhere at all. All those years of responsi-

bility and work, of schedules and obligations, were behind her now.

Why had she ever thought they mattered so much?

The water rolled toward shore, foamy lace at its edges, then waltzed back into its own heart with a sigh. She saw the silver flash and leap of dolphins at play, and beyond, so far beyond, the delicate line of the horizon.

It was perfect and peaceful and lovely. And so liberating to know she was completely alone.

She wondered why she'd ever felt compelled to work so hard, to worry, to care about what should be or had to be done, when all she really wanted was to be alone in a world of her own choosing.

A world, she understood without any sense of surprise or wonder, that she could change with a thought or on a whim.

There was no heartache unless she wished for it, no company unless she created it. Her life could spin out—color and movement and quiet and sound—like the pages of a book that never had to end.

If she wanted a companion, she had only to imagine one. Lover or friend.

But really, she needed no one but herself. People brought problems, responsibilities, baggage, needs that were not her own. Life was so much simpler in solitude.

Her lips curved with contentment as she wandered along the sickle curve of beach where the only footprints were hers, toward the lush green shade of palms and trees heavy with fruit.

Cooler here, because she wished it to be. Soft, soft grass beneath her feet, sprinkles of sunlight through the fronds overhead, and the sharp, bright flash of birds with feathers the rich colors of jewels.

She plucked fruit from a branch—a mango, of course—and took the first sweet, juicy bite.

It was chilled, almost icy cold, just the way she liked it best, rather than warmed by that streaming sun.

She lifted her arms, saw they were tanned a smooth and dusky gold, and when she looked down she grinned to see her toes were painted a bold and celebrational pink.

Exactly right, she realized. That's exactly what I wanted.

Her mind began to wander as she

roamed through the glade, watched gold-fish dance in a pool of clear blue water. She wanted the fish to be red as rubies, and they were. Green as emeralds, and they became so.

The wonderful flash of bright color in the water made her laugh, and at the sound of it, birds—more jewels—glided into that perfect bowl of sky.

This could be her forever place, she realized, changing only as she wished it to change. Here, she would never hurt again, or need, or be disappointed.

Everything would always be just the way she wanted it to be . . . until she wanted it to be different.

She lifted the mango again, and a thought passed through her mind: But what will I do here, day after day?

She seemed to hear voices, just the murmur of them, far off. Even as the breeze kicked up, whisked them away, she turned, looked back.

Flowers tangled on lush green vines. Fruit dripped, glossy as gems, from the delicate branches of trees. The sound of the surf, a seductive whisper, shivered through the air.

She stood, alone, in the paradise she had made.

"No."

She said it out loud, as a kind of test.

This isn't right. This isn't who I am, isn't what I want.

The fruit she held slipped out of her fingers and hit the ground at her feet with an ugly splat. Her heart jolted in her chest as she saw it was rotten at the core.

The colors around her were too harsh, she realized, the textures too flat. Like a stage set, like standing on an elaborate set built for an endless play.

"This is a trick." Angry wasps began to buzz around the spoiled fruit. "This is a lie!"

As she shouted it, the blue sky turned to boiling black. Wind screamed, ripping fronds, hurling flowers and fruit. The air turned bitterly cold.

She ran, with icy rain stinging her face, plastering the silk against her body.

In this wild and wicked world, trick or no trick, she knew she was no longer alone.

She ran, through the hurricane scream of the storm, through the lashing, razor-edged fronds that seemed to snatch at her arms and legs like grasping fingers.

Breathless, terrified, she spilled out onto the beach. The sea was a nightmare, walls of oily black water rising up, pounding down, eating away at the land bite by greedy bite. Palm trees crashed down behind her, and the white sand caved in on itself, like a world collapsing.

Even in the dark, in the cold, she felt the shadow spread over her. The pain shocked her to her feet again, had her stumbling forward as she felt something ripping inside her.

Ripping out of her.

Gathering all her strength, all her will, she made her choice, and plunged into the killing sea.

She reared up, gasping, shuddering, a scream tearing at her throat.

And found herself sitting up in her tub, chilly water sloshing over the side. Her book was floating, her candles pooling in their own wax.

Panicked, she crawled out of the tub, and for a moment simply curled shivering on the bath mat.

With her teeth chattering, she forced herself up, grabbed a towel and wrapped it around her. Suddenly the thought of being naked only added to the layers of fear. She stumbled out of the bathroom, her heart still heaving inside her chest, to fumble a robe out of her closet.

She'd wondered if she would ever be warm again.

He'd pulled her in. Kane. The dark sorcerer who had challenged the king of the gods and had stolen the souls of his daughters. Because they were half mortal, Dana thought, and that offended his sensibilities. And because he wanted to rule.

He had conjured the Box of Souls with its triple locks, and had forged the three keys that no god could turn. A kind of nasty joke, she thought as she struggled to catch her breath. A rude thumbing of his nose at the god who had had the bad taste to fall in love with a mortal woman.

The spell Kane had cast behind the Curtain of Dreams had held for three thousand years. Which meant he had plenty of punch—and he'd just given her a good hard shot to remind her that he was watching. He'd slipped into her head and pulled her into one of her own fantasies. How long? she wondered, hugging herself for warmth. How long had she been lying there, naked, helpless, out of her own body?

It was dark now, fully dark, and she switched on the light for fear of what might wait in the shadows. But the room was empty. She was alone in it, just as she'd been alone on that illusion of beach.

At the hard rap on her front door the scream started building again. She clutched a hand to her throat to trap it and all but sprinted to the door.

Whoever it was, it was better than being alone.

Or so she thought until she saw Jordan.

Oh, God, not him. Not now.

"What do you want?" she snapped. "Go away. I'm busy."

Before she could slam the door, he slapped a hand on it. "I want to talk to you about . . . What is it?" She was white as a ghost, her dark eyes enormous, and glassy with shock. "What's wrong?"

"Nothing. I'm fine." The shakes started up again, harder this time. "I don't want to . . . oh, the hell with it. You're better than nothing."

She simply fell against him. "I'm so cold. I'm so goddamn cold."

He scooped her right off her feet, then booted the door shut behind him. "Couch or bed?"

"Couch. I've got the shakes. I can't stop."

"Okay. It's okay." He sat, kept her cradled in his lap as he tugged the throw off the back of the couch. "You'll warm up in a minute," he comforted, and tucked the throw around her. "Just hold on to me."

He rubbed her back, her arms, then just wrapped his own arms around her and banked on body heat to do the rest. "Why are you wet?"

"I was in the tub. Then I wasn't. I don't know how it works." Her hand was fisted in his jacket, kneading there as she fought to steady herself. "The son of a bitch got inside my head. You don't even know it's happening, it just does. I'm not going to make any sense for a couple more minutes."

"It's okay. I think I'm following you." His stroking hands bumped the band that tied her hair up. Without thinking, he slipped it off, combed his fingers through. "It was Kane? He was here?"

"I don't know." Exhausted, she laid her head against his chest. She had her breath back at least. It no longer felt as if a hand was squeezing her racing heart. "Like I said, I don't know how it works. I wanted to take a bath, relax."

To give her something else to think about, he deliberately sniffed her neck. "You smell terrific. Tasty. What is that?"

"Mango. Cut it out." But she made no attempt to get off his lap. "I did the bubble bath routine. Lit candles, got my bath book. It's got a Caribbean setting—the book, so that's why the mango and Buffett. I put a Jimmy Buffett CD on."

She was rambling, but he let her talk it out.

"So, I'm settling in—hot bubbles, Buffett, beer and book. The book's a romantic thriller, nice fast pace, sharp dialogue. The scene I'm reading was from the heroine's viewpoint, during one of her breathers. She's on the terrace of her room at this tropical resort, that's actually a front for . . . Never mind, not important."

She closed her eyes, soothed by the steady stroking of his hand over her hair. "So she's standing there, looking out at the water. You've got the surf, the breeze, gulls. The writer paints a good picture, so I'm seeing it.

"Then I'm not just seeing it in my head, in the words on the page. But I don't even realize everything shifted, that I'm inside the image in my own head. That's the scariest part. You don't *know.*"

She rubbed her hands over her face. "I've got to get up." She tossed the throw aside and stood, then as an afterthought tightened the loose belt of her robe. "I was on the beach. Not just thinking about the beach, not just seeing it. I was there. I could smell the water, and flowers. Lilies, there were pots of white lilies. Didn't seem the least bit strange that I was all of a sudden walking over the sand, feeling the sun, the breeze. My feet are bare, my toes are painted, I'm tanned and I'm wearing this long silk thing, just a wrap. I can feel it fluttering around my legs."

"I bet you looked terrific."

She glanced over at him, and for the first time since he'd come in, the dimples winked into her cheeks. "You're trying to keep me from freaking again."

"That's a definite yes, but I still bet you looked terrific."

"Sure I did. It was my fantasy. My own, personal tropical island. Perfect weather, blue sea, white sand, and solitude. I was even thinking, as I walked the beach, how foolish I'd been to ever worry about responsibilities. I could do or have anything I wanted."

"What did you want, Dane?"

"At that moment? Just to be alone, I guess, not to worry about anything. Not to think how upset I was that the evil Joan had manipulated me out of a job I really loved, and how I'm a little scared about starting Act Two of the Life of Dana."

"That's human. That's normal."

"It is." She glanced back at him—big, handsome Jordan Hawke watching her with those deep blue eyes. He understood she wasn't looking for meaningless words of comfort or sympathy.

"It is," she repeated, as soothed by his understanding as she'd been by his hands. "I walked toward this grove of palm and fruit trees. I picked a mango. I could taste it," she paused, touching her fingers to her lips. "Basically, I just walked along thinking, boy, this is the life. But it wasn't the life, it wasn't *my* life. And it's not what I want, not really."

She came back to the couch, afraid her legs might go weak again when she told the rest. "That's the thought that came into my head—and then I heard voices. Off in the distance, but familiar. And I thought, this isn't real. It's just a trick. That's when it happened. Oh, God." As her chest tightened again, she pressed her fists between her breasts. "Oh, God."

"Easy now." He closed his hands over hers, squeezing lightly until she met his eyes. "Take your time."

"Storm came in. That's a mild word for it. When I realized it wasn't real, the world went to hell. Wind, rain, dark, and the cold. Jesus, Jordan, it was so cold. I starting running. I knew I had to get away, because I wasn't alone after all. He was there, and he was coming for me. I got back to the beach, but the ocean was insane. Walls of black water, fifty, sixty feet high. I fell. I felt him over me, around me. That cold. And the pain. Horrible, tearing pain."

Her voice was breaking. She couldn't stop it. "He was ripping out my soul. I knew

I'd rather face anything but that, so I jumped into the sea."

"Come here. Come here, you're shaking again." He gathered her close.

"I woke up, or came back, whatever it is. In the tub, strangling for air. The bathwater had gone cold. I don't know how long I'd been out of it, Jordan. I don't know how long he had me."

"He didn't have you. He didn't," he insisted when she shook her head. Gently, he eased her back so he could see her face. "A part of you, that's all. He can't get the whole, because he can't see the whole. A fantasy, like you said. That's how he works. And he can't push you into it so deep that a part of your mind doesn't surface again and question. And know."

"Maybe not. But he sure knows how to go for the gut. I've never been that scared."

"Once you move past that into pissed-off, you'll feel better."

"Yeah, you're probably right. I want a drink," she decided and pushed away from him.

"You want water?" He realized she was coming back fast when the question had her curling her lip at him.

"I want a beer. I never had my bath beer." She rose, seemed to hesitate. "You want one?"

Still watching her, he laid his fingers on his own wrist as if checking for a pulse. "Yeah."

He liked the way she snickered at him before she walked away. It was a normal sound, a Dana sound. There'd been nothing normal in the way she'd collapsed on him.

If he hadn't come by . . . but he had, he reminded himself. He was here, she wasn't alone. And she'd gotten through it.

He got to his feet, took his first real look around her place. Pure Dana, he thought. Strong color, comfortable furniture, and books.

He wandered after her, leaned on the wall. More books, he noted. Who but Dana would keep Nietzsche in the kitchen? "First time I've been in your place."

She kept her back to him as she opened two beers. "You wouldn't have gotten in this time if I hadn't been wigged."

"Despite that lack of welcome, I like it. Suits you, Stretch. And because it does, I don't suppose you'd consider bunking at Flynn's for the next little while. I can take my stuff over to Brad's and hang there if that's a factor."

She turned back slowly. "Are you being accommodating because I was hysterical?"

"I'm being accommodating because I want you to feel safe. To be safe."

"No need to put yourself out."

"I care about you." He shifted, blocking her exit before she could move past him. There was a quick flash of rage over his face, almost as quickly banked.

Where had that been hiding? she wondered. And how did he tuck it away again?

"I care, Dana. Just for a minute, one damn minute, set aside the way things ended up. We cared about each other, and if you'd feel safer at Flynn's, I'll get out of your way."

"All the way back to New York?"

His mouth thinned as he took one of the bottles out of her hands. "No."

Maybe it was unfair to poke and prod at him. But what the hell did she care about fair when it came to Jordan? "I wouldn't feel safer at Flynn's—with or without you around. In spite of my condition when you knocked on the door, I can take care of myself. I *did* take care of myself. I got out of it without your help. And nobody, not you, not that bastard Kane, is going to run me out of my own apartment."

"Well." He took a sip of beer. "I see you've moved to the pissed-off stage of tonight's entertainment."

"I don't like being manipulated. He used my own thoughts against me, and you're using old feelings. We cared about each other?" she shot out. "Maybe we did, but remember, that's past tense. If you want to be such a nice guy and get out of my way, then get out of it now. You're crowding me."

"I've got things to say to you, and if I've got to block you in to get you to hear them, then that's the way it is. I didn't know you loved me. I don't know what it would have changed, I just know it would've changed . . . something. Just like I know I wasn't ready for it. I wasn't smart enough or steady enough."

"You were smart and steady enough to do what you wanted."

"That's exactly right." With his eyes locked on hers, he nodded. "I was self-absorbed, broody, and restless. What the hell did you want with me, anyway?"

"You idiot." Because she'd lost her taste

for it, she set the beer aside. "You've just described the sort of guy every girl falls for at least once. Then you add those whiffs of recklessness, the brain, the looks, and the chemistry, and I didn't have a chance. How can you make a living writing about people when you don't understand half of them?"

When she tried to push past him, he took her arm. The look she sent him could have melted steel. "Buy a clue, Hawke. I said girls fall for *once.* Girls generally evolve into smart and steady women who put away the childish things like self-absorbed assholes."

"That's good. I prefer women." He put his beer on the counter. "I've always preferred you."

"Do you think that makes my heart go pitty-pat?"

"Not yours, Stretch. But this might."

He caught her face in his free hand, allowed himself the perverse pleasure of seeing her fury leap out of her eyes, then covered her mouth with his.

Thank God, he thought, thank God she was angry enough that he could do what he hadn't been able to do when she was pale and shaken.

There'd never been a taste he'd craved

the way he craved Dana's. He had never understood it. And never worried that he should. It simply was. She might rake him to the bone for it, but he had a point to prove. To both of them.

He wasn't gentle. She'd never seemed to expect or need gentleness from him. He simply pressed her back to the wall and took.

Heat flooded her, as enervating and nearly as terrifying as the cold she'd experienced earlier. There was no point in lying to herself, she wanted to feel this *involved* again, this aware of self, this needy.

But lying to him was a different matter entirely, so she shoved at him, struggled with herself, and refused to yield to either.

He laid a hand on her heart, and with his mouth only a breath from hers now, stared into her eyes. "Yeah. That got it going."

"Get this. It's not going to happen. It's never going to happen again."

"Somebody once said, 'What's past is prologue.' "

"Shakespeare, you ignorant jerk. *The Tempest.*"

"Right." Amused admiration flickered over his face. "You were always better at remembering that stuff than I was. But, in any case, I'm not looking to repeat myself. However much we're the same, we're that much different. We're not the same people we were, Dana. I want a chance to see who we would be together now."

"I'm not interested."

"Sure you are. You've got a curious mind, and you're wondering, the same as I am. But maybe you're afraid that being around me will prove too much for your self-control."

"Please. You arrogant pig."

"Well, then, why don't we test your self-control and satisfy my curiosity, and have ourselves a date?"

He'd managed to throw her off. "A what?"

"You remember what a date is, Dane. Two people going out to a prearranged location." Idly, he ran the lapel of her robe between his thumb and forefinger. "Oh, I see, you thought I meant we'd just jump straight into bed, rock and roll. Okay, if that's the way you want it—"

"Stop it." Baffled, annoyed, and more than half amused, she elbowed him aside. "I was not thinking about sex." And because that was a complete lie, her tone was aloof. "There's not going to be any rock and roll, as you so succinctly put it. And the idea of a date is just ludicrous."

"Why? You'd get a free meal out of it. And the added pleasure of being able to shut me down when I put the moves on you, and send me home sexually frustrated."

"That does have some appeal."

"Saturday night. I'll pick you up at seven-thirty."

"How do you know I don't already have a date for Saturday night?"

He grinned at her. "I asked Flynn if you were seeing anybody. I know how to do my research, Stretch."

"Flynn doesn't know everything," she retorted as Jordan strolled away. "Wait just a damn minute." She rushed out into the living room, caught up with him at the door. "There are some basic requirements. The meal's in an actual restaurant. No fast food, and not the Main Street Diner. And when you say you'll pick me up at seven-thirty, that doesn't mean you get here at seven-forty-five."

"Agreed." He paused. "I know there's no point in asking if you want me to stay, bunk on the couch. But you could call Malory, and I could hang out until she got here."

"I'm okay."

"You always were, Stretch. See you."

Thoughtfully, she locked the door behind him before wandering back to the kitchen to pour the warm beer down the sink. It seemed to be her night to waste beer.

She didn't know if any of it brought her closer to the key, but she'd certainly learned some new things this evening. Kane already knew she was searching for the second key, and hadn't wasted any time putting the whammy on her. He'd wanted her to know he was watching.

And didn't that mean he was worried that she had a good chance of succeeding?

Yeah, that made sense. Malory had shut him down once. So maybe he would be less cocky this time up. And more vicious, she mused.

She'd learned that Jordan still had that core of decency that had always attracted her. She'd been scared, nearly ill with fear, and he'd given her exactly what she needed to find her feet again without making her feel foolish or weak.

She had to give him credit for that.

More, she admitted as she went to clean up the mess she'd left in the bathroom, she had to give him credit for being honest enough to say he'd been selfish.

She could still hate him for it, but she had to respect the fact that he acknowledged it.

She had to bear down hard just to cross the threshold into the bathroom. It gave her the willies to see the book still floating, bloated with water, in the tub.

It was symbolic, she thought, that he'd invaded this most personal of rooms. It told her there was no place that she would be completely safe until the key was found or the month was over.

She pulled the plug, watched the water begin to drain.

"Just have to deal," she ordered. "And it won't be so easy to scare me next time. I'll deal with you. With Jordan. With myself. Because I learned one more thing tonight. Goddamn it, I'm still in love with the jerk."

It didn't make her feel any better to say it out loud, but it did help to put her bathroom to rights again. Her apartment, her things, her life, she thought as she went into the bedroom.

As far as Jordan was concerned, it was

much more likely that it was the memory she still loved. The boy, the young, wounded man who'd been her first love. Didn't every woman have a soft spot for her first true love?

She settled on the bed, took her bed book out of the nightstand drawer. The paperback she kept there was only a front. The one she opened was *Cold Case,* by Jordan Hawke.

Wouldn't he crow if he knew she was reading his latest book? Worse, if he knew she was enjoying every damn word.

Maybe she was still in love with the memory of the boy, but she would rather eat live slugs than have the man discover that she'd read every one of his books.

Twice.

Chapter Six

They started work on the porch, taking advantage of the fine fall weather and Zoe's experience.

By unanimous agreement, Dana and Malory had elected her the goddess of remodel. In their oldest clothes, and with new tools for Dana and Malory, they worked at Zoe's direction prepping the porch for paint.

"I didn't know it would be so much work." Malory sat back on her heels and examined her nails. "I've ruined my manicure. And you just gave it to me a couple of days ago," she reminded Zoe.

"I'll give you another. If we don't scrape and sand off the peeling paint, the new paint won't stick right. It needs a good, smooth, porous surface, or we'll be doing this again in the spring."

"We bow to you," Dana told Zoe, and watched her wield the little electric sander. "I always thought you just sort of slopped the paint on, then waited for it to dry."

"That kind of thinking is why you bow to me."

"It's already gone to her head," Dana grumbled and attacked curls of peeling paint with her scraper.

"I wouldn't mind having a little crown, something delicate and tasteful." Even as she spoke, Zoe kept one eye on her underlings. "It's going to look great. You'll see."

"Why don't you entertain us during the drudgery?" Malory suggested. "Tell us about dinner with Brad last night."

"It was no big deal. He just played some video games with Simon, ate, then left. I shouldn't have gotten so worked up about it. I just haven't had a guy over in a while. And I'm not used to cooking for millionaires. I felt like I needed finger bowls or something."

"Brad's not like that," Dana protested. "A guy with money can still be normal. Brad used to eat at our place all the time when we were kids. And we hardly ever used the finger bowls."

"It's not the same. We didn't grow up together, for one thing. And your family and his have more in common. A hairdresser who grew up in a trailer in West Virginia doesn't have a lot to say to the heir to an American empire."

"You're not being fair to him, or yourself," Malory told her.

"Maybe not. Just realistic. Anyway, he makes me nervous. I guess it's not only the money, really. Jordan has money, he must with all those bestsellers. But he doesn't make me so nervous. We had a nice, easy time together when he came over and fixed my car."

Dana lost her rhythm and ended up with a splinter in her thumb. "Your car?" Scowling, she sucked viciously at the thumb. "Jordan fixed your car?"

"Yeah. I didn't know he used to work on cars. He really knows his way around an engine, too. He just came by the other afternoon with all these tools and said why didn't he have a look at my car for me. It was really sweet of him."

"He's just a big sugar cookie," Dana said

with a smile that clamped her teeth together.

"Oh, don't be like that, Dana." Zoe
switched off the sander, angled her head.
"He didn't have to bother, and he spent
over two hours messing with it, and
wouldn't take anything but two glasses of
iced tea."

"I bet he ogled your ass when you walked
in the house to get it."

"Maybe." Zoe worked hard to keep her
face sober. "But only in a healthy, friend-of-
the-family sort of way. A small price to pay
for saving me another trip to the garage.
And the fact is, my car hasn't run this well
since I bought it. Actually, it didn't run this
well then, either."

"Yeah, he always was good with cars."
And generous with his time, Dana was
forced to admit. "You're right, it was considerate."

"And sweet," Malory added with a meaningful look at Dana.

"And sweet," she mumbled.

"He let Simon hang around him when he
got home from school, too." Zoe flipped the
sander back on, bent to her work. "It's fun
to see Simon pal around with a man. I

guess I have to say Bradley was nice to Simon too, and I appreciate that."

"So neither of them put the moves on Simon's mother?" Dana wanted to know.

"No." With a half laugh, Zoe scooted farther down the porch. "Of course not. Jordan was just doing a favor for a friend, and Bradley . . . it's not like that."

Dana's opinion was a long *hmmm* as she got back to work.

By lunchtime the porch was sufficiently prepped to pass Zoe's inspection. They gave their tired muscles a rest and sat on the sanded boards eating tuna sandwiches.

With a morning's work behind them, the sun bright, and the mood mellow, Dana decided it was time to tell them her experience of the night before.

"So . . . I had a little run-in with Kane last night."

Malory choked, grabbed for her bottle of water. "What? *What?* We've been here for over three hours, and you're just getting around to telling us that?"

"I didn't want to start off the morning with it. I knew we'd all get freaked again."

"You're okay?" Zoe laid a hand on Dana's arm. "You're not hurt or anything?"

"No, but I've got to tell you, the little brush I had with him before was nothing compared to this. I knew what happened with you, Mal, but I still didn't get it. I do now."

"Tell us." Malory shifted so she and Zoe flanked Dana.

It was easier this time. She was able to relate the experience more calmly and with more detail than she'd done with Jordan. Still, her voice shook at times, and she had to reach for her Thermos of coffee, sip slowly to ease her throat.

"You could've drowned." Zoe put her arm around Dana's shoulder. "In the tub."

"I wondered about that. But I don't think so. If he could just, well, eliminate us, why not have us walk off a cliff, or step in front of a truck? Something like that."

"Boy, that's really cheery." Zoe stared out at the street, nearly winced when a car drove by. "I'm so glad you mentioned it."

"Come on. Seriously. It seems to me he can only go so far. Like it was with Malory. It comes down to us making a choice—to reaching down inside, holding on to enough of ourselves to recognize the illusion and reject it."

"But he hurt you just the same," Zoe pointed out.

"Oh, man." Remembering, Dana rubbed a hand over her heart. "I'll say. Even if the pain was an illusion, it did the job. Worse than the pain was knowing what the pain meant, then the fear that he could take that from me."

"You should've called." There was as much exasperation as concern in Malory's voice. "Dana, you should have called me, or Zoe. Both of us. I know what it's like to be caught in one of those illusions. You didn't have to be alone."

"I wasn't. Exactly. Afterward, I mean. I was going to call. In fact, I think I was just going to stand in the bedroom and scream for both of you, but then Jordan knocked on the door."

"Oh."

Dana stared at Malory. "There's no 'oh' in that meaningful tone. He just happened to be there at a moment when I'd have welcomed a visit from a two-headed dwarf as long as he could chase the bogeyman away."

"Funny coincidence, though," Malory said with a flutter of lashes. "I mean when you figure the elements of fate and destiny and connections."

"Look, just because you're all mush-brained over Flynn, don't assume the rest of the world has to fall in line. He came by, and he behaved very decently. At first."

"Let's hear about at second, then," Zoe insisted.

"Unlike Brad, apparently, Jordan rarely hesitates to make his move. He cornered me in the kitchen."

"Really?" Malory gave a sigh. "The first time Flynn kissed me was in the kitchen."

"Anyway, I'm going out with him Saturday night." She waited, then scowled when no one spoke. "Well?"

Zoe braced her elbow on her thigh, propped her chin on her fist. "I was just thinking that it'd be nice if the two of you could at least be friends again. And that maybe, from an entirely different perspective, becoming friends again is part of what you have to do to find the key."

"I think I need to get into this a little more before I start multitasking. I don't know if I can be friends with Jordan again, because . . . I'm still sort of in love with him."

"Dana." Malory took her hand, but Dana broke free, pushed off the steps.

"I don't know if I'm still in love—more or less—with *him* him, or with the him that I fell for all that time ago. You know, like this memory of him. This image, and it's no more than an illusion now. But I've got to find out, don't I?"

"Yeah." Zoe unwrapped the brownies she'd brought along and held one out to Dana. "You need to find out."

"And if I am in love with him, I can get over it." She took a huge bite of brownie. "I got over it before. If I'm not in love with him, then everything gets back to normal. Or as back to normal as possible until I find the key."

"What about his feelings?" Malory asked her. "Aren't they a factor?"

"He had it his way once. This time around it's my way." She rolled her shoulders, pleased that the weight seemed to shrug off with the statement. "Let's paint our porch."

While they broke out brushes and rollers, Jordan relayed Dana's experience to Flynn and Brad.

They sat in Flynn's living room, set up as an informal think tank. Jordan paced as he spoke, and Flynn's dog, Moe, watched every movement in hopes that Jordan might detour to the kitchen, and cookies.

Now and again, if Jordan's direction veered closer to the doorway, Moe's big black tail would thump in anticipation. So far it hadn't netted him any treats, but it did get him a few rubs on the back with Flynn's foot.

"Why the hell didn't you bring her back here?" Flynn demanded.

"I guess I could have. If I'd knocked her unconscious and hog-tied her. This is Dana we're talking about."

"Okay, okay, point taken. You could've told me all this last night."

"I could've—and you'd have rushed over there. Which would've annoyed her. You'd have tried to make her come here, which would have meant the two of you would've ended up fighting. I just figured she'd had enough for one night. Added to that, I wanted to tell you both about it at once, when Malory wasn't around."

"Now that we do know," Brad put in, "what do we do about it?"

"There you go." Jordan walked back to the couch, and burst Moe's cookie fantasy by sitting down on the crate that served as coffee table. "We can't get her, or any of them, out of this. Even if we could, I don't know if we should. There's a lot at stake."

"Three souls," Brad murmured. "I don't think I've adjusted to that yet. Even knowing what happened with Malory, it doesn't compute in my head. But I'll go along with this. We can't get them out of it. So the question comes down to two parts. What can we do to keep them safe, and how do we help them find the key?"

"We make sure none of them is alone any more than necessary," Flynn began. "Even though we know that he got to Malory when she was with Dana and Zoe, it's a precaution we ought to take."

"She won't move in here, Flynn. I offered to move out, and she still wouldn't go for it." Absently Jordan rubbed his chin, reminding himself that he hadn't shaved. "But one of us could move into her place. At least stay there with her at night."

"Oh, yeah, she'll go for that." Sarcasm dripped from Flynn's voice. "The minute I say I'm going to sleep at her place, she'll get her back up, or just brain me with the handiest blunt instrument. And she sure as hell isn't going to let you move in with her. Or Brad either."

"I was thinking of Moe."

The annoyance on Flynn's face changed to bafflement. "Moe?"

At the sound of his name, Moe leaped up happily, knocking magazines off the crate with the enthusiastic sweep of his tail before trying to climb into Flynn's lap.

"You said Moe sensed Kane, or danger at least, when you went into the building where he'd separated Malory from Dana and Zoe."

"Yeah." Remembering it, Flynn rubbed Moe's big head. "And he charged up those stairs ready to rip out throats. Didn't you, you wild thing?"

"So, he could be a sort of early-warning system. And if he carried on the way you said he did before, he would alert the neighbors. Potentially, he could keep Dana grounded."

"It's a good idea," Brad agreed, and began to pick a few of Moe's hairs off his trousers. "But just how are you going to talk Dana into taking Moe as a roommate?"

"I can cover that," Flynn said smugly. "I'll tell her I'm moving in at her place, and we'll have the expected argument. I'll give in, then ask her if she won't at least compromise by taking Moe so I can sleep at night. She'll feel sorry for me and agree so she doesn't come off as bitchy."

"I've always admired your sneaky, serpentine methods," Brad commented.

"Just gotta keep your eye on the goal. Which brings us back to the key."

"My schedule's still the most flexible," Jordan began. "I can take all the time needed to dig into this. Research, brainstorming, legwork. You've got your journalist's resources," he said to Flynn. "Plus Mallory's willing and able to work with you, and Dana and Zoe have already let you in—as far as women ever let men in—to their group. Brad's got the HomeMakers' advantage. He can drop by their building most anytime— How's it going, ladies? Looks good. Can I give you a hand with that?"

"I can do that. Maybe you could casually mention to Zoe that I'm not now, nor have I ever been, an axe murderer."

"I'll see if I can work it into our next conversation," Flynn promised.

*   *   *

It was time, Dana told herself, to roll up her sleeves and get to work. To do something positive, something to offset the nasty seed of helplessness Kane had planted inside her.

She'd be damned if she would let it take root.

If her key was knowledge, then she'd get smart. And what better place to seek knowledge than the library?

It galled her to go back as a patron rather than an employee. But she would just swallow the bile and do the job.

She didn't bother to go home first, to change, but in her paint-splattered clothes walked straight into what had been a key in her life.

The smell caught her instantly. Books, a world of books. But she buried the sentimentality. Inside books, she reminded herself as she headed straight to one of the computer stations, were answers.

She'd read everything available on Celtic lore and mythology, so now she would expand on that. She ran a search for titles that related to sorcery. Know your enemy, she thought. Knowledge isn't just a defense. Knowledge is power.

Noting down her top choices, she ran other searches using what she thought of as the main code words from Rowena's clue. Satisfied that she'd made a good start, she headed toward the stacks.

"Did you forget something?" Her irritating toothy smile in place, Sandi stepped into her path.

"I keep trying to, but it's tough when you keep getting in my face. Fuck off, Sandi," she said in her sweetest tone.

"We don't appreciate that kind of language here."

With a shrug, Dana skirted around her and kept going. "I don't appreciate your overly rosy perfume, but there you go."

"You don't work here anymore." Chasing after her, Sandi snatched at Dana's arm.

"This is a public building, and it happens I have a library card. Now take your hand off me, or I'm going to mess up those pearly whites that your daddy probably paid a lot of money for."

She took a deep breath to find her calm. She wanted to get her books and get the hell out. "Why don't you run up and tell

Joan I'm here, nefariously checking out library books. Unless she's off in Oz picking on a scarecrow."

"I can call the police."

"Yeah, do that little thing. It'll be interesting to see what my brother writes in the *Dispatch* about how card-carrying patrons are treated these days in the local library."

She flipped a little wave at Sandi's face and swung into the stacks. "Don't worry. I'll make sure he spells your name right."

Bile was a little harder to swallow than she'd thought, Dana admitted as she began selecting her books. It was painful, every bit as much as it was maddening, not to be able to come here, even as a patron, without being hassled.

But she wasn't going to be chased away by the yappy little pom-pom queen. And she wasn't going to be frightened off by some hell-bent sorcerer.

They had a lot in common as far as she was concerned. They were both riddled with petty jealousy that lashed out and caused pain.

Jealousy, she thought, pursing her lips. It was, in a way, the opposite of love. As lies were to truth, as cowardice to valor, and so on. Another angle, she decided, and detoured to grab a copy of *Othello,* the king of stories on jealousy.

As she carted her load to checkout, Dana worked up a smile for one of the women she'd worked with for years. She dumped the books on the counter, dug out her card. "Hi, Annie. How's it going?"

"Good. Fine." In an exaggerated motion, Annie slid her gaze to the right and cleared her throat.

Following the direction, Dana spotted Sandi, arms crossed, lips tight, watching. "Oh, for Christ's sake," Dana said under her breath.

"Sorry, Dana. Sorry about everything." Keeping her voice low, Annie scanned the books, stacked them.

"Don't worry about it." After jamming her card back in her purse, Dana scooped up her armload of books. She sent Sandi a wide, wide smile and walked out.

One of the perks of having a mature adult relationship with a woman, to Flynn's mind, was coming home from work and finding her.

The smell of her, the look of her, the simple presence of her, made everything just a little clearer.

And when that woman, that pretty, sexy, fascinating woman, was cooking, it added just one more delight to the day.

He didn't know what she had going on the stove, and he didn't care. It was more than enough to see her, stirring something in a pot while Moe sprawled under the table, snoring like a freight train.

His life, Flynn thought, had found its true rhythm when Malory Price had walked into it.

He stepped up behind her, wrapped his arms around her waist, and pressed his lips to the side of her neck. "You're the best thing that ever happened to me."

"I certainly am." She turned her head so she could meet his lips with hers. "How are things?"

"Things are good." He nudged her around for a longer, more satisfying kiss. "And better now. You didn't have to cook, Mal. I know you were working all day."

"I just punched up some jarred spaghetti sauce."

"Still, you don't." He took her hands, then

frowned as he turned them over. "What's this?"

"Just some blisters. I'm telling myself they're good for me. Shows I'm pulling my weight."

He kissed them. "You know, if you'd wait for the weekend, I could give you a hand with the place."

"We really want to do it ourselves, at least start on it ourselves. I've got a few blisters and pretty much ruined a pair of jeans, but we have the most beautifully painted porch in the Valley. I wouldn't complain if you poured me a glass of wine, though."

He got out a bottle and two of the wine-glasses she'd bought. It seemed to him there were more glasses in the cabinet than there had been the last time he'd looked.

She was always slipping things in.

Glasses, fluffy towels, fancy soaps that he hesitated to actually use. It was one of the oddities and interests of having a woman around the house.

"Jordan told me what happened with Dana."

"I thought he would." Though it wasn't quite dark, she lit the long oval candle she'd picked up for the table. "We both know how horrible it must have been for her. I know how much you love her, Flynn. I love her too. But we can't shield her from this as much as we can just be there for her."

"Maybe not, but Jordan had an idea that might do a little of both."

He poured the wine, told her about using Moe.

"It's brilliant," Malory decided, then laughed down at the still snoring Moe. "She'll certainly agree to it, and if nothing else, she won't feel so alone at night." After a sip of wine, she moved to the sink to fill a pot with water for the pasta. "I suppose Jordan told you they're going out Saturday night?"

He'd been staring at the candle, thinking how odd it was to see it flickering away on the ancient picnic table he used in the kitchen. "Who's going out?" As it hit him, Flynn swallowed wine in one hard gulp. "Jordan and Dana? Going . . . out?"

"So he didn't tell you."

"No, it didn't come up."

"And," she concluded as she set the pot on the stove, "you're not too keen on the idea."

"I don't know. I don't want to get into it.

Damn it, I don't want them messing each other up again." Knowing that Jordan was working upstairs, Flynn glanced at the ceiling. "It's the person who ends up in the middle, and that would be me, who gets his ass kicked from both sides."

"She still loves him."

"Loves who?" Shock jumped into his eyes. "Loves him? Jordan? She loves him? Shit. Shit! Why do you tell me these things?"

"Because that's what people in love do, Flynn." She got three woven place mats from a drawer he wasn't sure he'd known was there and set them neatly on the table. "They tell each other things. And I don't expect you to go running to Jordan with this information."

"Man." Pacing now, he shoved a hand through his hair. "See, if you didn't tell me, I wouldn't have to think about not saying anything to him, or not saying anything to her. I would just exist in a nice bubble of ignorance."

"And I think Zoe's interested—extremely reluctantly—in Brad."

"Stop it. Stop this flood of information right now."

"You're a newspaperman." Enjoying herself, she pulled out the salad she'd put together and began to dress it. "You're supposed to thrive on information."

He'd never seen the salad bowl before, or the wooden things she was using to toss the greens. "I'm going to get a headache."

"No, you're not. You want your friends to be happy, don't you?"

"Sure."

"We're happy, aren't we?"

Cautious now, he replied, "Yes."

"We're happy, and we're in love. Ergo, you want your friends happy and in love, too. Right?"

"This is a trick question. So rather than answer it, I'm going to distract you."

"I'm not making love with you while dinner's cooking and Jordan's upstairs."

"That wasn't my idea, but I really like it. I'm going to distract you by telling you that the kitchen guys are coming on Monday to start the remodel."

"Really?" As he'd planned, every other thought spilled out of her mind. "Really?" she repeated and leaped at him. "Oh, this is great! This is wonderful!"

"I thought that would do it. So, are you going to move in with me?"

She touched her lips to his. "Ask me again when the kitchen's done."

"You're a tough one, Malory."

After a day of manual labor, Dana longed for a soak in a hot tub before she dived into her new resource books. But she lacked the courage to do it.

Since that realization was too mortifying to dwell on, she fantasized about the house she'd buy one day. The big, secluded house. With a library the size of a barn.

And a Jacuzzi, she added as she pressed on the ache at the small of her back.

But until that happy day, she would settle for her apartment. Eventually, for *all* the rooms in her apartment, which included the one with the tub in it.

She could join a gym, she thought as she settled down to her books for an evening of research.

She hated gyms. They were full of people. Sweaty people. Naked people who would insist on sharing her Jacuzzi time.

It just wasn't worth the aggravation. Better to wait until she could afford her own place. Of course, when she could afford her own place—with Jacuzzi—it was unlikely that she'd be spending eight hours scraping and painting until her back ached.

Ordering herself to settle down, she started on *Othello.* She had her own copy, of course. She had a copy of everything Shakespeare had written, but she wanted a different volume. A kind of fresh look, she thought.

It was jealousy and ambition that had driven Iago, she mused. He had planted "the green-ey'd monster which doth mock the meat it feeds on" in Othello, then had watched it devour him.

It was jealousy and ambition that drove Kane, and so he watched as his monster devoured.

She could learn from this, she thought, of what made a man—or a god—soulless.

She'd barely started when the knock on the door interrupted.

"What now?" Grumbling to herself, she went to answer it. Her irritation only increased when the door opened on Jordan.

"This had better not become a habit."

"Let's go for a ride."

Her response was to slam the door, but he anticipated her, slapped a hand on it, braced it open. "Let me put that another way. I'm heading up to Warrior's Peak. Do you want to come?"

"What are you going up there for? You're a bystander in this deal."

"That's a matter of opinion. I'm going up because I have some questions. Actually, I decided to get out of Flynn's place after dinner. To give the lovebirds a little space." He leaned comfortably on the jamb as he spoke but kept that hand firm on the door. "Found myself heading out of town and up the mountain road. Figured I might as well keep going, have myself a chat with Pitte and Rowena. Then I thought, You know, it's just going to tick Dana off if I do that without running it by her. So I turned around and came back. I'm running it by you."

"I suppose you want points for that."

His mouth curved. "If you're keeping score."

"I don't see that you have anything to talk to them about."

"Let's put this one more way. I'm going, with or without you." He straightened, let his hand drop from the door. "But if you want to come along, you can drive."

"Big deal."

"My car."

The image of his gorgeous, muscular, classic T-Bird flashed into her mind. She had to make a conscious effort not to drool. "You fight dirty."

He took his keys out of his pocket. And dangled them.

Her internal war lasted about three seconds before she snatched the keys out of his hand. "Let me get a jacket."

Whatever his flaws, Jordan Hawke knew cars. The Thunderbird climbed the hills like a mountain cat, all sleek grace and muscle. It clung to curves and roared down straightaways.

Some might think of it as a vehicle, others as a toy. But Dana knew it was a *machine.* A first-class one.

Being behind the wheel wasn't just a sexy pleasure. It let Dana shift the situation as smoothly as she shifted gears. She was in charge now. The trip to the Peak might have been Jordan's idea, but by God, she was driving.

The evening was brisk, and grew brisker yet as they climbed to higher elevations, but the top was down. She was glad to trade chilly fingers and the bite of the wind for the sheer joy of zipping along the roads in the open air.

The trees were at their peak, the force of colors made only more brilliant by the sheen of gold from the setting sun. Fallen leaves skipped and skittered across the road where light and shadow danced.

It was like driving into a story, she mused, where anything could happen around the next turn.

"How's it handling for you?" Jordan asked her.

"She's got style. And muscle."

"I always thought the same about you."

She slid her gaze in his direction, balefully, then focused on the road. However much fun she was having, it didn't mean she couldn't take a poke at him.

"I don't see why you need a car like this when you live in an urban environment where mass transit is not only readily available but efficient."

"Two reasons. First, for those times when I'm not in an urban environment, such as now. And second, I lusted after her."

"Yeah." She couldn't blame him. "Fifty-seven was the primo year for T-Birds."

"No question. I've got a '63 Stingray."

Her eyes went glassy. "You do not."

"Four-speed, 327. Fuel injection."

She felt the long, liquid pull in her belly. "Shut up."

"I had her up to 120. She'd've given me more, but we were just getting to know each other." He waited a beat. "I've got my eye on this very sweet Caddy convertible. Fifty-nine. Single quadajet carb."

"I hate you."

"Hey, a guy's got to have a hobby."

"The '63 Stingray's my fantasy car. The one I'm going to have one day, when all my dreams come true."

He smiled a little. "What color?"

"Black. Serious business black. Four-speed manual tranny. Doesn't have to be the 327, though that'd be the cream. Gotta be the convertible, though. The coupe just won't do."

She fell silent for a few minutes, just enjoying the ride.

"Zoe mentioned you'd fixed her car."

"I stopped over. Timing was off, and the carb needed a little work. Nothing major."

She made herself say it. "It was a nice thing to do."

"I had the time." He shrugged a shoulder, stretched his legs out a little more. "Just figured she could use a hand with it."

Suddenly she understood, and felt ashamed for her initial reaction when she'd heard he'd gone to Zoe's. The hardworking single mother, raising a young boy.

Just like his mother.

Of course he'd gone by to help.

"She really appreciated it," Dana told him, but kept it light. "Especially since you don't make her nervous the way Brad does."

"I don't? I think I'm insulted and will now be honor-bound to work harder to make her nervous."

"What kind of watch you got there?"

"Watch?" Baffled, he turned his wrist. "I don't know. It tells time."

She shook her hair back and laughed. "That's what I thought you'd say. Sorry, you're never going to make her nervous."

She slowed, reluctantly, as they approached the gates. Then she stopped, looking at the house through them as she dug her brush out of her purse. "Some place," she commented, brushing out the knots and tangles the wind had tied into her hair. "You live in a place like this, you could have that classic 'Vette. Keep it in a big, heated garage like it deserves. I wonder if Pitte and Rowena drive."

"That's some segue."

"No, really. Think about it. They are what they are, and they've been around since way before anybody even thought about the combustible engine. They can do what they do, but has either of them ever taken driving lessons, stood in line at the DMV, haggled over insurance?"

She dropped the brush back in her purse, looked over at Jordan. His hair was as windblown as hers had been, yet, she noted, it didn't look unkempt. Just sexy.

"How do they live?" she continued. "We don't really know what they do, when it comes to ordinary things. Human things. Do they watch TV? Play canasta? Do they cruise the mall? What about friends? Do they have any?"

"If they do, there'd be a regular turnover.

Friends, being human, would have that annoying habit of dying."

"That's right." She said it quietly as she looked back toward the house. "It must be lonely. Painfully lonely. All that power doesn't make them one of us. Living in that great house doesn't make it their home. It's weird, isn't it? Feeling sorry for gods."

"No. It's intuitive. And just the kind of thing that's going to help you find the key. The more you know and understand them, the closer you come to figuring out your part of the puzzle."

"Maybe." Suddenly the iron gates swung open. "I guess that's our invitation."

She drove, in the twilight, toward the great stone house.

The old man she'd come to think of as the caretaker hurried up to the car to open her door. "Welcome. I'll see to the car for you, miss."

"Thanks." She studied him, trying to get a gauge on his age. Seventy? Eighty? Three thousand and two? "I never got your name," she said to him.

"Oh, I'd be Caddock, miss."

"Caddock. Is that Scots, Irish?"

"Welsh. I'd be from Wales, in the original way of things, miss."

Like Rowena, she thought. "Have you worked for Pitte and Rowena long?"

"Yes, indeed." His eyes seemed to twinkle at her. "I've been in their service a number of years now." He looked past her, nodded his head. "There's a fine sight, isn't it, then?"

Dana turned, and stared at the huge buck that stood on the verge between lawn and forest. His rump seemed to glimmer white in the soft haze of twilight, and his rack shone silver.

"Traditional symbolism," Jordan said, though he was no less struck by the buck's magnificence. "The seeker sees a white deer or hare at the start of a quest."

"Malory saw it," Dana murmured over the lump in her throat. "The first night we came here. But I didn't, Zoe didn't." She walked to stand beside Jordan. "Does that mean it was already ordained that Malory would search for the first key? That it had nothing to do with the luck of the draw? That was just show?"

"Or ritual. You still had to choose to reach

into the box for a disk. You decide to follow the deer, or turn away from it."

"But is it real? Is that deer really standing over there, or are we imagining it?"

"That's something else for you to decide." He waited until the deer faded back into the shadows before he turned.

Both the old man and the car were gone. After the initial jolt, Jordan slid his hands into his pockets. "You've got to admit, that is very cool."

The entrance doors opened. Rowena stood dead center, the foyer lights spilling over her fiery hair, glinting on the long silver dress she wore. "How lovely to see you both." She held out a hand in welcome. "I was just pining for company."

Chapter Seven

Pitte was already in the parlor, wearing a black shirt and trousers that echoed Rowena's casual elegance. Dana wondered if they sat around looking beautiful all the time. Something else to think about, she supposed. Like did they ever have bad hair days, indigestion, sore feet?

Or were those things too mundane for gods living in the mortal world?

"We were just enjoying the fire, and a glass of wine. You'll join us?" Rowena asked.

"Sure, thanks." Welcoming the heat, Dana walked toward the snapping fire. "You guys hang like this every evening?"

In the process of pouring wine, Pitte stopped, frowned at her. "Hang?"

"Hang out. You know, sit around in great clothes, drinking fine wine out of, what is that, Baccarat?"

"I believe it is." Pitte finished pouring, offered the glass to Dana. "We often take an hour or so to relax together at the end of the day."

"What about the rest of the time? Do you just putter around this place?"

"Ah. You wonder what we do to entertain ourselves." Rowena sat, patted the cushion beside her. "I paint, as you know. Pitte spends time on our finances. He enjoys the game of money. We read. I've enjoyed your books, Jordan."

"Thanks."

"Pitte enjoys films," Rowena added with a glance of affection toward her lover. "Particularly ones where a great many things blow up in impressive explosions."

"So you go to the movies?" Dana prompted.

"Ordinarily no. We prefer settling in at home and watching at our leisure."

"Multiplexes," Pitte muttered. "They call them this. Like little boxes stacked end by end. It's a pity the grand theaters have gone out of fashion."

"That's something you'd both be up on. The changes in fashion. There'd have been a lot of that in a couple of millennia."

Rowena lifted a brow at Dana. "Yes, indeed."

"I know this sounds like small talk," Dana continued, "but I'm just trying to get a handle on things. It occurred to me that you know everything about me. You've had my whole lifetime to watch. Did you watch?"

"Of course. You were of considerable interest to us from the moment you were born. We didn't intrude," Rowena added, running the jeweled chain she wore around her neck through her fingers as she spoke. "Or interfere. I understand your interest in us now. We are more like you than you may think and less like you than you could possibly imagine. We can and do indulge in what you'd call human pleasures. Food, drink, warmth, vanity. Sex. We love . . ." She reached up for Pitte's hand. "As genuinely as you. We weep and laugh. We enjoy much of what your world offers. We celebrate the generosity and resilience of the human spirit, and mourn its darker sides."

"But while you're here, you're of neither one world nor the other. Isn't that right?"

There was something about the way they touched each other, Jordan thought. As if they would wither away without that small contact. "You can live as you choose to live, but within limitations. Within the boundaries of this dimension. Even so, you're not of it. You might feel the heat, but you don't burn. You might sleep at night, but when you wake in the morning, you haven't aged. The hours haven't changed you. Millions of hours can't."

"And do you see that kind of . . . immortality," Pitte inquired, "as a gift?"

"No, I don't." Jordan's glance shifted to Pitte's face and held. "I see it as a curse. A punishment, certainly, when you're locked out of your own world and spend those millions of hours here."

Pitte's expression didn't change, but his eyes seemed to deepen, to heat. "Then you have excellent sight."

"I see something else clearly enough. The penalty, if Dana fails to find the key, is a year of her life. A year of Malory's and Zoe's as well. From your standpoint that's nothing. But it's a different matter when you're human and your life is already finite."

"Ah." Pitte draped an arm over the mantel. "So, have you come to renegotiate our contract?"

Before Dana could speak, tell Jordan to mind his own business, he shot her a look. "No, because Dana's going to find the key, so it won't be an issue."

"You have confidence in your woman," Rowena said.

"I'm not his woman," Dana said quickly. "Has Kane watched us, too? From the beginning of our lives?"

"I can't say," Rowena answered, then waved an impatient hand at Dana's dubious expression. "I can't. There are, as Jordan said, certain boundaries we can't cross. Something has changed—we know this because he was able to draw both Malory and Flynn into dreams and to cause Flynn harm. He wasn't able, or perhaps didn't choose, to do so before."

"Tell them what he did to you."

It wasn't phrased as a request, and this time Dana's anger was sparked. But before she could snap at Jordan, Rowena took her arm.

"Kane? What happened?"

She told them, and found that this time her voice remained steady throughout the telling. More distance, she thought, less fear.

At least there was less until she saw a flicker of fear cross Rowena's face.

She didn't care to think what it took to frighten a god.

"There wasn't any real threat, right?" Her skin was prickling, icy little ants rushing down her back. "I mean, I couldn't have drowned when I jumped into the sea, because the sea didn't actually exist."

"But it did," Pitte corrected. There was a grim chill to his face. A soldier's face, Dana thought, as he watched the battle from a rise and waited for the time to draw his sword.

And she was the one down in the field, she realized, waging bloody war.

"It was conjured first by your fantasy, then by your fear. That doesn't make it less than real."

"That just doesn't make sense," she insisted. "When he had Malory in that fantasy, when she was painting, we could see her. We all saw her, just standing there in that attic."

"Her body, perhaps part of her consciousness—she has a strong mind—remained. The rest..." Rowena drew a breath. "The rest of what she was had traveled to the other side. And if harm had come to her. To her body," Rowena explained, holding out one hand. "To what you can call her essence." Then the other. "On either side, the harm would be to all of her."

"If she cut her hand in one existence," Jordan said, "it would bleed in the other."

"He could prevent it." Obviously troubled, Rowena rose to pour more wine. "If, for instance, I wished to give you a gift, a harmless fantasy, I might send you into dreams, and watch over you to keep you from harm. But what Kane does is not harmless. He does it to tempt, and to terrorize."

"Why didn't he just shove my head under the bathwater while I was out of it?"

"There are still limits. To maintain the illusion, he can't touch your corporeal body. And as it is your mind that forms the texture of the illusion, neither can he force you to harm yourself. Lie, yes. Deceive and frighten, even persuade, but he can't make you do anything against your will."

"That's how she broke back through." It was the answer that Jordan had needed confirmed. "First, by choosing to see it as a trick, she changed the texture, as you said, of the world. Instead of paradise, nightmare."

"Her knowledge and fear, and Kane's anger, yes," Pitte agreed. "The fruit you dropped," he said to Dana. "Your mind saw it then as rotten in the center. This was not your paradise but your prison."

"And when she dived into the sea rather than let him take what she was, rather than accept the fantasy or the nightmare, she broke through both," Jordan concluded. "So her weapon against him is staying true to herself, whatever he throws at her."

"Simply put," Pitte agreed.

"Too simply." Rowena shook her head. "He's wily and seductive. You must never underestimate him."

"He's already underestimated her. Hasn't he, Stretch?"

"I can handle myself." His easy confidence went a long way toward quieting her nerves. "What's to stop him from hitting on Zoe, screwing with her while we're focused on him screwing with me?"

"She is not yet an issue for him. But precautions can be taken," Rowena mused, tapping a finger on the rim of her glass.

"She can be protected, to an extent, until her time begins."

"If it begins," Pitte corrected.

"He's pessimistic by nature," Rowena smiled. "I have more faith." She walked back to the sofa, sat on the arm with the fluid grace some women are born with. Reaching down, she took Dana's face in her hands.

"You know the truth when you hear it. You may turn your ear from it, close your mind to it. As my man is pessimistic, you are stubborn by nature."

"Got that in one," Jordan muttered.

"But when you choose to hear it, the truth rings clear for you. This is your gift. He can't deceive you unless you allow it. When you accept what you already know you'll have the rest."

"You wouldn't like to be a little more specific?"

A smile touched the corners of Rowena's mouth. "You have enough to think of for now."

Later, when they were alone, Rowena curled on the sofa beside Pitte, rested her head on his shoulder and watched the fire. In the flames she studied Dana, her hands competent on the steering wheel as she drove through the night toward the quiet valley below the Peak.

She admired competence, in gods and mortals.

"She worries him," she said quietly.

Pitte watched the fire, and the images in it as well. "Whom does she worry? The soul-stealer or the story-spinner?"

Absently, for comfort, Rowena rubbed her cheek against Pitte's shoulder. "Both, certainly. And both have hurt her, though only one with intent. But a lover's blade slices deeper than any enemy's. She worries Kane," she said, "but the man is worried for her."

"They have heat." Pitte turned his head to brush his lips over Rowena's hair. "He should take her to bed and let the heat seal old wounds."

"So like a male, to think bedding is always the answer."

"It's a good one." Pitte gave her a little shove, and when she fell, it was onto the big bed they shared.

She cocked an eyebrow at him. Her silver

dress had melted away so that she wore only her own skin. Such things, she knew, were one of his more playful, and interesting, habits.

"Heat isn't enough." She spread her arms, and dozens of candles flared into flame. "It's warmth, my love, my only love, that heals the wounded heart."

With her arms still open wide, she sat up and welcomed him to her.

Dana had hardly gotten back in the door—and kept Jordan out—had barely settled down with *Othello* again and cleared her mind enough to focus on the task at hand, when there was another knock.

Figuring Jordan had come back with some new ploy to wheedle his way in, she ignored it.

She was, by Jesus, going to spend two hours working on this book angle, and then she was going to think about the drive to the Peak, what had been said there. What hadn't been said on the drive home.

If she had to think about Jordan, she sure as hell wasn't going to do it when he was around.

He'd sniff it out of her head like a blood-hound.

There was another knock, more insistent this time. She merely bared her teeth and kept scanning the play.

But the barking got her attention.

Realizing that she would get nowhere until the door was answered, she got up and opened it. "What the hell are you doing here? Both of you." She scowled at Flynn, then leaned down to rub Moe's floppy ears and make kissing noises. "Did Malory kick you out? Poor baby." Her sympathetic tone turned icy as she straightened and peered at her brother. "You're not sleeping here."

"Don't plan to."

"Then what's in the bag?"

"Stuff." He squeezed inside, around his dog and his sister. "I hear you had a rough one last night."

"It was an experience, and I'm not in the mood to rehash it. It's after ten. I'm working, then I'm sleeping."

With, she thought, every light in the apartment burning, just as she had the night before.

"Fine. Here's his stuff."

"Whose stuff?"

"Moe's. I'll haul over the big-ass bag of dog food tomorrow, but there's enough in there for his breakfast."

"What the hell are you talking about?" She looked in the bag he'd shoved into her arms and saw a mangled tennis ball, a tattered rope, a box of dog biscuits on top of about five pounds of dry dog food.

"What the hell is this?"

"His stuff," Flynn repeated cheerfully, and grunted when Moe leaped up to plant his paws on his shoulders. "Moe's your new temporary roommate. Well, gotta go. See you tomorrow."

"Oh, no, you don't." She tossed the bag on a chair, beat him to the door by a step, and threw herself against it. "You're not walking out that door without this dog."

He gave her a smile that was both mildly quizzical and wholly innocent. "You just said I couldn't sleep here."

"You can't. Neither can he."

"Now look, you've hurt his feelings." He looked sorrowfully at Moe, who was trying to nose his way into the bag. "It's all right, big guy. She didn't mean it."

"Give me a break."

"You don't know what dogs understand. Scientific tests are inconclusive." He gave Dana a brotherly pat on the cheek. "So anyway, Moe's going to stay for a couple weeks. Play guard dog."

"Guard dog?" She noted that Moe was now chewing on the bag. "Give me a serious break."

Obviously not finding the brown paper to his taste, Moe wandered off to sniff for crumbs, and Flynn sat down, stretched out his legs. He'd reconsidered his strategy and decided that this tack was foolproof with Dana. "Okay. I'll stay and be guard dog since you have no faith in Moe. Let's flip a coin for the bed."

"I'm the only one sleeping in my bed, and I have less faith in you than I do in that big mutt, who is currently chasing his own tail. Moe! Cut that out before you wreck my place."

She considered just tearing out her own hair when Moe bashed against a table in his desperate attempt to latch teeth onto tail, and sent books thudding down on his head.

He gave a startled bark and scrambled toward Flynn for protection.

"Go away, Flynn, and take your klutzy dog with you."

Flynn simply lifted his legs and used Moe as a footstool. "Let's just go over our options," he began.

Twenty minutes later Dana stomped into the kitchen. She stopped short, hissed through her teeth when she saw the contents of her trash can strewed from one end of the floor to the other and Moe happily sprawled over the mess of it, chewing on a wad of paper towels.

"How does he do it? How the hell did he talk me into this?" And that, she admitted, was the mystery of Flynn Hennessy. You never knew just how he managed to box you into the corner of his choice.

She crouched down, got nose to nose with Moe.

Moe rolled his eyes to the side, avoiding hers. Dana swore that if dogs could whistle, she'd have heard the I-wasn't-doing-anything tune coming out of the dog's mouth. "Okay, pal, you and I are going to go over the rules of the household."

He responded by licking her face, then flopping over to expose his belly.

*   *   *

She woke with the sun streaming over her face and her legs paralyzed. The sun was easy to explain. She'd forgotten to draw the curtains again. And her legs weren't paralyzed, she realized after a moment of panic. They were trapped under the massive bulk of Moe.

"Okay, this is no way to begin." She sat up, then shoved the dog hard. "I said no dogs allowed on the bed. I was very clear about that rule."

He moaned, an oddly human sound that made her lips twitch. Then he opened one eye. Then that eye brightened with manic joy.

"No!"

But it was too late. In one leap, he'd trapped not only her legs but her entire body. Dancing paws pressed into her belly, her breasts, her crotch. His tongue slathered her face with desperate love.

"Stop it! Down! Mary Mother of God!" And she was laughing hysterically, wrestling with him, until he leaped off the bed and raced out of the room.

"Whew." She pushed at her hair. It was

definitely not the way she cared to wake, as a rule. But for one day she could make an exception.

Now she needed coffee. Immediately.

Before she could throw back the covers, Moe bounded back in.

"No! Don't you do it! Don't you bring that horrible, disgusting ball into this bed."

Her usual morning speed approximated that of a snail on Valium, but one look at the tennis ball in Moe's mouth had her moving like an Olympic sprinter. She hit the floor, causing Moe to change direction and go into a skid. He thudded against the bed frame, then, undaunted, spat the ball at her feet.

"We do not play fetch the ball in the house. We do not play fetch the ball when I'm naked, which, you may notice, I am. We do not play fetch the ball before I have coffee."

He cocked his head charmingly and lifted a paw.

"We're going to have to compromise. First I'll get unnaked." She went to the closet for her robe. "Then I'll have my first cup of coffee. After which I'll take you for a very, very brief walk during which you can relieve your bladder and play fetch the ball for exactly three minutes. Take it or leave it."

She didn't know how he did it—like master, like dog, she supposed—but she ended up spending a good twenty minutes playing with Moe in the park.

This was *not* her morning routine, and if there was anything that was sacrosanct to Dana, it was her morning routine. She could admit that she felt more energized and more cheerful after the interlude with the goofy dog. But she wasn't going to tell Moe that, or anyone else.

He gobbled down his breakfast while she ate hers, then fortunately for all involved, plopped down for a quick morning nap while she substituted *Othello* for her current breakfast book.

To stay fresh, to let it all simmer in her head, she switched gears after thirty minutes, and chose one of the books on sorcery. However wily and amoral Iago was, Kane was more so—and he had power. Maybe there was a way to undermine it, or deflect it, while she searched for the key.

She read of white magic, and of black. Of sorcery and necromancy. And it was different, she realized as she made her notes, when you knew the fantastic you read of was real.

Not fantasy. Not lies, but truth.

She had to remember that, she thought as she closed the book. It was essential that she remember the truth.

It was very satisfying, Dana discovered when she was hip-deep in work at Indulgence, to prime the dull wall with fresh white paint.

Our place, she thought.

As they painted, she briefed Zoe and Malory on her visit to the Peak and what she'd learned.

"So he *can* hurt us." Frowning, Zoe added more paint to the automatic roller for Malory. "Or we can hurt ourselves. I guess that's what it really means."

"If we drift too far beyond actual reality, yeah," Dana agreed. "I think that's what it means."

"But he can't hurt us unless we allow it,"

Malory put in. "The trick is not to allow it, which is not as easy as it sounds."

"You don't have to tell me." The memory of her brush with Kane still made Dana shudder. "It's not just finding the last two keys, it's protecting ourselves."

"And the people around us," Zoe reminded her. "He went after Flynn, too. If he tries anything with Simon—anything—I'll spend the rest of my life hunting him down."

"Don't worry, Mom." Dana reached over to squeeze Zoe's shoulder. "When your turn comes, we'll all look after Simon. We can always send Moe to protect him," she added to lighten the mood. She sent a steely look at Malory. "A true friend would've called and warned me I was about to get a dog."

"A true friend knew you'd sleep better at night with a dog snoring beside the bed."

"Beside, my ass. He snuck onto the bed when I was sleeping. Which means I'd have slept through an earthquake last night, as he's not what we can call stealthy. And Moe-proofing the apartment is no snap, just let me add. Not to mention I'm not allowed to have dogs in my building in the first place."

"It's just for a few weeks and mostly at night," Malory reminded her. "You did sleep better, too. I can tell by your mood."

"Maybe I did. Anyway, I should fill you in on what I'm doing about the key."

With the first room primed, they moved to the next and the more tedious chore of cutting in around the trim.

"Jealousy, sorcery, getting inside Kane's skin." Standing on the new stepladder, Malory took on the task of painting the ceiling. "That's very smart."

"I think so. The answer's in a book. It's got to be. Yours dealt with painting, and one of the daughters, the one who looks like you, is an artist. Well, a musician, but that's an art."

Zoe glanced over. "I sure as hell hope that means I don't have to take up fencing because my goddess carries a sword."

"She also has that cute little puppy," Malory put in.

"I can't get a dog right now. I know Simon would love one, but—oh, you were taking my mind off the sword."

"There you go."

Dana sat back on her heels, stretched her back. "Puppy, sword—metaphors for something. We'll figure it out when the time comes. But if we follow this theme, Malory's key dealt with painting. Malory's dream was being an artist, but she didn't have the chops for it . . ."

She stopped, considered biting her tongue in half. "Sorry. That sounded harsh."

"No, it didn't. It sounded true." Malory stared up at the ceiling. She seemed to have the knack for this kind of painting. "I didn't have the talent to paint, so I directed my energies into a career where I could be part of the art world in other ways. It doesn't hurt my feelings, Dana."

"Okay, but you get a free kick later if you want it. Kane used Malory's desire to paint to pull her in, to distract her from the search. But our heroine proved much too clever for him and turned the tables."

Malory inclined her head regally. "I like that part."

"It's one of my favorites," Zoe agreed. "Do you want to write, Dana?"

"No." She pursed her lips for a moment, thought about it. "No, I don't. But I have to be around books, have them around me.

I'm fascinated with the people who can and do write them."

"Including Jordan?"

"Let's not go there, at least not yet. What I'm saying is books are personal to me, the way art is to Mal. So that's why I think my key is connected to books. I've got this gut instinct that it has to do with a book I've read. Something personal again."

"I'm going to do another title search, one using 'key,' and see what books I come up with." Her brows drew together as she tried to puzzle it out. "The whole key-in-the-title angle may be too simple, too obvious, but it gives me another place to look."

"We could split it up," Malory suggested. "If you make a list of the books you think might be the one, we could divide it into three and each take a chunk."

"That would help. We don't know what we're looking for," Dana continued. "But we've got to believe we'll know it when we see it."

"Maybe you should put together a list with 'goddess' in the title, too," Malory told her. "My key had to do with the singing goddess, from Rowena's clue. Yours might link to the goddess who walks, or waits, in your clue."

"Good thinking." With her section of wall finished, Dana got to her feet. "God, our eyes are going to bleed. There's this other thing." Wanting to keep busy, she went back to her brush roller. "Your key had to do with this place, Mal, with the way he—or your head—transformed it into your fantasy of happy home, family, painting in your studio. So far, mine's been a deserted tropical island. I don't think I'm going to find its root here in the Valley."

"You don't know where you'll go next time."

Dana set down the brush and stared. "Well, gee. That's a happy thought."

Chapter Eight

She may have been unemployed, but Dana doubted that she'd ever worked harder or put in longer days.

There was Moe to deal with, which she equated with having an eighty-pound toddler on her hands. He needed to be fed, walked, scolded, entertained, and watched like a hawk.

There was the sheer physical demand of painting for several hours a day, which had considerably upped her respect for anyone who did it for a living. But as Moe came with comfort and amusement, so did the work on the building bring satisfaction and pride.

Maybe it didn't look like much yet— they'd decided to prime *all* the walls before starting on color—but when you had three determined, dedicated women working as a unit, you saw considerable progress.

There was the design and strategy of the business she would debut in a matter of months. She had long, long lists of books, intriguing sidelines, possible styles for shelves and tables, for glasses and cups.

It had been one thing to fantasize about owning a bookstore, but it was another matter entirely to deal with the thousands of details involved in creating one.

Added to that were the hours of midnight oil she burned searching for the key. Reading had always been a passion, but now it was a mission. Somewhere in a book was the answer. Or at least the next question.

And what if the answer, or the question, was in one of the books she'd assigned to her friends? What if they missed it because it would only resonate with her?

That way lay madness, she told herself.

On top of everything else she had to do, had to think about, had to worry about, she had to get ready for a date. A date, she reminded herself, that she should never have agreed to.

Talk about the road to madness.

If she canceled, Jordan would either nag and harangue her until she sliced him to pieces with a butcher knife and spent the rest of her life in prison, or, even worse, he'd get that smug, told-you-so look on his face and claim he'd only proven that she was afraid to be around him.

In which case, it was back to the kitchen knife and life in the women's penitentiary.

The only choice left was to go—and to go fully armed. She would not only prove she wasn't the least bit concerned about spending a few hours with him, she would drive him mad while she was at it.

She knew he was a sucker for scent, so she slathered herself in perfumed body cream before slipping into what she thought of as her tonight's-the-night underwear. Not that she would give Jordan the chance to see it, but *she* would know she was wearing the sexy black bra, the lacy panties, the lace-trimmed garter belt and sheer hose.

And they would make her feel powerful.

She checked herself in the mirror—front, back, sides. "Oh, yeah, I look just fine. Eat your heart out, Hawke."

She picked up the dress she'd laid on the bed. It looked deceptively simple, one long, fluid line of black. But when you put a body into it, everything changed.

She slipped it on, gave it a few tugs, then did another turn before the mirror.

The scoop neck took on a whole new dimension when there were breasts filling it out, rising teasingly over the edge. The column turned seductive when the slightest movement parted that long side slit and revealed the length of leg.

She slipped on her shoes, delighted that the stiletto heels added three inches to her already impressive height. She'd never been sensitive about being tall. She *liked* it.

She had Zoe to thank for the hair. She'd done it sleek and loose, with a little jeweled clip anchored between the crown and the tip of her left ear. Just another tease, Dana mused. The clip didn't *do* anything but sit there and sparkle.

She dabbed perfume at her collarbone, in the valley between her breasts, at her wrists. Then tossed her head. "You are a dead man, pal. You are meat."

It occurred to her that she was actually looking forward to the evening. It had been weeks since she'd dressed herself up for a date. Plus, she had to admit she was curious. How would Jordan handle himself? How, for that matter, would they handle each other? She wondered what it would be like to be with him, within the ritual of a date, now that they were man and woman rather than boy and girl.

It was, she had to admit, exciting. Particularly exciting since she was certain he intended to win her over and she had no intention of being won.

She leaned toward the mirror, slid murderous red on her lips, then dropped the tube of lipstick in her purse. She pressed her lips together, opened them again with a cocky little pop. "Let the games begin."

When Jordan knocked at exactly seventhirty, she couldn't have scripted his reaction any more perfectly.

His eyes widened, blurred. She actually saw the pulse in his throat jump. Then he fisted a hand and rapped it twice against his own heart as if to get it started again.

"You're trying to hurt me, aren't you?"

She angled her head. "Absolutely. How'd I do?"

"Kill shot. Am I drooling?"

Now she grinned and turned back inside to get her coat. He stepped in behind her, leaned down and sniffed. "If I whimper, try to . . ." He trailed off as he saw the books. Piles and stacks of them beside the sofa, another stack on the coffee table, a sea of them on her dining table.

"Jesus Christ, Dane, you need treatment."

"They're not just for reading, not that there's anything wrong with that. They're for work and for research. I'm playing an angle on the key *and* I'm preparing to open a bookstore."

She slipped into the coat, trying not to be miffed that he now appeared to be more interested in the books than in how incredible she looked.

"*The Key to Rebecca, Key Witness, A House Without a Key.* I see where you're going here. *The Key to Sexual Fulfillment?*" He sent her a long, smirking look.

"Shut up. Are we going to eat?"

"Yeah, yeah. You've got your work cut out for you." He crouched down, began flipping through pages. "You want me to take some of these?"

"I've already split the load with Malory and Zoe." She knew he'd start reading in a moment; he wouldn't be able to help himself. In that area, they were identical twins.

"That's enough. Hungry here."

"What else is new?" He set a book back on a tower of its fellows, straightened and took another good long look at her. "Wow-zer."

"Aw, that's so sweet. Are we going?"

He moved to the door to open it for her. "Where's Moe?"

"Romping in the park with his best friend. Flynn's dropping him off before he goes home. Where are we eating?"

"Just get in the car, Miss One Track Mind. You'll get fed. How's the painting brigade doing?" he asked once she was settled and he was behind the wheel.

"We rock. Seriously. I can't get over how much we're getting done. And I have the body aches to prove it."

"Anything you want me to rub, just let me know."

"That's a kind and selfless offer, Jordan."

"Just the kind of guy I am."

She crossed her legs, making sure the move was slow and parted the slit of her dress well up to her thigh. "But I have Chris to take care of that for me."

His gaze traveled down, all the way to the sharp heel of her shoe, then back up again.

"Chris?" He didn't snarl it, but he wanted to.

"Mmm-hmm."

"And who's Chris?"

"A very talented massage therapist with magic hands." She stretched, as if under those magic hands, and added a quiet little moan. Oh, yes, she thought at the quick hitch of Jordan's breathing, she had entirely new weaponry to aim at him this time around.

"A recommendation from Zoe," she added. "Zoe's going to offer a variety of treatments in the salon."

"And would that be Christine or Christopher?"

She shrugged. "I got a neck and shoulder treatment this afternoon, a kind of audition. Chris passed with flying colors." She frowned when he zoomed past the town limits. "We're not eating in town?"

He couldn't breathe without breathing whatever she'd doused herself in to drive him crazy. And by the way, he thought, in case he'd forgotten she had legs that went all the way to her ears, she was going out of her way to remind him.

If his voice was a bit tight, there were

good reasons for it. "I'm feeding you and paying the bill. Venue's my pick."

"It better be worthy of my outfit and my appetite, or you'll be paying more than the bill."

"I remember your appetites." He ordered himself to relax. She might be playing a hell of a game, but he hadn't come up to bat yet. "So tell me, what is the key to sexual fulfillment?"

"Read the book. You tell me, what pops into your head when you think of 'key' when it comes to literature?"

"Locked-door mysteries."

"Hmm. Could be another angle. How about goddess, other than in mythology?"

"Your femme fatale character. Like the mystery woman in *The Maltese Falcon*."

"How is she a goddess?"

"She has the power to weave spells over a man, with sex, beauty, and lies."

"Huh." Deliberately, she skimmed her fingers down the long curve of her hair. "Not bad. Something to think about." As she did, she lost track of direction and time. It was nearly eight when she brought herself back and blinked at the big white house tucked into the hillside.

Batter up, Jordan thought as he saw her eyes go wide.

"Luciano's?" Her jaw dropped. "It takes a congressional edict to get a reservation at Luciano's this time of year. You have to book weeks in advance out of season, but in October you can't get in even by donating blood."

"You'll only have to give them a pint." He climbed out, tossed his keys to the valet.

"I've always wanted to eat here. Way out of my league."

"I tried to get us in for your birthday once. They didn't laugh at me, but it was close."

"You couldn't have afforded to . . ." She trailed off, and couldn't help but go to goo inside. It was just the sort of thing he'd have done, she remembered. Unexpectedly, recklessly done. "It was a nice thought," she told him and kissed his cheek.

"This time I pulled it off." He shocked her speechless by lifting her hand to his lips. "Happy birthday. Better late than never."

"You're being charming. Why are you being charming?"

"It goes with your outfit." And still holding her hand, he led her up the steps.

The restaurant had once been the mountain getaway of a Pittsburgh family of some wealth and influence. Dana didn't know if it qualified as a mansion, but it certainly met all the requirements for villa with its columns and balconies and porticos.

The grounds were lovely, and in spring and summer, even early fall, alfresco dining was offered in the courtyard so patrons could enjoy the gardens and the views along with a superbly prepared meal.

The interior had been restored, and maintained the elegance and ambience of a well-appointed home.

The entrance hall offered marble floors, Italian art, and cozy seating areas. Dana barely had time to absorb the light, the color, before the maître d' hurried over to greet them.

"Mr. Hawke, we're so pleased you could join us this evening. *Signorina,* welcome to Luciano's. Your table's ready if you'd like to be seated. Or if you prefer I'll have you shown into our lounge."

"The lady's hungry, so we'll take the table, thanks."

"Of course. Shall I take your wrap?"

"Sure."

But Jordan beat the maître d', and with a

trail of fingertips along her shoulders, slipped her coat off. It was whisked away, and they were led up the grand staircase and into what she realized was a private room already prepared with a single table for two.

A waiter materialized with champagne.

"As you requested," the maître d' said. "Is this suitable for your evening?"

"It's perfect," Jordan told him.

"*Bene.* If you wish for anything, you have only to ask. Please, enjoy. *Buon appetito.*"

He slipped away, leaving them alone.

"When you pull it off," Dana said after a moment, "you really pull it off."

"No point in doing things halfway." He lifted his glass, tapped it gently against hers. "To moments. Past, present, future."

"That seems safe enough to drink to." She sipped. "Jeez. You know what old Dom meant about drinking stars when he had his first sip of the bubbly stuff." She took another sip, then studied him over the rim. "Okay, I'm impressed. You're quite the big cheese these days, aren't you, Mr. Hawke?"

"Maybe, but it's more knowing to use what works. And the local boy who makes good can usually get a table at a restaurant."

She looked around the room, so softly lit, so private, so romantic.

There were flowers and candles, not only on the table but on the antique server, on the long, carved buffet. The room smelled of both of them, and music—something soft with weeping violins—drifted through the air.

A low fire burned in a black marble hearth, more candles, more flowers on the mantelpiece above it. A wide scalloped mirror reflected off it, creating a strong sense of intimacy.

"Some table," she said at length.

"I wanted to be alone with you. Don't spoil it," he said, and covered her hand with his before she could move it out of reach. "It's just dinner, Stretch."

"Nothing's *just* in a place like this."

He turned her hand over, ran his finger down the center of her palm while he watched her face. "Then let me try my hand at romancing you. Just for one evening. I could start by telling you that just looking at you right now almost stops my heart."

Hers did a quick bounce, and then went *thud.* "You're pretty good at it, for a beginner."

"Sit tight. I'll get better."

She didn't tug her hand away. It seemed wrong, a small, mean gesture when he'd gone to such trouble to give her something special. "It's not going to mean anything, Jordan. We're in different places than we were."

"Seems to me we're both right here. Why don't we relax and enjoy it?" He nodded to the waiter stationed discreetly just outside the room. "You said you were hungry."

She took the offered menu. "You've got that one right."

It would, Dana discovered, take considerable effort and a great deal of determination not to relax and enjoy. And it would be mean-spirited. He might have cornered her into the date, but he'd gone out of his way to make it a memorable, even magical one.

Then there was the fact that, by his own terms, he was romancing her. That was something new. As long as they'd been together, as much as they'd meant to each other, old-fashioned romance had never been particularly a part of their relationship.

Oh, he'd certainly been capable of sweetness, if he was in the mood. And surprise.

But no one, not even the most sympathetic, would ever have called the Jordan Hawke she remembered smooth or traditionally romantic.

Then again, she'd liked his edges. They'd attracted her and they'd aroused her.

Still, she wasn't about to complain about being courted for one evening by a charming, entertaining man who seemed intent on providing her with a dream date.

"Tell me what you want for the bookstore."

She took another bite of truly incredible sea bass. "How much time do you have?"

"All you need."

"Well, first I want it to be accessible. The kind of place people feel free to stroll into, just browse around, maybe settle in for a while and read. But at the same time, I don't want them to treat it like their private library. What I want to establish is the neighborhood bookstore, where customer service is the priority, where people like to gather."

"I wonder why no one ever tried that in the heart of the Valley before."

"I'm trying not to think about that," she admitted. "If no one did, there might be a good reason."

"They weren't you," he said simply. "What else are you after? Are you shooting for general stock, or are you going to specialize?"

"General. I want a lot of variety, but I worked in the library long enough to know what people in this area lean toward. So certain sections—romance, mystery, local interest—will outweigh some of the more esoteric titles. I want to coordinate with the local schools, know what teachers are assigning, and see if I can get at least one book club formed within the first six months."

She picked up her wine. "And that's just for starters. Mal and Zoe and I will be working together, and ideally we'll overlap our customer base. You know, somebody comes in for a book and thinks, Wow, look at that terrific blown-glass vase. It's just perfect for my sister's birthday. Or someone's going up to Zoe's for a haircut and picks up a paperback to read while she's getting done."

"Or they come in to look at paintings and decide they could really use a manicure."

She toasted him, sipped. "That's the plan."

"It's a good one. The three of you look good together. You fit together, complement each other. You've all got different styles, but they mesh nicely."

"Funny, I was thinking almost exactly that just the other day. It's like if anyone had suggested I'd be going into business—putting basically every penny I have on the line—with two women I've known only about a month, I'd have laughed my butt off. But here I am. And it's right. That's one thing I'm absolutely sure of."

"As far as the bookstore goes, I'd bet on you any day of the week."

"Save your money. I may have to borrow some before it's done. But following along, tell me what you would look for in a good neighborhood bookstore. From a writer's perspective."

Like Dana, he sat back, a signal to the waiter to clear. "You called me a writer without any derogatory adjectives."

"Don't get cocky. I'm just maintaining the mood of the evening."

"Then let's order dessert and coffee, and I'll tell you."

*   *   *

By the time they were done, she was wishing she'd brought a notebook. He was good, she had to give him that. He touched on aspects she hadn't thought of, expanded on others that she had.

When they spoke of books themselves, she realized how much she'd missed that perk. Having someone who shared her absolute devotion to stories. To devouring and dissecting them, to savoring and wallowing in them.

"It's a nice night," he said as he helped her to her feet. "Why don't we walk around the grounds before we drive back?"

"Is that your way of saying that I ate so much I need to walk it off?"

"No. It's my way of stretching out the time I have alone with you."

"You really have gotten better at this," she replied as he led her from the room.

Her coat reappeared nearly as quickly as it had been whisked away. And, she noted, Jordan didn't miss a beat when the maître d' presented one of his books and asked to have it signed.

He did that well, too, she thought. He kept it light, friendly, added some casual chatter and his thanks for the evening.

"How does it feel?" she asked when they'd stepped outside. "When someone asks you to sign a book?"

"A hell of a lot better than it does if they don't give a damn."

"No, seriously. Don't brush the question off. What's it like?"

"Satisfying." Absently, he smoothed down the collar of her coat. "Flattering. Surprising. Unless they've got a crazed look in their eye and an unpublished manuscript under their arm."

"Does that happen?"

"Often enough. But mostly it just feels good. Hey, here's somebody who's read my stuff, or is about to. And they think it'd be cool if I signed it." He shrugged. "What's not good about that?"

"That's not very temperamental of you."

"I'm not a temperamental guy."

She snorted. "You always used to be."

"You used to be argumentative and pig-headed." He smiled broadly when she scowled at him. "See how we've changed?"

"I'm just going to let that go, because I've had a really good time." She breathed deep as they wandered a bricked path, and looked up at the thick slice of waxing moon. "Into week two," she murmured.

"You're doing fine, Stretch."

She shook her head. "I don't feel like I'm getting to the meat of it. Not yet. The days are going by really fast. I'm not panicked or anything," she added quickly, "but I've got serious concerns. So much is depending on me. People I care about. I'm afraid I'll let them down. Do you know what I mean?"

"Yes. You're not alone in this. The brunt may be on you, but you're not carrying all the weight." He laid his hands on her shoulders, drew her toward him a little, until her body rested against his. "I want to help you, Dana."

She fit well with him. She always had. And her realization of that made little warning bells sound in some dim part of her brain. "We already know you're connected, somehow or other."

"I want more." He bent his head to brush his lips over her shoulder. "And I want you."

"I've got enough to worry about right now."

"Whether it worries you or not isn't going to change a thing." He turned her to face him. "I'm still going to want you. You're still going to know it." His lips curved as he ran his hands up and down her arms. "I've always liked that look."

"What look?"

"That mildly irritated look you get when somebody gives you a problem to work out. The one that puts this little crease right here." He touched his lips to her forehead, just between her eyebrows.

"I thought we were taking a walk."

"We did. Now I'd say this evening calls for one more thing."

He loved the way her lips curled just as much as he loved the flicker of surprise over her face when instead of kissing her, he slid her into a slow, swaying dance.

"Pretty clever," she murmured, but she was moved.

"I always liked dancing with you. The way everything lines up. The way I can smell your hair, your skin. The way, if I get close enough, look close enough, I can see myself in your eyes. Your eyes always did me in. I never told you that, did I?"

"No." She felt herself tremble, and the warning bells were lost under the thunder of her own heart.

"They did. Still do. Sometimes, when we

managed to spend the night together, I'd wake up early to watch you sleep. Just so I could see you open your eyes."

"It's not fair." Her voice shook. "It's not fair to tell me something like that now."

"I know. I should've told you then. But now's all I've got."

He touched his lips to hers, rubbed softly. Nipped gently. He felt her body slide toward surrender, and fought the urge to plunder.

He went slowly, for both of them, savoring what they'd once devoured, lingering where once they'd rushed. In the starlight, with her arms lifting to come around him, he wouldn't allow himself to demand. Instead, he seduced.

He was still circling her in a dance. Or was it just that her head was spinning? His lips were warm, and patient, all the more arousing with the hints of heat and urgency she sensed strapped down inside him.

She sighed, drew him closer. And let him take her deeper.

Soft, slow, moist. The chill of the air against her heated skin, the scent of the night, the whisper of her name through lips moving, moving over her own.

If all the years between had formed a gulf

between them, this one kiss in a deserted autumn garden began to forge the bridge.

It was he who drew back, then shook her to the core by grasping both of her hands, bringing them to his lips. "Give me a chance, Dana."

"You don't know what you're asking. No, you don't," she said before he could speak. "And I don't know the answer yet. If you want one that matters, you're going to have to give me time to figure it out."

"Okay." He kept her hands in his, but stepped back. "I'll wait. But I meant what I said before, about helping you. It hasn't anything to do with this."

"I have to think about that, too."

"All right."

But there was one thing she knew, Dana realized as they walked back for his car. She wasn't still in love with him. They were, as he'd said, different people now. And what she felt for him now made the love she'd had for the boy seem as pale and thin as morning mist.

Jordan let himself into the house, switched off the porch light. It had been a very long time, he reflected, since anyone had left a light on for him.

His choice, of course. That was what everything came down to. He'd chosen to leave the Valley, to leave Dana, and his friends and all that was familiar.

It had been the right choice; he would stand by that. But he could see now that his method of making it had been the flaw. The flaw that had left a crack in what had been. Just how did a man go about building something new on a faulty foundation?

He started toward the steps, then stopped as Flynn came down them.

"Waiting up for me, Dad? Did I miss curfew?"

"I see your night on the town put you in a cheery mood. Why don't we step back into my office?"

Without waiting for assent, Flynn strolled back to the kitchen. He took a look around. Okay, it was a hideous room, even he could see that. The ancient copper-tone appliances, the ugly cabinets and linoleum that possibly had looked fresh and jazzy in his grandfather's generation.

But he still couldn't visualize how it could, or would, look when Malory got done with it. No more than he could understand why the prospect of ripping it apart and putting it back together made her so happy.

"The guys are coming in Monday to bomb this place."

"Not a moment too soon," Jordan commented.

"I was going to get around to it, sooner or later. It wasn't like I was using it. But since Malory, stuff actually gets cooked in here." He bumped the stove with his foot. "She has a deep and violent hatred for this appliance. It's kind of scary."

"You brought me back here to talk about Malory's obsession with kitchen appliances?"

"No. I wanted cookies. Malory has this rule against eating them in bed. This is something else I can't figure," he continued as he got a bag of Chips Ahoy out of the cupboard. "But I'm an easygoing guy. You want milk?"

"No."

His friend was wearing gray sweats and a T-shirt that might have been new during his sophomore year of college. His feet were bare, his expression easy.

Looks, Jordan knew, could be very deceiving.

"And you're not easygoing, Hennessy. You pretend to be easygoing so you can get your own way."

"I'm not eating these in bed, am I?"

"Small potatoes, son. You got the woman in your bed."

"Yeah." Grinning, Flynn poured a glass of milk, then sat down, stretched out his legs. "I do. Of course, she's up there reading instead of offering me intriguing and varied sexual favors, but I can bide my time."

Jordan sat. Flynn, he knew from long experience, would get to his point eventually. "So, you want to talk about your sex life? Is this going to be a bragging session, or are you looking for advice?"

"I'd rather do it than brag about it, and I'm doing just fine on my own. But thanks for the offer." He dunked a cookie. "So, how's Dana?"

And there would be the point, Jordan thought. "A little anxious about the task at hand, I'd say, but diving in head-first. You must have seen the mountain range of books she's hiking through when you dropped off Moe."

"Yeah, I got eyestrain just thinking about reading half of them. And otherwise?"

"It looks like she's steadied herself after what happened to her the other night. She may be spooked by it, but she's just as curious. You know how she is."

"Mmm-hmm."

"Why don't you just ask me how things are with us?"

"And pry into your private and personal lives? Me?"

"Up yours, Hennessy."

"Wow, that was so creative, so succinct. I immediately see why you're a successful novelist."

"Sideways." And though he had absolutely no desire for one, Jordan pulled a cookie from the bag. "I screwed up with her, all those years ago. 'I'm going, it's been fun, see you around.' "

It caused a low burn in his gut to remember it now.

"Maybe not that cut and dried, but close enough." He bit into the cookie as he studied his friend's face. "Did I screw up with you, too?"

"Maybe some." Flynn nudged Malory's pretty candle aside so he could move the cookie bag between them. "I can't say I didn't feel a little deserted when you took off, but I got why you had to leave. Hell, I was planning on doing the same myself."

"The business exec, the struggling writer, and the dedicated reporter. Hell of a trio."

"Yeah, we all got there, too, didn't we? One way or the other. I never left the Valley to do it, but I thought I was going to, so I could look at you, and Brad, as sort of the advance guard. But then again, I wasn't sleeping with you."

"She was in love with me."

Flynn waited a beat, absorbed the baffled frustration on Jordan's face. "What, did that lightbulb just go off? You've got some faulty wiring in there, pal."

"I knew she loved me." Disgusted, Jordan shoved up to get a glass of milk after all. "Hell, Flynn, we all loved each other. We were as much family as any who share blood. I didn't know it was the big L for her. How the hell is a guy supposed to know that sort of thing unless the woman looks him in the eye and says, 'I'm in love with you, you asshole.' Which would," he continued, working up to fury, "have been something you'd expect from Dana. That's just how she does things. But she didn't, so I didn't know. And I'm the slug because of it."

Because he'd been concerned by Jordan's steady cool, the spike of temper relieved him. "Yeah, but you're a slug for a lot of reasons. I could write up a list."

"The one I'd write up on you would be longer," Jordan muttered.

"Great, a contest." Not just angry, Flynn noted as he studied Jordan's face, but unhappy. Still, it had to be finished out, had to be said.

"Look, when Lily dumped me and took off for fame and fortune in the big bad city, it hurt. And I wasn't in love with her. You and Brad had that one right. But I thought I was, I was ready to be, and her brushing me off messed me up. Dana *was* in love with you. You've got to expect that your going, whatever your reasons, messed her up."

Jordan sat again, thoughtfully broke a cookie in two. "You're telling me not to mess her up again."

"Yeah, that's what I'm telling you."

Chapter Nine

Dana tried working off her sexual and emotional frustration with the books. She focused on the goal, and spent half the night sifting through data, words, notes, and her own speculations about the location of the key.

Her primary reward was a massive headache.

What little sleep she managed to get was restless and unsatisfying. When even Moe failed to perk up her morning mood, she decided to give physical labor a try.

She dropped Moe back at Flynn's by simply opening the front door with her key and letting him bullet inside. Since it was still short of nine of a Sunday morning, she imagined the household was sleeping.

In her current mood, the machine-gun barking that sprayed through the quiet as Moe charged up the stairs made her lips curve in a dark, wicked smile.

"You go, Moe," she cheered, shut the door, and strolled back to her car.

She drove directly to the building. Indulgence, she corrected herself as she parked. It was going to be Indulgence, so she needed to start thinking of it that way instead of as "the house" or "the building."

When she unlocked the door and stepped inside, the strong smell of fresh paint hit her. It was a good smell, she decided. The smell of progress, of newness, of accomplishment.

Maybe the white primer wasn't pretty, but it was sure as hell bright, and looking at it, she could see just how far they'd come already.

"So let's keep going."

She pushed up her sleeves and headed to the supplies and tools.

It occurred to her that this was the first time, the only time, she'd been alone here. On the heels of that came the thought that maybe she was asking for trouble being alone in a place where Kane had already wielded his sorcery.

She glanced uneasily up the steps. And thought of cold blue mist. As if the chill of it crept over her skin, she shuddered.

"I can't be afraid to be here." The way her voice echoed made her wish she'd brought along a radio. Anything to fill the silence with normal sound.

Won't be afraid to be here, she corrected herself as she opened a can of paint. How could she, or any of them, make this place their own if they were afraid to come into it alone?

There were bound to be times when one of them came in early or stayed late. The three of them couldn't be attached at the hip. She—all of them—would have to get used to the quiet of the place, and the settling noises. Normal quiet, normal noises, she assured herself. Hell, she *liked* being alone and having a big, empty house all to herself. It was tailor-made Dana time.

The memory of Kane's nasty games wasn't going to scare her off.

And since she was alone, she didn't have to compete for the super paint machine.

Still, as she began to work she wished she could hear Malory's and Zoe's voices, as she had before, turning all those empty rooms into something bright and cheerful.

She comforted herself that they'd finished priming Malory's section and had a good start on hers. It would be a kick to finish her own space with her own hands.

She could begin to play with different setups in her head. Should she shelve mysteries here, or was this a better spot for nonfiction? Local interest?

Wouldn't it be fun to display coffee-table books on, ha ha, a coffee table?

Maybe she could find an old breakfront somewhere for the café section. She could display tins of tea, mugs, books. Should she go with those cute round tables that reminded her of an ice cream parlor, or the more substantial square ones? Wouldn't this room be the perfect place to set up a cozy reading corner, or would it be smarter to use that space for a small children's play area?

It was therapeutic to watch the clean white paint cover the dull beige, stroke by stroke marking the room as her own. No one could push her out of here as she'd been pushed out of the library. She was working for herself this time, and setting the rules herself.

No one could cut her off from this dream, from this love, as she'd been cut off from other dreams. From other loves.

"Do you think it matters? A little shop in a little town? Will you work, struggle, worry, pour your mind and your heart into something so meaningless? And why? Because you have nothing else."

"But you could."

She felt the cold shiver over her skin. It made her breath come too fast, tightened the muscles of her stomach toward pain. She continued to paint, guiding the roller over the wall, listening to the faint hum of the motor. She couldn't seem to stop.

"It matters to me. I know what I want."

"Do you?"

He was there, somehow there. She could sense him in the chill. Perhaps he *was* the chill.

"A place of your own. You thought you had one before, all those years of work, of serving others. Yet does anyone care that you're gone?"

It was a well-aimed arrow. Had anyone

even noticed she was no longer at the library? All the people she'd worked with, worked for? All the patrons she'd helped? Had she been so replaceable that her absence hadn't caused a single ripple?

Hadn't she mattered at all?

"You gave the man your heart, your loyalty, but he cast you off without a thought. How much did you matter to him?"

Not enough, she thought.

"I can change that. I can give him to you. I could give you a great many things. Success?"

The shop was full of people. The shelves were filled with books. The pretty tables were crowded with customers sipping tea, having conversations. She saw a little boy sitting cross-legged on the floor in the corner with a copy of *Where the Wild Things Are* open in his lap.

Everything about the scene spoke of pleasure—the combination of relaxation and brisk business.

The walls were exactly the right shade, she thought. Malory had been on the money there. The light was good, made everything friendly, and all those wonderful books temptingly arranged, on shelves, on displays.

She wandered like a ghost, passing through the bodies of people who browsed or bought, who sat or stood. She saw familiar faces, the faces of strangers, heard the voices, smelled the scents.

Attractive and intriguing sidelines were set up here and there. Yes, yes, those were the note cards she'd decided to carry. And the bookmarks, the bookends. Wasn't that the perfect reading chair? Roomy, broken in, welcoming.

It was very clever to use the kitchen as the hub of the three enterprises, with books, candles, lotions, and art all together to illustrate how nicely each complemented the others.

It was her vision, she realized. Everything she was hoping for.

"You'll enjoy it, of course, but it won't be enough."

She turned. He was there. It didn't surprise her in the least to see Kane standing beside her as people moved around them, through them.

Who were the ghosts? she wondered distantly.

He was dark and handsome, almost romantically so. The black hair framed a strong and compelling face. His eyes smiled into hers, but even now she could see something frightening lurking behind them.

"Why won't it be enough?"

"What will you do at the end of the day? Sit alone with only your books for company? Alone when everyone else gathers with their families? Will any of them give you a single thought after they walk out the door?"

"I have friends. I have family."

"Your brother has a woman, and the woman has him. You're not part of that, are you? The other has a son, and you'll never be inside what they have. They'll leave you, as everyone else has done."

His words were like darts in the heart, and as she bled from them she saw him smile again. Almost kindly.

"I can make him stay." He spoke gently now, as one did to the wounded. "I can make him pay for what he did to you, for his carelessness, for his refusal to know what you needed from him. Wouldn't you like him to love you as he has loved no other? Then, at your whim, you can keep him or discard him?"

She was in a room she didn't recognize, yet somehow *knew.* A large bedroom, saturated with color. Deep blue walls, an enormous bed covered in a ruby comforter, mounded with jewel-toned pillows. There was a generous sitting area, with two wing chairs facing a snapping fire. It was here that she sat, with Jordan kneeling at her feet. Her hands were clutched in his.

And his trembled.

"I love you, Dana. I never knew I could feel like this, as if there's no point in taking the next breath unless you're with me."

It was wrong. Wrong. His face never looked weak and pleading. "Stop it."

"You have to listen." His voice urgent, he buried his head in her lap. "You have to give me a chance to show you, to prove to you how much I love you. The biggest mistake of my life was leaving you. Nothing I've done, nothing I've touched since has meant anything. I'll do anything you want." He lifted his head and with some horror, she caught the gleam of tears in his eyes. "Be anything you want. If you'll only forgive me, let me spend every minute of every day for the rest of my life worshiping you."

"Get the hell away from me!" Shocked, panicked, she shoved at Jordan, knocking him back as she scrambled to her feet.

"Kick me. Beat me. I deserve it. Just let me stay with you."

"Do you think this is what I want?" She shouted it as she spun in a circle. "Do you think you can control me by making pictures out of my thoughts? You don't understand what I want, and that's why I'll beat you. No deal, asshole. And this is not only a lie, it's pathetic."

The fury in her voice echoed even when she found herself standing in the empty room with the paint roller on the floor at her feet.

Scrawled on the white wall in oily black was the message:

Drown thyself!

"Fat chance, you bastard." Though her hands shook, she picked up the roller and covered the black with fresh white primer.

Then they steadied, and her fingers dug

in on the handle of the roller. "Wait a minute, wait a minute!"

Her mind whirling, she dropped the roller with a splatter of paint, grabbed her bag and ran as though the gods were chasing her.

Minutes later, she charged into her apartment. She tossed her purse aside and grabbed the library copy of *Othello.*

" 'Drown thyself, drown thyself.' It's in here." She flipped pages, frantically pulling the scene and context into her mind as she searched for the quote.

It was one of Iago's lines, when he was doing one of his numbers on Roderigo. She *knew* that line.

When she found it, she sat down on the floor. " 'It is a lust of the blood and a permission of the will,' " she read aloud. " 'Come, be a man. Drown thyself! drown cats and blind puppies.' "

She fought for calm.

A lust of the blood and a permission of the will. Yes, that described Kane's vicious acts.

Jealousy, guile, betrayal, and ambition. What Iago knew, what Othello was ignorant of. Kane as Iago? The god-king as Othello.

The king hadn't killed, but still the daughters—those he loved—were lost to him through lies and ambition.

And the play—surely this play had beauty, truth, courage. Was it the key?

Ordering herself to be methodical, she paged through the book, searched its binding. Setting it aside, she found her own copy and did the same. She forced herself to sit again, to read through the entire scene.

There were other copies of the play. She would go to the mall bookstore, search through those. She could hit the library again on Monday. Rising, she began to pace.

There were probably dozens of copies of *Othello* in various forms around the Valley. She would go to the schools, the college. She'd knock on damn doors if she had to.

" 'Drown thyself,' my ass," she repeated and scooped up her purse. She would drive to the mall right now.

She'd already wrenched open the door when it struck her. Her own fury knocked her two steps back before she slammed the door shut again.

She was being a fool, a mark. An idiot.

Who had written the words on the wall? Kane. A liar quoting a liar. It wasn't a clue. It was misdirection. Something to have her running off on a tangent. Exactly as she had done.

"Goddamn it!" She flung her purse across the room. "Outright lies or twisted truth? Which *is* it?"

Resigned, she marched across the room to retrieve her purse. She had to find out, so it looked like she was taking that trip to the mall after all.

She was, Dana thought when she arrived home, probably as calm as she was going to get after spending the morning on what she was certain was a wild-goose chase. Still, she'd be happier when Malory and Zoe arrived. If nothing else, a girlfriend afternoon would cheer her up.

They'd have some food, they'd talk. And when Dana had called and said she needed them to come, Zoe had promised pedicures.

Not a bad deal.

She carried the Chinese food she'd picked up into the kitchen, set it on the counter. Then just stood there for a moment.

All right, she admitted, maybe she wasn't calm, maybe she wasn't steady. Not quite yet. And her head was screaming from the echoes of the morning fear, the frustration that had followed.

She walked to the bathroom, took a bottle of Extra-Strength Tylenol out of the medicine cabinet, and washed two down with tap water.

Maybe she should have opted for a nap instead of company. But despite the headache, the vague nausea, this was one time she didn't want to be alone.

She nearly flew to the door at the knock.

"Are you all right?" Zoe stepped in, dropped the bags she carried on the floor, then gathered Dana in her arms. "I'm sorry it took me so long to get here."

"It's okay. I'm all right." No, Dana realized, this was much better than a nap. "I'm just really glad you're here. What about Simon?"

"Flynn took him. It was really nice. He and Jordan are taking Simon over to Bradley's. He can run around with Moe, play with guys, eat junk food, watch football. Simon's thrilled. Isn't Mal here yet? She left before I did."

"Right behind you." Malory came hurrying down the hall, then held up a bakery box before she stepped inside the apartment. "I made a stop. Brownies—double fudge."

"I love you guys." Dana's voice broke as she said it and, appalled, she pressed her fingers to her eyes. "Oh, Jesus, I'm in worse shape than I thought. It's been a very crappy day so far."

"Sweetie, you come sit down." Taking charge, Zoe drew her across the room to the sofa. "You just relax for a minute. I'm going to fix you something to eat."

"I got Chinese. In the kitchen."

"That's fine. You just take it easy, and Malory and I will take care of everything."

They fixed plates, brewed tea, tucked a throw over her legs, and generally did all the things women instinctively know how to do to offer comfort.

"Thanks. I mean it. I didn't realize I was that close to cracking. Bastard really got to me."

"Tell us what happened." Malory stroked Dana's hair.

"I went over to our place, to paint. I woke up cranky and needed something to do." She slid a glance at Malory. "Sorry about siccing Moe on you so early."

"Not a problem."

"So." She soothed her throat with tea. "I started painting. It felt good, and I was thinking about how everything was going to look. Then he was there."

She started to tell them, as coherently as she could, and Zoe interrupted with an indignant oath.

"That's just bullshit! That's just a lie. Of course you matter. He doesn't know a damn thing about it."

"He's just playing on my weaknesses. I know it. Leaving the library bothered me, more than I've been willing to admit. I guess I've been feeling like what I did there didn't really matter to anyone but me. He uses things like that, then makes them bigger, more hurtful."

She picked up her tea again and told them how he'd transformed the rooms into her finished bookstore. "It was my vision of it," Dana said. "One I hadn't completely realized I had. Not just the way it looked but the way it felt, too. And, of course, loaded with customers."

Her dimples made a brief appearance in her cheeks. "He made it seem like it couldn't be that way unless he did it for me. That was a mistake, because it can be. Okay, maybe not bursting at the seams with customers, but the way it looked, the way it felt. It can be that way because it's mine. It's ours. And we'll make it that way."

"Damn straight." Seated on the floor at her feet, Zoe gave Dana's knee a squeeze.

"Then he shifted to Jordan. I've got to have a brownie now." She leaned forward and took one off the plate that Malory had loaded with them. "There's this fabulous bedroom, one of my dream rooms, you know? The place you build in your head if you could have a room done any way you want it? And Jordan's kneeling at my feet, like a supplicant. He's all but in tears, telling me how he loves me, how he can't live without me. All this junk he would never say in a million years. The kind of thing I've had him say in my head, so I could kick him in the teeth after. Payback stuff."

She blew out a breath. "Jeez, he's even telling me to kick him, beat him, whatever."

She broke off at the snicker and aimed a look at Zoe. Then her lips twitched. "Okay, maybe it is funny when you think about it. The Hawke, weeping at my feet, begging me to let him spend his life worshiping me."

Malory decided it was time for a brownie as well. "What was he wearing?"

After one long pause, Dana burst out laughing. All the aches, the tension, the illness vanished. "Thanks. Man, when I think I was next to sobbing like a baby. I was even feeling guilty because the deal with Jordan was close to a couple I used to toy around with. How he would realize his horrible mistake, come crawling back and beg. It seems satisfying in your head, you know. But let me tell you, when it really happens— or seems to—it's just horrible. So, basically, I told Kane he could kiss my ass, and I was back where I'd started."

Zoe took off Dana's shoes and began to rub her feet. "You had a pretty lousy morning."

"There's one more thing. There was writing on the wall, in this greasy black. 'Drown thyself!' I painted over it."

"That's horrible. He was trying to make you remember the island, the storm," Zoe muttered. "He's just huffing and puffing, that's all. He couldn't even make you think anything he did this morning was real. You knew it was him all along."

"I don't think he wanted it any other way," Dana mused. "I think he was trying a new line of attack. But the writing? Not about the island. It's a line from *Othello.* I recognized it almost immediately, just as I've now realized he knew I would. I went running out of our place like a maniac to get back here and look it up. To look for the key in the book."

"It's from a book?" Zoe swiveled around to pick up one of the copies from the coffee table. "I don't know how you'd remember something like that. It's a real talent. But why would Kane give you a clue to the key?"

"Now, quick wit—that's a real talent." Dana sighed. "I got suckered in. All I could think was that I knew the line, and how I'd been focused on that play, with the way Iago mirrored Kane in so many ways. So I went haring off, half-cocked, sure the key was going to fall right into my hot little hand."

She flopped back against the seat. "Even

when the light finally dawned, I just had to follow through. Hence, half a day wasted chasing the wild goose."

"It's not wasted if you figured it out. You knew he was lying about the bookstore," Malory pointed out. "Know the truth from his lies? Isn't that how it went? You did. And you realized he'd written a kind of lie to throw you off. But if you hadn't followed through, you wouldn't be sure."

"I guess. I'm still going to be snatching at every copy of that play I come across."

"I'll tell you something important you figured out today." Malory patted her knee. "You knew the truth was we're in this together, so you called us. And you know, however satisfying the fantasy might be when you're hurt or mad, you don't want Jordan to be a lapdog."

"Well . . . maybe just for a couple of days. Especially if Zoe can teach him how to give a foot rub." She leaned her head back, tried to relax.

"The thing is . . . I'm in love with him. Stupid jerkoff." She let out a long, long sigh. "I don't know what the hell I'm going to do about it."

Malory picked up the plate. "Have another brownie."

If she dreamed, Dana didn't remember it when she woke in the morning. And when she woke, the drum of rain and the gloom had her turning over, with the plan to go directly back to sleep.

Moe had other ideas.

Without much choice, she threw on clothes, added a fielder's cap and her oldest boots. Choosing a mug of coffee over an umbrella, she walked Moe in the rain and revved up her system with caffeine.

They were both soaked when the deed was done, forcing her to drag him into the bathroom. He whined, cried, tried to dig his paws into the floor as if she were taking him to slaughter.

By the time she'd toweled him off, she smelled as much like wet dog as he did.

A shower and another hit of coffee helped. She was just about to decide which one of her books to settle in with for the rainy morning when her phone rang.

Ten minutes later, she was hanging up the phone and grinning down at Moe.

"You know who that was? That was Mr. Hertz. You may not be acquainted with Mr. Hertz or Mr. Foy, who are involved in the longest-running trivia contest in our fine county. Apparently, the contestants assumed yours truly was on vacation and therefore unable to play master of ceremonies in my usual fashion."

Amused and ridiculously delighted, she walked into the kitchen to pour her third cup of coffee. "However, this morning Mr. Foy stopped into the library and was informed I was no longer on staff."

She leaned back on the counter, sipped coffee as Moe appeared to listen with avid attention. "Questions were asked and answered, mostly answered by the detestable Sandi. Mr. Foy, according to Mr. Hertz, gave the opinion that my departure was, quote, a downright, dirty shame, unquote, and vacated the premises."

As if riveted, Moe cocked his head and panted.

"Shortly thereafter, the two trivia aficionados held an informal meeting over at the Main Street Diner and decided that if the powers that be at the Pleasant Valley Library didn't appreciate a treasure such as myself, they no longer wished to have that institution involved in their daily information pursuit. I've just been asked if I would continue as emcee on a freelance basis."

Because it was just Moe, and he was nothing if not sympathetic, she didn't feel embarrassed when a tear trickled down her cheek. "I know it's probably stupid to feel this touched, but I can't help it. It's just nice to know I've been missed."

She sniffed back the tears. "Anyway, I've got to go on-line and find out when Chef Boy-Ar-Dee manufactured its first box of pizza mix." She headed off, coffee in hand, to her desktop. "Where do they think up these things?"

It kicked her into gear. Dana decided it was symbolic. She'd received validation of her purpose, her place in the community. The simple fact was, the Valley was vital to her, and this in-between stage—post-library, pre-bookstore—had left her feeling disenfranchised.

It wasn't the amount of work she had to do but the fact that the work she'd done in the past hadn't seemed to have any significance to anyone other than herself.

She dived in with a vengeance, placing orders for books, opening accounts, ordering her displays. Her mood was lifted to the point that when she was deep into the key books and the knock interrupted, she wasn't irritated.

"Time to come up for air anyway." She pulled open the door, then frowned at the young man who stood there, holding a single red rose in a clear bud vase. "Trolling for girls? You're pretty cute, but a little young for me."

He flushed, red as the rose. "Yes, ma'am. No, ma'am. Dana Steele?"

"That's right."

"For you." He passed her the vase, then took off.

Still frowning, Dana closed the door, then tugged off the card tied to the vase.

Reminded me of you,
Jordan

In his mind, Jordan was in the forest of the Pacific Northwest. Hunted. He had his wits, his will, and his need to see his woman again as his weapons. If he could survive for the next five minutes, he could survive for ten. For ten, he could survive an hour.

For the hunter wanted more than his life. It wanted his soul.

Fog slithered, gray snakes along the ground. The blood from the hastily bound wound in his arm seeped through the bandage and dripped into the mist. The pain kept him sharp, reminded him that he had more than blood to lose.

He should have seen it for a trap. That had been his mistake. But there was no going back, no point in regrets, no point in prayers. His only option was to keep moving. And to live.

He heard a sound. To his left? A kind of whispering the fog could make when parted by mass. He melted into the trees, pressed his back against bark.

Flight, he asked himself, or fight?

"What the hell game are you playing?"

"Christ Jesus." He popped back from the world in his mind, the one speeding onto the screen through the rush of his fingertips over keys.

The speed of the trip had the blood roaring in his ears as he stared at Dana.

She stood in the doorway, hands on hips, eyes full of suspicion.

"This is the little game I call writing for a living. Go away, come back later."

"I'm talking about the flower, and I've got just as much right to be here as you do. It's my brother's house."

"And this is, currently, my room in your brother's house."

She gave it one derisive scan. There was a bed, unmade, her own childhood dresser that she'd passed to Flynn when he'd bought the house, an open suitcase on the floor. The desk where Jordan worked had been Flynn's during his teenage years and was missing one of the three drawers that ran down the side. On it was a laptop, some files and books, a pack of cigarettes, and a metal ashtray.

"Looks more like a weigh station," she commented.

"It doesn't have to be pretty." Resigned, he reached for his cigarettes.

"That's a brainless habit."

"Yeah, yeah, yeah." He lit it, deliberately blew out smoke. "Half a pack a day, and mostly when I'm working. Get off my back. What're you riled up about, anyway? I thought women liked getting flowers."

"You sent me a single red rose."

"That's right." He considered her more thoughtfully now. Her hair was pulled back, so she'd been working. She hadn't bothered with makeup, so she hadn't planned on leaving the house. She was wearing jeans, a very faded Penn State sweatshirt, and shined black-leather boots with a stubby heel.

Which meant, he deduced from his knowledge of her, that she'd been planning to work around the apartment, then had grabbed the first pair of shoes that came to hand because she'd been in a hurry.

And that meant the flower had done the job.

"The single-red-rose gambit is supposed to be romantic." He smiled when he said it, just a little smugly.

She stepped into the room, skirted the suitcase. "You said it reminded you of me. Just what's that supposed to mean?"

"It's long and sexy, and it smells good. What's the problem, Stretch?"

"Look, you went for the big splashy date

Saturday. Good job. But if you think I can be taken in by a fancy meal and a rosebud, you're sadly mistaken."

He hadn't shaved, she noted, and could have used a haircut. Damn it, she'd always been a sucker for that heading-toward-scruffy look on him.

Then there was the expression on his face when she stepped in the door, before he'd known she was there. Half dreamy, half gone. And his mouth had been sort of grim and determined.

She had to grip the doorjamb to stop herself from rushing over and biting that mouth.

And now he was just watching her, that cocky half smile on his face. She didn't know whether to punch him or jump him.

"I'm not some starry-eyed kid this time around, and . . . what are you grinning at?"

"Got you over here, didn't it?"

"Well, I'm not staying. I'm just here to tell you it doesn't work."

"I missed you. The more I'm around you, the more I realize how much."

Her heart fluttered and was ruthlessly ignored. "That doesn't cut it with me either."

"What does?"

"You might try straight-up honesty for a change. Saying what you mean without any of the goofy touches. Which are clichés, by the way," she added as he stubbed out the cigarette and got to his feet.

And clichés became clichés, she thought, because they goddamn worked.

"All right." He stopped in front of her, hooked his fingers in the neck of her sweatshirt and tugged her forward. "Can't get my mind off you, Dana. I can tuck you away in it for stretches of time, but you're still in there. Like a splinter."

"So yank me out." She thrust up her chin. "Go ahead."

"I like you there, which makes me a glutton for punishment. I like you here, curling your lip at me and smelling of rain."

He reached up, tugged the band out of her hair and tossed it aside. Then he wrapped his fingers where the band had been. "I want to take you to bed, right now. I want to sink my teeth into you. I want to bury myself inside you. And when we're done, I want to do it all over again."

He angled his head, kept his eyes on hers. "How's that for straight-up honesty?"

"Not half bad."

Chapter Ten

He stared at her, trying to gauge her mood. "If that wasn't a yes," he decided, "you'd better run for the door. Fast."

"It—"

The rest of the words spilled down her throat when he swung her off her feet. "Too late. I win by default."

She did her best to frown, but it wasn't easy with the giddy thrill pumping through her. "Maybe I only want you because you're one of the few guys who can cart me around like I'm in the featherweight division."

"It's a start. I like your build, Stretch. Lots of territory to explore. What are you carrying now?" He juggled her a bit. "About one-fifty?"

A dangerous glint sharpened her eyes. "You think a comment like that's going to make me go gooey?"

"And every ounce exquisitely packed."

"Nice save."

"Thanks. I like your face, too."

"If you're about to say something about it being full of character, I'm going to hurt you."

"Those deep, dark eyes." He laid her on the bed as he looked into them. "I never could get the image of those eyes out of my head. Then there's that mouth. All soft and ripe and tasty." He nipped into her bottom lip, tugged gently. "I could spend hours thinking about your mouth."

She wasn't going gooey, exactly, but she had to admit something inside was definitely warming up. "You're better at this than you used to be."

"Shut up. I'm working here." He cruised his lips over her cheeks. "Then there's the dimples. Unexpected, capricious, strangely sexy. I've always loved the look of you."

He took her mouth again, long, slow, and deep until the pleasure spread from that point of contact through her body and straight down to her toes.

Oh, yes, she thought, he was much, much better at it now.

"Remember that first time with us?"

She arched a little, shifted a little as he nuzzled at her neck. "Since we all but set the living room rug on fire, it's a little tough to forget it."

"All that pent-up passion and energy. It's a wonder we survived it."

"We were young and resilient."

He eased back, smiled at her. "Now we're older and smarter. I'm going to drive you crazy, and it's going to take a very long time."

The muscles in her belly quivered. She needed to be touched. She needed to be shared, and with him—always with him— she could have both.

She'd known they would end up here when she'd walked out of her apartment. Maybe she'd known, down deep, they'd end up here the minute she'd opened Flynn's door and seen Jordan standing out- side.

She wanted, he wanted. She could only hope that could be enough for her.

"It happens I have some time on my hands just now."

"Let's start . . . right here."

His lips took hers with a kind of restrained urgency that shot shock waves of hot need through her system. Even as her heart leaped, he changed the tone, gentled it until that raging beat went slow and thick.

She floated back on the memory of what had been between them. The fire and the sinew of it. And forward again, to what was now. A kind of wonder and depth.

Helpless to resist either, hungry for the familiar and the new, she wrapped herself around him.

His body was familiar. The years hadn't really changed it. Long, broad at the shoulder, lean at the hips. The play of muscles under her hands, so much the same. The good solid weight of him, the shape of his mouth, his hands, so much the same.

How she'd missed this *knowing* of another. And the rush of love that streamed through the pleasure of being known by him.

Yet even as she slid into the old rhythm, he eased back and just looked at her.

"What? What is it?"

"I just want to look at you." He unbuttoned her shirt, taking his time about it, skimming the backs of his fingers over the exposed skin. And never taking his eyes off hers. "I want you to look at me. Who we were, who we are. Not so far apart, really." Still watching her face, he trailed his fingers over the thin cotton of her bra. "But just far enough to be interesting, don't you think?"

"You want me to think?" She shivered as those lazy fingers brushed her nipples.

"You're always thinking." He drew her up, slipped the shirt away. "Such a busy mind. Just one more thing about you that appeals to me."

As his hands stroked her back, she linked her arms around his neck. "You're awfully chatty, Hawke."

"Just gives you one more thing to think about, doesn't it?"

He opened the clasp of her bra, then walked his fingers over her shoulders to nudge the straps down.

His lips touched hers, retreated, touched and retreated until her arms locked around him and with a catch of breath her mouth fused to his.

He'd wanted that—that quick flash of need. For him. Because no, he didn't want her to think, but only to feel what they could bring to each other. Here and now.

His fingers tangled in her hair, then his hands fisted there, drawing her head back so that he could plunder her mouth, her throat. So that he could, for a moment, release the restless animal that prowled inside him.

He could have devoured her in one reckless bite. But that was too fast, that was too easy. Instead he let the heat rage and tormented them both.

He feasted on her, then sampled. His hands rushed over her, then slowed and lingered. When she trembled, so did he.

Her body had always been the purest of pleasures to him. Not just the shape and texture, but its eagerness to enjoy, its openness to the adventure of sex. The thunder of her heart under his lips aroused him as much as the ripe breasts.

All that lovely smooth skin that shivered under the pass of his tongue, the scrape of his teeth, was only more of a thrill when the woman urged him to take more.

Her hands rushed over him, tugging at his shirt. And the throaty purr of approval as her nails scraped his flesh had his blood burning so he had to fight a vicious war not to hurry.

But he wasn't going to gulp when he could sip.

Where had this patience come from? He would drive her mad with it. How could his mouth be so fevered and his hands so exquisitely controlled? His muscles quivered under her hands, and she knew him, oh, she knew him well enough to exploit his wants and weaknesses. Yet even as he met her demands, even as he pushed her to the trembling edge, he held back and left her quaking.

"For God's sake, Jordan."

"You're not crazy enough yet." His breath tore out of his lungs, but he pinned her arms down and continued to fuel the flames with his mouth. "Neither am I."

There was so much of her, and he needed it all. The sumptuous body, the questing mind, and that part of her heart he'd lost through carelessness. He needed more than her desire and heat. He needed her trust again, and would settle for a glimmer of the affection they'd once shared. He wanted back what he'd given up in order to survive.

He released her hands to embrace her, to hold her tight, tight as they rolled over the bed.

Her skin was slick with sweat, and she was hot and wet and ready. He had only to cup her to fling her over the edge. She sobbed out his name as her body erupted. And he knew when she went limp beneath him she'd given him something he hadn't known he'd craved.

Her surrender.

"Dana." He said her name over and over as his lips rushed over her face. When her eyes, so dark and heavy, opened and looked into his, he slid silkily inside her.

It was coming home and finding that what you'd left was only richer, truer, stronger than what had been. Impossibly moved, he linked his fingers with hers, gripped tight, and gave himself.

Accepting, she arched to him, then lifting her lips, found his and joined them. The sweetness of it brought an ache to her throat as pleasure built on top of pleasure. They matched, beat for beat, then thrust for thrust when sweetness became desperation.

They were still joined, lips, hands, loins, when they fell.

It could be, Dana thought as she lay sprawled over Jordan, that she had just experienced the most intense, spectacular sex of her life.

Not that she intended to mention it. Despite the afterglow and the filmy haze of love, she didn't have to feed his ego.

But if she *were* going to mention it, she would have to say her body had never felt more deliciously used. She wouldn't object to having it used in just that way on a regular basis.

Then again, sex had never been their problem. Wasn't their problem the fact she didn't know *what* their problem had been? Or was. Or might be.

Hell with it.

"You're thinking again," Jordan murmured, and ran a finger slowly down her spine. "You think so damn loud. I don't suppose you could put it off another few minutes, just until I regenerate some brain cells."

"When they're dead they're dead, smart guy."

"That was a metaphor, a delicate euphemism."

"Nothing delicate about you, especially your euphemism."

"I'm going to take that as a compliment." He tugged on her hair until she lifted her head. "You sure look good, Stretch, all rumpled and had. Are you going to stay?"

She cocked her head. "Am I going to get rumpled and had again?"

"That's the plan."

"Then I guess I can stick around for round two." She rolled aside, sat up and raked her fingers through her hair. And when he reached out, she cocked her brows knowingly.

Until he frowned and trailed his fingers gently over her breast. "Rubbed you a little raw here and there." He scraped his knuckles over his own chin. "If I'd known you were dropping by, I'd have shaved."

"I take it 'dropping by' is another euphemism." She needed to keep it light or her heart was going to melt right into his hands. "Besides, it was that unshaven, bohemian look that helped get me into bed with you."

She gave his cheek a friendly rub, then stretched. "God. I'm starving."

"Want to order a pizza?"

"I can't wait for pizza. I need immediate fueling. There's got to be something that passes for food in the kitchen."

"Wouldn't count on it. Kitchen's pretty torn up. Construction zone."

"A real man would go down and hunt up provisions."

"I hate when you do that. I always did."

"I know." It absolutely warmed her cockles. "Does it still work?"

"Yeah. Shit." He got out of bed, dragged on his jeans. "You're going to take what you get. No bitching."

"Deal." Satisfied, she lay back down on her side, snuggled into the pillow. "Problem?" she asked when he only stood, staring at her.

"No. Brain cells regenerating."

Her dimples flashed. "Food."

"I'm on it."

She felt quite smug as he walked out of the room. Maybe it was just a little small of her to gloat, even mentally, that she still knew how to push his buttons. But it brought her such a nice glow, how wrong could it be?

And it was better, wasn't it, than letting herself get all worried and churned up about what was going to happen next. This time around she would be smarter, enjoy the moment and restrain herself from expecting more.

They enjoyed each other's company, even when they were poking at each other. They shared people who mattered, very much, to both of them. And they had a strong sexual connection.

It was the basis of a good, healthy relationship.

So why the hell did she have to be in love with him? If not for that one little thing, it would be perfect.

Still, when you approached it realistically, it really was her problem. Just as it had been her problem before. He wasn't obliged to love her back, and whatever she put into or took out of the situation was her own doing.

He cared about her. She closed her eyes and bit back a sigh. Jesus, that was a sting. Was there anything more painful or lowering than being in love with someone who sincerely *cared* about you?

Better not to think about it, to turn that part of herself off, as long as she could manage it. She didn't have any illusions this time around about them being together forever, building a home, making a family, forging a future.

His life was in New York, and hers was here. And God knew she had enough in her life to satisfy and occupy her without adding to it by spinning dreams that included Jordan Hawke.

He'd only hurt her before because she'd let herself be hurt. She wasn't just older, she decided. She was smarter and stronger now.

While she was trying to convince herself, she stared at his laptop. His screen saver had come on, and was nothing but a shifting spiral of color that was already making her dizzy.

How did he stand it?

As soon as she thought it, she had the answer. It would irritate him enough to push him back to work.

Considering, she sat up. He hadn't turned the machine off when she'd interrupted him. He hadn't closed the document . . . had he?

She bit her lip, glanced toward the doorway.

That meant whatever he'd been writing was still on the screen, and if she just happened to give the mouse a little shake, it would pop right up. And if she just happened to read what he'd written, what was the harm?

Keeping an ear out for footsteps, she slid out of bed, tiptoed over to the desk. She tapped the mouse gently with a fingertip to flick the screen saver off.

With one last glance toward the doorway, she scrolled back two pages in the document, then began to read.

She was caught up quickly, though she hit what was obviously the middle of a descriptive paragraph. He had a way of pulling you into the scene, surrounding you with it.

And this one was dark and cold and quietly terrifying. Something lurked. By the first page she was in the hero's head, knowing his sense of urgency and the underlying fear. Something hunted, and was already feeding off pain.

When she came to the end of what he'd

written, she swore. "Well, damn it, what happens next?"

"That's a hell of a compliment from a naked woman," Jordan commented.

She jumped. She cursed herself, but she all but jumped out of her skin, which was all she was wearing. And she flushed, which was considerably worse. She felt the heat spread over her as she whirled to see Jordan standing in the doorway, jeans carelessly unbuttoned, hair mussed, a bag of Fritos, a can of Coke, and an apple in his hands.

"I was just . . ." There wasn't any way out of it, she realized, and so she simply told the embarrassing truth. "I was curious. And rude."

"No big deal."

"No, really, I shouldn't have poked around in your work. But it was just there, which is your fault for not closing the file."

"Which would make it your fault for interrupting me, then distracting me with sex."

"I certainly didn't use sex just so I could . . ." She broke off, heaved out a breath. He was grinning at her, and she could hardly blame him. "Hand over the Fritos."

Instead, he walked to the bed, sat back against the pillow. "Come and get them." He reached into the bag, took out a handful, and began to munch.

"Anyway, it was the screen saver. It was making me cross-eyed." Casually, she thought, she sat back down on the bed and tugged the bag of chips out of his hand.

"I hate that bastard." He crunched into the apple, handed her the soda. "So, you want to know what happens next?"

"I was mildly interested." She popped the top of the Coke, took a long sip. She ate some Fritos, traded them for the apple, traded them back. And, she thought in disgust, he wasn't going to crack.

"Okay, who is he? What's after him? How did he get there?"

He took the Coke. Was there anything more satisfying than having someone who shared your love of books being so interested in one of yours? he wondered.

If you added the fact that your literary partner was a very sexy, very naked woman, it was just gravy.

"It's a long story. Let's just say he's a man who's made mistakes, and he's looking for a way to fix them. Along the way he finds out there aren't any easy answers, that re-demption—the real thing—carries a price. That love, the kind that matters, makes the price worth paying."

"What did he do?"

"Betrayed a woman, killed a man." He ate more chips, listened to the rain drum and patter—outside the window, and in the for-est in his mind. "He thought he had reasons for both. Maybe he did. But were they the right reasons?"

"You're writing it, you ought to know."

"No, *he* has to know. That's part of the price of redemption. The not-knowing haunts him, hunts him as much as what's with him in the woods."

"What is with him in the woods?"

He chuckled. "Read the book."

She bit into the apple again. "That's a very underhanded method of making a sale."

"A guy's gotta make a living. Even if it is with 'mundane and predictable commercial fiction.' One of your pithy reviews of my work."

She felt a twang of guilt, but shrugged it off. "I'm a librarian. Former librarian," she corrected. "And I'm about to become a bookstore owner. I value all books."

"Some more than others."

"That would be a matter of personal taste rather than a professional outlook." Now she wanted to squirm. "Certainly your commercial success indicates you write books that satisfy the masses."

He shook his head and abruptly craved a cigarette. "Nobody damns with faint praise better than you, Dana."

"I didn't mean it that way." She was, she realized, digging a hole for herself. But she could hardly confess to being a fan of his work when she was sitting in his bed naked and eating corn chips. It was a sure way to make both of them feel ridiculous.

And would make any honest praise seem like pandering.

"You're doing what you always wanted to do, Jordan, and successfully. You should be proud of yourself."

"No argument there." He polished off the Coke, set the can aside. Wrapped his fingers around her ankle. "Still hungry?"

Relieved that the topic had been tabled, she rolled up the bag of chips, tossed it on the floor beside the bed. "As a matter of fact," she began, then jumped him.

It shouldn't bother him so much, and it irritated the hell out of him that it did. He didn't expect everyone to like his work. He'd long ago stopped being bruised or deflated by a poor review or a disgruntled comment from a reader.

He wasn't some high-strung, temperamental artist who fell into funks at the slightest criticism.

But damn it, Dana's dismissal of his work dug holes in him.

It was worse now, Jordan thought as he gazed out the bedroom window and brooded. Worse that she'd been kind about it. It had been easier to take her scathing and unsolicited opinions of his talent, her snotty, elitist dismissal of his field than her gentle and kindly meant pat on the head.

He wrote thrillers, often with a whiff of something *other,* and she dismissed them as hackneyed commercialism that appealed to the lowest common denominator.

He could handle that, if she *was* an elitist book snob, but she was far from it. She simply loved books. Her apartment was crammed with them and there was plenty of genre fiction on her shelves.

Though he'd noted there was nothing on them by Jordan Hawke.

And, yeah, he thought, it stung more than a little.

He'd been ridiculously pleased to come back into the bedroom and see her bent over his laptop, to see what he'd believed had been avid interest in the story he was building.

Curiosity, as she'd said. Nothing more.

Best to put that one away, he told himself. Lock it away in a box before it dug in too deep and started to fester.

They were lovers again, and thank God for it. They were, he hoped, halfway to being friends again as well. He didn't want to lose her, lover and friend, because he couldn't get past her disinterest or disapproval of his work.

She didn't know what it meant to him to be a writer. How could she? Oh, she knew it was what he'd wanted and hoped for. But she didn't know why it was so vital to him. He'd never shared that with her.

There was a great deal that he hadn't shared with her, he admitted.

His work, yes. He'd often asked her to read something he'd done, and naturally had been pleased and satisfied when she'd praised it—intrigued and interested when she'd discussed the story and offered her opinions.

The fact was, on a purely practical level, hers was one of the opinions he valued most.

But he'd never told her how much he'd needed to make something of himself. As a man, as a writer. For himself, certainly. And for his mother. It was, for Jordan, the only way he knew to pay his mother back for all she'd done for him, all she'd given up for him, all she'd worked for.

But he'd never shared that with Dana, or anyone else. Never shared with anyone that private grief, the drowning guilt or the desperate need.

So, he would put it away again and concentrate on rebuilding what he could and starting fresh with what he couldn't rebuild.

His current hero wasn't the only one looking for redemption.

* * *

Dana waited until she'd painted an entire wall in what was to be Zoe's main salon area. She'd bitten her tongue half a dozen times that morning, had talked herself out of saying anything, then had taken the internal debate full circle again.

In the end she convinced herself that it was an insult to friendship not to speak.

"I slept with Jordan." She blurted it out, kept her eyes trained on the wall she was painting, and waited for her friends to burst out with comments and questions.

When five long seconds ran by in silence, she turned her head and caught the look passing between Malory and Zoe.

"You knew? You already knew? You mean to tell me that arrogant, self-satisfied son of a bitch ran right to Flynn to brag that he'd banged me?"

"No." Malory barely swallowed a laugh. "At least not that I know of. And I'm sure if Jordan had said anything about it to Flynn, Flynn would've told me. Anyway, we didn't know. We just . . ." She trailed off, then studied the ceiling.

"We were wondering how long it would

take before the two of you jumped each other," Zoe put in. "Actually, we thought about starting a pool on it, but decided that would be a little crass. I'd've won," she added. "I had today as spontaneous combustion day. Malory figured you'd hold out another week."

"Well." Dana fisted her hands on her hips. "That's a hell of a note."

"We didn't actually bet." Malory chimed back in. "And see what good friends we are, not even pointing out that you're telling us, though Jordan telling Flynn would make him an arrogant, self-satisfied son of a bitch."

"I'm rendered speechless."

"Oh, no, you don't." Zoe shook her head. "At least not until you tell us how it was. You want to use the scale of one to ten, or do a descriptive retrospective?"

The laugh escaped before Dana could stop it. "I don't know why I like the two of you."

"Sure you do. Come on," Zoe urged. "Tell. You're dying to."

"It was great, and not just because I was ready to spontaneously combust. I missed being with him. You think you forget what it's like to feel so . . . connected to some-body. But you don't. You really don't. We were always good in bed. We're even better now."

Zoe let out a long sigh. "Was it romantic or insane?"

"Which time?"

"Now you're bragging."

With a laugh Dana started painting again. "Been a while since I had anything to brag about."

"How are you planning to handle it?" Mal-ory asked her.

"Handle what?"

"Are you going to tell him you're in love with him?"

The question brought a little shadow creeping in on the edge of her bright mood. "What's the point of it? He'd either back off or feel guilty about not backing off."

"If you're honest with him—"

"That was your way," Dana interrupted. "It's the way you needed to deal with what you felt for Flynn. It was right for you, Mal, and for him. But for me . . . well, I don't have any expectations of Jordan this time around, and I'm willing to take responsibility for my own emotions and the consequences. What I'm not willing to do is put my big, gooshy heart in his hands and force him into making a choice. What we've got right now is good enough for me. For now. We'll worry about tomorrow when it gets here."

"Um . . . I'm not going to disagree with you," Zoe began. "Maybe you need to take some time, let things settle or evolve. But more, maybe you're meant to. Maybe it's part of the quest."

The roller jumped in Dana's hand. "My sleeping with Jordan is part of the quest? Where the hell does that come in?"

"I don't mean the sex, specifically. Though sex is, let's face it, powerful magic."

"Yeah, well, maybe the gods sang and the faeries wept." Dana ran her roller over the wall again. "But I'm not buying that doing the wild thing with Jordan's going to lead me to the key."

"I'm talking about the relationship, the connection, however you want to say it. What was between you, what *is* between you, what's going to be."

Zoe paused as Dana lowered the roller, turned with a speculative look on her face. "Isn't that following along with what Row-

ena said to you about the key?" she continued. "Couldn't it be part of the whole
thing?"

Dana said nothing for a moment, then
dredged her roller in paint. "Well, that's another hell of a note. It's got some logic to it,
Zoe, but I don't see how it helps. Somehow
I don't think I'm going to find the key to the
Box of Souls tangled in the sheets the next
time Jordan and I make love, but it's an interesting angle, which should also be fun to
explore."

"Maybe it's more something, or some
place, that meant something to you, or both
of you, before. And now. And later." Zoe
threw up her hands. "I'm not making
sense."

"Yeah, you are," Dana corrected as a line
formed between her brows. "I can't think of
anything right offhand, but I'm going to
think harder. Maybe talk to Jordan about it.
No way to deny he's an integral part of this,
so he might as well be useful."

"I'm just going to say one thing." Malory
squared her shoulders. "Love's not a burden, not to anyone. And if he feels otherwise, he's not worthy of you."

After a moment's surprise, Dana set

down her roller. She walked over, bent down and kissed Malory's cheek. "You're a sweetheart."

"I love you. I love both of you. And anyone who doesn't love you back is a moron."

"Jeez, for that you get a hug, too." Dana gave Malory a squeeze. "Whatever the hell happens, I'm glad I've got the two of you."

"This is so nice." Zoe stepped over to swing an arm around each of them. "I'm really glad Dana had sex so we could have this moment."

On a bray of laughter, Dana gave them both a little nudge. "I'll see what I can do tonight, and maybe we can have a real weep fest after settlement tomorrow."

Chapter Eleven

Jordan slept with his arm flung over Dana's waist, his leg hooked over hers, as if he would hold her in place. Though she hadn't been the one to leave, this time around he was far from sure she would let him stay.

In her bed, or in her life.

But he held on to her as he wandered in dreams. Through the moonstruck night in the high summer heat where everything smelled ripe and green and secret.

The woods were locked in shadows, with the flicker of lightning bugs quick blinks of gold against the black. In dreams he knew, somehow knew, he was a man instead of the boy he'd been when he'd walked through the wild grass at the verge of those

woods. His heart pounding with . . . fear?
Anticipation? Knowledge? As he'd stared
up at the great black house that rose regally
toward the swimming moon.

His friends weren't close by, as they had
been on that hot summer night of his memory. Flynn and Brad weren't there, with their
contraband beer and cigarettes, the camp-
ing gear, or the youthful courage and carelessness three teenage boys made together.

He was alone, the warriors of the Peak
guarding the gate behind him and the
house empty of life and silent as a tomb.

No, not empty, he thought. It was a mistake to think of houses, old houses, as being empty. They were filled with memories,
with the faded echoes of voices. Drops of
tears, drops of blood, the ring of laughter,
the edge of tempers that had ebbed and
flowed between the walls, into the walls,
over the years.

Wasn't it, after all, a kind of life?

And there were houses, he knew it, that
breathed. They carried in their wood and
stone, their brick and mortar a kind of ego
that was nearly, very nearly, human.

But there was something, something he

needed to remember about this house, about this place. This night. Something he knew but couldn't quite bring clear in his mind. It drifted in and out, like a half-remembered song, teasing and nagging at him.

It was important, even vital, that he turned whatever was in his mind, like a camera lens, until the image came into sharp focus.

In the dream he closed his eyes, breathed slow and deep as he tried to empty his mind so what needed to come would come.

When he opened them, he saw her. She walked along the parapet under the white ball of moon. Alone as he was alone. Dreaming, perhaps, as he was dreaming.

Her cloak billowed up, though there was no wind to lift it. It seemed to him the air held its breath, and all the sounds of the night—the rustles and peeps and hoots—fell like a crash into terrible silence.

In his chest his heart began to pound. On the parapet, the woman began to turn. In a moment, he thought, in just a moment, they would see each other.

Finally . . .

The sun was a violent flash that shocked

his brain, blinded him. He staggered a bit from the displacement of being shot from inky night to brilliant day.

Birds sang with a kind of desperate joy in music that sounded of flutes and harps and pipes. And he heard the rushing sound that water makes when it falls from a great height, then thunders into itself.

He struggled to orient himself. There were woods here, but not any he recognized. Leaves were verdant, shimmering green or soft and glowing blue, and limbs were heavy with fruit the color of rubies and topaz. The air had a ripe, plummy scent, as if it too could be plucked and tasted.

He walked through the trees, on ground springy and richly brown, past a waterfall of wild blue where golden fish danced in the rippling pool at its base.

Curious, he dipped his hand into it. He felt the wet, the fresh coolness. And as he let it pour from his cupped hand, he saw that the water falling from his palm wasn't clear, but that same deep blue.

It was, he thought, almost more than the senses could bear. The sheer beauty was too intense, too vivid for the mind to translate. And once seen, once experienced, how did anyone survive without it, in the pale, dim reality?

Fascination had him reaching toward the water again when he caught sight of the deer drinking on the opposite side of the pool.

The buck was enormous, its coat sleek and golden, its rack a shining silver. When it lifted its great head, it stared at Jordan with eyes as green and deep as the forest around them.

Around its neck it wore a jeweled collar with the stones catching the streams of sunlight and tossing them back in colored prisms.

He thought it spoke, though there was no movement, and no sound other than the words that formed in his head.

Will you stand for them?

"Who?"

Go, and see.

The deer turned, and walked, silver hooves silent on the ground, into the woods.

This is no dream, Jordan thought. He straightened, started to circle the pond and follow the deer.

But no, it hadn't said *come* and see, but

go. Trusting instinct, Jordan took the opposite path.

He stepped out of the trees to a sea of flowers so saturated with color they shocked the senses. Scarlet, sapphire, amethyst, amber glinted in that streaming sun as if every petal were an individual facet cut perfectly from each gem. And in the center of that sea, like the most precious of blooms, were the Daughters of Glass, trapped in their crystal coffins.

"No, I'm not dreaming." He spoke aloud, to prove that he could, to hear the sound of his voice. To center himself before he walked across the sea of flowers to stare down at the faces he already knew.

They seemed to be sleeping. Their beauty was undiminished, but it was cold. He saw that, the cold beauty that could never change but was forever trapped in one instant of time.

He felt pity and outrage, and as he stared into the face so like Dana's, a tearing grief he hadn't experienced since his mother's death.

"This is hell," he said aloud. "To be trapped between life and death, to be unable to take either."

"Yes. You have it precisely." Kane stood on the other side of the glass coffin. Elegant in black robes with a jeweled crown atop his dark mane of hair, he smiled at Jordan. "You have a keenness of mind sadly lacking in much of your kind. Hell, as you call it, is merely the absence of all without an end."

"Hell should be earned."

"Ah. Philosophy." His voice held a touch of amusement, and a canny calculation. "Occasionally, you will agree, hell is merely inherited. Their sire and his mortal bitch damned them." He swept a hand toward the coffins. "I was merely an instrument, so to speak, who . . ." He lifted the hand, twisted his wrist. "Turned the key."

"For glory?"

"For that. For power. For all of this." He spread his arms wide, as if to encompass his world. "All of this, which can never, will never, be theirs. Soft hearts and mortal frailties have no place in the realm of gods."

"Yet gods love, hate, covet, scheme, war, laugh, weep. Mortal frailties?"

Kane cocked his head. "You interest me. You would debate, knowing who and what I am? Knowing I brought you here, behind the Curtain of Power, where you are no more than an ant to be flicked off a crumb? I could kill you with a thought."

"Could you?" Deliberately, Jordan walked around the crystal coffin. He wouldn't have even the reflection of Dana between them. "Why haven't you? Maybe it's because you prefer bullying and abusing women. It's a different matter, isn't it, when you face a man?"

The blow knocked him back ten feet. He tasted blood in his mouth, and spat it out onto the crushed flowers before he got to his feet. There was more than power on Kane's face, he noted. There was fury. And where there was anger, there was weakness.

"Smoke and mirrors. But you haven't got the guts to fight like a man. With fists. One round, you son of a bitch. One round, my way."

"*Your* way? You have no terms here. And you will know pain."

It gripped his chest, icy claws with razor tips. The unspeakable agony dropped him to his knees and ripped a cry from his throat that he couldn't suppress.

"Beg." Pleasure purred into Kane's voice. "Beg for mercy. Crawl for it."

With what strength he had left, Jordan lifted his head, stared straight into Kane's eyes. "Kiss my—"

His vision dimmed. He heard shouting over the roaring in his ears, felt a flood of warmth over the hideous cold.

And the fury of Kane's voice seemed to scream through his mind: "I am not finished!"

Jordan fell into unconsciousness.

"Jordan! Oh, God, oh, God, Jordan, come back."

He thought perhaps he was on a boat, one that rocked fitfully in the sea. He might have drowned, he supposed. His chest was on fire, his head dull and throbbing. But someone was bringing him back, pressing warm lips to his. Dragging him back to life whether he liked it or not.

But why the hell was a dog barking like a maniac out in the open sea?

He blinked his eyes open and stared up at Dana.

Though pale as glass, she was a welcome sight. She was running a trembling hand over his face, pushing it through his hair as she clamped her arms around him and rocked.

Outside the closed bedroom door, Moe barked and threw himself against the wood.

"What the hell?" he managed and stared dully when she began to laugh.

"You're back. Okay, you're back." Hysteria was trying to bubble and brew in her chest. "Your mouth's bleeding. Your mouth's bleeding, and your chest, and you're—you're so cold."

"Give me a minute." He didn't try to move, not yet, as he'd already discovered that just turning his head brought on a hideous wave of pain and nausea.

But what he could see was a blessed relief. He was in Dana's bedroom, sprawled on the bed, mostly over her lap, while she clutched him to her breast as she might a nursing baby.

If he didn't feel as though he'd been run over by a truck, it wouldn't have been half bad.

"I was dreaming."

"No." She pressed her cheek to his. "No, you weren't."

"At first . . . or maybe not. Stretch, you

got any whiskey around here? I need a shot."

"I've got a bottle of Paddy's."

"I'll give you a thousand dollars for three fingers of Paddy's."

"Sold." Her laugh was too close to a sob for comfort. "Here, just lie down. I'll get it. You need to cover up, you're shaking."

She hauled the covers over him, tucked him up like a bug in a cocoon. "Oh, Jesus God." She shook herself as she dropped her forehead to his.

"Two thousand if you get it here within the next forty-five seconds."

She fled the room, and Jordan figured he couldn't be in such bad shape if he could still appreciate the beauty of a naked Dana on the run.

An instant later Moe leaped on the bed and tripled every ache in his body. He started to curse, then settled for a sigh as the dog growled low, sniffed all around the bedcovers, then slurped Jordan's face.

"Yeah, that'll teach us to boot you out of the bedroom just because we want to have sex in private."

Moe whined, bumped Jordan's shoulder

with his nose, then turned three ungainly circles and settled down at his side.

Dana sprinted back, a bottle in one hand, a glass in the other. After pouring considerably more than three fingers of whiskey, she hooked an arm behind his head and lifted the glass to his lips.

"Thanks. I can handle it from here."

"Okay." Still, she eased him gently back against the pillows before lifting the bottle again and taking a long pull straight from it herself.

She imagined the heat of it hit Jordan's belly just as shockingly as it did hers. Steadier, she went to the closet and pulled out a robe.

"Do you have to put that on? I like looking at you."

She didn't want to tell him her skin felt as if it had been rubbed with ice. "We shouldn't have locked the dog out of the room."

"Yeah, Moe and I were just discussing that." He laid his hand on Moe's wide back. "Is he what woke you?"

"Him, and your screaming." She shuddered once, then sat on the side of the bed. "Jordan, your chest."

"What?" He looked down at himself as she eased the covers aside. There were five distinct grooves, like a talon pattern, over his heart. They were shallow, he noted, and thanked God for it. But they bled sluggishly and were viciously painful.

"I'm messing up your sheets."

"They'll wash." She had to swallow, hard. "I'd better take care of those cuts. While I'm at it, you can tell me what the hell he did to you."

She went into the bathroom for antiseptic and bandages, then just braced her hands on the sink and ordered herself to breathe until she could manage it without feeling like she was sucking razor blades into her throat.

She knew what fear was now. She'd felt it when the storm had ripped over the island and the black sea had rushed to take her. But even that, she realized, even that bone-deep terror, had been a shadow of what she'd gone through when the shocked agony of Jordan's scream had torn her out of sleep.

She fought back her tears. They were a useless indulgence when action was needed. Instead, she gathered what she needed and went back in to tend his wounds.

"I brought you some aspirin. I don't have anything stronger."

"That'll work. Thanks." He downed three with the water she offered. "Look, I can handle this. I remember you don't do well with blood."

"I won't be a baby if you won't." Ignoring the queasiness, she sat down to mop him up. "Talk to me, and I'm less likely to pitch over in a faint. What happened, Jordan? Where did he take you?"

"I started out somewhere else. I can't quite pull it back, so maybe I was dreaming. I was walking. It was dark, but with a full moon. I think it might've been up at the Peak. I can't remember for sure. It's hazy."

"Keep going." She concentrated on his voice, on the words. On anything but the way the cloth she was using reddened as she pressed it against the cuts.

"Next thing I knew, it was broad daylight. It was . . . sort of the way I always imagined the transporter in *Star Trek* works. Instant and disorienting."

"It wouldn't be my favorite mode of transportation."

"Are you kidding? It's got to beat the hell out of . . . Christ on a crutch!"

"I know. I'm sorry." But she gritted her teeth and continued to swab the disinfectant over the cuts. "Keep talking. We'll get through this."

Alarmed, Moe deserted the field by slinking off the bed and crawling under it.

Jordan did his best to breathe through the pain. "The Curtain of Power. I was behind it," he said and told her.

"You provoked him? Deliberately?" She sat back, all the interest and concern on her face shifting into irritated impatience. "Do you have to be such a man?"

"Yes. Yes, I do. Added to that, he was going to do whatever he was going to do. Why shouldn't I get a couple of swings in first, even if they were only verbal?"

"Oh, I don't know. Let me think." Sarcasm dripping from each word, she tapped a finger to the side of her head. "Maybe because . . . he's a god."

"And you'd've stood there, of course, hands folded, having a polite conversation?"

"I don't know." She blew out a breath and finished the bandaging. "Probably not." Deciding that she'd done her best, she bent over and dropped her head between her knees. "I don't ever want to have to do that again."

"That makes two of us." Stiff, still achy, he turned so he could run his hand up and down her back. "I appreciate it."

She managed what passed for a nod. "Tell me the rest."

"You just cleaned and bandaged the rest. Whatever he did felt just the way this looks. Actually, it felt considerably worse."

"You screamed."

"Do you have to keep saying that? It's embarrassing."

"If it makes you feel any better, I screamed, too. I woke up and you were—it looked like you were having a convulsion. You were dead white, bleeding, shaking. I didn't know what the hell to do. I guess I panicked. I grabbed you, started shouting. You went limp. Almost as soon as I touched you, you went limp. I thought—for a minute I thought you were dead."

"I heard you."

She stayed where she was another moment, fighting back tears again. "When?"

"After I hit the dirt the second time. I heard you calling for me, and it was like getting sucked back into the old transporter. I heard him, too, right as I was fading out. I heard him, but more inside my head. 'I'm not finished,' he said. 'I am not finished.' And he was royally pissed. He couldn't keep me there. He wasn't done with me, but he couldn't keep me there."

"Why?"

"You woke up." Reaching out, Jordan ran his fingers over her cheek. "You called me. You touched me, and that brought me out."

"Human contact?"

"Maybe as simple as that," he agreed. "Maybe just that simple—when the humans are connected."

"But why you?" She picked up the cloth and dabbed at the cut on his lip. "Why did he take you behind the Curtain?"

"That's something we have to figure out. When we do—ouch, Dana."

"Sorry."

"When we do," he repeated as he nudged her hand away, "we'll have more of the pieces for this particular puzzle."

* * *

Simple or complex, Dana needed answers. With Moe hanging his head blissfully out the passenger window, she drove to Warrior's Peak to get them. Research and speculation were one thing, but her lover's blood had been shed. Now she wanted cold, hard facts.

The trees were still bright, and their color splashed across a dull gray sky layered with sulky clouds. But more leaves littered the road and the floor of the forest.

Already past their peak, she thought. Time was moving forward, and her four weeks were down to two.

What did she think? What did she know? She ran through everything that came to mind as she drove the last miles and then through the gates.

Rowena was in the front garden, gathering some of the last of the fall blooms. She wore a thick sweater of deep blue speckled with dull gold, and to Dana's surprise, well-worn jeans and scuffed boots.

Her hair was tied back and rained in a sleek tail between her shoulder blades.

The country goddess in her garden, Dana thought, and imagined Malory would see it as a painting.

Rowena lifted a hand in a wave, then a smile lit up her face as she spotted Moe.

"Welcome." She ran to the car as Dana parked, opened the door for the exuberant Moe. "There's my handsome boy!" Her laugh rang out as Moe leaped up to kiss her face. "I was hoping you'd pay me a visit."

"Me or Moe?"

"Both are a delightful surprise. Why, what's this?" She put her hand behind her back, then brought it out again. She held out a huge Milk Bone that caused Moe to moan with pleasure. "Yes, it certainly is for you. Now if you'll sit and shake hands like a gentleman . . ."

The words were barely out of her mouth when Moe plopped his butt on the ground, lifted his paw. They exchanged a shake, a long look of mutual admiration. He nipped the treat delicately out of her fingers, then sprawled at her feet to chomp it to bits.

"Is it a Dr. Doolittle thing?" Dana wondered, and got a puzzled glance from Rowena.

"I'm sorry?"

"You know. Talking to the animals."

"Ah. Let's say . . . in a manner of speaking. And what can I offer you?" she asked Dana.

"Answers."

"So sober, so serious. And so attractive this morning. What a wonderful outfit. You have such a smart collection of jackets," Rowena commented as she ran a finger down the sleeve of the dull-gold tapestry fabric. "I covet them."

"I imagine you can whip one up just as easy as you did that dog biscuit."

"Ah, but that would take the fun, and the adventure, out of shopping, wouldn't it? Would you like to come in? We'll have some tea by the fire."

"No, thanks. I don't have a lot of time. We're settling on our property early this afternoon, so I'm going to have to start back pretty directly. Rowena, there are some things I need to know."

"I'll tell you what I can. Why don't we walk? Rain's coming," she added, casting a look at the sky. "But not for a bit. I like the heavy, anticipatory feel to the air before a rain."

Since Moe had made short work of the Milk Bone, Rowena opened her hand and revealed a bright red rubber ball. She threw it over the lawn toward the woods.

"I should warn you, Moe will expect you to keep throwing that for him for the next three or four years."

"There's nothing quite so perfect as a dog." Rowena tucked her arm companionably in Dana's and began to walk. "A comfort, a friend, a warrior, an amusement. They only ask that we love them."

"Why don't you have one?"

"Ah, well." With a sad smile, Rowena patted Dana's hand, then bent down to pick up the ball Moe dropped at her feet. She ruffled his fur, then flung the ball for him to chase.

"You can't." The realization struck, had Dana tapping her fingers to her temple. "Duh. I don't mean you couldn't, but realistically . . . A dog's life span is woefully shorter than that of your average mortal."

She remembered what Jordan had said about them being alone, about their immortality on this plane being curse rather than gift.

"When you factor in the spectacular longevity of someone like you, and the finite life span of your average mutt, that's a problem."

"Yes. I had dogs. At home, they were one of my great pleasures."

She picked up the ball, already covered with teeth marks and dog spit, in her elegant hand and threw it for the tireless Moe.

"When we were turned out, I needed to believe that we would do what needed to be done and return. Soon. I pined for many things of home, and comforted myself with a dog. A wolfhound was my first. Oh, he was so handsome and brave and loyal. Ten years."

She sighed, and skirted along the edge of the woods. "He was mine for ten years. The snap of a finger. There are things we can't change, that are denied to us while we live here. I can't extend a creature's life beyond its thread. Not even that of a beloved dog."

She scooped the ball up for Moe, threw it in another direction.

"I had a dog when I was a kid." Like Rowena, Dana watched Moe streak after the ball as if it were the first time. "Well, it was my dad's dog, really. He got her the year before I was born, so I grew up with her.

She died when I was eleven. I cried for three days."

"So you know what it is." Rowena smiled a little as Moe pranced back, doing a full-body wag with the rubber ball wedged in his mouth like an apple. "I grieved, and I swore I wouldn't indulge myself again. But I did. Many times. Until I had to accept that my heart would simply break if I had to go through the death of another I loved so much, after so short a time. So, I'm so pleased . . ."

She bent down to catch Moe's face in her hands. "And so grateful that you brought the handsome Moe to visit me."

"It's not all it's cracked up to be, is it? Power, immortality?"

"Nothing is without pain or loss or price. Is this what you wanted to know?"

"Part of it. There are limitations, at least when you're here. And Kane has limitations when he's here. Limitations when he deals with something from our world. Is that right?"

"That's a fine deduction. You are creatures of free will. That's as it must be. He can lure, he can lie, he can deceive. But he cannot force."

"Can he kill?"

Rowena threw the ball again, farther this time to give Moe a longer chase. "You're not speaking of war or of defense, of protection of innocents or loved ones. The penalty for taking the life of a mortal is so fierce I can't believe that even he would risk it."

"The end of existence," Dana supplied. "I've done my research. Not death, not the passing through to the next life, but an end."

"Even gods have fears. That is one. More is the stripping of power, the prison between worlds that allows entry to none. This he would risk."

"He tried to kill Jordan."

Rowena whirled, gripped Dana's arm. "Tell me. Exactly."

She related everything that had happened in the middle of the night.

"He took him behind the Curtain?" Rowena asked. "And there shed his blood?"

"I'll say."

She began to pace, her movements so fretful that Moe sat quietly holding the tooth-pocked ball in his mouth.

"Even now we're not permitted to see, to

know. They were alone, you say? There was no one else about?"

"Jordan said something about a deer."

"A deer." Rowena went very still. "What sort of deer? What did it look like?"

"It looked like a deer." Dana lifted her hands. "Except I guess it was the sort you'd expect to find in places where the flowers look like rubies and so on. He said it was gold and had a silver rack."

"It was a buck, then."

"Yes. And, oh, yeah, it had a collar, a jeweled collar."

"It's possible," she whispered. "But what does it mean?"

"You tell me."

"If it was him, why did he allow it?" Agitated, she began to stride up and down the verge, between wood and lawn. "Why did he permit it?"

"Who and what?" Dana demanded and dragged Rowena's attention back to her by shaking her arm.

"If it was the king," she said. "If it was our king taking the shape of the buck. If this is true, why did he allow Kane to bring a mortal behind the Curtain without consent?

And to harm, to spill his blood there? What war is being waged in my world?"

"I'm sorry, I don't know. But the only one wounded, as far as I can tell, was Jordan."

"I will talk to Pitte," she declared. "I will think. He saw no one else—only these two?"

"Just the buck and Kane."

"I don't have the answers you want. Kane has interfered before, but it's never gone this far. The spell was of his making, and the boundaries of it, his own. But he breaks them and is not stopped. I can do more, will do more. But I'm no longer certain of the scope of his power or protection. I can no longer be certain that the king rules."

"If he doesn't?"

"Then there is war," Rowena said flatly. "And still we are not brought home. This tells me, whatever is or has happened in my world, it remains my fate to finish what I was sent here to do. I have to believe it's your fate to help me."

She took a deep breath, calming herself. "I'll give you a balm for your man's wounds."

"We're sleeping together. I don't know if that makes him my man."

With an absentminded gesture, Rowena brushed this aside. "I must speak with Pitte. Strategy is more his area than mine. Come, I'll get you the potion."

"Just a minute. One thing. Jordan. He's essential to my key?"

"Why do you ask what you already know?"

"I want confirmation."

In answer Rowena laid her fingertips on Dana's heart. "You already have that as well."

"Is he part of this because I love him?"

"He's part of you because you love him. And you are the key." She took Dana's hand. "Come. I'll give you the balm for your warrior, then send you on your way." She cast another look at the darkening sky. "The rain's coming."

Chapter Twelve

Brad dumped ice in a galvanized bucket, creating a cold if humble nest for a bottle of Cristal. He covered the exposed neck with a clean paint rag.

Behind him, Flynn and Jordan set up a card table. "The cloth for that's in the bag over there."

Flynn glanced over. "Cloth?"

"Tablecloth."

"Why do they need a tablecloth? Table's clean."

"Just put it on the damn table."

Jordan walked over to the bag and ripped it open. "And look, he got one with pretty pink rosebuds on it."

"Matching napkins," Flynn added, pulling them out of the bag.

"What a sweetie. I didn't know you had a feminine side."

"When we're done here, I'm going to kick your asses just to reestablish my manhood—and because I'll enjoy it." Brad took out the champagne flutes he'd brought along, held them up to check for smudges. "Then maybe I'll tell the women this was my idea and negate your points."

"Hey, I sprang for the flowers," Flynn reminded him.

"I bought the cookies." Jordan shook the bakery box.

"Ideas get more points than cookies and flowers, my friends." Brad twitched the tablecloth to straighten it. "It's all about ideas and presentation. Which proves being in touch with your feminine side bags more women."

"Then how come Flynn and I are the only ones here getting laid?"

"Give me time."

"I really should clock you for saying that as regards my woman and my sister." Flynn studied Jordan's grin. "But it's not only an accurate statement, it rubs it in Brad's face, so I'm letting it pass. How much time we got?"

"A while yet," Jordan said. "Settlement should be pretty straightforward, but you've got lawyers, bankers, and papers, so it'll take twice as long as you think it will."

He stepped back, looked at the table set up in the foyer. He had to admit it was a nice touch there among the drop cloths and paint supplies. A splash of color and celebration against the primer-coated walls.

The women, he knew, would melt like ice cream in July.

"Okay, damn good idea, Brad."

"I've got a million of them."

"I don't see why we have to clear out before they get here," Flynn complained. "I'd like champagne and cookies, not to mention the big sloppy kisses this is going to generate."

"Because it's their moment, that's why." Satisfied, Brad leaned against the stepladder. "Recognizing that will only generate more big sloppy kisses in the long run."

"I like instant gratification." But Flynn paused, looked around. "It's going to be a hell of a place, really. Innovative idea, good location, attractive setting. It's good for the

Valley. Good for them. You should see some of the stuff Mal's setting up for stock. Over the weekend we went to see a couple of the artists she's going to feature. Cool stuff."

"He went with her to see art," Jordan pointed out, and with a grin tucked a finger in his mouth, then pulled up the side to mime a hook. "Can opera be far behind?"

"We'll see who's smirking when you're sitting in Dana's bookstore drinking herbal tea."

"That's not so bad. Brad here's probably going to have to get a facial to win Zoe over."

"There are lines that can't be crossed, no matter what the prize." But Brad looked up the stairs. "They're going to need to decide on lighting. And some of the trim needs to be replaced. Could use a new sink in the john up there."

"You're planning on seducing Zoe with bathroom fixtures?" Flynn asked. "You devious bastard. I'm proud to call you friend."

"Seducing her could be a very satisfying side benefit—after all, the stepladder got me a chicken dinner."

"Chicken dinner? You can get a chicken dinner at the Main Street Diner, Tuesday-night special." Sorrowfully, Flynn shook his head. "My pride in you is waning."

"I'm just getting started. But the fact is, they could use a little help here. There's some tile work, some carpentry, a little plumbing and electrical. They've got to upgrade some of the windows. We could pitch in with more than champagne and cookies."

"I'm in for that," Jordan agreed.

"Sure. Already figured on it." Flynn shrugged. "Hell, it looks like my house is going to be Remodel Central for a while anyway. Might as well spread the wealth. And driving a few nails should help keep us all from going crazy over the keys."

"Now that you mention it." Jordan glanced toward the windows as rain began to splat. "I'd better fill you in on what happened last night."

"Something happened to Dana?" Flynn pushed away from the wall. "Is she okay?"

"Nothing happened to her. She's fine. Hell, I need a smoke. Let's go out on the porch."

They stood outside, the rain drumming on the overhang. He took them through it— the colors, the sounds, the movements, building the story much as he'd done for them in tents pitched in a backyard, or around a campfire in the woods.

But this time it hadn't come out of his imagination. However active and agile that imagination was, it couldn't rake slashes down his chest. They burned still. It was some consolation to hear Flynn's sharply drawn breath and see Brad's wince of sympathy when he tugged up his shirt to show them.

"Christ, those look nasty." Flynn studied the raw, red grooves. "Shouldn't they be bandaged or something?"

"Dana put something on them last night, but she's not exactly Nurse Betty. I smeared some more crap on them this morning. Point is, our guy was seriously pissed— enough to take a genuine shot at me. Where does that leave the women?"

Heat flashed into Flynn's eyes. "He didn't touch Malory. Never physically touched her. It was bad enough, scary enough, the way he messed with her mind. But this . . . We've got to take him down."

"I'm open to ideas." Jordan spread his hands. "Problem is, as far as magic goes, I can't even pull a rabbit out of my hat."

"Some of it's just misdirection, tricking the eye," Brad mused.

"Let me tell you, son, when that guy's got his claws in you, it's no trick of the eye."

"No, I mean from our stand," Brad told Jordan. "We direct him toward us, it gives the women more space. He had a reason for going after you. If we can figure that out, exploit it, it might take his attention away from Dana for the next couple of weeks. And from Zoe when her time comes around."

"I haven't got anything concrete. It just feels like I know something, but I can't reel it in." Frustrated, Jordan jammed his hands into his pockets. "Something I know, or did, or have, that's the answer. Or one of them. Something from before, that plays into the now."

"Something between you and Dana," Brad prompted.

"Has to be connected, doesn't it? Otherwise it wouldn't follow the pattern. And if it isn't something important, why did he fuck with me?"

"Maybe it's time for a meeting," Brad began.

"For you suits, it's always time for a meeting," Flynn shot back.

"I'm forced to point out that I'm not wearing a suit."

"Inside you are. It's probably pin-striped. And I bet you're wearing a tie too. But I digress. Maybe the suit's right," he said to Jordan. "The six of us should put our heads together. Your place." He patted Brad on the shoulder. "You've got more furniture and better food."

"That works for me. The sooner, the better." Brad glanced at his watch. "Ha-ha, I have a meeting. Set it up with the women, let me know."

He stepped back inside to snag his jacket, then jogged out into the rain toward his car.

Jordan stood watching as Brad drove away. "We get through this one and get to the last round, his head's going to be on the block."

"You think he doesn't know that?"

"No, I figure he does. I was wondering if Zoe does."

The only thing Zoe knew at that moment was that this was one of the biggest days of her life. She clutched the keys, *her* keys, in her fist. They were brand spanking new, to go with the brand spanking new lock sets she'd bought to replace the old ones.

She was going to put the lock on the main door herself—she knew how—first thing. A kind of rite, she decided. A kind of claiming.

She parked, ran through the rain to the front porch, then waited as her friends pulled in behind. Malory had the original keys. Besides, it was right that the three of them went in together.

And wasn't it right, somehow symbolic, that Malory had the original key? That she and Dana would wait while Malory unlocked the door. The first door.

Malory had completed her part of the quest, and had held her key. Now it was Dana's turn. Then, God willing, it would be hers.

"Rain's going to strip a lot of the leaves off the trees," Malory commented as she rushed under the overhang. "There won't be much color left after this."

"It was nice while it lasted."

"Yes, it was." Malory started to unlock the door, then stopped. "It just hit me. It's ours now. Really ours. Maybe we should say

something profound, do something symbolic."

"I'm not carrying either of you across the
threshold." Dana scooped back her damp
hair.

"Booty shake," Zoe decided and made
Dana laugh.

"Booty shake," she agreed. "On three."

The few people driving by might have
been slightly surprised to see three women
standing on a pretty blue porch wiggling
their butts in front of a closed door.

Giggling, Malory turned the key. "That felt
right. And here we go." She opened the
door with what she considered a very nice
flourish, then her mouth dropped open.

"Oh, my God, look!"

"What?" Instinctively, Zoe grabbed her
arm to yank her back. "Is it Kane?"

"No, no! Look. Oh, this is so sweet! Look
what they did." She rushed inside and all
but buried her face in the roses set on the
card table. "Flowers. Our first flowers.
Flynn's going to get such a big reward for
this."

"It was really thoughtful of him." Zoe
sniffed at the flowers, then opened the bak-

ery box. "Cookies. The fancy kind. What a sweetheart you've got, Malory."

"He didn't do it alone." Dana pulled the champagne out of the bucket, arched her eyebrows at the label. "This has Brad's fingerprints all over it. Not just champagne but stupendous champagne."

Zoe frowned over the label. "That's expensive, isn't it?"

"Not only, but very classy. Only time I ever had it was when Brad gave me a bottle for my twenty-first birthday. He always had style."

"The three of them did this together, for us." With a long sigh, Malory danced her fingers over petals. "I'd say all three of them have style."

"Let's not disappoint them." Dana popped the cork, poured champagne into the three flutes set on the table.

"We need to have a toast." Zoe picked up the flutes, passed them out.

"Let's not do one that makes us cry." Malory took a steadying breath. "The flowers have me half started already."

"I've got it." Dana raised her glass. "To Indulgence."

They clinked glasses, sipped. And cried a little anyway.

"I've got something I want to show you." Malory set down her glass, picked up her briefcase. "Just something I was playing with. I don't want you to feel obligated. You won't hurt my feelings if you don't like the concept. It's just . . . just an idea."

"Stop killing us with suspense." Dana picked up a cookie. "Give."

"Okay. I was thinking about a logo, you know something that incorporates all three businesses. Of course, we might all want separate ones anyway, but we could use one logo for letterhead, business cards, the Web page."

"Web page." Pursing her lips, Dana nodded. "You're way ahead of me."

"Pays to plan. You remember Tod."

"Sure. Really cute guy you worked with at The Gallery," Dana supplied.

"Right. He's a good friend, too, and he's great at computer design. We could ask him to fiddle with looks and features for a Web page. Actually, I'm hoping to be able to offer him a job here. Down the road a little, but being optimistic, I'm going to need help. We all will."

"I haven't thought that far ahead," Dana admitted. "But yeah, I'll need at least one part-time bookseller who can handle brewing tea, serving wine. I guess I might need two people, realistically."

"I've got feelers out for a stylist, a nail consultant. Some others." Zoe pressed a hand to her jumpy stomach. "Jeez. We're going to have *employees.*"

"I like that part." Dana lifted her champagne glass again. "It's good to be boss."

"We're also going to need a tax consultant, office equipment, signage, an advertising budget, phone systems . . . I have lists," Malory finished.

Dana laughed. "I bet you do. Now what else is in the briefcase?"

"Okay. For the logo. This is just something I did from an idea I had."

She pulled out a folder, opened it, then set the drawing on the table.

The figure of a woman sat in a salon chair, tipped back in a pose of easy relaxation. A book was open in her hands, a glass of wine and a single rose in a bud vase on the table beside her. All this was inside an ornate border that framed it like a stylized portrait.

Above the border was the single word: IN-DULGENCE.

Below the name, it read FOR THE BODY, THE MIND, AND THE SPIRIT.

"Wow." Managing only the single word, Zoe put a hand on Malory's shoulder.

"It's just a thought," Malory said quickly. "Something to unify what we're all doing. Since we're using the one name for everything. Then we could have this sort of thing on our individual cards, letterheads, invoices, whatever, with something like—I don't know—'Indulgence. For Beauty. Indulgence. For Books. Indulgence. For Art.' And that would differentiate each aspect while keeping it under one umbrella."

"It's wonderful," Zoe exclaimed. "It's just wonderful. Dana?"

"It's perfect. Absolutely perfect, Mal."

"Really? You like it? I don't want to box you in just because—"

"Let's make a pact," Dana interrupted. "Any time any of us feels boxed in, she just says so. We're girls, but we're not weenies. Okay?"

"That's a deal. I can give this to Tod," Malory went on. "He could make up a sample letterhead. He'd do it as a favor. He's better at the desktop-publishing stuff than I am."

"I can't wait!" Zoe let out a hoot and did a little dance around the room. "First thing in the morning, we're going to start some serious work around here."

"Hold on." Dana spread her arms to indicate the walls. "What do you call all this painting we've been doing?"

"The tip of the iceberg." Still dancing, Zoe grabbed her champagne.

Dana had never considered herself a slacker. She was willing to work hard, insisted on pulling her weight, and she got the job done. Anything less was unacceptable.

She'd always viewed herself as a woman with high personal standards—both personally and professionally, and she tended to sneer at those who skimmed over work, who complained that the job they'd agreed to take on turned out to be too hard, too involved, too much trouble.

But compared to Zoe, Dana decided as she dashed into the market to pick up a few supplies, she was a malingerer. She was a wimpy-assed crybaby. The woman had worn her out in the first twenty-four hours.

Paint, wallpaper, trim samples, light fixtures, hardware, windows, floor coverings—and the budget for all that and more. And it wasn't just the thinking and deciding, Dana realized as she pondered a bunch of bananas, that was enough to make your head explode. It was the labor as well.

Scraping, hauling, stacking, unstacking, drilling, screwing, hammering.

Well, there was no doubt about it, she mused as she picked through the oranges. When it came to the organization, delegation, and implementation of labor, Zoe McCourt was in charge.

Between the work, the decisions, the worrying search for the key, and her struggle to keep her head above her heart regarding Jordan, she was completely worn out.

But could she just go home, fall on the bed, and sleep for ten hours? Oh, no, she thought with a hiss as she moved on to the dairy aisle. No, indeed. She had to attend a big meeting at Brad's place on the river.

She really needed about two solid hours of absolute solitude and quiet, but she'd had to trade a portion of that for groceries if she didn't want to starve to death in the coming week.

On top of that, she no longer had any confidence that she would find the answer to the key in the stacks of books she'd accumulated. She'd read and read, followed every lead, but she didn't seem to be any closer to a concrete theory, much less a solution.

And if she failed, what then? Not only would she let down her friends, her brother, her lover. Not only would she disappoint Rowena and Pitte, but her inadequacy would doom the Daughters of Glass until the next triad was chosen.

How could she live with that? Depressed now, she tossed a quart of milk in her basket. She'd seen the Box of Souls with her own eyes, ached to watch those blue lights battering frantically at their prison walls.

If she couldn't find the key, slide it into the lock as Malory had done with the first, everything they'd done would be for nothing.

And Kane would win.

"Over my dead body," she declared, then jolted when someone touched her arm.

"Sorry." The woman laughed. "Sorry. It looked like you were arguing with yourself. I usually don't get to that point until I hit the frozen dessert section."

"Well, you know. Whole milk, low fat, two percent? It's a jungle in here."

Then the woman angled her cart so another shopper could get through.

Pretty, brunette, late thirties, Dana observed, trying to place her. "Sorry. I know you, don't I? I just can't place it."

"You helped me and my son a couple of weeks ago in the library." She reached for a gallon of milk. "He had a report due the next day for American history class."

"Oh, right, right." Dana made the effort to tuck her dark thoughts away and answer the smile. "U.S. history report, Mrs. Janesburg, seventh grade."

"That's the one. I'm Joanne Reardon." She offered her hand. "And the life you saved was my son, Matt's. I stopped back in the library last week to thank you again, but I was told you weren't there anymore."

"Yeah." That brought some of the dark thoughts back into play. "You could say I retired abruptly from library service."

"I'm sorry to hear that. You were terrific

with Matt. And you made a big difference. He got an A. Well, an A-minus, but anything with Matt's name on it that includes an A is cause for wild celebration in our house."

"That's great." And particularly good to hear at the end of a long day. "He must've done a good job. Mrs. Janesburg doesn't pass out the A's like doughnuts."

"He did, which he wouldn't have done if you hadn't pointed him in the right direction. More, if you hadn't found the right key to turn in his head. I'm glad I got the chance to tell you."

"So am I. You picked up my day considerably."

"I'm sorry about whatever happened with the job. It's none of my business, but if you ever need a personal reference, you can sure have mine."

"Thanks. I mean that. Actually, some friends and I are starting our own business. I'm going to be opening a bookstore in a month or so. Probably a little more 'or so,' but we're putting it all together."

"A bookstore?" Joanne's hazel eyes sharpened with interest. "In town?"

"Yeah. A combination thing. A bookstore, an arts and crafts gallery, and a beauty salon. We're fixing up a house over on Oak Leaf."

"That sounds fabulous. What an idea. All that in one place, *and* in town. I only live about a mile and a half from there. I can promise to be one of your regular customers."

"If we keep up the pace, we'll have it up and running for the holiday season."

"Terrific. You wouldn't be hiring, would you?"

"Hiring?" Dana eased back, considered. "Are you looking for a job?"

"I'm thinking about slipping back into the workforce, but I want something close to home, something fun, and something with fairly flexible hours. What you'd call a fantasy job. Especially when you consider I haven't worked outside the home in over a decade, have only recently become computer literate—actually, it may be a stretch to say that—and my main job experience was as a legal secretary for a mid-level law firm in Philadelphia—where I did not shine—right out of high school."

She laughed at herself. "I'm not giving myself a very glowing recommendation."

"You like to read?"

"Give me a book and a couple hours of quiet, and all's right with the world. I'm also good with people, and I'm not looking for a big salary. My husband has a good job, and we're secure, but I'd like to pull in a little of my own. And I'd like to do something to earn it that doesn't have anything to do with laundry, cooking, or browbeating an eleven-year-old into picking up his room."

"I find those excellent qualifications in a potential employee. Why don't you come by the building sometime. It's the house with the blue porch. You can take a look at the place, and we'll talk some more."

"This is great. I will. Wow." She let out a laugh. "I'm so happy I ran into you. It must've been fate."

Fate, Dana mused when they'd parted ways. She hadn't been giving enough credit to fate. Needing to restock her pantry had brought her here, to the dairy section of her local supermarket.

A small thing, she thought as she continued through the aisles. An everyday sort of thing. But hadn't it put her here at just the right moment? Bumped her right into a woman who might become another spoke on the wheel of her life?

And more than that. She'd bumped into the woman who'd said exactly what she'd needed to hear.

You found the right key to turn in his head.

Was it just coincidence that Joanne had used that phrase? Dana wasn't going to blow it off as coincidence. No, her key—the right key—was knowledge.

She would find it, Dana promised herself. She would find it by keeping her mind open.

Chapter Thirteen

In Dana's opinion, there were a lot of things you could say about Bradley Charles Vane IV.

He was fun, smart, and great to look at. He could, depending on his mood and the circumstances, present a polished, urbane image that made her think of James Bond ordering a vodka martini in Monte Carlo— and then turn on a dime and become a complete goofball ready to spray seltzer down your pants.

He could discuss French art films with the passion of a man who didn't require the subtitles, and be just as fervent in a debate over whether Elmer Fudd or Yosemite Sam was a more worthy adversary for Bugs.

Those were just some of the things she loved about Brad.

Another was his house.

Towners called it the Vane House, or the River House, and indeed it had been both for more than four decades.

Brad's father had built it, a testimony to the lumber that formed the foundation of the Vane empire. Using that lumber, and with a skilled eye for the surroundings, B. C. Vane III had created both the simple and the spectacular.

The golden frame house spread along the riverbank, edging itself with spacious decks and charming terraces. There were a number of rooflines and angles, all of them balanced into a creative harmony that showcased the beauty of wood.

It offered lovely views of the river or the trees or the clever hodgepodge of gardens.

It wasn't the sort of place you looked at and thought, Money. Rather, you thought, Wow.

She'd spent some time there, tagging along after Flynn when she was a kid and tagging along with Jordan when she was older. It was a place where she'd always felt comfortable. It seemed to her it had been created with comfort as its first priority and style running a close second.

Another thing you could say about Brad, she decided, was that he didn't skimp on the refreshments when he had a gathering.

It wasn't anything fancy, at least it wasn't presented that way. Just some sort of incredible pasta salad that made her contemplate going back for more, a lot of interesting finger food, ham slices, and some dense, dark bread for sandwich making.

There was a round of Brie skirted by fat red raspberries, and crackers nearly thin enough to see through that crunched with satisfying delicacy at every bite.

There was beer, there was wine, there were soft drinks and bottled water.

She already knew she wasn't going to resist the mini cream puffs mounded in a tempting island on a platter the size of New Jersey.

All this was spread out casually in the great room, where a fire snapped and sizzled and the furniture was the kind you could happily sink into for weeks at a time.

Not fancy, not so you felt like you couldn't rest your feet on the coffee table. Just classy.

That was Bradley Vane, right down to the ground.

Conversation buzzed and hummed around her, and she was drifting into a happy coma brought on by good food, warmth, and contentment.

Or would, she thought, if Zoe would stop squirming beside her.

"You're going to have to do something about those ants in your pants," Dana told her.

"Sorry." Zoe shot another look toward the archway. "I'm just worried about Simon."

"Why? He had a plate with enough food piled on it to feed a starving battalion, and he's hunkered down in the game room. A nine-year-old's wet dream."

"There's so much stuff in this house," Zoe whispered. "Expensive stuff. Art and glassware and china and *things.* He's not used to being around all of this."

Neither am I, she thought, and struggled not to squirm again.

"What if he breaks something?"

"Well." Lazily, Dana popped another raspberry into her mouth. "Then I guess Brad'll beat him to a bloody pulp."

"He hits *children*?" Zoe exclaimed.

"No. Jesus, Zoe, get a grip. The place has survived nine-year-old boys before—at least three of them are alive and in this room. Relax. Have a glass of wine. And while you're at it, get me some more raspberries."

Half a glass, Zoe thought and got to her feet. But even as she reached for the bottle, Brad lifted it.

"You look a little distracted." He poured the wine into a glass, handed it to her. "Is there a problem?"

"No." Damn it, she'd only wanted half a glass. Why didn't he stay out of her way? "I was just thinking I should check on Simon."

"He's fine. He knows where everything is in the game room. But I'll walk you back if you want to take a look," Brad added when she frowned.

"No. I'm sure he's fine. It's very nice of you to let him play." She knew her voice was stiff and tight, but she couldn't help it.

"That, rumor has it, is what a game room's for."

Since Brad's voice echoed her tone, Zoe simply nodded. "Um. Dana, she wanted some more. Of these." Mortified for no reason she could name, she scooped some of the berries into a bowl, then carried them and her wine back to the couch.

"Pompous ass," she said under her breath and had Dana blinking at her.

"Brad?" Dana snatched the bowl of raspberries. "Sorry, honey, you got the wrong number."

Jordan wandered over, sat on the arm of the couch beside Dana and stole a couple of berries before she could stop him.

"Get your own."

"Yours are better." He reached out to play with her hair. "So, how'd you get this blond stuff in here?"

"I didn't. Zoe did."

Nipping one more berry, he eased forward to look past Dana, wink at Zoe. "Nice job."

"Any time you need a haircut, it's on the house."

"I'll remember that." He sat back again. "So, I'm sure you're all wondering why we've brought you here tonight," he began and made Dana laugh.

"Now there's a pompous ass." But she laid a hand on his thigh. "I guess since we're here to talk about the key, and I'm the one who's supposed to find it, I'll start."

Handing Jordan what was left of the

berries, she pushed herself off the couch and snagged her wineglass from the coffee table. Even as she took the first step, Jordan slid down into her seat. He gave her a quick grin and draped his arm behind Zoe over the back of the couch.

"Come here often?" he asked Zoe.

"I would have, if I'd known you'd be here, handsome."

"You guys are just a riot," Dana muttered, then eased past a frowning Brad to the wine bottle. What the hell, she wasn't driving.

"Now, if everybody's all comfy and cozy?" She paused, sipped her wine. "My key deals with knowledge, or truth. I'm not sure the words are interchangeable, but both, either, or a combination of them applies to my quest. There's also a connection to the past, the now, the future. I'm taking this, after some fiddling around and dead-ending, to be personal, as applies to me."

"I think you're right about that," Malory put in. "Rowena stresses that we're the keys. The three of us. And mine was personal. If we're going to consider a pattern, that's part of it."

"Agreed. The male-type people in this

room are part of my past, and of my now. Odds are, I'm probably going to be stuck with them one way or the other, so they're part of my future as well. We know, too, there are connections among all six of us. My connection to each of you, and yours to me, to each other. There are the paintings from Mal's part of it that added a link."

She, as did the others, glanced at the portrait Brad had hung over the mantel. Another of Rowena's works, it showed the Daughters of Glass, after the spell that had taken their souls. Each lay pale and still in their crystal coffin.

"Brad bought that at auction, without knowing what was going to happen here, just as Jordan bought one of Rowena's paintings, the young Arthur on the point of drawing the sword from the stone, at the gallery where Malory used to work. Also years before we knew what we know now. So . . . this, in turn, connects all of us with Rowena and Pitte and the goddesses."

"And Kane," Zoe added. "I don't think it's smart to leave him out."

"You're right," Dana agreed. "And Kane. He's messed with most of us already, and it's pretty clear he'll mess with us again. We know he's bad. We know he's powerful. But those powers aren't without limits."

"Or someone or something limits him. He took a slice out of me," Jordan continued. "Then Rowena sends a little potion home with Dana. You guys saw this yesterday." He opened his shirt. The cuts were now only fading welts. "They started healing minutes after we slapped the stuff on them. The point is, whatever he did couldn't hold up against Rowena. And whatever she did to counter it couldn't erase it completely."

"To which we conclude," Dana finished for him, "that they're pretty evenly matched."

"He has weaknesses." Absently Jordan rebuttoned his shirt. "Ego, pride, temper."

"Who said those were weaknesses?" Dana wandered over, sat on the arm of the chair Brad had taken. "Anyway, it's more. He doesn't really get us—the whole human or mortal thing. He doesn't get us as individuals. He skims the surface, picks up on our little fantasies or fears, but he doesn't really get to the core—or hasn't. That's how Malory beat him."

"Yes, but when he has hold of you, it's hard to see clearly, hard to know." Malory shook her head. "We can't underestimate him."

"I'm not. But up to now, I think, he has underestimated us." Thoughtfully, Dana studied the portrait. "He wants them to suffer, simply because part of them is mortal. Rowena talked of opposing forces: beauty and ugliness, knowledge and ignorance, courage and cowardice. How without one the other loses its punch. So he's the dark, and you can't have light without dark. I figure he's essential to the whole deal, not just an annoyance."

She hesitated, then took a drink. "It's no secret that Jordan and I were intimate. I don't think it's any secret that we're . . . intimate now."

Jordan waited a beat. "I've never known you to get flustered talking about sex, Stretch."

"I just want to make it clear to . . . people. To you, that I'm not sleeping with you as a way to find the key. Even if that has something to do with it," she continued quickly, "because as somebody told me recently, sex is powerful magic—"

"If you do it right," Jordan interrupted.

"So let's see what we know," Brad said,

trying to get back on track. "None of this would have happened—past—without Kane." Brad tapped his index fingers together. "His presence and manipulations influence the search for the key. Present." He held up a second finger. "And there's no finish to the spell without him." And a third. "He's a necessary factor. There's no reward without work, no victory without effort, no battle won without risk."

"It's another traditional element of a quest," Jordan added. "An evil to be overcome."

"I understand all this," Zoe said. "And it's important. But how does it help Dana find the key?"

"Know your enemy," Brad told her.

"That nutshelled it," Dana agreed.

"But there's more," Flynn noted. "Blood has been shed. Another traditional quest element. I can read, too," he said. "Why was it Jordan's blood? There's a reason for it."

"Might be because Jordan pissed him off, which he's really good at doing," Dana said. "But more likely it's because I need Jordan to find the key."

"Stretch, you need me for so many things."

"Let's ignore the ego burst and stay focused." Dana gestured with her glass. "The key's knowledge. Something I know, or have to learn. A truth that has to be sifted out from lies. Kane mixes his truth and lies. What is it he's said or done that's truth? That's one of the angles I'm playing. Then there's the last bit of the clue. Where one goddess walks another waits. That's a stumper so far. Malory's goddess was singing, and she re-created that moment, and the key, by painting it. Following that, my goddess, Niniane, should be walking. But where, why, when? And which goddess waits? Would that be Zoe's?"

"Maybe you're supposed to write it," Zoe suggested. "Like a story, I mean. The way Malory painted hers."

"That's not bad." Dana considered. "The thing is, I never wanted to write, not like Malory wanted to paint. But maybe it's something I'm supposed to read, and God knows I'm not hitting on anything in the six million books I've gone through so far. So maybe I have to write it myself, first."

"Maybe Jordan does." Flynn played absently with Malory's hair as he thought it through. "He's the writer—not to diminish my own considerable talent, but I report. He just makes shit up."

"Really good shit," Jordan reminded him.

"Goes without saying. I'm thinking here that if for nothing other than the cohesion and the exercise, Jordan could write all this out. In story form. Maybe when Dana reads it, the scales will fall from her eyes, she'll pull out the key, and we can all have a party, with cake."

"It's not an entirely stupid idea," Dana decided.

"I think it's great." Zoe shifted in her seat to beam at Jordan. "Will you do it? I just love reading your books, and this would be even more fun."

"For you, gorgeous?" He picked up her hand and kissed it. "Anything."

"I'm feeling a little queasy." Dana patted her stomach. "How soon will you have something I can see?" she asked Jordan.

"Okay, now you sound like an editor. It could force me to have a creative tantrum and slow everything down."

"Do you? Have creative tantrums, I mean." To Zoe, the idea was fascinating. "I've always wondered how it works, with artists and all."

"Oh, God, now she's called him an artist." Dana got to her feet. "I must go home and lie down."

Ignoring her, Jordan gave Zoe his attention. "No, not really. It's a job, just happens to be a really great job. My editor—my *real* editor," he added with a glance at Dana, "is a woman of discerning taste, skill, and diplomacy."

"Your editor's a woman? How does it work? Do you work with her all the way through a book, or does she tell you what she wants you to do, or . . ." She trailed off, shook her head. "Sorry. Way, way off topic."

"It's okay. Do you want to write?"

"Write? Me?" The idea had her exotic eyes going wide before she laughed. "No. I just like knowing how things work."

"Speaking of work, we've got a full day of it tomorrow." Malory gave Flynn's hand a pat.

"That's my cue. I'll go round up Moe for you," Flynn told Dana.

"I'm running low on dog food. He eats like an elephant."

"I'll drop some off." He caught her face in his hands. "Keep him close, okay?"

"He doesn't give me a lot of choice."

"Flynn, would you round up Simon, too?" Automatically, Zoe began stacking dishes. "He's probably attached to Moe at the hip, so he shouldn't give you any trouble."

"Sure."

"We'd better cut out too. I'm going to see if I can get this one started on his homework." Dana jerked a thumb at Jordan. "Any tips for that, Zoe?"

"Bribery. That's my method."

Brad stepped over, laid a hand on Zoe's. And made her jump like a rabbit. "You don't have to bother with those."

"Sorry." She instantly set the plates down. "Habit."

It seemed to Brad that the woman deliberately misinterpreted every second word out of his mouth. "I just meant you don't have to pick up. Anybody want coffee?"

"I do."

"No, you don't." Dana gave Jordan a nudge toward the doorway. "It's work for you, pal. You can have coffee when you've gotten a couple of pages done."

"Bribery." Zoe nodded approval. "It never fails."

Moe bounded into the room, a wild blur of fur. In his delight to see everyone, he leaped, licked, swept glasses off the coffee table with an exuberant tail, and nosed his way into a plate of cocktail shrimp before he could be controlled.

"Sorry, sorry." With one hand hooked in Moe's collar, Flynn dragged the dog, or was dragged by him, toward the door. "I'll put him in Jordan's car. Bill me for damages. See you. Oh, Zoe, Simon needs a few more minutes to finish a game. Jesus Christ, Moe! Hold up!"

"This is my life now," Malory said happily. "It's kind of great. Thanks, Brad, sorry about the dishes. See you tomorrow, Zoe, Dana. 'Night, Jordan."

"I have to go save my upholstery." Jordan grabbed Dana's arm and pulled her toward the door. "Later."

"Stop yanking me. Smooches, Brad. See you in the morning, Zoe."

The door slammed behind them, and there was absolute silence.

It had all happened so fast, was all Zoe could think. She'd never intended to be the last one to leave. It was horrible. Horrifying.

She considered running into the game room and grabbing Simon, but she wasn't exactly sure where it was. And she could hardly stand where she was and shout for him. Still, she needed to do *something.*

She bent down to pick up the glasses Moe had knocked to the floor. At exactly the same moment, so did Brad.

Their heads bumped. Each of them straightened quickly, then stood taut as bows.

"I'll get them." He crouched, gathered up the glasses, set them on the coffee table. He was close enough to catch her scent now. It was always different, sometimes earthy, sometimes light, always very female.

It was one of the fascinating things about her, he mused. The variety of her.

"Coffee?"

"I really should just get Simon. It's nearly his bedtime."

"Oh. Well. Okay."

When he just stood, looking at her, Zoe felt embarrassed heat creeping up the back of her neck. Had she done something wrong? Left out something?

"Thanks for having us."

"Glad you could make it."

During the next long pause, she had to make a conscious effort not to bite her lip. "Simon? I don't know exactly where he is."

"The game room. Oh." Amused at both of them, Brad laughed. "You don't know where the game room is. Come on, I'll take you back."

The more Zoe saw of the house, the more in love with it, and intimidated by it, she was. To begin with, there was so *much* of it, all of it charming or stunning or just lovely. She imagined the things she noticed on tables or shelves were several levels up from knickknacks.

Brad veered off through an archway into what she assumed was some sort of library. The soaring ceiling was done in wood and made the room feel open while still managing to be cozy.

"There's so much room." She stopped, appalled that she'd spoken out loud.

"The story is, once my father got started, he couldn't stop. He'd get another idea, add it into the design."

"It's a wonderful house," she said quickly. "So much detail without being fussy. You must've loved growing up here."

"I did."

He stepped into another room. Zoe already heard the roar of engines, the vicious gunfire, the breathless chant—*come on, come on, come on*—of her son.

The video game was some sort of urban car war that flashed over an enormous wall-size TV screen. Simon sat cross-legged on the floor rather than in one of the cushy recliners in a room that fulfilled every boy's fantasy.

A pool table, three pinball machines, two video-arcade games. Slot machines, a soda machine, a jukebox.

The ceiling here was coffered, framed in honey-toned wood that shielded strips of lights.

There was another fireplace, with cheerful flames snapping, as well as a small, glossy bar and a second television with an entire cabinet devoted to various components.

"Gosh. This is Simon Michael McCourt's personal version of heaven."

"My dad loves toys. We spent a lot of time in here."

"I bet." She stepped up behind her son. "Simon. We have to go."

"Not yet, not yet." His face was fierce with concentration. "This is Grand Theft Auto Three! I'm really close, really close to having them call out the National Guard. Tanks and everything! I'm kicking Swat Team butt. I could set a record. Ten more minutes."

"Simon. Mr. Vane needs his house back."

"Mr. Vane is fine with this," Brad corrected.

"Please, Mom. *Please.* Tanks."

She wavered. She saw more than the heat of competition on his face as he stared at the screen. She saw joy.

Someone died on-screen with a great deal of splashing blood, and from the delighted cackle she figured it wasn't Simon.

"It's a little violent," Brad realized and winced. "If you don't want him playing this sort of thing—"

"Simon knows the difference between reality and video games."

"Right. Good. Why don't we go have that coffee?" Brad suggested. "A few more minutes can't hurt."

"All right. Ten minutes, Simon."

"Okay, Mom, thanks, Mom. I'm going to do it," he mumbled, already back in the groove. "I'm going to *do* it."

"It's nice of you to let him play with your things," Zoe began as they left Simon to the battle. "He talked about being out here before for days."

"He's a great kid. Fun to be around."

"I certainly think so."

She found herself in the kitchen with him—another spacious, stunning room. This one done in bright, cheerful white and toasty yellows that would make it seem sunny even on a gloomy day.

She coveted the acres of counter space, the forest of cupboards, some with gorgeous seeded glass. She admired the sleek appliances that had to make cooking a creative joy rather than a mundane chore.

Then it occurred to her that she was, once again, alone with him.

"You know, I should just go back with Simon, and let you . . . do whatever. We'll be out of your way quicker."

He finished measuring out coffee before he turned to her. "Why do you think I want you out of my way?"

"I'm sure you have things to do."

"Not so much."

"Well, I do. A million things. I should really be ready to pry Simon away before he loses control and starts another game. I'll just go get him, and we'll let ourselves out."

"I don't get it." Forgetting the coffee,

Brad stepped closer to her. "I really don't get it."

"What?"

"You're comfortable enough with Flynn and Jordan to flirt with them, but two minutes with me and you're not only blowing cold, you're halfway out the door."

"It's not flirting." Her voice went sharp. "Not like that. We're friends. They're Malory's and Dana's boyfriends, for Pete's sake. And if you think I'm the sort of person who'd—"

"Then there's that," Brad continued with what he considered admirable calm. "The way you automatically jump to conclusions, usually the wrong ones, when it comes to me."

"I don't know what you're talking about. In the first place, I barely know you."

"That's not true. People get to know each other pretty quickly in intense situations. We're in one, and we've been in one for close to two months now. We've spent time together, we have good mutual friends, and you've cooked me dinner."

"I didn't cook you dinner." Her chin came up. "You happened to be at the house when I cooked dinner. You ate. That's different."

"Point for you," he acknowledged. "You know, for some reason your response to me causes me to start sounding like my father when he's annoyed. There's this tone he gets in his voice, this change of body language. Used to bug the hell out of me when I was a kid."

"I have no intention of bugging the hell out of you. We'll leave."

In Brad's mind there was a time for talk and there was a time for action. When you were fed up, it was time for action. He closed a hand over her arm to keep her in place, watched temper and nerves rush across her truly spectacular face.

"There it is," he told her. "Your usual response to me. Annoyance and/or nervousness. I've been asking myself why that is. I spend a lot of time asking myself questions about you."

"Then you must have a lot of time to waste. Let go. I'm leaving."

"And one of my theories is," he continued easily, "this."

He cupped his other hand at the nape of her neck, pulled her forward, and kissed her.

He'd wanted to kiss her for weeks. Maybe for years. He'd wanted the taste of her on his lips, on his tongue, in his blood. And the feel of her, he thought as he slipped an arm around her waist to bring her more firmly against him.

Her mouth was so full, so ripe, and much more potent than he'd anticipated. Her body quivered once against his, in shock, in response. At the moment it didn't matter.

Just as it didn't matter if this single act was taken as a declaration of war or an offer of peace. He only knew he'd slowly been going mad waiting to hold her.

She'd hesitated instead of pushing him away. And that, she would think later, when thinking was an option again, was her mistake.

He was warm and hard, and his mouth was skilled. And God, it had been so long since she'd been pressed against a man. She felt the need lift inside her, from the toes to the belly to the throat, followed by that long, lovely pull and flutter that took it all the way back down.

For one mad moment, she drew him in. The male scent and flavor, the strength and the passion, and let it tumble through her in a kind of joyful spree.

It was like a carnival, like the giddiest of

rides when you couldn't be sure—not absolutely—that you wouldn't be flung out of
your seat and into the air.

And wasn't that fabulous?

Then she slammed on the brakes. What
choice did she have? She knew what happened when you rode too fast, too hard, too
high.

And this wasn't her place, this wasn't her
man. What was hers—her child—was playing in the next room.

She pulled out of Brad's arms.

He was shaken, right down to the soles
of his feet, but he stared into her eyes and
nodded coolly. "I think that made my point."

She was no quaking virgin, and a long
way from being an easy mark. She didn't
step back, that would have been retreat,
but stood firm and kept her eyes level with
his. "Let's get a few things straight. I like
men. I like their company, their conversation, their humor. I happen to be raising one
of my own, and I intend to do a good job of
it."

She looked, he thought, like an angry,
and aroused, wood nymph. "You are doing
a good job of it."

"I like kissing men—the right man, the

right circumstances. I like sex, under the same conditions."

His eyes warmed to a deep, foggy gray that was unexpected and compelling. The charming creases in his cheeks—too manly, Zoe thought, to be called dimples—deepened. Her fingers itched to trace those creases, and the sensation warned her she was in trouble.

"That's a relief to me."

"You'd better understand that I make the conditions at this point in my life. The fact that I have a kid and I'm not married doesn't make me easy."

Angry shock leaped into his face. "For Christ's sake, Zoe. Where did we veer from me finding you interesting and attractive and wanting to kiss you to finding you easy?"

"I want to be clear, that's all. Just like I'm going to be clear that nobody uses my kid to get to me."

The shock, the anger iced over. The chill hit him from a foot away. "If you assume that's what I'm doing, you're insulting all three of us."

She felt twin jolts of guilt and embarrassment. As she started to speak, Simon flew into the room. "I rule! Beat your high score, sucker!" He danced around Brad, shaking his index fingers in the air in a victory dance.

With effort, Brad folded his emotions further inside, then hooked an arm around Simon's neck. "A momentary event, I promise you. Gloat while you have the chance, you midget."

"Next time I'm beating your butt in the NBA play-offs."

"Never happen. And when I humiliate you, you will crawl to me on your belly like the insignificant worm you are."

As she watched the exchange, saw their obvious enjoyment of each other, her guilt only increased. "Simon, we have to go."

"Okay. Thanks for letting me mop the floor with ya."

"I'm just luring you in, so crushing you will be more gratifying." With his arm still around the boy, he looked at the mother. "I'll get your coats."

Chapter Fourteen

Since it became apparent, very quickly, that Dana wasn't handy with home improvement chores that involved tools, she was designated head painter. Which meant, she thought, a little sulkily, that she spent all day slapping paint on walls while Zoe went around doing stuff with a cool little electric screwdriver or drill and Malory putzed around with the leak under the kitchen sink.

The fact that Malory was the girliest girl of Dana's acquaintance and that *she* got a wrench was lowering.

It wasn't that she minded painting so much—even though it was incredibly boring, despite the magic roller machine. She just could've used a little variety on her job list.

Still, watching the walls take on color was satisfying. Malory and Zoe had been on the money in the choice. Her bookstore section was going to look not only warm but stylish.

Zoe swore that once the floors were sanded and sealed, they would glow.

She knew how it could look. Kane had shown her. And if he'd used her own fantasy to build the image, that was fine. This was one fantasy she was going to make sure came true.

As an idea struck, she stopped, turned off the machine, set the roller aside.

The truth in his lies. Her fantasy, and his manipulation of it.

What if the key was here, as Malory's had been? Why couldn't it be that simple? He'd shown her, hadn't he? Look what you can have, if you only cooperate with me: your dream bookstore, full of customers and stock. Not real, she thought now, not truth. But there'd been truth in it. It was what she wanted, what she intended to work for. What she could have, with her own effort and on her own merits.

Maybe the key was right here, if she

could only see it. If she could bring it out as Malory had.

She took some deep breaths, shaking her arms, rolling her shoulders, like a diver about to spring off the high platform.

Then she closed her eyes, tried to let herself drift.

She could hear the whirr of Zoe's drill, and the cheerful music that Malory had playing on the radio.

What was that? ABBA? Jesus, couldn't she find a station that recognized music from this millennium?

Annoyed with herself, Dana struggled to erase the image of a teenage dancing queen from her mind.

The key. The pretty gold key. It was small, shiny, with that looping Celtic pattern at the hilt. Was it a hilt when it was a key? she wondered. It wasn't a damn sword, so there had to be another word for it. She'd have to look that up.

Oh, stop it!

She huffed out another breath, and focused.

The whirr of the drill, the tinkle of music, and beyond that, the muffled sound of cars passing on the street outside. The hum of the furnace as it kicked on.

And if you listened hard enough, she realized, the creaks and whispers of an old house settling into its own bones.

Her house. Hers. The first she'd ever owned. A step out of the past toward the future. A single, definite move that changed the pattern of what had been toward what would be.

She could smell fresh paint, a testament to a new start.

Those things were real, as real as her own flesh and blood. Those things were truth.

The key was real. She had only to see it, to touch it, to take it.

She saw it now, floating on a field of peacock green, shimmering against that deep color. But when she reached out, her hand passed through it as if it, or she, was insubstantial.

I'm the key. It's meant for me.

She tried again, again, bearing down with the effort until sweat pearled on her forehead.

It's mine, she kept thinking. And this place is mine. Soon books will be lined along this wall, other walls. Knowledge.

"Dana!"

She snapped back, swayed even as Zoe's hands caught her arms. "What did he do to you? What did he do? Malory!"

"No, I'm okay. I'm fine."

"You don't look fine. Hold on to me. Mal!" she shouted again.

Dana calculated she had a good thirty pounds on Zoe, but her friend managed to hold her upright and steady.

"What is it? What's wrong?" With a crescent wrench gripped like a weapon in her hand, Malory rushed in. For some reason, seeing the pretty, feminine blonde in her plumber's gear of sexy black leggings and slim green sweater—with matching hair tie—wielding a wrench had Dana giggling weakly.

"Kane. Kane had her. She was in some sort of trance."

"No. It wasn't Kane. I'm a little dizzy. Maybe I should just sit down."

She slid to the floor, taking Zoe with her.

"Oh, God. Are you pregnant?"

"What?" The shock went a long way toward clearing her head as she goggled at Zoe. "No. Jeez. I just started having sex again, remember? Would you two stop staring at me as if I were about to start speaking in tongues?"

"Here. Have some water." Zoe pulled a bottle from the holster on her tool belt.

"I'm okay." But she gulped down the water. "I was just experimenting with a little self-hypnosis."

"Here, let me have that." Malory reached for the water, took a deep drink. "You scared the hell out of me."

"Sorry. I had this idea that the key's here. Yours was—and the whole past, present, future thing. The store, our businesses. The books I'm going to be hauling in here. Truth in lies. How Kane showed me the place all finished and full of those books and customers buying them."

"Okay. I'm following." Zoe pulled out a red-and-white bandanna and dabbed at Dana's brow. "But what happened? When I walked in you were standing in the middle of the room with your arm out in front of you. Kind of swaying, with your eyes closed. Honey, you looked really spooky."

"I was trying to, you know, bring the key out. See the key. Be the key. Shit, that sounds stupid."

"No, it doesn't." Handing the water back

to Zoe, Malory considered. "It's a good idea. It could be here. Hell, it could be anywhere, so why not here?"

"A good idea," Zoe agreed. "But I don't think you should try something like that alone. It could be like opening yourself up to him, with nobody around to keep you steady. Like a control group, or backup. You really looked out of it, Dana."

"You've got a point." But she smiled. "Stop fussing, Mom." To lighten the mood, she pinched Zoe's biceps. "You're a lot stronger than you look. You work out regular?"

"A little here and there. Mostly I'm just built." And her heart rate settled down again. "You look better now. Maybe we could try something like this, with the three of us."

"It might be worth a shot," Malory agreed.

"If you're up to it, Dana. We could sit right here, link hands. Mal and I could sort of *push* our energy toward you."

"Perhaps you recall a small incident last month involving a Ouija board?" Dana asked.

"Not likely to forget." Zoe gave a quick

shudder. "But we wouldn't be using any-thing but our own connection. It's not like we're playing around with the dark arts, or whatever it is."

"Okay." Lips pursed, Dana looked around. "But it seems kind of silly. The three of us sitting on a drop cloth in an empty, half-painted room trying to conjure up a magic key. But . . ." She gripped Zoe's hand, then Malory's. "I'm in."

"Mal, maybe you could give her some tips. What it was like for you, what you did."

"I don't know if I can explain it. So much of it just happened. It's like being in a dream, but knowing you're dreaming, and at the same time knowing it's not a dream."

"That's a big help." But with a half laugh, Dana squeezed her hand. "Actually, I know what you mean. It's the way I felt when he took me into the bookstore."

"I don't know how I understood what to do, but it was suddenly so clear. The one thing was focusing on what I had to do without letting him know I was focusing on it. And that was hard, really hard, but part of that was because I was so scared. For me, it helped to concentrate on painting, the actual art and act. The colors, the tone, the detail. I don't know if that helps you."

"I don't know either. So let's find out."

"We're not going to let anything happen to you," Zoe told her. "We're going to be right here."

"Okay."

Taking that long breath, Dana shut her eyes. It was a comfort to feel the hands gripped on hers. Like an anchor, she supposed, that would prevent her from floating off somewhere she shouldn't go.

She let herself listen again to the sounds of the house, to her own quiet, steady breathing matching the rhythm of her friends'. She smelled paint, and perfume.

There was the key again, shining on the colored field she now realized was the wall she'd just painted. Her wall, with the color chosen by the woman flanking her.

But when she reached out for it with her mind, she could bring it no closer.

She struggled with impatience and tried to imagine how the key would feel in her hand. Smooth, she thought, and cool.

No, it would have heat. It held power. She would feel that fire from which it was forged, and when she closed her fist over it, it would fit easily in her palm.

Because she was meant to hold it.

The color washed away to a strong white lined with black. The key seemed to melt into it, a shimmering gold pool that dripped over black and white, then faded away.

In her mind she heard a long sigh. A woman's sigh. And felt, heard, a rush of wind that smelled like autumn burning.

She walked at night, and was the night with all its shadows and all its secrets. When she wept, she wept for day.

The words that ran through her mind brought such an ache she thought her heart might bleed dry from it, as from a mortal wound. In defense, she shut them off.

Everything faded again. And she could smell the paint, and the perfume.

She opened her eyes, saw her friends watching her.

"Honey, are you all right?" Zoe spoke gently as she freed her hand from Malory's and touched Dana's cheek.

"Sure. Yeah."

"You're crying." Zoe dried Dana's cheek with the bandanna.

"Am I? I don't know why. Something hurt,

I guess. You know." She pressed a hand to her heart. "In here. I don't know where it is. I still don't know where the key is."

She scrubbed the heels of her hands over her face and told them what she'd imagined.

"She walks at night," Malory repeated. "The goddess walks."

"Yeah. It sounded sort of familiar, but I could've made it up. Or it could apply to Niniane. I just know it made me horribly sad."

She got to her feet, walked to the window to open it. She needed air. "She's alone in the dark—that's how I think of her. They're all alone in the dark. If I don't do what needs to be done, they'll stay in the dark."

Zoe walked over to press her cheek to the back of Dana's shoulder. "They've got each other, and they've got us. Don't beat yourself up. You're trying."

"And I think you're getting somewhere." Malory joined them at the window. "I'm not saying that to be annoyingly optimistic. You're putting the different parts of Rowena's clue together. Your brain's working them out, shifting them around, trying to make them fit. And I think with this last attempt, you've started to use your heart.

"It's not just your mind that has to be open," Malory added when Dana turned her head to stare at her. "Your heart has to be. That's one thing I learned. You can't take that last leap otherwise. You won't be ready to risk what's on the other side."

She didn't know why it bothered her, bothered her to the point of anger. Open her heart? What was that supposed to mean? Was she supposed to strip her emotions bare so anyone could come in on a whim and dance all over them?

Wasn't it enough that she was working her ass off, giving herself headaches with hours of research, note-taking, calculating, and supposition?

She cared, damn it, she thought as she slammed into her apartment. She cared about those three young women, half goddess, half mortal, and trapped for eternity inside a glass prison.

She had shed tears for them, would shed blood if necessary.

How much more open did she have to be?

Tired, achy, irritable, she strode to the kitchen, popped the top on a beer, ripped open a bag of pretzels to go with it. She dropped into a chair in the living room to sip, munch, and sulk.

Take the last leap?

She was going up against an ancient and powerful sorcerer. She was risking nearly every cent she had on a new business. She'd ordered shelving and tables, chairs, and books. Let's not forget the books.

Then there was the cappuccino machine, the individual teapots, the glassware, the paper products that would max out her credit card in very short order.

And she was doing it all without any projected income. If that wasn't a goddamn leap, what was?

Easy for Malory to talk about open hearts and last leaps. She'd already done her part, and was all cozied up with Flynn in connubial bliss.

Got your house and your dog and your man, Dana thought with a scowl. Congratulations all around.

And, God, she was being such a bitch.

She let her head fall back and stared up at the ceiling.

"Face it, Dana, you're jealous. Not only did Malory come through the test with a big fat A, she earned all the goodies. And here you are, spinning your wheels, sleeping with a man who's already broken your heart once, and terrified you're going to blow it all."

She hauled herself up at the knock on her door, and took the beer with her to answer.

Moe shoved his nose into her crotch by way of greeting, then rushed past her to claim the mangled rope he'd left on the rug during his last visit.

He pranced back, ears flopping, to whack the rope hopefully against her knees.

"You didn't come by to get Moe," Jordan commented.

"I forgot." She shrugged, then walked back and dropped into the chair again.

Jordan closed the door behind him, tossed the manila envelope he carried on a table. He knew that look, he thought as he studied Dana's face. She was sulking and working her way up to a serious mad.

"What's going on?"

"Nothing much." Since Moe was trying to

crawl into her lap, she tugged the rope out of his teeth and tossed it to Jordan.

It had the expected and for her, gratifying, result of causing Moe to charge him like a bull charges a matador. And like a matador uses his cape, Jordan flicked the rope down and to the side. Man and dog played tug-of-war while dog growled playfully and man stared at woman.

"Long day? I was going to come by and give you a hand, but I got caught up in stuff."

"We're managing everything."

"An extra pair of hands couldn't hurt."

"You want to put your hands to good use?"

"It's a thought."

"Fine." She pushed out of the chair, headed toward the bedroom. "Bring them along with you."

Jordan lifted a brow at Moe. "Sorry, kiddo, you're on your own. I think I'm about to play a different sort of game."

He followed Dana into the bedroom, shut the door. He heard Moe collapse on the other side with a huge doggie sigh.

She'd already stripped off her sweatshirt

and shoes and was unbuttoning her jeans. "Lose the clothes."

"Got an itch, Stretch?"

"That's right." She wiggled out of the jeans, tossed back her hair. "Got any problem scratching it?"

"Can't seem to think of one." He shrugged out of the coat, threw it aside.

He got rid of his shoes, his shirt, while she pulled down the covers. He'd been off about her mood, he realized. She'd already worked herself up to a good mad and was looking for a handy place to put it.

When she reached up to unclasp her bra, he stepped over, gripped her hands, trapping them—for one erotic moment—behind her. Then he released her to trail his fingers down her spine. "Leave something for me, will you?"

She shrugged, then fisting a hand in his hair, yanked his mouth to hers.

She used her teeth, her nails, setting the mood for fast, hot sex with just a hint of mean. She wasn't looking for fancy touches or soft flourishes but for sweat and speed.

She felt his body's instant response, the hard hammer blow of his heart, the lightning strike of heat that punched out of him and straight through her. His mouth fed off hers, and his hands began to take, fingers digging in to brand and bruise.

She was already wet and ready when she shoved him back on the bed.

She would have straddled him and made quick work of it, but he flipped her over, trapped her body under his. Set his teeth on her breast. Her hips jerked, her hands clamped on his, and she ground herself against him in frantic, furious demand.

His vision hazed with red as the fierce bite of need tore through his system. He yanked her bra down to her waist, filled his mouth with her even as he shoved his hand between them, drove his fingers into the heat of her and shot her brutally over the edge.

She exploded under him, her body writhing, straining, then gathering itself for another leap. Her nails bit into him, her hips pistoned until he was as wild as she.

They rolled, grappling for more in a slippery, mindless battle that had thrill ramming into thrill. Her mouth was fevered and ravenous, her hands greedy and swift.

He knew he'd rather die warring with her than live in peace with anyone else.

With her breath sobbing, she rose over him and took him inside her with one hard thrust.

The dark glory of it gushed through her, flooded her until the anger and doubts drowned.

This was real, she told herself. This was enough.

And she watched him watch her take him.

Fast and hot, focused on those twin goals of pleasure and release. She rode him with a ruthless energy that turned her own body into a morass of greed. For speed, for passion. For *more.*

When she felt his fingers vise her hips, when she saw those brilliant blue eyes go blind, she threw her head back and flew off the end of the world with him.

She was still shuddering as she slid down to him. Her breath was as ragged as his when her head fell heavy on his shoulder. He managed to hook an arm around her and decided he would probably regain feeling in his extremities at some point.

For now, it was just fine to lie there bruised, battered, and blissful.

"Feel better?" he asked her.

"Considerably. You?"

"No complaints. When my ears stop ringing, you might want to tell me what set you off today."

"No one thing." She lifted her head just enough to sweep her hair aside so she could feel her cheek against his flesh. "I just feel like I'm fumbling at most everything, but then I remembered this is one thing I do really well."

"You won't hear any argument from me on the last part. What's the fumble?"

"You want the list? I feel like I'm so close to finding the key, then I don't. Then I feel like I'm miles away from it, and the whole business is going to crash and burn. I spent most of the day painting because I exhibited very little, if any, aptitude for hand tools."

"Then you probably don't want me to mention you've got some paint in your hair."

She heaved a sigh. "I know it. Even Mallory's better with a screwdriver than I am, and she's a total girl. And Zoe? She's a regular Bob Vila with breasts. Did you know she's got her belly button pierced?"

"Really?" There was a long pause.

"Really," he repeated with enough male interest to make her laugh.

"Anyway." She flopped over on her back. "There was all that, then I started doing some mental number crunching and got depressed realizing how close to the edge financially all this stuff is taking me. All the output, no income—and without the output there'll never *be* an income. And even when the income comes, it's going to be a serious juggling act for the foreseeable future."

"I could lend you some money, give you some breathing room." Her silence spoke volumes. "It'd be an investment. Writer—bookstore. Makes sense."

"I'm not interested in a loan." Her voice had chilled, and just under the chill was a sulk. "I'm not looking for another partner."

"Okay." He shrugged it off, then tugged on her hair. "I've got it. I can pay you for sex. Like you said, you are really good at it. But I'd get to set the price for each specific act, and I think there should be something in the rates about buy three, get one free. We'll work it out."

Since he was watching her face, he saw her dimples flutter as she struggled with a grin. "You're a pervert." She rolled over on her stomach, braced herself on her elbows. "It was nice of you to reach down into the gutter to cheer me up."

"We do what we can." He trailed a finger down her cheek. "I bet you could use some food. You want to go out to eat?"

"I absolutely don't want to go out."

"Good. Neither do I." He shifted a bit, worked considerable charm into his expression. "I don't suppose you'd care to cook."

"I don't suppose I would."

"All right. I will."

She blinked, then sat up and tapped her fingers on her head. "Excuse me, did you just say you'd cook?"

"Don't get excited. I was thinking of something along the lines of scrambled eggs or grilled-cheese sandwiches."

"Let's damn the cholesterol and have both." She leaned down, gave him a quick kiss. "Thanks. I'm going to grab a shower."

When she came out, comfortable in sweats, he was in the kitchen, pouring eggs into one skillet while sandwiches browned in another, and the dog inhaled a bowl of kibble.

He was missing the frilly apron, Dana

noted, but all in all, he made a hell of a picture.

"Look at Mr. Domestic."

"Even living in New York, it pays to be able to throw an emergency meal together. You want to get out plates?"

New York, she thought, as she opened a cabinet. It wouldn't do to forget the guy lived in New York and wasn't going to be making her grilled-cheese sandwiches on a regular basis.

She pushed the thought away, set the table, and added a couple of candles for the fun of it.

"Nice," she said over the first bite when they'd settled down. "Really, thanks."

"My mother used to make me grilled-cheese sandwiches when I was feeling out of sorts."

"They're comforting—the toasty bread, the butter, the warm, melty cheese."

"Mmm. Look, if you're interested in my hands doing more than driving you wild with passion, I can give you some time tomorrow."

"If you've got it."

"I'd have come by today, but I had homework." He pointed toward the envelope he'd dropped when he'd come in.

"Oh. You wrote everything up."

"Think I got it all. You can look it over, see if I left anything out."

"Cool." She got up, hurried across the room to fetch the envelope.

"Didn't anyone ever tell you it's impolite to read at the table?"

"Certainly not." Tossing back her hair, she settled back down. "It's never impolite to read." She tapped out the pages, surprised to see how many there were. "Busy boy."

He forked up more eggs. "I figured it would work better to get it down in one big gush."

"Let's see what we've got here."

She ate and she read, read and ate. He took her back to the very beginning, to the night she'd driven through a storm to War-rior's Peak. He made her see it again, feel it again. That and all that had happened since.

That was his gift, she realized. His art.

He told it like a story, each character vivid and true, each action ringing clear, so that when you came to the end, you wanted more.

"Flynn was right," she said as she turned the last page over. "It helps to see it like this in my head. I need to absorb it, read it again. But it puts everything that's happened on one winding path instead of having a lot of offshoots that just happen to run into each other."

"I'm going to have to write it."

"I thought you just did," she replied, shaking her head.

"No, that's only part of it. Half of it at best. I realized today when I was putting it all down that I'm going to have to write it when it's all done, turn it into a book. Do you have any problem with that?"

"I don't know." She smoothed her fingers over the pages. "I guess not, but it feels a little strange. I've never been in a book before."

He started to speak, then stopped himself and polished off his eggs. She hadn't been in a book she'd read before, he thought. Which, when it came down to it, amounted to the same thing.

Chapter Fifteen

"Look," Kane said, "how you betray your-self in sleep."

Dana stood looking down at the bed where she and Jordan slept. On the floor beside them, Moe twitched and made ex-cited sounds.

"What did you do to Moe?"

"I gave him a dream, a harmless, happy dream. He chases rabbits on a sunny spring day. It will keep him safe and occupied, as we have much to talk about, you and I."

She watched Moe's back right leg swing as if he were running. "I don't have much to say to anyone who sneaks into my bed-room at night to play Peeping Tom."

"I don't peep, I watch. You interest me,

Dana. You have intelligence. I respect that. Scholars are valued in my world, in any world. And there we have the scholar and the bard." He gestured toward the bed at her and Jordan. "One would think a fine combination. But we know better."

It both frightened and fascinated her to see the couple on the bed, wrapped together in a tangle of limbs. "You don't know us. You never will. That's why we'll beat you."

He only smiled. The dark suited him, cloaked him like velvet and silk and left his eyes burning bright. "You search, but you don't find. How can you? Your life is pretense, Dana, a dream as much as this. Look how you cling to him in sleep. You, a strong, intelligent woman, one who considers herself independent, even willful. Yet you throw yourself at a man who tossed you aside once and will do so again. You allow yourself to be ruled by passion, and it makes you weak."

"What rules you if not passion?" she countered. "Ambition, greed, hate, vanity. They're all passions."

"Ah, this is why I enjoy you. We could have such interesting conversations. No, passions are not owned by the mortal world. But to invite pain merely for love and the pleasures of the flesh." He shook his head. "You were wiser when you hated him. Now you let him use you again."

He lies. He lies. She couldn't let herself fall into the trap of that seductive voice and forget how it lied. "Nobody uses me. Not even you."

"Perhaps you need to remember more clearly."

It was snowing. She felt the flakes—soft, cold, wet, on her skin, though she couldn't see them fall. They seemed to hang suspended in the air.

She felt the bite of the wind but couldn't hear it, nor did it chill her.

The world was a black-and-white photograph. Black trees, white snow. White mountains rising toward a white sky, and there, far up, the black silhouette of Warrior's Peak.

All was still and cold and silent.

There was a man all the way down the block, frozen in the act of shoveling his walk. His shovel was lifted, and the scoop of snow was caught in its flight through the air.

"Do you know this place?" Kane asked her.

"Yes." Three blocks south of Market, two blocks west of Pine Ridge.

"And this house."

The tiny two-story box, painted white with black shutters. The two small dormer windows of the second floor, one for each small bedroom. The single dogwood, with snow adorning its thin branches, and the narrow driveway that ran beside it. Two cars in the driveway. The old station wagon and the secondhand Mustang.

"It's Jordan's house." Her mouth was dry. Her tongue felt thick and clumsy. "It's . . . it was Jordan's house."

"Is," Kane corrected. "In this frozen moment."

"Why am I here?"

He stepped around her, but left no mark, no print, in the snow. The hem of his black robe seemed to float just an inch above that white surface.

He wore a ruby, a large round cabochon on a chain that fell nearly to his waist. In the black-and-white world it shone there like a fat drop of fresh blood.

"I give you the courtesy of allowing you to

know this is memory, of letting you stand with me and observe. Do you understand this?"

"I understand this is memory."

"With the first of you, I showed her what could be. So I showed you. But I realize you are a more . . . earthbound creation. One who prefers reality. But are you brave enough to see what is real?"

"To see what?" But she already knew.

Color seeped into the world. The deep green of pines beneath the draping snow, the bright blue mailbox on the corner, the blues and greens and reds of the coats the children wore as they built snowmen and forts in the yards.

And with the color came the movement. The snow fell again, and the shovelful from the walk on the corner landed with a thump, even as the man bent to scoop up another. She heard the shouts, high and pure in the air, from the children playing, and the unmistakable *thwack* of snowballs striking their targets.

She saw herself, bundled in a quilted jacket the color of blueberries. What had she been thinking? She looked like Violet in *Charlie and the Chocolate Factory.*

A knit cap was pulled over her head, a knit scarf wrapped around her throat. She moved quickly, but stopped long enough for a brief and energetic snow battle with the little Dobson boys and their friends.

Her own laughter drifted out to her, and she knew what she'd been thinking, what she'd been feeling.

She was going to see Jordan, to convince him to come out and play. He was spending much too much time closed up in that house since his mother died. He needed to be with someone who loved him.

The past few months had been a nightmare of hospitals and doctors, suffering and grief. He needed comfort, and a gentle, gentle push back into life. He needed her.

She trooped up the unshoveled walk, stomped her feet. She didn't knock. She'd never needed to knock on this door.

"Jordan!" She pulled off her cap, raked her fingers through her hair. She'd worn it shorter then, a chopped-off experiment she hated, and willed, daily, to grow back.

She called him again as she unzipped her coat.

The house still smelled of Mrs. Hawke, she noted. Not of the lemon wax she'd always used on the furniture, or the coffee she'd habitually had on the stove. But of her sickness. Dana wished she could fling open the windows and whisk the worst of the sorrow and grief away.

He came to the top of the stairs. Her heart did a tumble in her chest, as it always did when she saw him. He was so handsome, so tall and straight, and just a little dangerous around the eyes and mouth.

"I thought you'd be at the garage, but when I called Pete said you weren't coming in today."

"No, I'm not going in."

His voice sounded rusty, as if he'd just gotten up. But it was already two in the afternoon. There were shadows in his eyes, shadows under them, and they broke her heart.

She came to the foot of the stairs, shot him a quick smile. "Why don't you put on a coat? The Dobson kids tried to ambush me on the way over. We can kick their little asses."

"I've got stuff to do, Dana."

"More important than burying the Dobsons in a hail of snowballs?"

"Yeah. I have to finish packing."

"Packing?" She didn't feel alarm, not then, only confusion. "You're going somewhere?"

"New York." He turned and walked away.

"New York?" Still there was no alarm. Now there was a thrill, and she bounded up the stairs after him with excitement at her heels. "Is it about your book? Did you hear from that agent?"

She rushed into his bedroom, threw herself on his back. "You heard from the agent, and you didn't tell me? We have to celebrate. We have to do something insane. What did he say?"

"He's interested, that's all."

"Of course he's interested. Jordan, this is wonderful. You're going up to have a meeting with him? A meeting with a New York literary agent!" She let out a crow of delight, then noticed the two suitcases, the duffel, the packing crate.

Slowly, with that first trickle of alarm, she slid off his back. "You're taking an awful lot of stuff for a meeting."

"I'm moving to New York." He didn't turn to her, but tossed another sweater, a pair of jeans into one of the open suitcases.

"I don't understand."

"I put the house up for sale yesterday. They probably won't be able to turn it until spring. Guy at the flea market's going to take most of the furniture and whatever else there is."

"You're selling the house." When her legs went weak, she sank onto the side of the bed. "But, Jordan, you live here."

"Not anymore."

"But . . . you can't just pack up and go to New York. I know you talked about moving there eventually, but—"

"I'm done here. There's nothing for me here."

It was like having a fist punched into her heart. "How can you say that? How can you say there's nothing for you here? I know, Jordan, I know how hard it was for you to lose your mother. I know you're still grieving. This isn't the time for you to make this kind of a decision."

"It's already made." He glanced in her direction, but his eyes never met hers. "I've got a few more things to deal with, then I'm gone. I'm leaving in the morning."

"Just like that?" Pride pushed her back on her feet. "Were you planning on letting me in on it, or were you just going to send me a postcard when you got there?"

He looked at her now, but she couldn't see into his eyes, couldn't see through the shield he'd thrown up between them. "I was going to come by later tonight and see you, and Flynn."

"That's very considerate."

He raked his fingers through his hair, a gesture she knew reflected impatience or frustration. "Look, Dana, this is something I have to do."

"No, this is something you want to do, because you're done with this place now. And everyone in it."

She had to keep her voice low, very low. Or it would shrill. Or scream. "That would include me. So I guess the past couple of years haven't meant a damn thing."

"That's bullshit, and you know it." He slapped one suitcase closed, fastened it. "I care about you, I always did. I'm doing what I need to do—what I want to do. Either way it comes to the same thing. I can't write here. I can't fucking think here. And I have to write. I've got a chance to make something of myself, and I'm taking it. So would you."

"Yeah, you're making something of yourself. A selfish bastard. You've been planning
this, stringing me along while you planned
to dump me when it was most convenient
for you."

"This isn't about you, this is about me
getting out of this fucking house, out of this
goddamn town." He rounded on her, and
the shield cracked enough for her to see
fury. "This is about me not busting my ass
every goddamn day working in a grease pit
just to pay the bills, then trying to carve out
a few hours to write. This is about my life."

"I thought I was part of your life."

"Christ." He dragged a hand through his
hair again before yanking open a drawer for
more clothes.

He couldn't be bothered to stop packing,
she thought, not even when he was breaking her heart.

"You are part of my life. You, Flynn, Brad.
How the hell does me moving to New York
change that?"

"As far as I know you haven't been sleeping with Flynn and Brad."

"I can't bury myself in the Valley because
you and I had the hots for each other."

"You son of a bitch." She could feel herself beginning to shake, and the stinging tears gathering in her throat. Using all her strength, she channeled the hurt into rage. "You can make it cheap. You can make yourself cheap. But you won't make me cheap."

He stopped now, stopped packing and turned to look at her with regret, and what might have been pity. "Dana. I didn't mean it that way."

"Don't." She slapped his hand away when he reached for her. "Don't you ever put your hands on me again. You're done with the Valley? You're done with me? Fine, that's fine, because I'm done with you. You'll be lucky to last a month in New York, hacking away at that crap you write. So when you come crawling back here, don't call me. Don't speak to me. Because you're right about one thing, Hawke—there's nothing for you here anymore."

She shoved past him and fled.

She'd forgotten her hat, she realized as she watched herself run out of the house. A snowball winged by one of the Dobson boys splatted in the middle of her back, but she didn't notice.

She didn't feel the cold, or the tears streaming down her face.

She felt nothing. He'd made her nothing.

How could she have forgotten? How could she have forgiven?

She didn't see then, nor did she see now, that he'd stood in the narrow window of the dormer and watched her go.

She woke to thin autumn sunlight, her cheeks wet, her skin chilled.

The grief was so real, so fresh, she rolled away, curled up in a ball and prayed for it to pass.

She couldn't, wouldn't, go through this again. Had she worked so hard to get over him, to push herself out of the grief and misery and hurt only to lay herself open to it all again?

Was she that weak, that stupid?

Maybe she was, when it came to Jordan. Maybe she was just that weak and stupid. But she didn't have to be.

She eased out of bed and left him sleeping. She pulled on a robe, a kind of armor, then headed to the kitchen for coffee.

Moe scrambled up from the foot of the bed and bounded after her. With his leash between his teeth, he danced in place in the kitchen.

"Not yet, Moe." She bent to bury her face in his fur. "I'm not up to it yet."

Sensing trouble, he whined, then dropped the leash to lick her face.

"You're a good dog, aren't you? Been chasing rabbits, huh? That's okay, I've been chasing something, too. Neither one of us is ever going to catch it."

She drank the coffee where she stood, and was pouring a second cup when she heard Jordan's footsteps.

He'd pulled on his clothes, but still looked sleepily rumpled. He grunted when Moe's paws hit his chest, and managed to nip the coffee mug out of Dana's hand. He drank deep.

"Thanks." He handed it back, then stooped to pick up Moe's leash. The act had Moe running around them in desperate circles.

"Want me to take him out?"

"Yes. You can take him back to Flynn's."

"Sure. Want to go for a run before breakfast?" he said to Moe as he clipped on the leash. "Yeah, you bet."

"I don't want you to come back here."

"Hmm?" He glanced up, saw her face. "What did you say?"

"I don't want you to come back here. Not this morning, not ever."

"Down, Moe." Something in the quiet tone had the dog obeying. "Did I sleep through an argument, or . . . Kane," he said and gripped Dana's arm. "What did he do?"

"It has nothing to do with him. It's about me this time. I made a mistake letting you back in. I'm correcting it."

"What the hell brought this on? Last night—"

"We have great sex." She shrugged, sipped her coffee. "That's not enough for me. Or maybe it's too much for me. Either way it doesn't work. You ripped me to pieces once."

"Dana, let me—"

"No, that's just it." She stepped back from him. "I won't let you, not again. I've got a good life, all in all. It satisfies me. I don't want you in it. I don't want you here, Jordan. I can't have you here. So I'm telling you to go while there are no hard feelings.

I'm telling you while we still have some chance of being friends."

She moved past him quickly. "I'm going to shower. Don't be here when I come out."

He was still in a daze when he walked into Flynn's. Was this what she'd felt like? he wondered. Was this what he'd done to her? Had he left her feeling hollowed out and numb?

And what happened when the numbness passed? Was it pain, or anger, or both?

He wanted the anger. Christ, he wanted to find his anger.

Trailing the leash that Jordan forgot to unclip, Moe dashed back toward the kitchen, and Flynn's cheerful greeting followed the sound of thumps.

"A boy and his dog." Malory jogged down the stairs, morning fresh in khakis and a navy sweatshirt. "You're back early this morning," she began, "or I'm running behind." Then she stopped, stared at him. "What is it? What's wrong?" A bubble of fear came into her voice. "Dana—"

"No, nothing. She's fine."

"But you're not. Come on. Let's go sit down."

"No, I need to—"

"Sit down," she repeated, and taking his arm, pulled him toward the kitchen.

Flynn was at the card table, a temporary measure in the evolving kitchen. The walls had been painted a strong teal blue that set off the golden wood of the new cabinets. The floor was stripped down in preparation for the hardwood Malory had selected. A piece of plywood sat on a stretch of base cabinets as a makeshift countertop.

Flynn was eating cereal, and from the guilty look on both his and his dog's faces, he'd been sharing it with Moe.

"Hey, what's up? You want food, you've got about fifteen minutes before the crew gets here."

"Sit down, Jordan. I'll get you some coffee."

Flynn studied his friend's face. "What's the deal? You and Dana have a fight?"

"No, no fight. She just told me to go."

"Go where?"

"Flynn." Malory set a mug of coffee in front of Jordan and laid a hand on his shoulder. "Can you possibly be that dense?"

"Well, Jesus, give me a minute to catch up. If you weren't fighting, why did she kick you out?"

"Because she didn't want me there."

"So you just left?" Flynn tossed out. "Without finding out what pissed her off?"

"She wasn't mad. If she'd been mad I could've handled her. Handled it. She just looked . . . tired, and sad. And finished." He rubbed his hands over his face. So it wasn't going to be anger after all, he realized. It was just pain.

"Whatever she felt, Jordan, whatever's behind it, you have to find out." Malory gave his shoulder a quick shake. "Doesn't she mean anything to you?"

He shot her a look storming with emotions, and with a sigh she moved in to wrap her arms around him. "All right, then," she murmured. "All right."

"She means enough," he managed, "that I'm not going to put that look on her face again. She wants me gone, I'll go."

"Men are such morons. Haven't you considered that she wants you gone only because she already expects you to go?"

*   *   *

Zoe met Malory at the front door, then
nudged her back out. "I've been watching
for you. Dana's in there, painting your side.
Something's wrong. I can see it. But she
won't talk about it."

"She broke up with Jordan."

"Oh. If they've had a fight—"

"No, it's something else, and nothing as
simple as an argument. I'm going to see
what I can do."

"Good luck." Zoe went back in.

"What's that noise, anyway?"

"Just one more complication. Bradley's
over in Dana's section with an electric floor
sander. He won't let me use it. Yes, it was
very nice of him to lend it to us," she continued when Malory lifted her eyebrows. "But
I'm perfectly capable of sanding the floors.
With him here, it's that much harder to get
Dana to open up."

"Keep him busy, I'll deal with Dana."

"I don't want to keep him busy. The last
time I was alone with him for ten minutes,
he put the moves on me."

"Which moves?"

Zoe glanced over her shoulder toward

the sound of the sander. "The night we were at his place, after everyone else left. I was having a simple conversation with him, then he kissed me."

"He kissed you? That perverted maniac! Get the rope."

"Oh, ha, ha."

"Okay, did you have to fight him off? Was it a scarring experience?"

"No, but . . ." She lowered her voice, though she could have shouted and not been overheard. "He really *kissed* me, and my head went wonky for a minute, so I kissed him back. I've got entirely too much on my plate for fun and games right now. Besides, he makes me nervous."

"Yeah, great-looking guys who take time out of their day to sand floors for me always make me nervous. Listen, I've got to talk to Dana. When I've taken care of her, I'll run over and, if necessary, save you from Brad's nefarious clutches. Unless, of course, you don't think you can handle yourself."

"Okay, that was low. Very low."

"Just make sure he doesn't wander over while I'm talking to Dana. Scoot." She

waved Zoe away, then headed in the opposite direction.

Her first thought was: Oh! Her walls were
coming to life with that pale, delicate burnt
gold she'd chosen. It was right, just so
right. Already she could see what a perfect
backdrop it would make for art.

Her second thought was how set and
blank Dana's face was as she worked.

And that was wrong, just so wrong.

"It looks wonderful."

Obviously jolted out of long thoughts,
Dana turned her head. "Yeah. You've got a
knack for bull's-eyeing color. I figured this
would look bland, even a little dingy. Instead it has this nice, quiet glow."

"You don't. You don't have any glow at all
today."

Dana shrugged, and continued to work.
"Can't be Mary Sunshine all the time."

"I saw Jordan this morning. He wasn't
glowing either. In fact," she continued as
she walked to Dana, "he looked devas-
tated."

"He'll get over it."

"Do you really think that, or do you need
to think it because it gets you off the hook?"

"I'm not on any hook." She stared hard at

the wall as she painted. Gold over white, gold over white. "I did what was right for me. It's none of your business, Malory."

"Yes, it is. I love you. I love Flynn, and he loves you."

"We're just one big, gooey family."

"You can be angry with me if you want, if it helps. But you have to know I'm on your side. Whatever happens, I'm on your side."

"Then you should understand why I broke things off and you should support my decision."

"I would, if I thought it was what you really wanted." Malory rubbed a hand over Dana's back. "If it made you happy."

"I'm not looking for happy yet." Her friend's comforting stroke made her want to sit down on the floor and wail. "I'll settle for a little stretch of smooth road."

"Tell me what happened between yesterday and today."

"I remembered—with a little help from Kane."

"I knew it." As she snapped it out, Malory's face went bright with anger. "I knew he was behind this."

"Hold on. He took me on a trip down memory lane. That makes him a son of a bitch, but it doesn't change the facts." God, she was tired. She just wanted to be left alone to paint the walls. Paint away the ache and fatigue. "He didn't change what happened or make it worse. He didn't have to. I just knew that after seeing it again, feeling it again, I was making a mistake."

"Why is it a mistake to love a decent man?"

"Because he doesn't love *me.*" She yanked the band out of her hair, as if doing so would relieve the headache simmering at the base of her skull. "Because he's going to leave as soon as he's done here. Because the more I'm with him, the deeper in I get, and I can't control how I feel the way I thought I could. I can't be with him and not be in love with him."

"Did you ask how he felt?"

"No. And you know what? I just wasn't up to hearing the old 'I care about you' routine. Sue me."

No one spoke for a moment. There was only the sound of Dana's labored breathing, the hum of the paint machine, and the steady buzz of the sander from the other side of the house.

"You hurt him." Malory stepped over,

flicked off the machine. "Maybe his feelings aren't as simple and weak as you think. The man I saw this morning had been cut straight down to the bone. If you wanted payback, Dana, you got it."

She whirled around, vibrant with fury, trembling with insult. The roller fell out of her hand and left a dull gold smear on the drop cloth. "For Christ's sake, what do you take me for? Do you think I've been sleeping with him just so I could kick him out and get back some of my own?"

"No, I don't. I'm just thinking, if you really want that smooth stretch of road, you don't get it by running somebody else into a ditch, then leaving him there bleeding."

Dana heaved the hair band to the floor and wished viciously she had something more satisfying to throw. "You've got some goddamn nerve."

"Yes, I guess I do."

"This is my fucking spin on the wheel, Malory. I don't need you or anyone else telling me who to let into my life, or who to close out."

"Seems to me that's just what you're letting Kane do. He had a direction he wanted you to take, and you're going right along with it. You're not even asking yourself why he gave you the push."

"So now I should stay with Jordan because of the key? You're lecturing me about my own life, my own decisions, so I won't risk screwing up your deal?"

Malory drew a long breath. It wasn't the time for her to lose her temper, or, she decided, to blame Dana for losing hers. "If you believe that, you don't know me, and more, you don't know what it is you've agreed to do. So you can keep on painting, and congratulating yourself for avoiding all those bumps in the road, or you can stop being a coward and settle this with Jordan."

Finished, Malory started out. "He shouldn't be hard to find," she called back. "He told Flynn he was going to see his mother this morning."

Chapter Sixteen

He brought her carnations. Tulips had been her favorite, but it was the wrong season. Still, she'd liked simple flowers the best. Tulips and daffodils, rambling roses and daisies. The carnations were simple, it seemed to him, and feminine in a soft, old-fashioned pink.

She'd have appreciated them, made a fuss, and put them in her good vase—the one her mother had given her some long ago Christmas.

He hadn't thought to buy anything to put them in, so the florist's paper would have to do.

He hated the cemetery. All those stones and markers popping out of the ground like a crop of death in gray and white and black. All the names and dates inscribed on them were as much a reminder that no one beat fate in the end as a memorial to a lifetime.

Morbid thoughts, he supposed, but this was the place for them.

The grass was bumpy and weedy, so the green was marred with brown patches where it had worn away, spindly where it hadn't been clipped close enough to the stones. Others had brought flowers to their dead, and some of the offerings were faded and withered. Some solved this remembrance of death by laying artificial blooms at the markers, but the bright colors struck him as false.

More lie, he thought, than tribute.

It was too windy here on the north end, and too cold, without the shelter of the small grove of trees to the east or the sunny rise just to the west.

He'd had the marker replaced a few years before with smooth white granite. She'd have considered that a foolish expense, but he'd needed to do something.

It held her name. *Susan Lee Hawke.* And the span of her life, that short forty-six years. Beneath, in script, was the line he'd paraphrased from Emily Dickinson.

Hope perches in the soul

She'd never lost hope. She'd lived her life believing in the power of hope, and faith, leavened with good, hard work. Even when the sickness had eaten away her beauty, had whittled her down to brittle bones she'd had hope.

For him, Jordan thought now. She'd had hope for him, believed in him, and had loved him without qualification.

He crouched down to lay the flowers on her grave.

"I miss you, Mom. I miss talking to you, and hearing you laugh. I miss seeing that look in your eye that told me I was in trouble. And even when I was, you were there for me. You were always there for me."

He stared at the words on the stone. It looked so formal. She'd always been Sue. Simple, straightforward Sue.

"I know you're not in there. This sort of thing, it's just a way of letting other people know you were around, that you were loved. Sometimes I feel you, and it's such a strong feeling it's as if I could turn around and there you'd be. You always believed in stuff like that, in the possibilities of what we are."

He rose, slid his hands into his pockets. "I'm wondering what the hell I am. I've screwed up. Not everything, just one vital thing. I've got the one thing I always wanted, and I lost the one thing I didn't know I always needed. I'd say maybe it's cosmic justice. Maybe you just can't have it all. But you'd give me that look."

He gazed out toward the hills she'd always loved, and the way the sky held a strong blue over the flame of the trees. "I don't know if I can fix it. Fact is, I don't know if I should even try."

He closed his eyes a moment. "It hurts to be here. I guess it's supposed to." He touched his fingers to his lips, then pressed his fingers to the stone. "I love you. I'll come back."

He turned, and stopped when he saw Dana standing on the edge of the access road, watching him.

He looked so sad, she thought. More than that, it was as if the sorrow had stripped away his defenses and left the emotions behind them open and raw. It was painful to see him this vulnerable, to understand that they both knew she'd caught him unguarded in a moment meant to be private.

No longer sure what she would say, could say, she walked across the grass to stand with him by his mother's grave.

"I'm sorry. I didn't want to . . . disturb you," she began. "That's why I was waiting over there."

"It's all right."

She looked down at the grave, the fresh flowers spread over the grass. Perhaps she did know what to say. "Flynn and I come here once a year." She cleared her throat. "His father, my mother . . . and yours. We, ah, try to come right after the first real snowfall. Everything's so peaceful and white and clean. We bring her flowers."

She shifted her gaze from the flowers and saw he was staring at her. "I thought you'd like to know we always bring her flowers when we come."

He didn't speak, but his eyes said everything. Then he simply lowered his forehead to hers.

They stood like that, silent, while the wind

whipped around them and fluttered the petals of the pink carnations.

"Thanks." He straightened slowly, as if he were afraid something in him might break. "Thank you."

She nodded, and they stood, silent again, looking out at the hills.

"This is the first time I've been out here since I've been back," he told her. "I never know what I'm supposed to do in a place like this."

"You did it. Carnations are nice. Simple."

He let out a little laugh. "Yeah, that was my thought. Why are you here, Dana?"

"I had things to say to you, that maybe I didn't say the right way this morning."

"If it's along the lines of we can still be friends, maybe you could wait a couple of days on that."

"Not exactly. I don't know if this is the appropriate time or place to talk about this," she began, "but after Malory finished reaming me out this morning, I decided she had a few points, and that I owed you—myself—I owed both of us something better than the way I ended things."

"I hurt you. I could see it on your face. I don't want to hurt you, Dana."

"Too late for that." She lifted her shoulders, let them fall. "You were careless with me, Jordan. You were careless and you were callous. And though I might have spent some happy hours over the years dreaming about paying you back in kind, I realize that's not really what I want. So my being careless and callous with you this morning wasn't any more satisfying for me than it was for you."

"Why did you do it?"

"I went back last night, courtesy of Kane." She frowned up at his pithy comment. "I don't think you should use that sort of language over your mother's grave."

For some reason, the remark loosened a knot in his belly. "She's heard it before."

"Nevertheless."

He shrugged, and there was something of the boy she'd loved in the gesture. Just enough of him to twist her heart again. "Where did you go?"

"I went back to the day you were packing to move to New York. I experienced it again. Watched myself experiencing it. It was very strange, and no less horrible knowing I was watching a rerun. It was like standing on both sides of a one-way mirror. Watching us, and still being a part of it. Everything you said to me, everything you didn't say to me, was just as painful as when it happened."

"I'm sorry."

She tipped her face up to his. "I actually believe you are, which is why I'm here rather than burning you in effigy. But you see, it hurt, all over again. And I have the right, I have the responsibility to myself, to step back from that. I'm not willing to let my heart spill at your feet again, and I can't be with you and keep it intact. Maybe we can be friends, maybe we can't. But we can't be lovers. I just needed to explain that to you."

When she stepped back, he laid a hand on her arm. "Would you walk with me?"

"Jordan—"

"Just walk with me for a few minutes. You said what you had to say. I'm asking you to listen."

"All right." She put her hands in her pockets to warm them, and to avoid contact with his.

"I didn't handle it well when my mother died."

"I don't know that you're supposed to handle things like that well. My mother's

buried over there." She lifted a hand to gesture. "I don't really remember her. I don't remember losing her. But I miss her, and
sometimes still I feel cheated. I have some
of her things—a blouse my father saved
that was her favorite, some of her jewelry,
and photographs. I like having them. The
fact that I don't remember her, that I was
too young to remember losing her, doesn't
mean I don't understand what it was like for
you. You wouldn't let me help."

"You're right. I wouldn't let you help. I
didn't know how." He took her arm briefly to
steady her over the uneven ground, then let
her go as they walked toward the trees.

"I loved her so much, Dana. It's not the
sort of thing you think about every day
when things are normal. I mean I didn't
wake up every morning thinking, boy, I sure
love my mother. But we were a unit."

"I know."

"When my father left us . . . well, I don't
remember him very well either. But I remember that she was a rock. Not cold, not
hard, just sturdy. She worked like a fucking
dog, two jobs until we were out of the debt
pit he'd put her in."

Even now, he could almost taste the bitterness of it. "She must've been so tired, but she always had time for me. Not just putting a meal on the table or handing me a clean shirt, but for me."

"I know. She was so interested in everything you did, without breathing down your neck over it. I used to pretend she was my mother."

He glanced down. "You did?"

"Yeah. You didn't think I was hanging around your house when I was a kid just to annoy you and Flynn and Brad, did you? I liked being around her. She smelled like a mother, and she laughed a lot. She'd look at you—sometimes she'd just look over at you, and there was such love in her face, such pride. I wanted a mother who would look at me that way."

It moved him to hear her say it, and the faint tang of bitterness washed away. "She never let me down. Not once. Not ever. She read everything I wrote, even when I was a kid. She saved a lot of it, and she would tell me that one day, when I was a famous writer, people would get a big kick out of reading my early stories. I don't know if I would be a writer today if it wasn't for her. Her steady, constant faith in me."

"She'd be thrilled with what you've done."

"She didn't live to see me published, not with a book. She wanted me to go to college. I wanted it, too, but I figured on putting it off a year or two, earning more money first. She laid down the law—and she was damn good at that when it was important to her. So I went."

He was silent for a moment, and a cloud slipped over the sun, deadening the light. "I sent some money home, but not much. Wasn't that much to spare. I didn't come home as much as I should have. I got caught up. There was so much out there. Then I went to grad school. There were a lot of years I wasn't there for her."

"You're being too hard on yourself."

"Am I? She put me first, every time. I could've come back here sooner, earned a good living at the garage and taken some of the weight off her."

She put a hand on his shoulder so he would turn and face her. "That's not what she wanted for you. You know it wasn't. She was over the moon about what you were doing. When you had those stories published in magazines, she was thrilled."

"I could've written them here. I did write when I finally came home. I got my teeth into a book, wrote like a crazy man at night after work. When I wasn't being crazy over you, that is. I was going to do it all, have it all. Money, fame, the works."

He spoke quickly now, as if the words had been dammed up too long. "I was going to move her out of that broken-down house, buy her someplace beautiful, up in the hills. She would never have to work again. She could garden or read, or whatever she wanted to do. I was going to take care of her. But I didn't. I couldn't."

"Oh, Jordan. You're not to blame for that."

"It's not a matter of blame. She got sick. I'd spent all that time away, now I was back, going to make it right. And she got sick. Just a little tired, she'd say. Just a little achy. Getting old. And she'd laugh. So she didn't go to the doctor in time. Money was tight, time off work was tough to get, so she didn't go until it was too late."

Unable to hold out against it, she took his hand in hers. "It was terrible. What both of you went through was terrible."

"I didn't pay attention, Dana. I was

wrapped up in my own life, in what I wanted, what I needed. I didn't see that she was sick until she . . . Jesus, she sat me down and told me what they'd found inside her."

"It's stupid to blame yourself for that. Stupid, Jordan, and she'd tell you exactly that."

"She probably would, and I've come around to that since. But during it, after . . . It happened so fast. I know it took months, but it seemed so fast. The doctors, the hospital, the surgery, the chemo. Christ, she was so sick through that. I didn't know how to take care of her—"

"Wait. Just wait. You did take care of her. You stayed with her, you read to her. God, Jordan, you fed her when she couldn't feed herself. You were her rock then, Jordan. I saw it."

"Dana, I was terrified, and I was angry, and I couldn't tell her. I locked it in because I didn't know what else to do."

"You were barely in your twenties, and your world was crashing down around you."

Even as she said it, she knew she hadn't understood that at the time, not completely.

"She was fading away in front of me, and I couldn't stop it. When we knew she was dying, when there wasn't much time—she was in such pain—she told me she was sorry she had to go, that she had to leave me. She said there wasn't a single day of my life she hadn't been proud of me, and grateful for me.

"I fell apart. I just lost it. Then she was gone. I don't know if I said good-bye, or told her I loved her. I don't even know what I said or did."

He turned back, walking once more toward the stones that bloomed out of the patchy grass. "She'd made all the arrangements already, so all I had to do was follow through. One foot in front of the other. The memorial service—the dress she wanted to wear, the music she wanted played. She had some insurance. She'd scraped money together for that every month. Christ knows how. There was enough to pay off most of the debts that had built up and give me some breathing room."

"You were her child. She wanted to provide for you."

"She did, in every possible way. I couldn't stay here, Dana. Not then. I couldn't live in that house and grieve for her every time I took a breath. I couldn't stay in this town,

where I would see people I knew everywhere I went.

"You'd think it would be a comfort, the familiar. But for me it was constant pain. One
minute I'd feel like I was suffocating, the
next like I was going to explode. I had to get
away from it. I had to bury some of that pain
the way I'd buried her."

"You wouldn't talk to me about it."

"I couldn't. If I'd had the words, I'd have
choked on them. I'm not saying it was right.
It wasn't. But it's the truth. I had to make
something of myself, and I couldn't do it
here. Or I believed I couldn't, so what's the
difference?"

"You had to go," she murmured, "or you
wouldn't be who you are." How could it
have taken her so long to see that?

"I hated what I was here, and I was afraid
of what I would become if I stayed. I saw
myself working in the garage day after day,
year after year, and throwing away everything she'd worked for, everything she'd
wanted for me because I couldn't do any
better. I was angry and in pain, so wrapped
up in both I didn't give a damn about anything else."

He came back to the edge of his mother's

grave, stared down at the flowers. "I didn't know you loved me. I don't know what I'd have done differently if I had, but I didn't know. You always seemed so strong, so sure of yourself, so easy with the way things were, that I didn't see inside that."

He reached out to brush the hair back from her cheek, then dropped his hand again. "Maybe I didn't want to. With all that happened to her, I didn't have any room to love anyone. But I hurt you, and I meant to. Because it was easier on me if you walked away. I'm ashamed of that, and I'm sorry for it. You deserved better."

"I don't know what to say to you. It helps, hearing all this. I know it wasn't easy to tell me."

"Don't cry, Dana. It rips me."

"It's a little tough to get through otherwise." But she swiped her fingers under her eyes. "We were young, Jordan, and we both made mistakes. We can't change what happened, but we can put it in place and try to be friends again."

"We're grown up now, and we've got today to deal with. You want to be friends, I'll be your friend."

"Okay." She managed a wobbly smile and held out a hand.

"There's just one more thing you need to know." He clasped her fingers firmly in his. "I'm in love with you."

"Oh." Her already unsteady heart stumbled. "God."

"I never got over you. Whatever I felt for you back then, it was like the root. Time went on, I'd keep trying to kill that root, but it wouldn't die. I'd breeze back into town to see Flynn, catch a glimpse of you, or you'd take a shot at me, and what was growing on that root would nudge a little further up from the ground."

"Damn it, Jordan. Damn it."

Whatever it cost him, he had to get it out. "This last time, when I knocked on Flynn's door and you opened it, it was like that vine shot up another ten feet and wrapped around my throat. I'm in love with you, Dana. I can't kill it off, and I wouldn't if I could. So, I'm spilling my heart at your feet this time. It's yours, whatever you do with it."

"What do you think I'm going to do, you jackass?" She leaped into his arms.

Relief, joy, pleasure rushed through him

like a flood as he buried his face in her hair. "That's what I was hoping you'd say."

The first thing Dana heard when she walked back into Indulgence was arguing. Just one of the essential elements, in her opinion, that made a house a home. She cocked an ear toward her section of the building, and held up a hand for quiet when Jordan stepped in behind her.

"I'm not going to hurt myself. I'm perfectly capable of running an electric sander. You just don't want anyone else to play with it."

"In the first place, it's not a toy." There was such chilly exasperation in Brad's voice that Dana had to muffle a snort. "In the second, once I've finished this area—which I would already have done if you didn't keep nagging—"

"I don't nag." There were equal parts venom and insult in Zoe's response.

Dana gave Jordan's arm a tug. "You go referee the Irritable Twins," she whispered. "I need to talk to Malory."

"Why can't I talk to Malory?"

"A real man wouldn't be afraid to—"

"Oh, stop that." He hunched his shoulders, jammed his hands in his pockets, and strode off in the direction of the spat.

Dana buffed her nails on her jacket. "Works every time." Then she huffed out a breath, squared her own shoulders, and headed in the opposite direction to swallow her serving of crow.

The walls in what would be Malory's main showroom were finished. And looked, Dana decided, just swell. She could hear the music from the radio jingling out from the room beyond, and Malory's singing along with Bonnie Raitt.

She was also, Dana noted as she stepped in, grooving. As Malory swiped the roller up and down, her hips bumped to the jumpy Delta beat.

"You got that up so loud just to keep up your rhythm, or to block out the sexual tension from across the hall?"

Malory turned, set down her roller to give her arms a rest. "A little of both. How're you doing?"

"How do I look?"

"Better." Malory took a closer study. "In fact, you look pretty damn good."

"I feel pretty damn good. First, I'm sorry. I

was feeling miserable and I took it out on you. You were only trying to help."

"Friends do that. Take their moods out on each other, and try to help. Both of you looked so unhappy, Dana."

"Well, we were. We had reason to be. Whatever Kane's motives, he showed me the truth. I couldn't just bury what happened before, all that hurt. It had to be dealt with, taken out, looked at. Understood, at least."

"You're right."

"No, you were right." She peeled off her jacket, tossed it on the window ledge. "I wasn't dealing with it, not by starting things up with Jordan again, or cutting them off. I just had it buried in a very shallow grave. We both did."

"You needed time together first, to get to know each other again."

"You're right. You're batting a thousand today."

"Though I've never understood exactly what that means, let me see if I can keep it up. You went to see Jordan, you talked some of this out, and you reached the understanding, at last, that you're in love with each other."

"Sign her up. He loves me." When Dana's eyes filled, Malory whipped the kerchief off her head and rushed over to offer it. "Thanks. He said things to me he didn't say before. Couldn't say, or wouldn't. I don't guess it matters. He wasn't ready, and if I'm going to be honest about it, we weren't ready. I loved him, but that wasn't enough to let me see what he was going through, what he needed. What I needed, for that matter. It was blinding, so all I could see was 'I want Jordan.' Period. I never thought about what we'd do together, or be together, what either of us needed to do separately to make it strong. It was all just right that minute."

"You were young, and in love." Malory took the kerchief back and dried her own eyes.

"Yeah, I was. I loved him with everything I had. But I have more now. And it's so amazing, really, to be able to take one step back and look at the man he is, the man he's made of himself and realize he's more. To know it was worth the wait."

"Dana."

Her damp eyes went wide on Malory's face, then she blinked rapidly before turning to where Jordan stood in the doorway. "This is girl stuff here."

"Dana." He said her name again, then crossed to her. She saw the emotion swirling in his eyes, blazing in the blue before his arms banded around her. He hitched her up to her toes as his mouth swooped down to hers.

"Oh." Undone, Malory buried her face in the kerchief.

"Okay, I'd just like to say—" Zoe stormed halfway into the room before she skidded to a halt. Staring at the couple wrapped in each other, she pressed a hand to her heart. "Oh." She reached back to dig the bandanna out of her pocket, but Brad stepped up beside her, pushed his into her hand.

"Thanks." She sniffled into it. "But I did have my own."

"Shut up, Zoe."

Because the moment was too precious to spoil, she did.

Jordan eased back. "There's something I have to do."

Her eyebrow winged up, and her smile was quick and wicked. "Right here? In front of all our friends?"

NORA ROBERTS

"Cool," was Brad's response, which earned him Zoe's elbow in his belly.

"This isn't the time for gutter thoughts."

"It's always the time."

"Ignore them," Jordan murmured and pressed his lips to Dana's forehead.

"I am."

"There's something I have to do," he said again. "So I have to renege on giving you a hand around here today."

"But—"

"It's important," he interrupted. "I'll explain it tonight."

"We all need to get together tonight and go over what you wrote. I'm running out of time."

"Why don't we meet at Flynn's? It's the most central." He glanced over. "Is that okay with you, Malory?"

"Sure. The kitchen's not finished yet, so we won't get food like we did at Brad's. Actually, even with the kitchen finished we wouldn't get food like we had at Brad's."

"Pizza and beer works for me," Dana said.

"That's my girl." Jordan kissed her again. "I'll see you there."

"You've got something up your sleeve."

Dana narrowed her eyes. "I can see it. If you're thinking about messing with Kane—"

"He's got nothing to do with this. I've got to go, or I'm not going to get it all done. Brad, you're coming with me."

"I haven't finished here."

"You go. Take him," Zoe said, pointing at Brad. "Leave the sander. All will be well here."

"You're not hauling that thing upstairs by yourself."

"It's not that heavy, and I'm not that weak."

"You're not carrying it up those stairs."

"Jesus, Vane, cart the thing up and be done with it." Grinning, Jordan slung his arm around Dana's shoulder. "Don't you know how to handle a woman?"

"Kiss my ass." Brad turned on his heel and strode away.

"I can do it myself," Zoe began.

"Zoe." Basking in the glow of love rediscovered, Dana shook her head. "Stop being a jerk."

"I can't help it." Zoe lifted her hands, let them fall. "He brings out the jerk in me." She heard him cursing under his breath as he carried the sander toward the steps, and folded her arms over her chest. "I'm not going to say anything. I'm not going to do anything."

"Good plan. Why don't you grab a roller?" Malory suggested. "We can finish in here, then start upstairs."

"Can I just say you women are doing a hell of a job with this place?"

"There, see?" Delighted, Zoe walked over and gave Jordan a loud kiss on the cheek. "Here's a secure man who has respect for a woman's abilities."

"Absolutely. Nothing sexier than a self-sufficient woman."

"Lap it up, Hawke, lap it up." Dana nudged him aside. "Now take your playmate and run along. We've got work to do."

She waited until Jordan and Brad had gone out, then dashed to the window to spy on them. "What's he up to? Yeah, yeah, Brad's asking him what gives right now. I can tell. But he's not saying. He's not saying because he knows I'm standing here watching. Damn it!"

She jerked back with a laugh as Jordan looked straight at her through the glass. "You just can't pull one over on Jordan. God, I love that about him."

"I'm so happy for you." Malory sighed. "And if we're not careful, we're going to start another weep-o-rama."

"Since I've leaked more in this one day than I have the entire past year, let's paint." Dana turned, gave her biceps an exaggerated flex. "He's right, you know. We're doing a hell of a job with this place."

They worked downstairs until the walls were done, then took a coffee break, sitting on the floor to admire them.

"The floors in Dana's section need to be damp-mopped. You need a clean surface before they're sealed."

"I don't know how the sealing part goes."

"It's easy," Zoe told her. "I'll show you. Once they're sealed, dried good and hard, you can start moving stuff in."

"Wow!" Since Dana's stomach jumped, she pressed a hand to it. "It gets more real every day. I ordered the shelves. If they get here when they're supposed to, along with the other stuff I ordered—and the first shipments of books—I should be setting up in a couple of weeks. Maybe less. And I have a potential employee."

"You didn't say anything about that." Zoe punched her lightly on the arm. "Who is it?"

"It's a woman I met when I was working in the library. I ran into her at the grocery store, and one thing led to another. She's personable, presentable, likes to read, wants a job, and isn't looking for a big salary. She's going to come by sometime and get a look at the place. If she doesn't run screaming, I think I've got myself a bookseller."

"Zoe, how soon do you think I can start moving stock in?" Malory asked.

"I think next week." Zoe sipped coffee, glanced around the room. "It's all coming together so well, I don't want to jinx it, but I really think next week. It's going to take me a little longer. There's more to set up in a salon. And we still have to replace some of these windows. Plus there's going to be a good, long list of punch-out work."

"I love it when she talks the manly talk," Dana commented. "Now let's go up and play with the sander like men."

"First," Zoe said in a fair imitation of Brad's most clipped tone, "it's not a toy."

"Jeez." Dana laughed her way to her feet. "You slay me."

Chapter Seventeen

"You sure about this?" Brad studied Jordan, and the square-cut ruby ring in his hand.

"Yeah. I think. She'd like this better than the traditional diamond."

"I don't mean the ring. I mean what you're buying the ring for."

"I'm sure. A little queasy, but sure."

"I'm not going to take offense," Flynn decided. "I could take offense that asking my sister to marry you makes you queasy, but I won't."

Jordan smiled a little as he turned the ring under the light. He'd wanted them both with him when he took this step. A kind of circle, he supposed, just as the ring was a circle. He couldn't say either of them had been thrilled to be hauled off to Pittsburgh and into a jewelry store, but they'd come through.

They always did.

"I think this is the one. I know she is." He offered the ring to Brad. "You know more about this stuff than either of us. Give me an opinion of the rock."

Behind the counter, the jeweler began to make noises.

"Yeah, yeah." Jordan waved him off. "I know the spiel. I'd rather hear what my pal here has to say."

"I can assure you that stone is an excellent quality. Burmese ruby at three carats, set in eighteen-karat gold. The craftsmanship of the—"

"Why don't you get me a loupe?" Brad suggested pleasantly. "The guy's buying an engagement ring. It's a moment."

He might not have been happy, but the potential sale had him producing a jeweler's loupe and offering it to Brad.

Playing it out, Brad hemmed, hawed, and hmmmed before setting both the ring and the loupe on the black velvet pad. "You're buying yourself a hell of a rock," he said. "It hits the three C's—color, cut, clarity, and at three substantial carats, rounds it out nicely. She'll love it."

"Yeah, that's what I thought. Wrap it up," he told the jeweler.

"We should go get a beer now, right?" Flynn glanced warily at the other rings in the glass case. "And Jordan should buy, in a symbolic gesture of . . . oh, hell with all that. I just want a beer."

"All in good time, my pretty." Jordan pulled out his wallet, dug out his credit card. "We've got another stop to make on the way back."

The way he looked at it, he was going to make a clean sweep. A kind of romantic hat trick. He got the girl, he'd bought the ring. Now, he thought as they pulled through the gates of Warrior's Peak, he was going to see if he could finesse the house.

"This is wild," Flynn said from the backseat where Moe snored beside him, exhausted by the thrill of the car trip. "I think I'm in some sort of shock."

"Pretty wild," Jordan agreed. "But the fact is, I always wanted this place. Even when I was a kid."

"Okay, before you go in there and make some sort of insane offer, let's just take one more pass through the routine." Brad shifted. "Let me point out, once again, that this place is enormous."

"I like big."

"It's isolated."

"I like isolated."

"You haven't asked Dana if she wants to live up here."

"I don't have to. I know how she'll feel about it."

"It's like talking to a brick," Brad muttered. "Okay, if you're set on going through with this, at least take the I'm-a-big-sucker-with-a-lot-of-money sign off your ass."

"They're gods, son." Jordan parked, pushed open the door. "I don't think a poker face is going to make much difference."

"I don't know why you think they'll consider selling the place to you," Brad continued. "They only bought it a couple of months ago. Gods or not, there are the small matters of equity, taxes, capital gains."

"Listen to the suit." Flynn grinned as Moe leaped over him and out of the car.

"Shut up. You're in shock, remember? Takes a good thirty minutes to get down to the Valley from here," Brad continued.

"The way you drive, it does," Jordan muttered under his breath.

"I heard that. Thirty minutes," Brad repeated, "for a mature adult who has respect for the speed limit. And that's in good weather. Fine for you, you can stay home and write in your underwear. Dana's going to be running a business in town, six days a week."

"Six?" Jordan turned from studying the house. "How do you know they're planning on being open six days?"

"I got that from Zoe in between her sniping at me. The point is, she's going to have to travel down there most every day. And in the winter—"

"I'll buy her a four-wheel, a goddamn Humvee. Stop fretting, Mary."

"Just for that, I hope—if they're in the market for a buyer—they hose you."

Rowena opened the door and was already laughing as she bent down to greet Moe. "Welcome! How lovely. Three handsome men and a handsome dog."

"You call that dog handsome," Jordan commented. "It must be love."

"And so it is." She straightened, smiled brilliantly as she looked into Jordan's eyes. "So it is. Come in."

Moe didn't need a second invitation. He raced by her, skidded on the tiles, bumped into the archway on his turn into the parlor. When they caught up with him, he was curled into a chair, his chin resting on its velvet arm, his tail thumping.

"Hey! Off the furniture, you ingrate."

Even as Flynn moved over to haul him down, Moe's big brown eyes shifted to Rowena. His tail thumped harder.

"No, please. He's perfectly welcome to sit there. After all." She hurried over to intervene. "After all, he's a guest."

"He's an operator."

"Yes." She stroked one of his floppy ears. "And he . . . what's the phrase? He has my number. No harm. Now what can I offer you? Coffee, tea?" The corner of her lips twitched as she looked at Flynn. "Perhaps a cold beer."

"Did you read my mind or do I just look like a guy who wants a beer right now?"

"Perhaps a bit of both. Please, follow

Moe's lead, and sit. Be comfortable. I'll just be a moment."

"Is Pitte available?" Jordan asked.

"Certainly. I'll ask him to join us."

Brad waited until she'd left the room, then turned to Jordan. "Okay, I can't stand it. Don't just blurt out how you want this house and always have, or something lame-brained like that."

"Do I look like I just fell out of the nest?"

"Ever bought a house before?"

"No, but—"

"I have. You're a successful author with a string of bestsellers. They know you've got money. Add some sparkly childhood dream to that and you're just asking to get taken."

Jordan took a seat. "You know, I'm beginning to see why you irritate Zoe."

Brad looked down his nose. "I don't irritate her, I make her nervous. The irritation is merely a side effect of the nerves."

"Yeah, I'm starting to get it, too," Flynn put in, and flopped down in his chair, much like his dog. He perked up as Rowena came back, carrying a tray.

"Hey, let me give you a hand with that." Flynn pushed to his feet, took the tray that held five pilsners of beer.

"Thank you. Please, help yourselves. Pitte will be right along." She sat on the sofa, curled up her legs, and sent Flynn a silky smile when he offered her one of the glasses. "It's an important day."

He felt his stomach clutch when she looked at him. "Yeah. I guess it is."

"You're allowed to feel a bit off-center. It's human. Ah, here's Pitte."

"Good afternoon. Rowena tells me we've things to talk about." He sat on the sofa beside her, reached for a beer. "You're well?"

"Seem to be," Jordan answered. "Maybe I should start with what's happened."

He told them first of Kane's taking Dana back into their past.

"It's interesting." Pitte studied his beer, considered. "More straightforward than one expects from him."

"A method that matches his quarry," Rowena said. "Clever of him. He doesn't attempt to trick or deceive her. Rather he tells her precisely what he's doing, allows her to see, and still experience. Yes, it was a very good strategy."

"It might have worked. Nearly did. I don't think we'd be where we are, at least not now, if Malory hadn't given us both a push."

"The six of you are part of one whole. Vital and individual," Rowena added, "but stronger yet for your connection. How did you resolve this thing with Dana?"

"Do I have to tell you? I can just about see the little red hearts circling over my head myself."

"I'd still like to hear what you say, and how you say it."

As he complied, she nodded, slid her hand into Pitte's. "It's difficult," she said, "to know what to let go of, what to hold. I'm happy for you both, that you held each other."

"So am I, for purely personal reasons. But it plays into the rest, doesn't it?" Jordan watched her face, wished he could read it. "It's part of the quest."

"In a tapestry, every thread matters. The length, the texture, the hue. He wished to separate you; you didn't allow it. The thread between you is long, and rich, and strong."

"Why is it so important that he separate us?"

"You're more together than you are apart. You know that."

"It's not only that." He leaned forward. "Help me help her."

"You have. You will. I believe that."

"She's nearly out of time."

"You've come farther than you think, so be careful. He'll do whatever he can to break that thread."

Jordan sat back. "He won't break it. There's another reason I'm here. I'm starting to wonder if it's not part of the tapestry as well. I want to buy this house."

Brad made a strangled sound in his throat that had Pitte shooting him a dryly amused glance. "Would you care for some water?"

"No. No." With a sigh, Brad drank more beer. "No."

"The big businessman over there figures I should tap-dance around, and we'll play let's negotiate for an hour or two. I don't see the point. I don't know what your plans are for the place once this is all done, but if you're willing to sell, I'm ready to buy."

Why doesn't he just give them a blank check? Brad thought to himself. Access to his brokerage account, the deed to his condo in New York?

"Your business-minded friend has some excellent points." Sending Brad a nod of acknowledgment, Pitte swirled his beer.

"I've developed a number of business interests over time. I enjoy . . ." He gave Rowena a questioning glance.

"Wheeling and dealing."

"Yes. It's an entertaining hobby. This
property, beyond suiting our needs during
this period, is quite desirable. A house of
this size and material, with its history and its
location—which includes twenty-five point
three acres, both cleared and wooded, a
six-car garage, an indoor swimming pool,
with steam room and . . ."

"Whirlpool tub," Rowena supplied on a
bubble of laughter. "We quite enjoy the
whirlpool tub."

"Yes." He lifted her hand, nipped her
knuckles. "As well as a number of other details and amenities—"

"Please." Unable to hold back, Brad lifted
a hand. "This place is an enormous white
elephant. Amenities and history are one
thing, but it's twenty miles away from the
Valley—"

"Eighteen point six," Pitte corrected
blandly.

"On a narrow road that twists straight up
the mountain," Brad continued. "It's bound
to cost a fortune to heat and cool. You put it

on the market tomorrow, you'd be lucky to get a serious offer within the next decade."

Pitte stretched out his legs, crossed his ankles. It occurred to Jordan that this was the most relaxed he'd seen Pitte in the weeks of their acquaintance.

"I would enjoy doing business with you," he told Brad. "Perhaps, at some point, there will be an opportunity. I believe it would be very stimulating."

"Right now you're doing business with me," Jordan reminded him.

"Yes, that's true." Pitte's gaze shifted to Jordan.

"I have a question first." Rowena patted Pitte's arm to hold him off, then looked at Jordan. "Why do you want this house?"

"I've always wanted it."

Brad rolled his eyes toward heaven. "Have pity on him."

"The question is why."

"It . . . spoke to me. I don't mean that literally."

"No." Rowena nodded. "I understand you. Go on."

"When I was a kid, I would look up here and I'd think: That's my house. It's just waiting for me to grow up. I remember telling my mother that I was going to buy it for her one day, and she'd be able to stand up here, on the top of the world."

He shrugged. "When I was older, I would drive up here sometimes, look at the place and tell myself that one day I'd drive through the gates and walk right in the front door. It's beautiful, and it's strong, and it may be all the way up here, but it's part of what makes the Valley what it is. I couldn't give it to my mother. I want to give it to Dana. I want to build a life with her here, raise children with her here. I want to be able to look down at the Valley and know we're all a part of something solid and real and important."

"You can have the house."

The gleam in Pitte's eyes winked out. "Rowena!"

"For its appraised value," she continued, wagging a finger at her lover. "And not a penny more."

"You wound me, *a ghra.*"

"You won't charge him for the legal business of it, the settlement, the transfer, whatever it is. You will pay the fees and the . . . what are they called?" she asked Brad.

"Points." He had to swallow a laugh. "I think you mean points."

"Yes, all of that sort of business." She thought for a moment. "I think that's everything."

Pitte hissed out a breath. "Women are a trial to a man. Why don't I just wrap bows around the place and gift it to him?"

"Because he wouldn't accept." She leaned over to kiss Pitte's cheek while he scowled. "It's always been his," she said. "You know that as well as I."

"Be that as it may." He drummed his fingers on his knee. "You and I," he said to Jordan, "will work out the details of the thing without the female buzzing about."

"At your convenience."

"Shake hands on it, Pitte." Rowena gave him a nudge. "Shake hands on the terms just set."

"Bloody hell." He shoved himself to his feet, held out a hand. "Might as well do it, then, or she'll nag me hairless."

Jordan clasped Pitte's hand, felt a quick jolt. It might have been power, he mused, or simple frustration. It was hard to tell when you were closing a deal with a god. "Thank you."

"So you should thank me. Your friend over there will know I could turn considerably more than the appraised value in this current market."

"That handshake binding?" Brad wondered.

"It is."

"Without a full inspection of the property, I'd say you'd have gotten ten percent over appraisal. Minimum."

"More like fifteen." Though he'd been carefully silent during the transaction, Flynn spoke up now. "When you publish the local paper, you know these things. There's a hotelier who's tried to buy it up, turn it into a resort. He got close a couple of times," Flynn continued conversationally. "But something always screwed the deal. Bad luck for him."

Rowena met his quiet look, and smiled. "Indeed. Would you care to go through some of the house now, Jordan?"

Before he could open his mouth, Flynn tapped his watch. "We're running a little short on time."

"Ah, well. Soon, then." She took Jordan's hand as well, squeezed it once. "You must see more of it, and the views, of course, from the terraces and balcony and parapet."

"I'll look forward to it. I'll bring Dana and we'll . . ."

He trailed off, staring at her, the way she stood. Slim and quiet and somehow apart from the rest of them.

And he saw the woman standing on the parapet under a gleaming moon with her dark cloak billowing in the wind.

"It was you. All those years ago, I saw you."

"I saw you." She touched a hand, very gently, to his cheek. "A young, handsome boy, so troubled, so full of thoughts. I wondered when you'd remember me."

"Why did I see you? Why didn't they?"

"They didn't need to."

He wasn't sure what it all meant, and Rowena had left him wondering. What he needed, Jordan decided, as he let himself into Dana's apartment, was a little time to get his thoughts into some sort of order.

Maybe he should write them down, as he had with the sequence of events. He would sit down at Dana's computer and just let it flow.

But when he walked into the bedroom, he heard the shower running. He hadn't noticed her car parked out front, which meant, he concluded, that his mind was somewhere else. He poked into the bathroom to let her know he was there.

Her scream could have shattered brick when he tugged back the shower curtain.

With one hand over her heart, the other shoving at her dripping hair, she gasped for air. "Why don't you just make that squeaky violin music and finish the job?"

"Hey, it's not like I'm wearing a dress and carrying a knife. I just wanted to tell you I was here, so I wouldn't scare you when you came out."

"Yeah, better to scare me when I'm wet and naked and helpless."

He pursed his lips. She'd always looked good wet and naked. "Helpless?"

"Okay, maybe not helpless." She reached out, grabbed a fistful of his shirt. "Get in here, big guy."

"Tempting, very tempting, but I need to talk to you about some stuff, and we need to get to Flynn's."

"Talk later, hot, steamy sex now."

"It's really hard to argue with that." He toed off his shoes.

She waited until he stepped in behind her, then handed him the soap and an over-the-shoulder invitation. "Wash my back?"

"I can start there."

"Mmm. I'm going to get all . . . slippery and . . . slick and . . . That's not my back."

He slid his soapy hands over her butt. "It's behind you, so it counts." Bending his head, he skimmed his teeth over her shoulder. "You've got the most incredible body. Have I mentioned that before?"

"Maybe once or twice, but I don't mind redundancy under certain circumstances." She dipped her head back as his hands sleeked up her torso, slithered over her breasts. "Such as that."

"Then I'll risk repeating myself." He turned her around. "I love you." He laid his lips on hers. "I'm so in love with you."

With a sound of pleasure and joy, she hooked her arms around his neck, poured herself into him.

Water sluiced over them, and the steam billowed up. Flesh slid over flesh, and soapy hands glided to tease and arouse.

Lips rubbed and nibbled, then began to hunger.

Her heart was so full she wondered it didn't burst like light and rock the room. "It's different." She kissed his mouth, his throat, his mouth. "It's different now, knowing you love me." She fisted her hands in his hair to draw him back an inch. "It's different now, when I can tell you I love you."

"Then it's always going to be different, because I'm never going to stop."

Their mouths met again.

It was different. Every touch, every taste, every need was gilded with a sense of belonging. Water showered over them as he anchored her, as he slipped inside her. The beauty of it brought her a thousand sweet aches.

Hers now, he was hers now. And she was his.

She held tight, and matched him beat for beat.

Emotions swamped him, sensations drowned him, and all he could see was her. The dark eyes, the sleek hair, the strong mouth, and water streaming down her face like tears. She held him, body and heart. And, he realized, she always had.

He felt her tremble, heard her breath shudder and catch, then her eyes went beautiful and opaque as she came.

As she tightened around him, he pressed his mouth to hers again, and gave himself to her.

After, a long time after, they simply stood holding each other.

"This is good, Jordan. This is really good."

"Yeah."

"Even though the water's getting cold. I feel all lazy and sleepy. I wish we could slide into bed instead of getting dressed and going over to Flynn's."

"If you're too tired to go—"

"That's not it. I just want to lie around in bed with you."

He drew her back. "I can't argue with that either."

"But we're going to get dressed and go over to Flynn's because lying around in bed would be wrong." She kissed him lightly. "Jesus, the water *is* getting cold."

He reached behind her and switched it off. "We can go over, then leave early and come back and lie around in bed."

"Good plan." She stepped out of the

shower, grabbed a towel. "So, what's this mysterious mission you went on today?" She wrapped her hair in the towel, grabbed a second one.

He held out a hand, thinking it was for him, but she started drying her legs with it. He shook his head, got yet another towel for himself.

"We'll talk about it later."

"What's wrong with now?"

"Because we're in the bathroom, naked. It's just not the right place for it."

"That's silly. We've had naked conversations before. In fact, we've had some very interesting naked conversations. Where did you go, and why did you need Brad and Flynn along? Because I know they went with you. I have ways of getting that sort of information."

She grabbed a bottle of body cream and poured some into her hand.

"I'll tell you later. You'll appreciate the fact that we get into this in a more appropriate setting."

"See, now you're making me crazy." She slathered on cream. "Which forces me to grill you. You were gone for hours. Where did you go? What did you do?"

"We went to a titty bar and drank cheap booze while women with fascinating man-made breasts slid around on long, shiny poles."

"You think that'll irritate me and I'll leave you alone, but you're wrong." She took the towel off her head and finger-combed her hair. "Personally, I don't have a problem with guys going to strip clubs and making jackasses of themselves. So you might as well tell me the truth."

"Fine. Here and now, then." He picked up his pants, dug the jeweler's box out of the pocket. He held it out to her, flipped up the lid with his thumb.

"Oh, my Jesus Christ," she said and sat down heavily on the lid of the toilet.

"Yeah, that's romance. You like it or what?"

She had to swallow. "Depends."

"On what?" He scowled, turned the box around to study the ring. It looked great, he decided, but there was never any certainty with women. "I figured you'd like this better than the standard diamond. But if you'd rather go that route, I can exchange it."

She shivered, but she didn't feel cold.

Not in the least. "Then that would be an engagement ring you've got there."

"What the hell do you think it is? Would you stand up? This is just a little too bizarre."

"Sorry." She got to her feet. "I wasn't sure what it meant."

"It means marry me, Dana." He had to push his dripping hair back. "It means I love you, and I want to spend my life with you. I want to make children with you, and grow old with you."

She'd thought her heart was full, but it hadn't been. There was still room, so much room for him. "Oh, well, that clears things up nicely. It's a beautiful ring. It's the most beautiful ring I've ever seen. You were only wrong about one thing."

"What's that?"

"I don't mind the time and place, Jordan." She looked up at him now with a brilliant smile. "I don't mind it at all. In fact, if you would put that on my finger, I'd like it to be the only thing I'm wearing for the next few minutes." Holding out her hand, she took one quick, catchy breath. "I'd really love to wear that ring. I'd love to marry you, and all the rest of it, too."

He took it out, set the box aside, then lifted her left hand. "This is one more beginning for us."

"I'm looking forward to the rest of them."

He slipped the ring on her finger. There was a little buzz of heat, then a lovely spread of warmth where the gold circled her finger. "It's beautiful. It even fits."

"Yeah? None of us knew your ring size, so that's a bonus." He turned her hand, watched the stone sparkle. "It looks good on you."

She rose to her toes, took his mouth with hers. "You're so full of surprises."

"You've got that right. I might as well tell you the next one. I bought—or I'm buying—Warrior's Peak."

She blinked twice, very slowly. "Sorry. I thought you said you were buying the Peak."

"That's right. I want us to live there. I want us to make a family there."

"You . . ." Though her knees wobbled, she didn't give in and sit down again. "You're not going back to New York?"

"Of course I'm not going back to New York." Bafflement moved over his face. "How the hell am I supposed to be married to you and live in New York while you run a business in the Valley? Dana."

"I thought . . . It's where you live."

He cupped her chin, unsure if he was impatient or amused. "You think I'd ask you to move to New York, throw away your store before it even gets started? I was never planning to go back there to live anyway, but if I had been, this would've changed it."

"You weren't going back?"

"No. There was a time when I had to leave. This was the time when I had to come back. I need to be here. I need to be with you."

"I would've gone with you," she managed. "I want points for that."

"We're not going anywhere. If the Peak doesn't suit you, we'll—"

"You're just trying to get points back." Overcome, she laughed and threw her arms around him. "You know it suits me. God, this is fantastic. It's amazing. But please tell me that's the last surprise. My head's going to spin right off my shoulders."

"That's pretty much it for now."

"Let's get dressed, get over to Flynn's." She pressed her hands palm to palm and

stared at her ring. "I can't wait to tell everyone."

"Flynn and Brad already know."

"Men." She flicked them away with a
wave as she walked into the bedroom.
"They don't know anything. Boy, oh, boy,
wait until Malory and Zoe get a load of this
ring! I've got to find a really cool outfit to set
it off."

"I like the one you're wearing now."

She shot a look over her shoulder before
she dived into her closet. "See? Men don't
know anything."

Chapter Eighteen

When Moe dragged Flynn into the house, they heard the single, high-pitched scream. Moe bared his teeth, Flynn bared his, and they raced toward the kitchen prepared to taste blood.

Malory stood in the center of the room, her hands crossed over her heart, laughing like an idiot.

"Where is he? What did he do? Son of a bitch."

"Who?" Malory braced herself for Moe's leap of love but wasn't prepared to have Flynn lift her off her feet. "What?"

"You were screaming."

"Oh. Okay, Moe, down you go. Flynn, put me down. I'm fine, I'm perfectly fine." Other than the fact that she was flushed with embarrassment and trying not to giggle. "I thought I was alone."

Reaction set in and made Flynn short of breath. He dropped Malory back on her feet with a little thump as his arms started to tremble. "You stand in the kitchen and scream when you think you're alone?"

"Well, not usually. But look! Just look." She did a fast-time step, followed by a neat little pirouette.

Clueless, Flynn tried again. "You've realized you want to fulfill a childhood dream and become a dancing star of stage and screen?"

"No!" With a laugh, she whirled Flynn into a circle that had Moe leaping again. "Look. We have a floor. A wonderful, beautiful hardwood floor."

She executed what Flynn thought might be some sort of clog dance. "Sounds like wood, all right."

"No more ugly linoleum for us. And look at this!" She whirled away from him and embraced the glossy new side-by-side refrigerator with the passion of a woman greeting a lover returning from the war.

"Isn't it wonderful? And see how it matches this?"

While Flynn watched, she spun to the range.

"It's so beautiful." She crooned it now. "So shiny and clean. And everything works. I tried all the buttons and dials, and it works! I actually can't wait to cook something. I walked in, saw all this, and I just had to scream. They put in the floor, Flynn, and brought in the appliances. See the new microwave?"

"Very sexy."

"It *is*." Whirling into a dance again, she tried out a rhumba. "And we have pretty new cabinets with pretty glass fronts. I'm going to put pretty dishes in them, and sparkly glasses. It's a kitchen. An actual kitchen."

He was getting it now, and the charge of watching her revel. She'd switched from the rhumba to . . . he wasn't sure what. But she looked really cute. "What was it before?"

"There is no name for what it was before. I'm so happy. I'm so grateful. You're the most wonderful man in the world." She caught his face in her hands and kissed him. "And I'm a terrible person."

"Why? Not the 'I'm wonderful' part, because, hey. But why are you a terrible person?"

"Because I wouldn't move in with you before you did this. I made the kitchen a kind of exchange. Remodel the kitchen and I'll live with you. It was selfish. It worked," she added, raining kisses over his face. "But it was selfish. You're doing this for me. I know I said I wouldn't move in until it was finished, and I even made snarky comments about the lamps up in the bedroom."

"Something about not being fit to light a cave inhabited by bats and blind spiders."

"Yes, that was one of them. Anyway, forgive me?"

"Okay."

"I know it's not quite finished. There's still the counters and the backsplash and, oh, a few more things, but I don't want to wait anymore. I'll move in tomorrow, and we can start, officially, living together."

"I don't want to live together."

Her face went blank.

"What?"

"Sorry, Mal." He gave her shoulders a squeeze. "I don't want to live together."

"But . . . but you asked me to move in

with you weeks ago. You've asked me half a dozen times."

"Yeah, well." He shrugged. "I changed my mind."

"You—you changed your *mind*?"

"That's right." Casually, he opened the new refrigerator. "Wow. Look at all this room. And it is shiny."

She couldn't do anything but stare at him. Her stomach had dropped to her feet, and those feet no longer felt like dancing. "I don't understand. I don't understand how you could just change your mind about something like this, from one minute to the next."

"Me either. Actually, I don't think I really changed it, I think I just realized it wasn't what I wanted."

"You just realized you don't want me." There was too much shock, too much anger for the pain to fight through. So she rode on the shock and the anger and stepped forward to give him a hard shove. "Well, that's just fine."

"I didn't say I didn't want you. I said I didn't want to live together."

"You can take your new kitchen and stuff

it. If you can't handle a committed, adult relationship then you can't handle me."

"There you go, we're right on the same
page. Committed, adult relationship." He
pulled the box from his pocket, opened it.
"This adult enough for you?"

Her mouth dropped open, and he
thought she'd never looked more beautiful
as she stared down, dumbstruck, at the diamond ring.

"Let's be really grown-up, Malory. Let's
get married."

"You want to marry me?"

"I do. Look, I already know my lines." He
grinned at her. "You look a little pale. I'm
going to take that as a good sign. The jeweler said this was a classic, and Brad gave
it a thumbs-up." Flynn removed the ring
from the box. "Brilliant-cut solitaire, blah-
blah, whatever. You go for the classic look,
right?"

A latch kept trying to slam shut in her
throat, but she forced it open. "Yes, I do."

"There, you know your lines, too." He
took her limp hand, slipped the ring on before she could say another word. "It fits. I
didn't think it would, you've got such deli-

cate fingers, but it looks like we won't have to have it sized after all."

She felt the snap of heat, the spread of warmth from the gold circling her skin. Yes, it fit, she thought dreamily. It looked as if it had been made for her finger. "It's beautiful. It's absolutely beautiful."

"You could say yes now."

She looked up from the ring, into his eyes. "Life's going to be a roller coaster with you. I used to be afraid of roller coasters because you just never know what they're going to do next. They don't scare me anymore."

"Say yes. I'll get rid of the lamps."

On something between a sob and a laugh, she leaped into his arms. "Yes. You know it's yes, even with the ugly lamps."

"I love you."

"I love you, too." With her cheek pressed to his, she held up her ring hand and watched the diamond glitter. "How could the same man who bought this gorgeous ring have bought those hideous lamps?"

"The many sides of Flynn Hennessy."

"Lucky for me." She heard the front door open and moved nearly as fast as Moe. "Oh, they're coming. I have to show it off."

She pushed away from Flynn, then nipped back to kiss him again. "I have to show somebody."

She hurried toward the front of the house, even as Dana hurried toward the back with Zoe at her heels.

"What is it?" Zoe demanded.

"Have to show you both at once. Boy, have I got news for you," Dana said when Malory rushed toward her.

"Whatever it is, it can't top mine. I've got news for *you.*"

Zoe pushed between them. "Jeez, somebody tell somebody something before I explode."

"Me first," Dana and Malory said in unison, then both held out their left hands.

There were screams, followed by a burst of unintelligible words. At least they were unintelligible to the three men and a boy who looked on.

Simon watched his mother and her two friends jump and squeal like the girls did on the playground at school. Wrinkling his brow, he looked up at Brad.

"How come they do that?"

"It's just one of the many mysteries of life, kid."

"Girls are dopey." He clapped for the dog, who was blindly joining in the female ecstasy, and hunkered down for some wrestling.

Flynn looked past the women to Jordan. "Beer?" he asked.

"Beer," Jordan agreed, and skirted the madness to seek the relative sanity of the kitchen.

"I can't believe it!" Zoe gripped both Malory's and Dana's hands and bounced on her toes. "Engaged! You're both engaged. At the same time. It's like magic. The rings. They're so beautiful. Oh, boy." She dug into her pocket for a tissue.

"Sheesh. Mom, get a grip."

Zoe sent her son a glare. "I'll give you a grip."

He snorted, rolled with a delighted Moe. "Are we getting pizza, or what?"

"Why don't you go back in the kitchen and ask Flynn? Politely," she added as he scrambled up.

"I've got to show you the kitchen," Malory remembered. "But first." She grabbed Dana's hand again to admire the ruby. "It's gorgeous. So perfect for you."

"So's he. Wait until I tell you how he asked me."

"I can top it," Malory claimed.

"Were you naked?"

"No."

Dana licked a finger, swiped it down an imaginary scoreboard. "I win."

"Mom!" Simon shouted from the kitchen door. "The guys say if you all want pizza you have to say what kind, or else you have to take what you get."

"Tell you what." Zoe draped an arm around her friends' shoulders. "When we don't have a bunch of guys cluttering things up, you can tell me, and each other, every detail. We'll have a little celebration at Indulgence in the morning."

"Works for me," Dana agreed. "I'm starved, and I don't want a bunch of onions and mushrooms messing up my pie."

An hour later, Dana was polishing off her third piece. She stretched out on the floor beside Simon and Moe and said, "Ugh."

"On that note," Flynn began, "let's talk about finding this key."

"Simon, why don't you take your book

upstairs? That's all right, isn't it?" Zoe asked Flynn.

"Sure. He knows the way."

"You and Moe can hang out. I'll call you when it's time to go."

"How come we can't hang out here while you talk about the magic stuff?"

"Where do you get that?" Zoe demanded. "Simon, have you been eavesdropping?"

"Jeez, Mom." He sent her an insulted, sulky frown. "I don't have to go sneaking around, I just have to have ears." He pinched them between his fingers, wiggled them. "Hey, look! I've got two of them."

"We'll talk about your ears later. Upstairs, to that horrible prison with a TV and a dog. You can write a letter of complaint to your congressman tomorrow."

"Man." Though his lips twitched, he rolled his eyes for form, then they widened and focused on what Brad held in his hand. "Holy Cow! WWF Smackdown!"

"Maybe you want to borrow it, take it for a few rounds."

"Yeah? Smackdown! It really kicks—" He caught himself, swallowed back the word that would get him in serious hot water with his mother. "Really kicks," he amended. "Thanks."

"No problem. This way when we go *mano a mano* and I humiliate you, you won't be able to whine that you didn't get to practice."

"Yeah, sure, right." Simon took the video disk. "This is so way cool. Thanks."

He streaked off, hooking his book bag under one arm and calling for Moe.

Zoe folded her hands in her lap. "That was very nice of you."

"He may not think so when I trounce him in the upcoming match."

"I don't want you to feel obligated to—"

"I don't." Brad cut her off, coolly, firmly, then deliberately looked at Dana. "You want to get this rolling?"

"As long as I can start it from the supine position. As previously discussed, Jordan wrote up the sequence of events."

"He gave me a copy," Malory interrupted. "And I made copies for everyone. I'll go get them."

"She's something, isn't she?" Dana commented as Malory left the room. "Our own Debbie Detail. Since Mal's already read it, and the rest of you will, I'll just say that it puts everything into a comprehensive and cohesive form. It's helpful to see just how everything's unfolded to this point. Malory, Zoe, and I getting the invitation to Warrior's Peak, meeting there for the first time. Our first contact with Rowena and Pitte, and hearing the story of the Daughters of Glass. Though we didn't know they were called that until Flynn stepped in."

"There's the way Flynn met Malory, and became a part of the quest," Jordan continued. "The fact that each of you was at a crossroads, jobwise."

"We were in trouble, jobwise," Zoe corrected. "And that made the offer of twenty-five thousand dollars for agreeing to look for keys—keys I don't think any of us really believed in—that first night too tempting to pass up."

"It's more than that." Malory came back in and distributed manila envelopes, neatly labeled with names. "There was the financial incentive, yes. But there was also a sense of mutual frustration, of being in flux, not knowing what we were going to do next. And that almost instant connection between us. Jordan caught that, very clearly, in writing it out."

"Add to that how those tendrils spread out," Dana went on. "How they hooked Jordan and Brad in. Connecting them to us, to the quest, to Rowena and Pitte, and to the daughters. I think that's an important point. Each of us has a role, each of us has to be here for this thing to go through."

"Then there's Kane." Malory slid her copy out of the envelope. "The way you describe him, Jordan, it's so spooky—and so accurate. As if you'd seen him through my eyes."

"Seeing him through my own was enough. I think we need to look at him as more than the bogeyman, more than a foe. He's another element to the quest."

"I agree with that." Brad nodded. "He's as essential to this as the rest of us are. In the end, I think, it's not going to be just a matter of outwitting him, as Malory did, or twisting his game to our advantage, as Dana's done so far. It's going to be a matter of destroying him."

"How do you destroy a god?" Zoe demanded.

"I don't know, but first I'd say by believing you can do it."

"Maybe. But right now I'll settle for getting my hands on the key." Dana sat up. "I've only got a few more days. And here's what I know. While I may have to find it on my own, Jordan is essential to the search. Kane has tried to separate us or pull us apart, and it's not just because he doesn't want us to live happily ever after. What he did, however, was push us closer together. He's not going to be pleased by that."

She reached over, peeled a round of pepperoni off a slice of pizza and nibbled. "And he miscalculated by showing me the past. That was one of the steps I had to take, and might not have, at least not as decisively, if he hadn't thrown me back in time. Past, present, and future. I've resolved and accepted the past, I've made my peace with the present, and . . ."

She held up her ring hand. "I'm looking toward the future. This is important stuff, not only to me personally but to what I'm meant to do. One of the constants in those three time frames is Jordan."

"Thanks, Stretch."

"Don't get all puffed up. Some of this is just fate. Now if you read some of this stuff . . ." She plucked the copy out of Malory's hands. "You start to feel it, see it, even if you weren't part of that particular event. You get a good, clear picture. Here—that blue fog that took over Indulgence. The bone marrow chill of it, the oddness of the light, the color, the texture. You start to feel it creeping over your skin."

"Writer's tools," Jordan said.

"Yeah, and you're damn good with them."

"Excuse me?"

Mildly annoyed with the interruption, she glanced up to see him staring at her with a kind of narrowed intensity that brought heat to her face. "I said you were good. So what?"

"So . . . there's a first time for everything. Need another drink," he said and walked out of the room.

Dana shifted, then huffed out a breath. "Short break," she announced, and followed Jordan to the kitchen.

"What's the deal?"

He pulled a soda out of the refrigerator. "No deal." He popped the top, then shrugged. "You never—well, since I moved to New York, you've never had a good word to say about my work."

"I was pissed at you."

"Yeah, I get that." He started to take a

swig, then set it down. Truth, he thought again. No matter how it exposed him, there had to be truth between them.

"The thing is, Dana, it mattered. There's nobody's opinion I respect or value more when it comes to books than yours. So it mattered what you thought of my work."

"You want to know what I think of your work? My honest opinion?"

"Yeah, let's be honest."

"Well, you did buy me this really terrific ring, so I guess I should come clean." She took the soda, sipped, handed it back. "You have such an amazing talent. You have a gift, and it's obvious that you nurture and appreciate it. Every time I've read one of your books I've been astonished by your range, your scope, your skill with the language. Even when I hated you, Jordan, I was proud of you."

"How about that," he managed.

"I'm not sorry I swiped at it before. Maybe it made you work harder."

He had to grin at her. "Maybe it did."

"Are we okay now?"

"We're a lot better than okay."

"Then let's go back, because I haven't finished. And I'm going to be very interested in what you think of what I have to say next."

She walked back out to the living room, settled down on the floor again. "Okay," she said, raising her voice over the conversations. "Break's over. The point I was trying to make was that however skilled Jordan might be, this is more than a writer's point of view. It's more than a series of events entertainingly woven together in story form. When you read it, you start to see how often he's linked to one of those events, or is to one of the people involved in the event. In fact, he was the first, years ago, to see or feel anything, well, otherworldly about the Peak. He once thought he saw a ghost there."

She stopped, amused to see Malory pick up a highlighter from the crate and begin to mark the sections under discussion on Flynn's copy.

"Jordan was the first of us to see, and own, one of Rowena's paintings," Dana continued. "Flynn's my brother, Brad's my friend, but Jordan stepped up from being a kind of brother, from being a friend, to being my lover."

"He broke your heart." Malory meticulously coated typed words with bright yellow. "A shattering of innocence. Sorry," she said to Jordan, "but there's a very strong kind of magic in that."

"And it was Jordan's blood that Kane shed." Nodding at Malory, Dana smiled. "He's the one who left home—orphaned, alone, young, on a quest. And came back," she concluded, meeting Jordan's eyes, "to finish it."

"You think I have the key." Fascinated, Jordan sat back. "I follow the logic, and the traditional elements of your theory, Dane, but where? How? When?"

"I can't know everything. But it makes sense. It just plays through. I haven't hammered it all out yet. There's still that business about goddesses walking and waiting. Walking where? Waiting for what? Then there's that image I saw when I was trying to put myself into a trance."

Something started to click in his head, then shut off again at her last statement. "When you did what?"

"An experiment. Like meditation. Blank out the mind, that sort of thing, and see what formed. I saw the key, just sort of floating on this blue-green field. Probably my wall at Indulgence, as that's what I'd been staring at. It was like I could reach out and touch it. But I couldn't."

Frowning, she looked back, imagined it all again. "Then the field changed. White with these blurry black lines running across it. And I heard these words in my head."

"You heard voices?" Brad asked her.

"Not exactly. But I heard the words. Wait a minute, let me think, get it right. 'She walks the night, and is the night with all its . . . all its shadows and secrets. And when she weeps, she weeps for day.'

"So, doesn't it make sense that she's the goddess—whoever the hell she is? That's got to be one of the last pieces to put into place."

"I can put it in place," Jordan told her. "It's mine. I wrote that. *Phantom Watch*."

There was a moment of stunned silence, then everyone began talking at once.

"Hold it!" Brad got to his feet, held up his hands. "I said hold it! Let's not lose the thread. First, let's eliminate any coincidence. Dana, did you read the book?"

"Yes, but—"

"You did?"

She rolled her eyes at Jordan. "I'm not

going into another round of pumping your creative ego. Yeah, I read it, but it was years ago. Even I don't remember every line of every book I've ever read. I didn't recognize it when I heard it."

"I read it, too." Zoe raised her hand like a girl in a schoolroom, then, mortified, immediately lowered it. "It was great," she said to Jordan. "But the woman, the one you wrote about walking at night, wasn't a goddess. She was a ghost."

"Good point," Brad put in. "But it's an interesting touch that Jordan wrote that book about Warrior's Peak, that he created that ghost because he thought he saw her one night."

"You did?" Zoe asked. "That's so cool!"

"We went up there to camp. Brad and Flynn and I. Brad managed to . . . liberate some beer and cigarettes."

Now Zoe turned to Brad. "Is that so?"

"We were sixteen," he muttered.

"As if that makes it better."

"Scold him later," Dana demanded. "Let's pull this thread through."

"I saw her walking on the parapet," Jordan continued. "In the moonlight. Washed in light and shadows with her cloak streaming in a wind that wasn't there. I thought she was a ghost, and when I wrote her I drew her as one. Lonely, trapped in the night and weeping for the day. But she wasn't a ghost."

Dana laid a hand on his knee. "She was a goddess."

"She was Rowena. I understood that today, when I went to see them at the Peak. I didn't know what it meant until now."

"You were the first to see her," Dana said softly. "And you wrote of her, in whatever form. You gave her another kind of substance, another kind of world. She, the key holder. The key's in the book."

Her hand trembled as it slid into place for her. "The white field with black lines across. Words on a page. And the key melted into it. Into the page. The book." She sprang to her feet. "Flynn, you've got a copy."

"Yeah." He looked around the room. "I'm not exactly sure where. I haven't unpacked everything yet."

"Why should you? You've only lived here nearly two years. Well, find it," Dana demanded.

He gave her a weary look, then rose. "I'll go upstairs and look."

"I've got a copy at home," Zoe put in. "A paperback. I've got all your books, but my budget doesn't run to hard-covers," she said in apology.

Jordan reached over, yanked her hand to his lips. "You are the sweetest thing."

"I could go get it. I might be able to bring it back before Flynn finds his."

"Give him a little time." Malory glanced at the ceiling, imagining Flynn upstairs rummaging through boxes. "I've got a copy, too, and my place is closer if it comes to that." Then she stopped, lifted the index fingers on both hands. "What do you want to bet we all have copies of *Phantom Watch*?"

"Well, I certainly do," Jordan confirmed.

"And me," Brad agreed.

"Yeah. Clink, clink, clink," Dana said. "That's the sound of links fusing on the chain. Come on, Flynn, how hard can it be to find a book?"

"When's the last time you've been up in one of those spare rooms?" Malory asked.

"Good point." She began to pace. "It's in there. It's in there. I know it. I'll go up and find it myself."

She spun toward the doorway just as Flynn came jogging down the stairs.

"Got it. Hah. It was in a box labeled 'Books.' I didn't know I had a box labeled 'Books.' " He handed the book to Dana.

She ran her hand over it, hoping for some sort of sign, and studied the silhouette of Warrior's Peak brooding under a full moon. She opened it, fanned the pages, and smelled paper and dust.

"Where's the line, Jordan?"

"It's the end of the prologue."

She turned the first few pages, read the words in her head, spoke them out loud. Waited.

"I don't feel anything. I should feel something. Malory?"

"There was an awareness, a kind of knowing. It's hard to explain."

"But I'd know it if I felt it," Dana finished. "And I don't. Maybe I have to read it, get the whole picture. The way you had to paint the whole portrait before you could reach the key."

"I wonder . . ." Zoe hesitated. "Well, I just wonder if maybe it's not in that book, because that book's not yours. Jordan wrote it, so all the copies are his in a way. But only one is yours. And you're the key, so wouldn't it make more sense for it to have to be your own book?"

Dana stared at her, then grinned. "Zoe, that's absolutely brilliant. Okay, troops, saddle up. Let's move this to my place."

"I'll be right behind you." Zoe picked up her purse. "I'll just run Simon home and see if my neighbor will sit with him."

"Let me just get rid of these boxes. Zoe, I'm going to wrap up some of this leftover pizza for Simon."

Life, Dana decided, didn't stop. Not even for magic keys and wicked sorcerers. And wasn't that why it was life?

"Meet us there after you're done the domestic stuff." She grabbed Jordan's hand, headed for the door. "And you could wrap up some slices for me while you're at it."

Chapter Nineteen

"Did you read the book, or did you just say you read the book?" Jordan asked as they drove back to her apartment.

"Why would I just say I read it?"

"Beats me. But you said just the other day that you'd never been in a book before. So I figured you'd never read *Phantom Watch*."

"You lost me."

"Did you read the book?"

"Yes, damn it. I hated that book. It was so good, and I wanted it to suck. I wanted to be able to say, See, he's no big deal. But I couldn't. I was going to toss it out, even fantasized briefly about burning it."

"Jesus, you were pissed."

"Oh, brother, let me tell you. Of course, I couldn't burn a book. My librarian's soul would wither and die. I couldn't toss it out, either, for much the same reason. And I could never bring myself to turn it in at the used bookstore or just give it away."

"I haven't seen any of my books in your apartment."

"You wouldn't. They're camouflaged."

He took his eyes off the road to laugh at her. "Get out."

"I didn't want people seeing I had your books. I didn't want to see I had your books. But I had to have them."

"So you read *Phantom Watch,* but you didn't recognize Kate."

"Kate?" She reached back in her memory. "The heroine? Ah . . . good brain, a little arrogant about it. Strong-willed, self-reliant, content in her own company—which is why she took all those long walks and ended up with that fascination for the Peak—or the Watch, I should say."

She dug back a little deeper, let the image form. "Had a mouth on her. I admired that. A tendency toward crankiness, especially toward the hero, but you couldn't blame her. He asked for it. A small-town girl, and happy to stay that way. Worked in, what was it, this little antiquarian bookshop, which is what put her in the villain's cross-hairs."

"That's our girl."

"She had a healthy outlook toward sex, which I appreciated. Too many women in fiction are painted as either virgin or slut. She used her head, which was a good one, but it was that and a stubborn streak that got her in a jam."

"No bells ringing?" Jordan said after a moment.

"What bells? I don't . . ." A ripple of shock had her gaping at him. "Are you saying you based her on me?"

"Bits and pieces. A lot of bits and pieces. Jesus, Dana, she even had your eyes."

"My eyes are brown. Hers were . . . something poetic."

" 'The color of chocolate, both rich and bitter.' Or something like that."

"I'm not stubborn. I'm . . . confident in my decisions."

"Uh-huh." He pulled up outside her building.

"I'm not arrogant. I simply have little patience for narrow minds or supercilious behavior."

"Yep."

She shoved out of the car. "It's starting to come back to me now. This Kate could be a real pain in the ass."

"At times. It's what made her interesting and real and human. Especially since she could also be generous and kind. She had a great sense of humor, the kind of woman who could laugh at herself."

Scowling at him, she unlocked her door. "Maybe."

As they walked in, Jordan gave her a friendly pat on the butt. "I fell pretty hard for her. Of course, if I were to write her today—" He backed Dana against the door, braced his hands on either side of her head.

"Yes?"

"I wouldn't change a thing." He lowered his mouth to hers, slid into the kiss. "I was so sure you'd read it, see yourself and get in touch with me. When you didn't get in touch, I figured you'd never read it."

"Maybe I wasn't ready to see myself. But you can be sure I'm going to read it again. The fact is, it's the only one of your books I never reread."

With a half laugh, he eased back. "You reread my books?"

"I can actually see your head swelling, so I'm going to get out of the way before somebody gets hurt." She ducked under his arm, headed toward one of the bookshelves.

"To the woman I lost. To the woman I found. To the only woman I've loved. How fortunate for me that all three are one."

She looked back at him as she reached for a book. "What was that about?"

"It's the dedication I just wrote in my head for the book I'm working on now."

She dropped her hand. "God, Jordan, you're going to turn me into a puddle of mush. You never used to say things like that to me."

"I used to think things like that. I just didn't know how to say them."

"This is the one I read a piece of. The one about redemption. I'll look forward to reading the rest of it."

"I'll look forward to writing it for you."

He watched her remove a book from the shelf, slip off the outer dust jacket to reveal the one beneath.

" 'Phantom Watch,' " he read, " 'Jordan

Hawke.' Covered up by . . ." The laughter rolled out of him. " '*How to Exterminate Pests from Home and Garden.*' Good one, Stretch."

"Worked for me. I have another of yours under the cover of a novel titled *Dog-Eaters.* A surprisingly dull and bloodless book, despite the title. Then there's . . . Well, doesn't matter. Just variations on the theme."

"I get it."

"Tell you what." She covered his hand with hers. "After we're done, you and I will have a ritual unveiling, after which I will, with some ceremony, place your books in their rightful place on the shelves."

"Sounds good." He looked down at the book, then back at her. "Going to wait for the others?"

"I can't." She could see he hadn't expected her to wait. "I'm too wound up. And I think, I feel, that this is something we're supposed to do. You and me."

"Then let's do it."

As she had with Flynn's copy, she ran her fingers over the cover, over the illustration of the Peak.

But this time, she felt . . . something.

What had Malory called it? An awareness. Yes, Dana decided, exactly that. "This is it, Jordan," she whispered. "The key's in the book." Hands steady, she opened it.

Focus, she told herself. Concentrate. It was there. She only had to see it.

He watched her skim her fingers down the title page, the tips running lightly over his name. Her breath quickened.

"Dana."

"I feel it. It's warm. It's waiting. She's waiting."

She flipped pages gently, then let out a single shocked gasp as the book fell out of her hands. He called her name again and caught her as she collapsed.

Stunned, scared, he lowered her to the rug. She was breathing, he could feel her breathing, but she'd gone pale and cold as ice.

"Come back. Dana, damn it, you come back." On a spurt of panic, he shook her. Her head rolled limply to the side.

"Where did you take her, you son of a bitch?" He started to haul her up, and his gaze landed on the book that had fallen, open, on the floor. "Oh, my God."

He picked her up, clamping her against

him to warm her, to protect. He heard the voices out in the hall and fumbled the door open before Flynn could knock.

"Dana." Flynn grabbed for her, ran his hands over her face. "No!"

"He's got her," Jordan spat out. "The son of a bitch pulled her into the book. He's got her trapped in the goddamn book."

She felt him take her. He'd wanted her to, she'd known that immediately. He'd taken her with pain so she would be sure to know he could. He'd ripped the consciousness from her body as gleefully as an evil boy rips wings off flies.

After the pain, there was cold. Bitter, brutal cold that shot straight to the bones, seemed to turn them brittle and thin as glass.

She was torn from the warmth and the light and thrust into the cold and the pain, through the damp, hideous fingers of the blue mist. It seemed to wrap around her, binding arms and legs, strangling her until she wheezed for even one breath of that cold air, wheezed for another even though it was like inhaling iced blades.

Then even the mist was gone, and she lay shivering, alone in the dark.

Panic came first, made her want to curl up tight and whimper. But as she sucked in air, she tasted . . . pine, autumn. Forest. She pushed to her hands and knees and felt, yes, pine needles, fallen leaves, under her hands. And as the first edge of fear eased, she saw the sprinkle of moonlight coming through the trees.

It wasn't so cold now, she realized. No, it was more brisk than cold, the way it was meant to be on a clear fall night. She could hear the sounds of night birds, the long, long call of an owl, the hushed music of the wind soughing through the trees.

A little dazed, she braced a hand on the trunk of a tree, nearly wept with relief at the texture of the rough bark. It was so solid, so normal.

Fighting a wave of dizziness, she pulled herself to her feet, then leaned against the tree while her eyes adjusted to the dark.

She was alive, she told herself. She was all in one piece. A little light-headed, a little shaky, but whole. She had to find her way back home, and the only way to get there was to move.

Which way, that was the question. She decided to trust her instincts and move forward.

The shadows were so deep, it seemed she might stumble into one and fall forever. The light that struggled through the trees was silver, the dull tone of unpolished swords.

The thought passed through her mind, absently, that there were too many leaves on the trees for so late in October.

She stepped on a twig, and the sound of it snapping under her heel was like a gunshot that had her stumbling forward in reaction.

"All right, it's all right." Her own voice echoed back to her, had her pressing her lips together to prevent herself from speaking again.

She looked down to check her footing, then simply stared, puzzling over her shoes. She was wearing sturdy brown hiking boots, not the dressy black leather pumps that she'd pulled on for the evening.

She'd wanted to dress up because . . . The thought faded in and out of her mind until she bore down, grabbed it. She'd wanted to show off her ring. Yes, she'd

wanted to look fabulous to match her engagement ring.

But when she lifted her hand, she wore
no ring.

Her heart jumped, and every other terror
faded to nothing at the idea of losing Jordan's ring. She swung around, raced back
through the woods, trying to find the place
where she'd fallen.

Wakened?

And running, searching the ground for a
glint of gold, she heard the first sly rustle
behind her, felt the bright chill sprint up her
spine.

She'd been wrong. She wasn't alone.

She ran, but not in blind panic. She ran in
a headlong rush to escape and survive. She
heard him coming behind her, too arrogant
to hurry. Too sure he would win this race.

But he would lose, she promised herself.
He'd lose because she was not going to die
here.

Her breath whistling, she burst out of the
trees and into the shimmering light of a full
white moon.

It was the wrong moon. Part of her mind
registered that as she loped across the
grass. It shouldn't be full. It should be in its

last quarter, waning toward the new moon, and the end of her four weeks.

The end of her quest.

But here the moon was full, swimming in a black glass sky over the shadow of Warrior's Peak.

She slowed to a walk, pressed a hand to her side to ease a stitch.

There was no white flag with the emblem of a key flying from the tower. There were no lights gleaming gold against the windows. It would be empty now, she thought, but for the busy spiders and the skittering mice.

Because that was how Jordan had written it.

She was in the book, walking through the pages of his book.

"You've a very strong mind."

She whirled. Kane stood behind her, just at the edge of the woods.

"This is false. Just another fantasy."

"Is it? You know the power of the written word, the reality created on the pages. This is his world, and was real to him when he built it. I've only brought you here. I wondered if your mind would hold up to it, and I see it has. That pleases me."

"Why should you be pleased? I'm only that much closer to the key."

"Are you? I wonder, do you remember what happens next?"

"I know this wasn't in the book. You weren't in the book."

"A few changes." He lifted an arm, swept it out in an elegant gesture. "That will lead to a different ending. You can run if you like. I'll give you a sporting chance."

"You can't keep me here."

"Perhaps not. Perhaps you'll find your way out. Of course, if you leave, you lose." He took a step closer, held up a hand that dangled a long white scarf. "If you stay, you'll die. Your man made death in Phantom Watch."

He gestured toward the great house that Jordan had called the Watch in his novel. "How could he know it would be yours?"

She spun toward the Watch, and ran.

"We have to get her back." Helpless, Flynn rubbed Dana's cold hand between his. They'd laid her on the bed, tucked blankets around her.

"If this is what she's meant to do," Brad began, "she shouldn't have to do it alone."

"She's not going to be alone." Seeing only one choice, Jordan got to his feet. "We're not bringing her back. The contact, calling her, being here. None of it's bringing her back. Brad, I need you to go get Rowena. I need you to get her here, and fast."

"That'll take an hour." Zoe, standing at the foot of the bed, now moved to the side. "An hour's too long. Malory, Rowena came to us before. We have to try to make her come to us again. Dana's not supposed to be alone. That's what he does. He separates us, isolates us. We don't have to let him get away with it."

"We can try. We're strongest when we're together." Malory reached across the bed for Zoe's hand, kept her other clasped around Dana's. "We'll ask her to come."

"Not this time." Zoe's fingers tightened, and the light of battle shone in her eyes. "This time we tell her."

"How do they intend to order a god to make a house call?" Flynn said.

Brad laid a hand on his shoulder. "It's going to be all right, Flynn. We're going to get her back."

"She looks like the portrait." His throat burned as he stared down at his sister's face. Her white, empty face. "Like the daughter in your portrait. After . . ."

"We're going to get her back," Brad said more firmly. "Look, I'll head out right now, get up to the Peak. I'll bring Rowena or Pitte, or both of them back if I have to do it at gunpoint."

"That won't be necessary." Rowena stood in the doorway, with Pitte behind her.

Dana ran toward the house, fled toward it, hoping that the stone and glass would offer some kind of protection.

What happened in the book? What chapter had she fallen into? Were her actions her own will, she wondered, or written?

Think! she ordered herself. Think back and remember. Once she'd read a story, it became part of her. It was in her memory. She just had to clear away the fear and bring it back.

She was so scared. The screech of an owl had her heart pounding at the base of her throat. Fog was eating over the ground now, thin and white, just edged with blue. It thickened, seemed to boil around her feet until it was as if she waded through smoke.

It muffled the sound of her running footsteps. And his, she realized. God, and his.

If she could reach the house, just reach the house, she could find somewhere to hide until she caught her breath. She could find a weapon, defend herself.

For he meant to kill her, he meant to wrap that long white scarf around her neck and pull, pull while she struggled for air, while her eyes wheeled frantically in her head, while her veins burst with her blood.

Because he was mad, and she had seen the madness too late.

No. No. Those were Kate's thoughts. The thoughts of a fictional character in a fictional world. It wasn't a fictional killer who hunted her now. It was Kane.

If he could, he would take something more precious than her life. He'd take her soul.

At the last moment she veered away from the door. She remembered now, remembered this last chance and battle. Kate had wasted precious time battering against the wood, pounding on it and calling for help before she'd snapped back and accepted that there was no one to help.

Edit out that bit, Dana thought, and setting her teeth, she smashed her elbow through the window. She ignored the shock of pain from jagged glass scraping her arm as she reached in, flipped the latch. With a grunt she shoved the window up, leaped onto the ledge, and rolled inside.

She landed hard enough to hear her own bones rattle, and lay stunned, gasping against the pain as she struggled to see through this new layer of dark.

The air was stale and damp, and the heels of her hands skidded on dust as she pushed herself up. No glossy floor, no dripping chandeliers or stunning antiques. No fire roaring in the hearth.

Instead the room was dank and chill, with the gray spill of cobwebs and the breath of ghosts.

This wasn't the Peak of her world, but the Watch of Jordan's. She gained her feet, holding her throbbing right arm with her left, and limped across the room over boards that creaked and groaned.

Good job with the atmosphere, Hawke, she thought, fighting to steady herself.

Class A haunted house you built here. The perfect place for our plucky heroine to battle the homicidal maniac.

Wincing, she reached down and rubbed her tender knee. Kate had banged up her knee, Dana remembered, but it hadn't stopped her.

She drew a breath as she came to the entrance hall, saw the shadows facing off with the streams of moonlight that snuck through the grimy windows.

She liked nothing better than diving into a book, Dana reminded herself, but this was a little more than she'd bargained for.

She closed her eyes for a moment and took stock. She'd jammed her knee, jarred her shoulder, sliced up her arm some. She was scared, so scared it hurt to breathe.

But that was all right, that was allowed. She could be hurt, she could be scared. She wasn't allowed to panic, and she wasn't allowed to give up.

"We'll see who pulls this story out in the end, you bastard. This goddamn ex-librarian is going to kick your ass."

She heard the sly tinkle of glass being crushed underfoot and made a dash for the stairs. And the big climax.

*   *   *

"You came." Zoe released Malory's hand, reluctantly let go of Dana's. "Do something."

Rowena stepped forward, touched her fingers lightly to Dana's wrist as if checking her pulse. "What happened here?"

"You're the god," Flynn shot out. "You tell us. And you get her back. You get her back now."

Jordan nudged Flynn aside, stepped between them. "Why don't you know what happened?" he demanded of Rowena.

"He's capable of blocking certain actions from us."

"And you from him?"

"Yes, of course. He doesn't have her soul," she said, gently, to Flynn.

"Whatever he's got, get it back." Flynn shoved forward again, pushing Malory's hand away. He only flicked a cold, hard stare at Pitte when he moved to flank Rowena. "Do you think you worry me right now?"

"You waste time in your fear for your sister."

"She's cold. Her skin's like ice. She's barely breathing."

"He took her into the book," Jordan said and had Rowena's attention snapping to him.

"How do you know?"

"I know." He picked up the book he'd set on the night table. "She opened this and she was gone."

She took the book from him. "It's gone. The key is gone from here. It was not to be this way," she murmured. "He crosses too many lines, breaks too many pacts. Why is he not stopped? This is not temptation, intimidation, or even threat."

She turned to Pitte, and there was a spark of fear in her eyes. "He's changed the field, and somehow he's moved the key."

"It was in the book?" Jordan interrupted.

"Yes. Now, somehow, he's taken it into the story, and her with it. He should not be permitted to do so."

"She's alone in there. Whether it's the story or whether it's Kane, her life's in danger." Jordan gripped Dana's hand. "Bring her out."

"I can't bring out what he put in. It's beyond my power. He must release her, or she must free herself. I can warm her," she began.

"The hell with that." Jordan snatched the book back. "Send me in with her."

"That's not possible." She turned away from him to lean over Dana, to run her hands gently over Dana's face.

On an oath, Jordan grabbed her arm, spun her back to him. "Don't tell me it's not possible." He felt a jolt, a shock that sang straight up his arm to his shoulder, but he kept his grip firm.

"Take your hand off my woman," Pitte said very softly.

"What are you going to do, smite me? *My* woman's lying there helpless, going through Christ knows what, because she gave her word to you. And you'd stand here and do nothing?"

"He conjured this world he took her into. It's his power that holds there." In a rare sign of agitation, Rowena pushed at her hair. "There's no way of knowing what he's done there, or what would become of you if I attempted it. And I'm not permitted to take you beyond your own world. To do so would break the vow I took when I came into this place, when I was given charge of the keys."

"I conjured this world," Jordan tossed

back, and threw the book on the bed beside Dana. "That's my mind in there, my
words, and I've got a real problem with
some self-serving god threatening the
woman I love, and plagiarizing me to do it. I
don't care how many vows you break,
you're not leaving her in there alone. You're
sending me after her."

"I can't."

"Rowena." Taking her shoulders, Pitte
turned her to face him. "He has the right.
Listen," he insisted as she started to speak.
"A man shouldn't be stripped and bound
while his woman fights alone. It was Kane
who broke an oath, and doing so crossed
beyond all honor. He was not meant to take
her life. He was not meant to touch the key
by hand or mind or sorcery. It's a different
battle now. We fight on his terms or we
lose."

"My love." She curled her fingers around
his arms. "If I do this, even if I succeed, you
know what it may cost us."

"Can we live, in this prison, and do nothing?"

The sigh ached in her breast as she lowered her forehead to his heart. "I'll need
you."

"You'll have me. Always."

She nodded, drew a deep breath, then looked at Jordan with eyes that seemed to burn. "Be sure. If I do this thing, her life, yours, and all are at risk."

"Do it."

"Send us all." Zoe grabbed Dana's hand again. "Send all of us in. You said we're stronger together, and we are. We'll have a better chance of getting her back if we all go."

"Valiant warrior." Pitte smiled at her. "This is not for you. But if gods are willing, you'll have your turn."

"Give him a weapon," Brad demanded.

"He can take nothing with him but his mind. Lie beside her," Rowena told Jordan, then picked up the book. She closed her eyes, and it began to glow. "Ah, yes, I see. Take her hand."

"I've already got it."

Rowena opened her eyes. The blazing blue was nearly black against the pure white of her skin. Her hair seemed to lift in an unseen wind. "Are you ready?"

"Yeah, I'm ready."

"Bring her back." Flynn drew Malory

close to his side as he looked down at Jordan. "Bring her home."

"Count on it."

He felt that wind blow through him, fast and warm. He felt it whirl him through time, through space, through shimmery silver curtains that parted with a sound like the sea.

And he was standing in the moonstruck night, staring at the black peaks and towers of Phantom Watch.

He sprinted toward it, noting the smoking fog, the scream of an owl. A dog would bay at that fat, full moon, he remembered, and felt a curious satisfaction when the sound echoed through the air.

Last chapter, he realized, and confirmed it when he saw the broken window.

Time to do a little revising, he thought, and climbed through the shattered glass.

Chapter Twenty

"What can we do?" Malory held tight to Flynn. "There must be something we can do besides stand here and wait."

"Keep close," Pitte told her.

"Perhaps there's a bit more." Rowena sat on the side of the bed, with the book in her lap. "We've already broken our vow," she said to Pitte. "If there is punishment, it won't change if we do more."

"Watch, then." He ranged himself beside her. "But they deserve the chance to win this on their own. Read." He laid his hand on her shoulders and merged his power with hers. "So the others can watch as well."

She nodded and opened the book to the last chapter.

" 'She took the stairs at a limping run, and the fear was all around her, crowded close in the shadows of the Watch.' "

At the landing Dana started to veer right. There were dozens of rooms, hundreds of places to hide.

But for how long?

He would find her. The dark was no barrier for him.

Would he kill her? Could he? Kate had saved herself in the end, but she had fought a man, flesh and blood against flesh and blood.

How could she know how much of this was Kane's world and how much was Jordan's? Even, she realized, how much was her own creation brought on by bits and pieces she remembered from the book, spiked by her own fear?

At the sound below, she whirled to see the shadow of Kane and the long white scarf glowing faintly blue in the path of the moonlight.

And she saw the fog, now cold and blue, begin to crawl up the steps toward her.

"I'll find you, Kate." He crooned it. "I'll always find you."

The killer's words, she thought. She heard her answer spill out of her mouth without conscious thought. "I won't make it easy for you. It won't be like the others."

She pivoted on the landing and charged up the next flight of stairs.

She needed distance, she thought frantically. Enough distance to buy enough time to clear her mind. Fear was clouding it, making it harder for her to separate herself and her actions from the character's.

She batted madly at cobwebs, had to stifle a scream as they clung to her hair and face. But somehow the innately human disgust steadied her.

Find the truth in his lies, she remembered, as her breath began to puff out in thin vapors.

"I'm Dana!" she shouted. "I'm Dana Steele, you bastard from hell, and you're not going to win this one."

His laughter chased her down the wide corridor where doors swung open, slammed shut with bulletlike snaps. The mist was sneaking along the floor, added a hideous glow to the dark and curling ice around her feet. The sweat sliding down her back and temples went clammy with cold as she stumbled into a maze of hallways.

Breathless, she turned in circles. There were dozens of corridors now, and each seemed to stretch for miles like some mad dream.

He was changing the story, she realized. Adding his own flourishes to confuse her. And doing a damn good job.

"Choose." His voice whispered inside her head. "Choose unwisely, you might tumble off the edge of the world, or rush toward a pit of fire. But stand, only stand and yield, and all this will be no more than a dream."

"You lie."

"Run and risk your life. Surrender and save it."

"Choose," he said again, and she felt the hot silk of the scarf wrap around her throat.

Horrified, she clawed at it, raked her own skin with the frantic swipes of her nails. She was choking, fighting the illusion of the strangling cloth as the blood roared in her head like the sea.

Then suddenly she was free, and there was only the single corridor leading to the last staircase.

Tears leaked from her eyes as she ran for it, dragging herself up by the banister as her injured knee gave out under her.

She threw herself at the door, yanked at the knob with slippery hands. Her breath sobbed out of her burning lungs, scored her abused throat when she stumbled out into the silver light of the moon.

She was at the top of the Watch, high above the valley, where light glowed against the dark. People, she thought, were tucked away in those houses. Safe and warm. She knew them, and they her. Friends, family, a lover.

All so far away now, beyond her reach. Beyond her world.

She was alone, and there was no place left to run.

She slammed the door closed, scanned the stone parapet for something to brace against the door. If she could keep the killer on the other side until day broke . . .

No, not the killer. Kane. It was Kane.

She was Dana, Dana Steele, and what chased her was worse than a killer.

She pressed her back against the door, using her weight as a wedge. Then she saw she'd been wrong. She wasn't alone.

The cloaked figure walked in the shower of moonlight, one hand, with its glitter of rings, skimming along the low stone wall. Her cloak streamed out in a wind that made no sound.

The phantom of the Watch, she thought, and closed her eyes for a moment of peace. The ghost. Jordan's ghost.

"He's coming." She was amazed how calm she sounded with a vengeful god or mad killer behind her, and a spirit of the dead in front. "To kill me, or stop me, or take my soul. It all comes to the same thing in the end. I need help."

But the figure didn't turn. She only stood, looking down at the forest where two hundred years before, love had killed her.

"You're Jordan's. You're Jordan's creation, not Kane's. In the book you helped, and the acl set you free. Don't you want to be free?"

But the phantom said nothing.

"Kate's dialogue," Dana murmured. "I need Kate's words. What are they?"

As she dug for them, the door burst open, throwing her forward onto the stone.

"She can't help you." Kane ran the scarf

through his hands as he stepped out. "She's only a prop."

"It's all props." She scrambled backward like a crab. "It's all lies."

"Yet you bleed." He gestured toward her arm, her throat. "Is the pain a lie? Is your fear?" His smile spread as he came closer. "You've been a challenging opponent. You have a clever mind and a strong will. Clever enough, strong enough to have changed some small pieces of my picture. Imagining the stairs and the door to this place took considerable strength. Bringing her here"— he gestured toward the cloaked figure— "even more. I commend you."

Her mouth trembled open, then she shut it again. Had she imagined it, the route, the door? Had she willed the ghost into being?

No, no she didn't believe she had. She'd been circling in confusion.

Jordan. It was Jordan's book. And he was a man with a clever mind and a strong will. Somehow he was trying to help her. Damned if she was going to let him fail.

She was Dana, she reminded herself. And she was Kate—Jordan's Kate. Neither one of them would cower at the end.

"Maybe I'll just imagine you jumping off that wall to your bloody, messy death."

"Still hissing. A cornered cat. Perhaps I'll simply leave you here, deep inside a book. You should thank me, as books are one of your pleasures."

He inclined his head as she got to her feet, as he saw her wince of pain. "Or perhaps I'll step back and let the killer come onstage. It would be interesting to see you battle him, though in my version you may not triumph. Either way, it would be entertaining. Yes, I believe I'd enjoy the theater of it."

The white scarf vanished from his hands. "Do you remember how she hears him shambling up the steps, what she feels run through her when she understands that she's trapped?"

Dana's breath began to hitch once more as she heard the slow, oncoming footsteps.

He couldn't force her to do anything, she remembered. He could only trick her mind.

"How the fear clutched in her belly as she understood that she had run exactly where he'd wanted her to run? And below, her lover sees her standing in the light of the moon, sees the phantom beyond her, and the killer as he steps out onto the stone.

"And he calls her name, in terror and despair, as he knows he can never reach her in time."

"Sure he can. All it takes is a rewrite."

Kane whirled as Jordan leaped out of the doorway.

The force of the attack knocked Kane back against the wall.

"You have no place here!"

"This *is* my place." Putting all his rage into it, Jordan rammed his fist into Kane's face. It burned as if he'd shoved his hand into fire. Still, he reared back to do it again. And was lifted off his feet and flung backward.

"Die here, then."

A sword shot up from the hand Kane raised. Dana sprang to her feet, and charged him, sprang onto his back to fight with teeth and nails and spitting fury. She heard someone howling, and realized as her throat opened again, that the sound came from her.

Kane knocked her away with a vicious backhand that sent her slamming hard against Jordan. She saw blood on his face, from wounds that both she and Jordan had inflicted.

And her heart danced.

"You will know pain," she shot out at him.

His eyes gleamed black as he raised the sword. "And you, worse. Your blood will seal you here."

But as he swung down to strike, his hand was empty.

"Let's see if gods fly," Jordan said. Both he and Dana rushed forward.

Dana felt her shoving hands connect, then they passed through him as he vanished.

There was a swirl of smoke, a flash of dull blue light. Then nothing but the moon and shadows.

"Did I do that?" She had to wheeze out the words. "Or did you?"

"I don't know." He caught her when her legs gave way, and lowered them both to the stone floor. "I don't care. Jesus, you're bruised and bleeding. But I've got you." He wrapped her tight in his arms. "I've got you."

"Ditto." Undone, she buried her face against his chest. "How did you get here?

He didn't bring you. He wasn't expecting you."

"He's not the only god in the Valley these days." Lifting her head, he pressed his lips to her cheek, her temple. "We've got to find our way back, Dana. I don't mind being sucked into a story, but this is a little much."

"I'm open to suggestions." Hold on, she ordered herself. Hold on until it's finished. "This is just about the end of the story. Heroine grapples with bad guy, and with a little help from the ghost—who was no help at all, by the way—fights him off, sends him over the wall just as the hero bursts out to save her. Kiss, kiss, frantic explanations and declarations of love. Then they watch the phantom of the watch fade away, freed by her final act of humanity."

"You remembered that pretty well for somebody who read it six years ago." He helped her to her feet, then looked toward the end of the parapet. The cloaked figure stood, looking out at the forest.

"She's not fading."

"Maybe she needs a little more time." When she put weight on her knee, the pain brought tears to her eyes. "Ouch! Damn.

Maybe you could write in an ice pack for this knee."

"Wait." Fascinated, he stepped forward. "Rowena."

"Her name wasn't Rowena. It was . . . I can't quite remember, but it wasn't—" She broke off, her eyes widening as the cloaked woman turned and smiled at her. "Except it is Rowena."

"I couldn't send you alone. We wouldn't let him take your lives here. Will you finish your quest?" she asked Dana.

"I haven't come this far to toss it in now. I was about to—" She cut herself off again. "It's not in the book, not anymore. Not on the white page with the black words. It's here now. In the story, like we are."

"I've already done more than I'm permitted to do. I can only ask you: Will you finish your quest?"

"Yes, I'll finish it."

She vanished, not with smoke and light as Kane had, but as if she'd never been.

"What the hell do we do now?" Jordan asked. "Go back—somehow—to the beginning of the book and start looking? The lines you remembered were from the prologue."

"No, we don't have to go back. I need a minute first." She stepped to the wall, breathed deep. "Autumn smoke in the air," she chanted. "The way the moon, a perfect ball, is carved into the sky. Everything—the trees, the valley . . . look, you can just see the river, the way the moonlight glints off the water at the bend of it. It's all here, every detail."

"Yeah, nice view. Let's finish up and go look at it in our world."

"I like your book, Jordan. I don't want to live here, but it's a fascinating place to visit. It's exactly the way I pictured it. You write a hell of a story."

"Dana, I can't do this. I can't stand thinking about the way you're lying there back home. You're so pale, so cold. You look like—"

"Niniane, from Brad's portrait. One walks." She gestured to where Rowena had been. "One waits. That would be Niniane, or in reflection, I guess it's me." She turned, held out a hand. "I need the key, Jordan."

He stared at her. "Honey, if I had the key, I'd've given it to you long before this."

"You always had it. You just didn't know it. I'm the key, and you're mine. Write it for me, Jordan. Put it in my hand, and let's go home."

"All right." He tried to wrap his mind around it. Then he touched her face and let himself see. "She stood bathed in moonlight. Goddess and lover, with eyes deep and dark with truths. He might have been born loving her, he wasn't sure. But he knew, without question, that he would die loving her.

"She smiled," he continued as Dana's lips curved, "and held out her hand to him. It glittered in her palm, a small, simple thing. The key she'd searched for, fought for. It was old, but bright with promise. A slim bar of gold topped with a swirl of connecting circles in a symbol as old as time."

She felt the weight of it, and the shape against her palm. Closing her fist around it, she reached for him with her free hand. "It'll take us back," she said, "for the epilogue."

She opened her eyes, blinked at the sea of faces, then blinked at her brother. "Auntie Em."

"Oh, Christ. Dana." He grabbed her,

hauled her up against him, and rocked them both.

"Ouch." But she was laughing as he hugged her tight enough to crack ribs. "Take it easy. I've already got more than enough bumps and bruises."

"You're hurt? Where are you hurt?"

"If you can bear to let her go a moment, I'll tend her." Rowena touched Flynn's shoulder.

"I have the key."

"Yes, I know. Will you trust me with it for now?"

"You bet." Without hesitation, she put the key in Rowena's hand. Reaching back for Jordan, she grinned at her friends. "What a ride."

"You scared the hell out of us." Malory swallowed back tears. "Both of you."

"Your face is bruised. Her face is bruised," Zoe said, and moved in immediately. "Her arm's bleeding. Oh, her poor throat. Where are the bandages?"

"She won't need them, little mother," Pitte stated calmly.

"I cut my arm on some glass, breaking into the Peak, or the Watch, I should say. And my knee feels about the size of a watermelon. As scary and weird as the whole thing was, I have to admit, it was also very cool. I was . . ."

She trailed off, looking down in surprise at the knee that had throbbed until Rowena laid hands on it. "Wow, that feels good. Better than usual."

"Maybe so, but I bet you can still use this." Brad pushed a snifter into her hand. "I remembered where you keep the brandy," he told her, then leaned down and pressed his lips to hers. "Welcome back, baby."

"Good to be back." She downed a swallow of brandy, then passed the snifter to Jordan. "There's a lot to tell."

"Would you prefer to stay here and rest, or are you feeling well enough to come to the Peak tonight and use the key?"

Dana studied Rowena as the woman stroked her fingers over her bruised cheek. "You'd wait?"

"The choice is yours. It always has been."

"Well, I'm up for it." She glanced at the clock, nearly goggled. "Nine? How can it be only nine o'clock? I feel like I was out for days."

"Sixty-eight of the longest minutes of my

life," Flynn told her. "If you want to do this tonight, we'll go with you."

"I have to call the baby-sitter." Zoe flushed as all heads turned toward her. "I know that sounds silly considering, but—"

"There's nothing silly about making certain your child is safe and well tended." Rowena rose. "Pitte and I will take the key, and wait for you."

"If there's a problem with the sitter," Brad began, "I'll go stay with Simon. You should be with the others for this."

"Oh, well." Flustered, she backed out of the room. "I'm sure Mrs. Hanson won't mind staying a bit later. But thanks. I'll just go call."

"We'll start up as soon as Zoe's ready." Dana turned back to look at Rowena, but she and Pitte were gone. "Man, they sure do poof in and poof out, don't they?"

"They'd have saved us an hour's driving time round-trip if they'd poofed us with them." Jordan danced his fingers lightly over her cheek, down the column of her throat. The bruise and scrapes were gone. "You sure you're up to this?"

"Not only up for it, raring. We'll fill you guys in on everything when we get to the

Peak. I'll feel better once the key's in the lock."

In the portrait room they were served good, rich coffee and small sugary cakes while Dana and Jordan took turns filling in those sixty-eight minutes.

"You were so smart," Zoe commented. "I don't know how you kept your head."

"There were moments when I lost it. I'd get confused, or I'd get scared, or he'd change the plot on me. It helped a lot when I realized that Jordan was either there or manipulating things, too. Getting rid of that maze Kane had created, pointing me toward the right door, made a big difference."

"I didn't care for his editorial input." Jordan took her hand, kissed it just above the ruby. "And, in this case, I decided the hero should take a more active role in the denouement."

"No complaints here."

"Do you think you killed him?" Malory wanted to know. "When you pushed him over the wall of the parapet?"

"No, I don't think so. He went, you know."

Dana wagged a thumb toward Rowena and Pitte. "Poof."

"But we hurt him," Jordan put in. "And not just his pride. He felt it when I punched him, just like he felt it when Dana tried to rip his face off. He bled. If he can bleed, he can be killed."

"Not completely." Rings sparkled on Rowena's hands as she poured more coffee. "Death is different for us, and some part of what we are remains. In the trees, in the stones, in the earth or the water or wind."

"But he can be defeated," Jordan insisted. "He can be . . . vanquished."

"It could be done," she said quietly. "Perhaps it will be."

"He retreated." Brad lifted his coffee cup. "He ran because he wasn't prepared to take you both on at once."

"He might've done us both in with that sword he pulled out of thin air. I think we owe Rowena for that one," Dana said.

"He was not to shed mortal blood, not to take mortal life. It should never have been allowed. We don't know why it has been, but since it has, we'll do whatever we can to prevent him from doing so again."

"At what cost to you?" Brad wondered.

"The responsibility is ours," Pitte said simply. "As is the cost."

"You may not get back now, isn't that it?" He'd worked it out while trying to keep his mind off his own fears for his friends. "You broke your vow, so even if all three keys are found and used, even if the souls of the Daughters of Glass are freed, you may not be able to go back. You'll be trapped here, in this dimension. Forever."

"That's not fair." Seeing the truth of it on Rowena's face, Zoe stood up. "That's not justice. That's not right."

"Gods are not always just, and often far from fair." Touched by Zoe's defense, Rowena rose. "This was our choice. One might say our moment of truth. And now, will you finish yours?"

She held out a hand, offering the key to Dana.

Odd, Dana thought, that she was wobbly in the knees now. But she stood, walked to Rowena. "Whatever promise or rule you broke, you did it to save lives. If you're punished for that, if that's the way your world works, maybe you're better off in ours."

"There would be no lock if we had

guarded them more closely. They are the innocents, Dana, and they suffer because I was weak."

"How long do you have to pay for that?"

"As long as they do, and longer if that is the law. Take this and open the second lock. You'll give them hope, and give it to me as well."

Pitte lifted the glass box, dancing with blue lights, out of the chest. He placed the Box of Souls with great care on a table, then stood at one side, warrior-straight, while Rowena stood on the other.

Watching those lights, Dana felt her heart ache.

There were two locks left, and she slid the key into the first, felt the gold heat against her skin, watched light shoot along the bar, along her fingers as she turned her wrist.

She heard the quiet click, a kind of sigh, then saw the frantic leap of those three lights. With a flash, both key and lock melted away.

And there was one lock remaining on the glass prison.

Rowena stepped forward and kissed

Dana on each cheek. "Thank you, for your vision." Turning, she smiled at Zoe.

"Looks like I'm up." Because her cup rattled in her saucer, she set it aside.

"Will you come, all of you, at seven on the night before the new moon?"

"The night before the new moon?" Zoe repeated.

"Friday, seven o'clock," Brad supplied.

"Oh. Yes. Okay."

"Will you bring your son? I enjoy children, and I'd like to meet him."

"Simon? I don't want to take any chances with Simon."

"Neither do I," Rowena assured her. "I'd like to meet him, and do what I can to see him safe. Whatever I can do, I will do to see that no harm comes to him. I promise you this."

Zoe nodded. "He'll get a big kick out of this place. He's never seen anything like it."

"I look forward to it. Dana? Could I have a word with you, in private?"

"Sure."

Rowena stretched out a hand, and took Dana's to lead her out of the room.

"Did I ever tell you I like what you've done with the place?" Dana scanned the colorful mosaics on the floor, the silky walls, the gleaming furniture. "I especially like it now that I've seen what it could look like under less hospitable circumstances."

"It will be yours soon."

"Still hard to imagine that."

"I keep meaning to show you this particular room." Rowena stopped in front of a double pocket door, swept it open.

And ushered Dana into a book lover's version of heaven.

It was a two-level library, with a lovely ornate rail encircling the second level. A fire was snapping away in a hearth of rosy granite, its light, and the light from a dozen lamps, glittering on the polished wood of the floor.

High above, a mural was painted on the domed ceiling. She saw dozens of figures from the most romantic of faerie tales. Rapunzel, spilling her golden hair out of a tower, Sleeping Beauty just wakened by a kiss, Cinderella slipping her foot into a delicate glass slipper.

"It's incredible," Dana whispered. "Beyond incredible."

Wide, deep chairs, long, deep sofas were done in leather the color of good port.

There were other small treasures in tables, in rugs, in art, but Dana was dazzled by the books. Hundreds, perhaps thousands, of books.

"I knew you would enjoy it," Rowena said on a peal of laughter. "You look as though you're about to be well pleasured by a particularly skillful lover."

"You know, I have to be impressed by your being a god and all that sort of thing. But this goes way over the top. I bow to you."

Delighted, Rowena perched on the arm of a chair. "When Malory completed her quest, I offered her a gift of her choosing. Any boon that was in my power to grant. I offer you the same now."

"We made a deal. We both kept our part of it."

"So she said, or something close enough to the same. I gave her the portrait she'd painted while Kane held her. It seemed to please her. I'd like to offer you these books, all that's in this room. I hope that will please you when you're mistress of this place."

"*All* of them?"

"Yes, all," she said with another laugh. "And all inside this room. Will you accept?"

"You don't have to twist my arm. Thank you." She moved toward one of the shelves, then stopped herself. "No, if I get started, I won't get out of here for the next two or three years. I'll take very good care of them. I'll treasure this room," Dana told her. "And everything in it."

"I know you will. Now, let your man take you home. Let him cherish you tonight, as he wants to."

"I can do that. You already gave me a gift," she said as they walked out of the room. "You gave him back to me."

"You took him back. That's entirely different." She paused when they reached the door to the portrait room. "He's very handsome, your warrior."

"Yeah." She studied him, watched the way he turned his head, the way his eyes met hers, held hers while he slowly smiled.

"See that look there?" she murmured to Rowena. "That's the one that turns me to jelly. If he knew that, he'd use it on me every time he wanted his way."

What were you and Rowena grinning about when you came back in?" Jordan asked.

"That's our little secret." Instead of opening the car door, she walked past it, then turned to look back at the Peak. "It's going to be ours. I'm still trying to get my head around that. We're going to live here, Jordan."

He moved behind her, wrapped his arms around her waist and drew her to him. "We'll be happy here. The house wants happiness."

On a sigh, she tilted her head, pressed her lips to his cheek. "I'm already happy."

They drove away from the Peak, and neither saw the cloaked figure standing on the parapet under the thin light of the crescent moon.

She watched them go. She wished them well.

And turned when her warrior touched her shoulder. Pressing her cheek to his heart, she wept a little for what was, and for what might be.

COMING IN JANUARY . . .
THE SEARCH FOR THE THIRD KEY BEGINS.

The Key of Valor

TURN THE PAGE FOR A SNEAK PEEK
AT ZOE'S STORY

Back in the parlor, where they found coffee and wedges of apple pie thick enough to make even Simon's eyes bug out, Malory rubbed a comforting hand up and down Zoe's back. "Are you ready for this?"

"I've got to be, don't I?"

"You've got us all with you. We're a good team."

"The best. It's just that I thought I'd be prepared. I've had the most time to get prepared. I didn't think I'd be this scared."

"It was easiest for me."

"How can you say that?" Baffled, Zoe shook her head. "You went into this knowing almost nothing."

"Exactly. And you've got everything

we've learned and experienced in the last two months running around in your head." Her smile sympathetic, Malory gave Zoe's hand a squeeze. "Plenty of it's scary. And there's more. When we started this we weren't as involved. With each other, with Rowena and Pitte, with the daughters. Everything matters more now than it did two months ago."

Zoe let out a shaky breath. "You're not making me feel any better."

"I don't mean to. You've got a big load to carry, Zoe, and sometimes you're going to have to carry it yourself, no matter how much we want to take some of it off your hands."

Malory looked up, pleased to see Dana coming toward them.

"What's up?" Dana asked.

"A quick pep talk before we get started." Malory took Zoe's hand again. "Kane will try to hurt you. He'll try to trick you. In fact— and I've thought a lot about this—because this is the last round, win or lose all, he's going to be only more determined to stop you."

Dana took Zoe's other hand. "Feeling peppy yet?"

"I've thought a lot about it, too. I'm afraid of him." Zoe squared her shoulders. "I think you're telling me I should be afraid. That if I'm really going to be prepared, I should be afraid."

"That's exactly it."

"Then I guess I'm as ready as I'm going to get. I need to talk to Rowena before she takes us into the portrait room. I've got one stipulation before we move to the next stage."

She looked over, hissed under her breath as she saw Rowena already in deep discussion with Brad. "Why is he everywhere I want to be?"

"Good question." Dana gave her a quick pat on the back.

Malory waited until Zoe started across the room. "Dana? I'm scared, too."

"Well, that makes three of us."

Zoe stopped in front of Rowena, cleared her throat. "I'm sorry to interrupt. Rowena, I need to speak to you for a minute, before we get started on the next . . . thing."

"Of course. I imagine it concerns what Brad and I were just discussing."

"I don't think so. It's about Simon."

"Yes." In invitation, Rowena patted the

cushion beside her. "Exactly. Bradley's been very insistent that I do something tangible, something specific, about Simon."

"Kane's not going to touch the boy." There was steel, cold and immovable, in Brad's tone. "He's not going to use the boy. Simon is to be taken out of the mix. That's not negotiable."

"And you are setting terms now for Zoe, and her son?" Rowena asked.

"No." Zoe spoke quickly. "I can speak for myself, and for Simon. But thank you." She looked at Brad. "Thank you for thinking about Simon."

"I'm not just thinking about him, I'm making this crystal clear. You and Pitte want the third key," he said to Rowena. "You want Zoe to succeed. Kane wants her to fail. There were rules, you said, about causing harm to mortals, shedding their blood, taking their lives. He broke those rules last time, and would have killed Dana and Jordan if he could have. There's no reason to think he'll go back to fighting fair this time. In fact, there's every reason to believe he'll fight even dirtier."

The muscles around Zoe's heart seemed to clench, leaving her breathless. "He's not touching my boy. You have to promise. You have to guarantee it, or this ends now."

"New terms." Rowena lifted her eyebrows. "And ultimatums?"

"Let's put it this way." Before Zoe could speak again, Brad silenced her with one sharp look. "If you don't do something to remove Simon from the board, if you don't shield him from Kane, he could be used against Zoe and cause her to fail. You're close, Rowena. Too close to let one stipulation stand in your way."

"Well played, Bradley." Rowena patted his knee. "Simon has a formidable champion in you. And you," she said to Zoe. "But it's already been done."

"What?" Zoe looked across the room at Simon, who was sneaking Moe a bit of crust from his pie.

"He's under protection, the strongest I can make. It was done while he slept, the night Dana found the second key. Mother," she said gently, touching a hand to Zoe's cheek, "I would not ask you to risk your child, not even for the daughters of a god."

"He's safe, then." She closed her eyes against the sting of relieved tears. "Kane can't hurt him?"

"As safe as I can make him. Kane would have to go through me, and Pitte. I can promise you, such an attack would cost him dearly."

"But if he got through—"

"Then he'd come up against us," Brad put in. "All six of us—and a big dog. Flynn and I talked about it earlier. You should take Moe with you, keep him around the way Dana did. An early-warning system."

"Take Moe? Home?" That big, clumsy dog in her tiny little house? "I'd think you'd consult with me before you made such decisions."

"It's a suggestion, not a decision." He angled his head, and though his voice was mild again, his face was set. "It's just a sensible and reasonable suggestion. Besides, a kid Simon's age ought to have a dog around."

"When I think Simon's ready for a dog—"

"Now, now." Swallowing a laugh, Rowena patted Brad's knee again, and Zoe's. "Isn't it silly to argue when you're both only thinking of what's best for Simon?"

"Can we just do what comes next? I'm getting all twisted up waiting for it to be official."

"All right. Perhaps Simon could take Moe out for a walk around the grounds. He'll be watched," she assured Zoe. "He'll be safe."

"Okay."

"I'll arrange it. Then we'll move into the next room."

Zoe found herself sitting on the sofa with Brad, without Rowena as a buffer between them. She linked her hands in her lap as he picked up his coffee cup.

"I'm sorry if I sounded ungrateful and rude," she began. "I'm not. Not ungrateful."

"Just rude?"

"Maybe." Knowing she had been brought heat to her cheeks. "But I didn't mean to be. I'm not used to anybody—"

"Helping you?" he prompted. "Caring about you? About Simon?"

There was a bite in his voice, but there was something both careless and cool about it that made her feel small. She countered it by shifting and looking him dead in the eyes. "That's right, I'm not. Nobody helped me raise him, or feed him, or love him. Nobody helped me put a roof over his head. I've done it myself, and I've done a decent job of it."

"You haven't done a decent job of it," he

corrected. "You've done an extraordinary
job of it. So what? That means you have to
slap away every helping hand?"

"No. No, it doesn't. You get me so mixed
up."

"Well, that's a start." He took her hand,
and had it to his lips before she could
protest. "For luck."

"Oh. Thanks." She got quickly to her feet
when Rowena came back into the room.

"If everyone's ready, we'd like to continue
the tradition of beginning the quest in the
next room."

Brad kept his attention on Zoe. She was
a little pale, but she was holding her own.
Still, as they started down the wide hallway,
he noted how Malory and Dana moved in to
flank her.

They'd become a team, a triad, even a
family over the last two months. He didn't
think anything would change that now. They
would need that unity through what was
coming.

His heart took a bump when he stepped
into the next room and looked up at the
portrait that dominated it.

The Daughters of Glass, moments before
their souls were stolen, gathered close. Just

as the three women who shared the faces of those tragic demigoddesses now gathered close.

Venora, with Malory's vivid blue eyes, sat with a lap harp in her hands and a smile just blooming across her face. Niniane, with Dana's strong features and dense brown hair, sat beside her on a marble bench and held a scroll and quill.

Standing, a sword at her side and a small puppy in the crook of her arm, Kyna looked back at him. Her hair was a long fall of inky black rather that the short, sharp, sexy style Zoe wore. But the eyes, those long, topaz eyes, were the same.

They pulled at him, as if they'd dug hooks into his heart.

The three daughters radiated beauty, joy, innocence, in a world sumptuous with color and light. Yet, a closer look showed the hints of darkness to come.

In the thick green forest was the shadowy shape of a man. Just slithering onto the bright tiles was the sinuous figure of a snake.

In the corner, the sky was bruised with a brewing storm that the daughters were yet unaware of. And the lovers who embraced in the background were too wrapped up in each other to sense the danger edging close to their charges.

To look closer yet was to see the three keys worked cleverly into the painting. One, disguised in the shape of a bird, seemed to fly through the cerulean sky. Another hid itself within the lush green leaves of the forest. And the third reflected deep in the pool behind the daughters who were sharing their last moment of peace and innocence.

He'd seen how they'd looked after the spell. White and still as death in the crystal coffins as Rowena had painted them.

He'd bought that painting, titled *After the Spell,* months before he'd even come back to the Valley or known of this quest and these women. Been compelled to buy it, he thought now, as he'd fallen in love, or into fascination or obsession—he wished to God he knew—with Zoe's face.

"Two keys are found," Rowena began. "Two locks are opened. Now there is but one." She moved to stand under the portrait as she spoke, with the fire snapping gold and red flames behind her.

"You agreed to this quest because you were curious, and you were each at a point where aspects of your life were unsettled and dissatisfying. And," she added, "because you were paid. But you've continued to quest because you're strong and you're true. No one else, not in three millennia, has come so far."

"You've learned the power of art," Pitte continued, and stepped over to join Rowena. "And the power of truth. The first two journeys bring you to the third."

"You have each other," she said to the women. "And you have your men. Together you make a chain. You must not let him break it." She stepped forward and spoke to Zoe as if they were alone in the room. "It is for you now. It was always for you to finish."

"For me?" Panic wanted to gush into her throat. "If that's true, why did we pick before? With Mal and Dana?"

"There must always be choice. Fate is the door, but you choose to walk through or turn away. Will you walk through?"

Zoe looked up at the portrait, and nodded.

"Then I'll give you your map, your clue to the key, and pray that it guides you." She walked over and took up a scroll.

"Beauty and truth," she read, "are lost without the courage to hold them. But one pair of hands can grip too hard, so that the precious slips through the fingers. Loss and pain, sorrow and will, blaze the rough path through the forest. Along the journey there is blood, and there is the death of innocence and the ghosts of what might have been.

"Each time the path forks, it is faith that chooses the way or doubt that blocks it. Is it despair, or will it be joy? Can there be fulfillment without risk of loss? Will it be an end, or a beginning? Will you move into the light, or return to the dark?

"There is one who stands on either side, with hands held out. Will you take one, the other, or close your hands in fists to hold what is already yours until it's ground to dust?

"Fear hunts, and its arrow strikes heart, mind, belly. Without tending, wounds fester, and scars too long ignored harden into shields that block the eyes from what needs most to be seen.

"Where does the goddess stand, her sword in hand, willing to fight each battle in its time? Willing, too, to lay down the sword when the time comes for peace. Find her, know her power, her faith, and her valiant heart. For when you look on her at last, you will have the key to free her. And you will find it on a path where no door will ever be locked against you."

"Oh, boy." Zoe pressed a hand to her stomach. "I can keep the paper, right? I'm never going to remember all that."

"Of course."

"Good." She worked hard to keep her voice calm and even. "It sounded a little . . ."

"Violent," Dana put in.

"Yeah, that." Zoe felt better, considerably, when Dana's hand came to rest on her shoulder. "But, it seemed, compared to the others, that my clue was more a lot of questions."

Rowena held out the scroll. "Answer them," she said simply.

Famous Horses

AND THEIR PEOPLE

Zachary Taylor on Old Whitey

Famous Horses

AND THEIR PEOPLE

EDNA H. EVANS

The Stephen Greene Press

BRATTLEBORO, VERMONT

The publisher is indebted to *Western Horseman* Magazine for the frontispiece picture of Zachary Taylor on Old Whitey; to Jeanne Mellin for her painting of Justin Morgan on page 51; to the University of Kansas for the photograph of Comanche on page 96; to the Keeneland Library for the photograph of Will Harbut and Man o' War by J. C. Meadows on page 132; and to the Museum of Modern Art Film Archive for the photographs of William Hart and Fritz on page 142 and of Tom Mix and Tony on page 150. The remaining pictures of Pegasus and Bellerophon, Alexander the Great on Bucephalus, Hernando Cortés and Warhorse in Armor, Napoleon on Marengo, Wellington on Copenhagen, Robert E. Lee and Traveller, Philip Sheridan and Rienzi, and Buffalo Bill on Charlie are courtesy of Culver Picture Service.

This book has been produced in the United States of America: designed by R. L. Dothard Associates, composed by American Book–Stratford Press, Inc., printed and bound by Colonial Press. It is published by the Stephen Greene Press, Brattleboro, Vermont 05301.

Evans, Edna Hoffman, 1913–
  Famous horses and their people.
  Bibliography: p. 176
  1. Horses. 2. Statesmen—Biography. 3. Horsemen—Biography. I. Title.
SF285.E93   636.1   74–31238
ISBN 0–8289–0231–3

        75 76 77 78 79 9 8 7 6 5 4 3 2

For my dad, George P. Hoffman

Contents

List of Illustrations

Author's Note

HORSES AND PEOPLE have been associated for thousands of years. No one knows when the first man tamed the first wild horse nor where. But it did happen and the effects have been historic. People can live without horses and horses can live without people, but as partners they have accomplished great things.

Horses have worked with people, have fought with them, have carried their burdens, have taken them on explorations and hunting expeditions, have raced for their entertainment, and have given them companionship. It has been a fine partnership, beginning with the dawn of history and continuing into the age of space.

Some people have owned one or many horses and have become famous because of this. Some horses have become famous because of their own particular abilities. In either case, fame has fallen to an individual person or an individual horse. In rarer cases one person and one horse have been so closely associated that the story of one is not complete without the story of the other. Notwithstanding the many horses that have lived, and the many people who have been associated with horses over the centuries, there are only a few whose names

1

have survived as a team. This book is an attempt to tell at least some of their stories.

Except for Pegasus the winged horse and Bellerophon his rider, who were the creations of ancient Greek mythology, the horses and people chronicled in this book were real. Some of the deeds, told and retold by poets and storytellers, have been preserved in literature. In more recent times, historians, professional writers, and even the participants themselves, have kept the record. But in each case, there was a real horse and a real person as springboard for each of the stories. For the places from which these stories have come, see the "Sources" section at the end of this book.

These are the stories of real horses and real people who, together, have become famous. I hope you enjoy them.

Edna H. Evans

Pegasus { *THE HERO'S HORSE*

A HORSE WITH WINGS, a horse that could gallop across the sky—what an exciting idea! The ancient Greeks, lovers of both horses and the heavens, were the first people to imagine such a glorious creature.

Pegasus, the winged horse they imagined, and Bellerophon, the hero who rode him, have never been forgotten. Although their creation was more than three thousand years ago, they are still as young and virile as on the day of their birth.

———

Some early Greeks believed that Pegasus was created by the sea god Poseidon in a contest with Athena, the goddess of wisdom. The two were vying to see who could give mankind the greatest gift. As her entry, Athena created the olive tree and the contest judges decided in Athena's favor. Although the judges agreed that Poseidon's horse was an important gift, they said that a man could walk on his own feet, whereas Athena's olive tree offered man food, olive oil and shelter—neces-

3

sities he could not provide for himself. So, while the Greeks thanked Poseidon for his gift, the city of Athens was named for Athena in honor of her victory.

In another story according to Greek mythology, Pegasus was the son of Poseidon, with his mother the once beautiful Medusa.

Medusa, because of certain misdeeds, had been transformed into a horrible monster with writhing snakes for hair. She was so hideous to look at, the story goes, that anyone who saw her was instantly turned to stone. Because Medusa had become such a dreaded creature, the king sent the hero Perseus to destroy her. It was a dangerous assignment as it was fully expected that Perseus would also be turned to stone as others before him had been.

The messenger god Mercury loaned the young hero his winged cap and sandals; Athena gave him her bright shield and a curved sword. And, by flying above Medusa and using Athena's shield as a mirror, to avoid looking directly at the frightful monster, Perseus was able to cut off Medusa's head with no harm to himself.

When Medusa's blood fell into the sea, the story continues, the winged horse Pegasus was created. Then, while Perseus was busy putting Medusa's head into a leather pouch, Pegasus spread his wings and flew away.

Since a flying horse, as any other, needs a stall and someone to feed him, Pegasus flew up to Olympus, the home of the gods, and found shelter in the stables of Zeus, king of the gods. There Zeus used Pegasus to carry thunderbolts—Zeus's most important weapon—from the forge of the giants who made them to a storehouse in the royal palace.

When he was not working for Zeus, the winged horse

spent a great deal of time on Mount Helicon where he was petted and trained by the goddess Athena. Once, when he was thirsty, Pegasus stamped on the ground with his hoofs and a clear spring of water gushed out. The spring was named Hippocrene, or horse fountain, and anyone who drank from it was instantly inspired to compose and recite poetry.

For a time, the myth continues, Pegasus also had a human master, a young hero named Bellerophon. Like the hero Perseus before him, Bellerophon was given a difficult task to do. He was to kill the much feared Chimaera, a fire-breathing monster with a lion's head, a goat's body and a snake tail.

Bellerophon knew he could not fight such a monster single-handed. He decided to appeal to the goddess Athena and went to her temple to pray for help. That night the goddess appeared to him in a dream and told him how to catch the winged horse which he would need for his dangerous mission. She also gave him a golden bridle and bit which he found lying beside him when he awoke from his dream.

Following Athena's advice, in his search for Pegasus, Bellerophon went to the well of Peirene, a place the winged horse often visited. There he waited patiently until a rush of wings and the sound of flying hoofs told him that the winged horse had arrived. Then, when the horse lowered his head to take a drink, Bellerophon stepped up close to him.

"Ho, Pegasus," he said. "Steady there, fellow."

The winged horse was not startled. He let Bellerophon pat him and rub his ears. Soon the young man slipped the golden bridle over Pegasus's head and the bit between his teeth. The winged horse did not object.

"Steady, Pegasus," Bellerophon repeated.

He took the reins in his left hand and grasped the horse's mane just behind the ears. Then, with his other hand on the withers, Bellerophon bounded onto Pegasus's back. When he was seated securely between the wings that sprouted from Pegasus's shoulders, Bellerophon swung a heel into the horse's side.

"Up, Pegasus," he said. "Let's go!"

The horse sprang into the air and, with his wings beating strongly, galloped off through the clouds. Bellerophon hung on, thrilled by the ride but a little afraid to look down at the earth so far below. After a while, Bellerophon felt at ease on Pegasus's back; he patted the horse's neck and spoke to him softly.

"Now, Pegasus, let's go back to earth."

Using the reins to guide him, Bellerophon turned the horse's head toward a familiar meadow. The winged horse responded and soon they were on firm ground once more, close to Bellerophon's home.

"Good boy," the young Greek said happily, giving the horse an affectionate pat. "Tomorrow we will go after that Chimaera."

The next morning they flew to the place where the monster lived. When it saw them, the Chimaera snorted smoke and fire wildly and lashed its snake tail. Bellerophon shot arrows at it from the flying horse's back, and as Pegasus swooped in closely, Bellerophon killed it with his spear. The Chimaera's fire suddenly went out and the monster collapsed in a heap of smouldering ashes.

As a reward for this deed, the king allowed Bellerophon to marry his daughter. He gave the young couple a palace to live in and presented Bellerophon with many honors. Pegasus had a special stall in the royal stables and helped his master fight many other monsters as well as pirates and the Amazons.

As time went on Bellerophon grew bored with doing good deeds and performing services for mankind. He also became proud and overconfident. One day, in a hasty moment, he sprang upon Pegasus's back and gave a dangerous command.

"Carry me up to Olympus, Pegasus," he said. "I'm tired of the people on earth. I want to visit the gods."

Pegasus whinnied a warning but Bellerophon paid no heed. He turned the horse's head upward and Pegasus obeyed. The winged horse knew the way.

Zeus, king of the gods, was surprised to see Bellerophon and Pegasus galloping upwards toward Olympus through the clouds.

"That young man can't come up here," he said indignantly. "Mortals are not allowed in Olympus."

And as Pegasus flew closer, Zeus sent a gadfly buzzing down through the air. It landed on Pegasus's back, close to his tail and gave the winged horse a mighty sting. Pegasus snorted in pain and kicked out wildly with his hind legs.

Startled by this sudden move, Bellerophon lost his balance and fell from the horse's back. It was a long way to earth and Bellerophon landed so hard he was crippled for the rest of his life. The Greeks believed that this was his punishment for trying to invade the privacy of the gods.

Pegasus, for his part, flew on and, with no one to guide him, finally returned to his former pasture on

Mount Helicon. There he became the pet of the Muses,
nine beautiful goddesses who presided over the arts.
Somehow it was fitting: a winged horse seemed just the
right pet for them.

As the years passed, Pegasus became known as the
poets' horse and whenever a poet wished to embark on
a flight of fancy he said he would mount the winged
horse and fly away.

———

There was, of course, no such creature as a winged
horse but to the ancient Greeks a horse was the symbol of beauty, grace and perfect motion, and Pegasus
the winged horse was the free airy creature that all
horses should be. To them, he was real and so was the
hero Bellerophon.

Bucephalus { *THE CONQUEROR'S HORSE*

THE YEAR WAS 343 B.C. and it was the time of the annual horse fair in the Greek kingdom of Macedonia. Traders had come from many lands, and there were many buyers. The field was crowded with men and horses. Philip, the king of Macedonia, was among them. He was anxious to buy a new warhorse to replace one recently killed in battle.

The great black horse was beautiful. His neck arched with pride and his hoofs stamped the ground impatiently. His mane and tail were long and flowing; his glossy coat shone like satin. Every hair of his coat was black except for a white blaze on his forehead. This mark was triangular; the point was toward his nose and the other two corners turned up, giving the white patch a look vaguely like the head of an ox.

The black horse was indeed beautiful—but his nostrils flared, his eyes rolled, and his ears were laid back. He kicked and snapped viciously at his grooms as they lead him across the field. Any discriminating horseman would say he was too wild, too nervous, and too mean

Alexander the Great on Bucephalus

to be worth the high price the horse dealer was asking
for him.

The trader had already written King Philip a letter
describing the horse's merits. He had written about his
beauty, his strength, his spirit—but had not added that
the horse was mean and unruly. Now, as the horse
fought against the grooms who were showing it, King
Philip could see for himself how vicious it was. A good
warhorse must obey its rider; in battle a soldier cannot
fight against his horse and an enemy at the same time.
King Philip shook his head and the grooms started to
lead the horse away.

"There goes the best horse on the field," a boy's voice
said loudly. "He deserves a better showing and a better
decision than he's getting." At that, the crowd of
traders and buyers grew quiet. People did not speak
out in criticism of King Philip's actions in such fashion.

"All it takes is someone with enough courage and
skill to manage him," the boy continued, his voice
sounding louder than ever in the silence.

King Philip knew the voice. It belonged to his young
son Alexander. Although only thirteen years old, Alexander had already killed a dangerous wild boar and
had taken part in a small skirmish with enemy raiders.
But even so, a king's son did not usually criticize the
king.

Philip of Macedonia looked squarely at his son. It
was quite a confrontation. The king was black haired
and black bearded; his skin was burned dark by the
sun and scarred with the wounds of many battles. Alexander was fair skinned and his hair was red-gold; in
looks he resembled his mother, but in pride and
strength of will he was like his father.

"That's the best horse on the field," Alexander repeated. "The men don't know how to handle him. They're afraid."

"I suppose you could do better," the king said evenly.

"Yes," the boy answered. "He is a fine horse and I could ride him."

"Will you bet on that?" the king asked scornfully. "The trader has set a high price—thirteen talents. If you can ride him, I will buy him for you. What will you pay if you fail?"

"I will pay for the horse," Alexander answered firmly.

The crowd, which had stood silent during the conversation between father and son, began to murmur. Men who knew horses agreed that the horse was good, but could the boy manage him? A wager of thirteen talents was a big one, even for a king's son. A talent was a large sum of money, equivalent to several thousand dollars.

King Philip laughed. "If you lose," he said, "your allowance is forfeit for years to come. I will keep my promise."

"So will I," the boy answered.

Alexander moved toward the horse, took the reins from the groom, and reached up to pat the glossy shoulder. He spoke softly and his voice seemed to calm the excited animal. Its laid-back ears straightened and its head stopped tossing nervously.

The boy continued to talk, moving his hand to the horse's head and then down its nose. The horse snorted but stood quiet.

"I don't know your name, fellow," the boy said, "but when you belong to me you will have a new name.

That white spot on your forehead is shaped like an ox's head. That's what I'll call you, Ox-Head—Bucephalus. We will do great things together, Alexander and Bucephalus."

As he talked, Alexander turned the horse so it faced the sun. The boy had noticed, while watching the grooms at work, that the horse shied whenever it saw its shadow. Now, turned facing the sun, the shadow was out of sight and the horse was quieter.

Alexander continued to talk quietly, urging the horse to move forward and trotting along beside it for a few steps. Then, holding the reins in his left hand, he grasped the horse's mane with his right hand, gave a little leap, swung his right leg over the horse's back and was mounted.

The crowd watched silently. Men at the horse fair knew horses; they knew that silence was better than noise in a contest like this. But, when they saw the boy kick his heels and urge the black horse forward, they gave a great shout of approval.

Alexander and Bucephalus galloped down the field and disappeared in the distance. The horse was not running away, everyone could see that clearly. The boy rider was in control and the horse was obeying.

In a few minutes they galloped back, the boy's red-gold hair flying in the wind as wildly as the horse's black mane and tail. Alexander pulled the horse to a stop and swung off its back to face his father. The crowd again roared its approval.

King Philip reached out and hugged his son, tears of pride were running down his cheeks and into his black whiskers. He thumped Alexander on the back and kissed him.

"My son," he said, "you have won the bet. The horse is yours. When you are grown you must look for a bigger kingdom than Macedonia because Macedonia will be too small for you."

———

King Philip spoke truly. The kingdom of Macedonia was too small for Alexander. As the boy grew older he studied warfare, politics and philosophy with the greatest teachers of his time and was given considerable responsibility. At eighteen Alexander rode Bucephalus to victory at the head of one wing of his father's army in the Battle of Chaeronea. And soon after that he rode Bucephalus on an important political mission to Athens —to try to persuade the Athenians to join his father in a war against the Great King of Persia.

When Alexander was twenty King Philip was murdered. The young man took command and soon was in firm control of his father's kingdom. He made himself master of Greece and Egypt, and finally fulfilled his father's dream to conquer Persia. Not one of the ancient empires was able to stand against him.

Bucephalus, the great black warhorse, took part in all these conquests. Alexander had other horses, and sometimes rode one of them in battle. Occasionally one of his horses was killed by enemy spears and arrows, but Bucephalus led a charmed life. The black horse was wounded several times, but Alexander took pains to see that Bucephalus was given the best of care and the horse always recovered.

As Bucephalus grew older, Alexander was careful not to overwork him. The man who ruled over millions of subjects, and could be cruel or kind as he wished, was always considerate of his faithful black warhorse.

Before the Battle of Arbela, in which he defeated the great Persian King Darius, Alexander rode another horse while he organized his battle line. But when the fighting began, Alexander rode Bucephalus.

In ten years' time Alexander had conquered a great empire. Men called him Alexander the Great and worshipped him like a god. No one before had ever ruled so many lands and peoples.

Alexander was not satisfied. He led his army into India where King Porus met him with two hundred elephants in the center of his battle line. The two armies faced each other across the Hydaspes River.

"I will ride Bucephalus today," Alexander said as he prepared for battle. "I want him to share in the victory."

Bucephalus was nearly thirty years old, but his black coat was still glossy and his neck still arched with pride. He seemed to know that he was the favorite warhorse of the world's most famous soldier.

All day Bucephalus carried Alexander as the tide of battle shifted. The great war elephants were hard to overcome; many of the Greek horses snorted with terror and tried to run away when they smelled the huge creatures, but Bucephalus was not afraid.

Finally, the enemy line was broken. King Porus was captured. Bucephalus tossed his head proudly, the triangular blaze on his forehead was grimy with sweat and dust. Alexander dismounted. The black horse drew a deep breath, his sides heaved, and slowly he sank to the ground. Age, exertion, and battle weariness were too much for his proud old heart. Bucephalus, the great black warhorse, was dead.

Alexander had his old friend buried with all the honors due the warhorse of a world conquerer. In his memory Alexander established a town near the horse's grave and called the place Bucephalia. The name is no longer used but there are several towns in the area; the horse's grave may be near one of them.

Bucephalus left many descendants. For hundreds of years the rulers of countries through which Alexander's armies had passed claimed that their horses issued from the line of Bucephalus. And they were still making this claim when Marco Polo, the Venetian traveler, visited India about seven hundred years ago—over sixteen hundred years later.

Alexander, himself, died three years after Bucephalus of a fever he contracted in Asia. He had ruled many countries and had had many followers but none was more faithful than his great black warhorse Bucephalus.

Incitatus { *THE MADMAN'S HORSE*

DOES HAY FROM AN IVORY MANGER or water from a golden bowl taste any better than hay from a wooden manger or water from a clay pot? Incitatus could have answered that question.

Incitatus was the favorite horse of Roman Emperor Caligula. He was a handsome and spirited animal, high stepping and fast moving and his name reflected this—Incitatus in Latin meant "Flyer" or "Go Ahead." Besides having an ivory manger and a golden bowl, Incitatus also had a palace of his own and many slaves to take care of him.

Caligula—absolute ruler of Rome for the nearly four years from 37 to 41 A.D.—was a cruel and excessive man. "Remember, I have a right to do anything to anybody," Emperor Caligula often claimed, and his actions testified that he believed what he said. Were Caligula alive today he probably would be confined to an institution for the criminally insane. But in his time such was not the practice.

If Caligula had one redeeming feature, it was his love

for his horse. And, as with everything else he did, Caligula went to extremes in showing this affection.

Because he was the emperor's favorite, Incitatus lived as no horse had ever lived before—or since. The rooms of his palace were filled with fine furniture; there were rugs on the floors and beautiful paintings and rich tapestries on the walls.

The palace had a large banquet hall where the emperor often entertained important people as guests of the horse. Written invitations were sent out in the name of Incitatus, and no one dared refuse to come and feast with the emperor's four-footed favorite. A refusal could only result in ruin, banishment, or death.

Incitatus's own stall was of fine marble and, as we have seen, he ate his hay and grain from his own ivory manger. On hot days the water in his golden bowl was cooled with snow brought by swift runners from the distant mountains. That was how the wealthy Romans in those days cooled their wine and obviously Caligula felt that what was good enough for a wealthy Roman was none too good for the emperor's horse.

Musicians played soft music to entertain Incitatus while slaves curried his coat. Other slaves curled his mane and wove silk ribbons into his long flowing tail. His hoofs were polished until they shone and on special days they were gilded.

In those days the Romans were just learning how to shoe their horses, so Incitatus may or may not have been shod. Nero, Caligula's successor as emperor, had his horses shod with silver, so perhaps Incitatus had silver shoes, too.

Incitatus had his own bottles of perfume and wore

a jeweled collar around his neck. At night and on damp, rainy days he was covered with purple blankets to protect him from the cold. On holidays, when games and races were held in Rome, the emperor ordered soldiers to stand guard outside the horse's palace. This was done to keep the enthusiastic crowds from making any noise that might disturb Incitatus or interfere with his rest.

Inviting important people to feast with him was not the only way Caligula chose to honor his horse. Sometimes, with Incitatus hitched to a jeweled and gilded chariot, the emperor invited Roman senators to go for a trot with him. The senators trotted along on foot while Caligula rode in the chariot and guided Incitatus with silver-trimmed reins. Sometimes he urged the horse to a canter or gallop and the dignified senators were obliged to sustain a fast run in order to keep up. Caligula would then laugh at them for puffing and panting, and brag that Incitatus was not breathing hard at all.

Among the many strange things that Caligula did, one of the strangest was to order a road built across the Gulf of Baiae near Rome. The gulf was more than three miles wide, but Caligula had all the merchant ships in the area brought together and anchored in a double line across the water. Then he had wooden planks nailed across the ships and covered with earth. When the road was finished, the emperor spent the day riding back and forth across it on his horse. For the occasion Incitatus was adorned with a jeweled bridle while Caligula wore a cloak made of cloth of gold and an oak leaf crown. A sword in a jeweled scabbard was buckled around his middle and he carried a golden shield.

The next day Caligula drove across the same causeway in a chariot drawn by two famous race horses. This

time he was dressed in the costume of a Roman
charioteer.

———

Chariot racing was a favorite sport in Rome at that time.
The Romans were ardent racing fans and everybody
made wagers on the races. The charioteers were divided
into four different factions, each known by its own
special color, and people made their bets according to
the color they favored. There were the Reds, the Whites,
the Blues, and the Greens. Caligula always favored the
Green teams and on the night before a race he would
often feast with the Green drivers, sometimes even
spending the night in the Green stables. At one feast
he gave two million gold pieces to a successful charioteer. Perhaps Incitatus won races on feast days; certainly his name indicates that he was a fast runner.

Finally, after giving the horse every other gift he
could think of, Caligula decided to appoint Incitatus
to the office of Consul. This was an important political
office in Rome and a position once filled by an an-
cestor of Caligula's—Julius Caesar. But three years, ten
months, and eight days of rule by such a madman was
enough for the Romans. Two officers of his own guard
finally stabbed Caligula to death while he was on his
way to his midday meal.

What became of Incitatus is not recorded. No doubt
he was moved out of his marble stall and had to eat his
hay from an ordinary manger, though it probably tasted
just as good to him.

A good horse is a good horse, regardless of how mad
his master may be. Incitatus was a good horse, even
though he never became a Roman Consul or served in
the Roman Senate.

Raksh { *THE WARRIOR'S HORSE*

RAKSH—THE LIGHTNING—was the name of a rose-colored horse that belonged to the Persian hero Rustum. The deeds of Rustum and Raksh are described in an old Persian epic poem called the *Shah-Nama* or *The Book of Kings.*

Rustum's father and grandfather were both famous warriors who had grown old in the service of the shahs of Persia, and Rustum wished to follow in their footsteps. Like most young heroes, the first thing he wanted was a good horse.

Zal, Rustum's father, owned great herds of horses of the best stock in Asia, and ordered all of them rounded up and brought to one place so the young man could take his choice from among them.

Much as an American cowboy does today, Rustum used a lasso to catch the horses he wished to try. He swung his rope with a noose at the end and caught them, one after another. Each one he tried was good, but not good enough to suit him. He knew his horse

must be as strong and fearless as he was if they were
to do great deeds together.

At last he saw a beautiful mare with strong shoulders
and a deep chest. She was followed by a reddish colored
colt that looked even stronger than she. The two kept
to themselves away from the rest of the herd and were
proud, powerful, and wild.

"That is the horse I want," Rustum said, pointing to
the colt. "From his looks he is already three winters
old and ready for the saddle."

"He is a good horse for you," the chief horse herder
agreed. "He is the offspring of Abresh, a famous sire,
born of a Diw or Demon. His name is Raksh, The
Lightning."

Rustum grinned with pleasure when he heard this.
He adjusted his rope and prepared to lasso the colt.

"Watch out for the mare," the herdsman warned.
"She is a Demon. She has already killed three men who
have tried to catch her colt."

Rustum laughed out loud. He swung his rope and the
noose settled over the young horse's neck.

When the mare saw that Rustum had lassoed her colt,
she charged at him with bared teeth, rearing up and
lashing out with her front hoofs in an effort to brain
him. Rustum held on to his rope and the herdsmen
managed to drive the mare away. The colt fought a
fierce battle for freedom, but finally Rustum was able
to spring onto his back. The colt knew it had met its
master and from that time on the two—Raksh and
Rustum—were inseparable companions.

Rustum spent half a year training Raksh, teaching
him to do all the things a warhorse should, until man
and horse seemed to move as one single creature. Raksh

became smooth-paced, soft-mouthed, and smart. Rustum boasted that the horse had eyes so sharp he could see an ant running on a black cloth two miles away.

The poets of ancient Persia wrote many verses praising the great rose-colored horse Raksh. They pictured him with a bright saffron-hued coat dappled with reddish markings—much like a lawn strewn with rose petals. His black mane and tail were long and flowing, and from the knees down his powerful legs were black. In the horseman's language of today, he probably would be called a blood bay or perhaps a strawberry roan.

———

Like his ancestors before him, Rustum served the shahs of Persia long and faithfully. When the wise old shah died, a new ruler took his place upon the Peacock Throne of Persia. The new shah was very young. Sometimes he foolishly listened to bad advice and, as the stories go, even did things suggested to him by evil spirits and demons disguised as musicians and fortune tellers.

As it happened, the shah and his army were captured by a powerful enemy called the White Demon. It befell Rustum and Raksh to make a difficult seven-day ride to rescue them.

On the first day of the ride the hero and his horse covered what was usually a two days' journey. That night Rustum made camp at the edge of a grassy plain where large herds of game were grazing. Raksh grazed with them, but stayed close to his master. During the night a lion crept out of the tall grass and crouched to spring on the sleeping man. Raksh attacked the lion, striking it with his sharp hoofs and sinking his white teeth deep into its back. Rustum awoke to find the lion lying dead on the grass and Raksh grazing peacefully nearby.

The next day's journey carried them across a desert where they almost died of thirst. The sand was deep and the sun was so hot that Rustum dismounted and led Raksh, pushing on until neither of them could go a step further. Just as he was sinking to his knees, Rustum saw a fat ram run past. He staggered to his feet and followed, pulling Raksh after him. The ram led them to a spring of clear water. Both drank thirstily, then, before seeking food and rest himself, Rustum bathed his horse in the cool stream that flowed from the spring. When night came, he slept beside the spring while Raksh grazed close at hand.

While Rustum slept, a huge fire-breathing dragon, eighty yards long, crawled out of the desert to see who had dared enter its territory. Raksh saw the dragon and galloped to his sleeping master, pawing the ground and neighing in alarm.

But when Rustum opened his eyes, the dragon vanished.

"What is the matter with you, Raksh?" Rustum grumbled. "Be quiet and let me sleep."

As soon as Rustum closed his eyes the dragon again appeared and crept nearer. Again Raksh neighed and stamped on the sand with his hoofs to warn his master. Rustum awoke, and once more the dragon vanished.

"Can't you be quiet?" Rustum asked angrily. "If you don't stop waking me, I'll chop off your head!"

With that threat, Rustum went back to sleep.

When the dragon appeared for a third time, Raksh tried to lure him away into the desert, but the fire-breathing monster only moved closer to Rustum. This time, when Raksh awoke him, Rustum saw his danger.

"Who are you?" he demanded.

"This is my land," the dragon retorted. "I am going to kill you, no matter who you are."

"I am Rustum, the son of Zal and champion of Persia," the warrior proclaimed, drawing his sword.

Together, the hero and his horse attacked the dragon. Raksh tore at its scaly hide with his sharp teeth and hoofs while Rustum fought it with his sword. Finally, after a great struggle, Rustum was able to cut off the dragon's head and the danger was past.

When morning came, Rustum and Raksh resumed their journey and went on to rescue the beleaguered shah.

After this adventure Rustum and Raksh were able to rest for a time, but soon they were busy again defending Persia from three foreign kings who had joined forces to attack the shah's army. Raksh, fat and rested, pranced before the assembled warriors while Rustum urged the men of Persia to fight on fiercely. When the battle began, the rose-colored steed and his warrior master charged through the enemy ranks as though they were playing a simple game of polo. Soon the three invading kings and their armies were defeated.

Once again there was a period of peace. Rustum and Raksh were glad to have the time to leave the capital and gallop out across the country. They traveled for many days, going nowhere in particular but enjoying their freedom. At night Rustum would sleep soundly while Raksh grazed quietly.

One night Raksh wandered farther from camp than usual and a band of strange tribesmen surrounded him. They knew their ruler would reward them if they could bring in this valuable horse as a captive. The rose-colored horse fought fiercely and, though none of the strangers could ride him, they finally threw a lasso over his head and surrounded him with their own horses. In this way they were able to drive him to their city.

When Rustum awoke, he looked around for Raksh. The rose-colored horse was gone. Rustum found his tracks and could tell from the torn-up ground that the horse had fought fiercely before being driven away. Furiously angry, Rustum picked up his weapons and followed the robbers on foot.

"I must find Raksh," he told himself. "My enemies will laugh out loud when they hear that Rustum slept while strangers stole his horse."

When Rustum reached the thieves' city he went directly to the king and announced that his horse had been stolen.

"I have tracked him to your city," the young warrior said, speaking as though he rode at the head of an army instead of being alone and on foot. "If he is found at once I will thank you for your honesty. If he is not found, some of your chieftains will lose their heads."

"Do not be angry," the king replied. "A horse as well known as your rose-colored Raksh cannot be hidden. He will be found; I will send my men to look for him. While they are searching, come and honor us with your presence at dinner."

Rustum accepted the invitation. While he was a guest in the far away city he and the king's daughter fell in love and were married. For a time the young warrior was so happy that he scarcely heard when the king told him that at last Raksh had been found. But after a while Rustum knew that he must mount his horse and ride back home to Persia.

The romance had a sad ending. Some years later, when Rustum's son Sohrab was old enough for warfare, he and his father met in a hand-to-hand battle. Without recognizing each other, they fought long and fiercely. Not until Rustum had given Sohrab a fatal wound did he find out who the young man was. Rustum was heart-broken when the son he had just found again died in his arms.

Time went on and, although Rustum's grief did not grow any less, duty again and again called him to fight for Persia. Rustum lived a long time, as did his horse Raksh. They served several shahs of Persia and no enemy was ever able to defeat them in battle.

Treachery, on the part of Rustum's jealous half-brother Shughad, finally brought about their downfall. This half-brother turned the most recent ruler against Rustum and suggested a way for the shah to kill him.

"Invite Rustum and Raksh to go hunting with you," Shughad advised. "Have your men dig deep pits in the road, big enough to hold a man and his horse, and plant several swords in each pit with their points and sharp edges up. Then have your men cover the pits lightly so Rustum will not know they are there."

The shah did as the evil Shughad suggested and

Rustum accepted the invitation. When the hunt began, Rustum rode Raksh down the middle of the road while the shah's followers rode on the sides. Suddenly the rose-colored horse stopped, refusing to move until Rustum used his whip. At the sting of the lash Raksh leaped forward and fell into one of the pits.

In spite of the swords that pierced them, the powerful Raksh leaped out of the pit, carrying his master with him, but soon he fell into another. When he escaped from that pit he fell into yet another. Six times the great rose-colored horse was able to carry his master to safety, but he fell exhausted at the edge of the seventh pit. Both horse and rider were fatally wounded.

Rustum managed to avenge himself and his horse before he died. He seized his great bow and took aim at his half-brother. Even though Shughad hid behind a tree, Rustum shot his arrow straight through the trunk to the other side where it pierced the traitor and killed him.

And so Rustum and his splendid rose-colored horse Raksh met their end. They had lived a long time—some stories say two whole generations—and they accomplished great deeds together. Persian poets and storytellers have kept their memory alive for more than a thousand years.

Babieca { *THE CID'S HORSE*

PEOPLE SOMETIMES give uncomplimentary pet names to the things they care for most. "You big bum" or "Hi, stupid," are familiar examples of expressions often used to show affection rather than the criticism they seem to imply. Perhaps this was true for the name El Cid, the Spanish national hero, gave to his horse— Babieca. In Spanish *babieca* means "dumbbell" or "idiot."

El Cid Campeador, the Lord Champion, was a famous Spanish warrior who lived a thousand years ago. In those days Spain was a collection of little kingdoms, each ruled by its own king—each king in turn jealous and suspicious of all the others. In addition to fighting among themselves, the little Spanish kingdoms also had to fight the Moors, the fierce Mohammedan warriors who had crossed over from Africa, invading Spain, and threatening to conquer all of Western Europe. The Moors had established a Mohammedan kingdom in Spain that was a constant threat to all the small Christian kingdoms already there. It was in these troubled times that El Cid and Babieca performed the deeds that made them famous.

Rodrigo Diaz de Bivar, who was later to become El Cid, was born in the small kingdom of Castille. His father was a nobleman in the service of the King of Castille. Young Rodrigo, who was also called Ruy by his friends, was taught to use the weapons of his time—the lance, broadsword, battle axe, and iron-spiked mace. He learned to ride both the heavy European warhorses and the smaller, fleet-footed steeds that the Moors had brought to Spain from the deserts of Arabia. In addition he learned the manners of his time, the rigid requirements of knightly honor, and the need for complete loyalty to God, king, and country.

When he was old enough to become a knight, the young man's father provided him with armor and went with him to the great horse fair where once a year all the horse dealers gathered. From the best horses in Spain, the young man was to choose his warhorse. There were heavy dark horses from France, not swift but sturdy enough to carry the weight of a man and armor in battle. There were slim graceful white steeds from Arabia, and Barbs that were larger than their Arabian ancestors but equally swift and enduring. Then, too, there were native Spanish horses, bred from a combined ancestry of the others.

"Take your choice, my son," the old Lord of Bivar told the young man. "Choose wisely. A warrior's fame in battle often rests on the strength and intelligence of his warhorse."

Young Ruy Diaz leaned on the top rail of the corral

fence and looked over the throng of horses with experienced eyes. He was a handsome young man, dark,
slender, and quiet. His face was smooth—the famous
beard of El Cid had not yet sprouted on his chin.

For a long time he stood watching the horses. Now
and then he would single out one and have it led before
him. He would run his hands over its legs, look into its
mouth, or pat its shoulders to feel the strong muscles.

"Now bring that one," Ruy Diaz said at last, pointing
to a scraggly colt that no one had judged worthy of
notice. It was a dirty gray color and the big bones of its
frame showed plainly through its shaggy, unbrushed
hide. Its tail was matted with burs and its mane was
tangled and ragged.

In spite of its unkempt appearance, the colt gave the
grooms a good chase before they could catch it. Its ears
were back and its eyes rolling when they finally led it to
the corral fence where Ruy Diaz and his father were
waiting.

The young man examined the horse carefully, feeling
the bones under its hide, looking at its hoofs, and finally
at its teeth.

"This is the horse for me," he said at last. "This is my
choice, father."

The Lord of Bivar looked disgusted.

"Surely you are joking, my son," he exclaimed in
amazement. "Only a *babieca,* an idiot, would choose a
horse like that from among the best that Castille has to
offer."

"This is my choice," the young man repeated. "In a
short time you will see that I am right. I will call him
Babieca so you will not forget how you doubted me."

The father shook his head in disbelief.

"And I tried to teach you to be a good judge of horses," he grumbled. *"Babieca, babieca, babieca."*

The Lord of Bivar paid the small sum the horse dealer wanted and had his servants lead the bony colt away. A few onlookers laughed, but they were quickly silenced by an angry glance from young Ruy Diaz.

From that time on Ruy Diaz spent most of his time in the stable and paddock supervising the care of his horse. He saw to it that the horse got proper food and exercise. Sometimes he groomed the shaggy coat himself, using the currycomb and brush with gentle, efficient hands. The colt soon learned to know him and whinnied with pleasure when it heard his master's voice.

In less than a month a great change began to take place in the horse's appearance. The bones disappeared as good food put flesh on them. The dirty gray hide got lighter and lighter in color as brush and currycomb removed the shaggy old hair. The new hair grew in white and lustrous. The mane and tail grew long and flowing; the horse's neck arched with pride and he pranced with spirit, strength, and good health.

Finally one day young Ruy Diaz rode the horse out to show it off to his father. The older man had to smile and nod in approval.

"You are a better judge of horses than I am, my son," he admitted gracefully. "Your *Babieca* is a fine horse and I, alas, am the idiot."

————

Life in those days was seldom peaceful for long. There was too much greed, suspicion and hostility at the royal courts and there were too many enemies outside the castle gates to permit life to remain calm.

The first warlike action for young Rodrigo Diaz de Bivar was to avenge an insult made to his father by a jealous rival. Next he fought and defeated five Moorish kings. He then entered the service of King Ferdinand of Castille and later served King Ferdinand's sons, King Sancho of Castille and King Alfonso of Navarre.

It was against the Moors that Rodrigo Diaz gained his greatest fame. Riding Babieca, his beautiful white warhorse, he was the Spanish commander and standard bearer. He fought many battles against the Mohammedan warriors and soon gained their fear, their respect, and their admiration. It was the Moors who gave him his first title—El Cid they called him, from the Arab word *Seid* which means the lord. To this, his Spanish followers added the title *Campeador,* the Champion. And so, Rodrigo Diaz de Bivar became the famous and feared El Cid Campeador.

One time, on returning victorious from a battle with the Moors, he was welcomed by the king and given many honors. Long speeches and high compliments were exchanged. The king praised El Cid, his fighting ability, his sword, and his powerful warhorse Babieca.

El Cid in turn made a speech acknowledging the king's praise and, in a gesture of great loyalty and generosity, said:

"You praise me and you say my warhorse is the best in Spain. He *is* the best, O King, and for that reason I present him to you. He is worthy of a king."

Fortunately, the king knew very well that a warrior without his warhorse was hardly a fighter. In those days horses fought as fiercely as men.

"If I accept the horse you give me," the King answered quickly, "Babieca would lose a good master.

Keep him and continue to ride against our enemies. God grant that no man ever takes Babieca from you, El Cid Campeador."

El Cid fought many battles during his lifetime, but he was not always victorious. Each time he was defeated, he allowed his beard to grow longer, and when he won a victory he refused to have it cut. The beard grew so long and so thick that he had to tie it with a cord and tuck it inside the coat he wore over his armor.

Later, when El Cid's life was near its end, El Cid and his forces found themselves inside the walled city of Valencia besieged by Moors. The dying warrior called his wife and officers to him to give them definite orders as to what they must do to defeat the enemy. Three days after El Cid's death they put the plan into action.

The great gates of the city swung open and out rode El Cid's entire army. At the head was Babieca, El Cid's white warhorse, and to the saddle on his back was lashed the warrior's embalmed body. A board in front and a board behind held him erect; his great beard was tied with a cord as always and in his right hand was his shining broadsword. Behind him on his right rode Doña Ximena, his widow, and on his left rode his faithful lieutenants.

The Spanish army advanced at a canter, closer and closer to the Moorish ranks drawn up for battle. Babieca stepped as proudly as ever, prouder perhaps, because on him rested his dead master's great military reputation. Nearer and nearer the white warhorse came to the Moorish soldiers.

The Moors began to murmur. El Cid—they had thought El Cid was dead. But there he was—his beard, his sword, and his great white warhorse.

Their murmurs grew louder. Suddenly someone shouted in terror.

"It is a ghost—a ghost on a white devil horse!"

To a man, the Moors broke ranks and fled. Each urged his horse to run as though the Devil himself were after them. El Cid and Babieca had won another victory, although only one of them was alive to know it.

Babieca lived for several years after El Cid's death. The great warhorse was forty years old when he died, and El Cid's followers remembered his dead master's orders.

"When my Babieca dies," El Cid had said, "be sure to bury him deep. Pile stones on his grave. Let no Moorish dogs tear him in death when he trampled so many of them in life."

El Cid was laid to rest inside the walls of the Monastery of San Pedro de Cardeña, and his followers buried Babieca just outside the main gate of that same monastery. The monks planted two elm trees to mark the noble warhorse's grave.

Living the life of a soldier of fortune, El Cid was involved in much of the intrigue surrounding the various Spanish rulers and even, for a time, fought on behalf of the Moors as well as the Christians.

Some of the things Rodrigo Diaz de Bivar did during his lifetime might not be considered admirable by modern standards, but he lived in fierce and lawless times. And over the years El Cid became a great national hero in Spain.

After El Cid's death in 1099, Spanish poets and storytellers added so much romantic embroidery to the adventurous career of Rodrigo Diaz de Bivar it is hard to tell where truth ends and imagination begins. But the poets, storytellers, and historians all agree that Babieca, the great white warhorse, was a most important partner in all his master's adventures.

Sharatz { *THE PRINCE'S HORSE*

A DRAGON MOUNTED on a dragon is the way old storytellers described Prince Marko of Serbia and his warhorse Sharatz. Together they did great deeds in the fourteenth century when the Serbs were fighting among themselves and against their chief enemies, the Turks.

Prince Marko was the eldest son of King Voukashin of Serbia, and like all young heroes he needed a horse strong and brave enough to share his adventures.

Several stories are told of how the prince chose his warhorse. One story claims that when Marko found the horse, it was suffering from leprosy. Because it was such a powerful looking creature, Marko decided to cure it of the dread disease by making the horse drink great quantities of red Serbian wine. The treatment was successful, but the horse's coat remained a spotted black and white, and so the prince named it Sharatz, or piebald.

Another story claims that a *veela,* or fairy queen, gave the horse to Prince Marko. She assured the young man that the piebald horse was as swift as the wind and would carry him faithfully on all his adventures.

A third story recounts how young Marko agreed to work three years for a lord who owned great numbers of horses. The only pay he asked was permission to choose a horse of his own from among those owned by his employer.

When the three years were ended, Prince Marko went to the meadow where the horses were grazing. He tested each horse, seizing it by the tail and whirling it around. Only one colt, a black and white, was able to stand firm and motionless; even Prince Marko's great strength could not move it. That was of course the colt he chose as his own.

———

Prince Marko and Sharatz had many adventures—some, as the stories go, with veelas and other powerful spirits, and some with dragons and similar monsters, but some also with men. Much disappointed when the Serbs did not choose him as king after his father died, for a time Marko joined the Turkish forces and fought with them. Eventually, however, he returned to the side of the Serbians.

Sharatz was a wise and well-trained horse. Some accounts say he and his master could talk together, and all agreed that the prince and his steed drank red wine together. The prince's golden wine bowl was said to hold three gallons of wine and Marko shared each bowl full equally with his horse.

In battle, Sharatz knew just when to kneel down so that the lance of a charging enemy would pass harmlessly over the prince's shoulder. He also knew when to rear and lash out with his front hoofs against an enemy warhorse. When he was angry, blue flames spouted from his nostrils, and when his hoofs hit the ground they sent sparks and rock fragments scattering in all directions.

Sharatz was swift as the wind. He could leap three lance-lengths into the air and each bound carried him four lance-lengths forward. He trampled Turkish soldiers under his hoofs and bit the ears off their horses. While Prince Marko held the reins in his teeth and swung his great war club or his magic sword against the enemy, Sharatz fought equally well with his own weapons.

When the two were simply traveling alone, Sharatz had such an easy gait that the prince could go to sleep in the saddle. He knew that wise and watchful Sharatz would stamp his right forefoot to awaken him if danger threatened. Prince Marko never rode any horse other than Sharatz, and the famed piebald horse never allowed any other rider on his back.

———

History tells us that Prince Marko was killed by the Turks during the Battle of Rovina in 1399, that Sharatz knew of his master's fate ahead of time, and that he stumbled and wept real tears of sorrow.

Legend tells us that Prince Marko never died. Instead, he threw his great war club into the ocean, thrust his magic sword up to the hilt in solid rock, and retired to his mountain castle at Prilep in what is now the country of Yugoslavia. There he waits and drinks red wine while Sharatz munches hay in his rocky stall in the castle stable.

Now and then, every century or so, Prince Marko looks out at the rock where he thrust his sword. When

Marko sees the sword rise from the rock and stand on its point, so the legend goes, he will know the time has come to mount Sharatz and ride forth again. Together, the two will restore the Empire of Serbia to its old-time strength and glory.

El Morzillo { *THE CONQUIS-TADOR'S HORSE*

HERNANDO CORTÉS rode a spirited black stallion named El Morzillo when he conquered the great Aztec Empire and made himself master of Mexico.

Horses were very important in the conquest of Mexico. The Aztecs, who had never seen horses before, were as much or more afraid of them than they were of Cortés and his soldiers. Without their horses, it is doubtful that Cortés and his handful of Spaniards could have overcome the multitudes of Aztec fighting men commanded by Emperor Montezuma. The Spaniards' guns were now and terrifying to the Indians, but in the long run it was the horses, not the flame-spitting guns, that brought terror to the hearts of the Aztecs. Was a man on horseback one monster or two, the Indians wondered. The first time the Aztecs saw a Spaniard fall from his horse, they thought the monster had broken in two and they ran away in terror.

The Spaniards, themselves, were quite willing to ad-

Hernando Cortés and Warhorse in Armor

mit the important role played by their horses. One Spaniard wrote: "Horses are the most necessary things in the new country because they frighten the enemy most, and after God, to them belongs the victory."

When Cortés began his conquest of Mexico in 1519 he had an army of between 400 and 600 men and just sixteen horses. The numbers and names of the men are not exact, but the Spaniards left accurate records of the names, colors, characteristics, and ownership of each one of the horses.

At the start of the expedition Captain Cortés was mounted on a horse described as "a vicious dark chestnut," not at all suited for the task of conquering an empire. That horse died about two months after the expedition landed in Mexico, and Cortés soon acquired a new horse, a black one owned jointly by two of his men. The word *morcillo* means reddish-black or all-black in Spanish so Cortés called his new steed *mi caballo Morzillo*, "my black horse." El Morzillo, the Black One, served his master long and faithfully.

Conquering an empire is not easy. Even after Cortés and his men reached Tenochtitlan, the Aztec capital which is now Mexico City, and captured Emperor Montezuma, the Aztecs would not admit they were defeated. They chose a new emperor and attacked the Spaniards so fiercely that Cortés and his men had to retreat. During one terror-filled night, they abandoned Mexico City while the Aztecs fought them fiercely on all sides. When the Indians destroyed a bridge to keep the Spaniards from escaping, El Morzillo made a magnificent jump across the ruins of the bridge, thereby saving his master's life.

The Spaniards' retreat was only temporary, they were

not defeated. In a few months' time Cortés rode El Morzillo back into Mexico City at the head of a new army of some 500 foot soldiers and 70 men on horseback. This time his victory was complete. The Aztecs were conquered and the Spaniards were masters in Mexico.

For a time the Spanish captain was busy organizing a new government, but he was a restless man and soon wanted more action. Looking around to find other outlets for his energies, Cortés decided that the country of Honduras was an inviting place for additional conquest. Honduras was a long way from Mexico City and many trackless miles of mountains and tropical jungles lay between. But such details do not always bother conquerors and, indeed, they did not bother Cortés.

In October of 1524 Cortés set out, again riding El Morzillo. Beside him on his right rode Doña Marina, the beautiful Indian girl who acted as interpreter when Cortés talked with the Mexican natives. On his left rode Cuauhtémoc, the Aztec prince who was Montezuma's heir. Cortés took him along so that he could not start a rebellion among the newly conquered Aztecs in Cortés's absence.

El Morzillo stepped out proudly. The expedition began like a triumphal procession with musicians and entertainers going along with the horsemen and foot soldiers. Behind them came the porters carrying the baggage, and a horde of servants driving flocks of cattle and pigs to supply food for the expedition.

For the first few days travel was easy, but soon the going grew very difficult. The musicians and entertainers turned back, the servants deserted, and the guides lost their way. But Cortés pushed on, over mountains and through jungles. The explorers crossed a huge swamp where the horses sank to their bellies in mud and the men had to struggle hard to save them. When at last they reached firm ground on the other side of the swamp, they were all so exhausted they could scarcely stand.

Finally, after months of wandering, the expedition reached Lake Peten Itza in what is now Guatemala. The country was pleasant and the people who lived on one of the lake's islands were friendly. Their chief came to the mainland to meet Cortés. His people were Mayas, he said, and their island city was called Tayasal. Like the Aztecs of Mexico, the Mayas had never seen horses before.

"Will you do us the honor of visiting our island?" the chief invited. "Bring your great beast with you, and as many men as you wish."

Cortés accepted the invitation—for himself, his horse, and twenty of his men.

Getting El Morzillo across the lake to the island was no simple matter. The Indians' dugout canoes were not large enough to carry a horse, but Cortés soon solved the problem. One canoe was not enough so he ordered two canoes lashed together. El Morzillo stood with his front feet in one canoe and his hind feet in the other, and he and his master were paddled to the island.

Canoeing is not an activity suited to horses. In maintaining his balance during that ride, the great black horse managed to run a splinter into his foot. And, in fact, El Morzillo was going lame when Cortés rode him into the city. Alas, it was their last ride together.

The Mayan chief showed Cortés the sights of his island city and entertained him at a feast. But when it was time for the Spaniards to return to the mainland, the black horse was so lame and his foot was so sore that Cortés knew El Morzillo could not make the canoe trip back to the Spanish camp. Nor could he continue the march to Honduras with the expedition.

Cortés made a hard decision—horse lover that he was, that decision probably hurt him more than the loss of much gold or fine treasure. He decided to part with his friend, to leave El Morzillo on the island in the keeping of the chief of Tayasal. The chief promised to take good care of him.

And so the Spanish conquistador and his black horse parted. El Morzillo probably whinnied lonesomely as he watched his master step into the Indian canoe and be paddled away. No doubt Cortés intended to return for his horse on his way back to Mexico, but he never did. He had to abandon his plans of Honduran conquest and return to face rebellion and troubles in Mexico and in Spain. He was never able to go back to the island city in Lake Peten to claim his black warhorse from the Mayan chieftain.

As for El Morzillo, fate gave him a strange destiny. The Indian chief did not know much about the care and feeding of lame horses, but he took his responsibilities seriously. He did know how to treat a god and El Morzillo seemed like a god to him.

The lame black horse was led to a temple and garlands of flowers were hung around his neck. The finest kinds of Mayan food—roasted chickens, cakes made from corn meal, honey, fruits and melons—were placed before him. The most beautiful Indian maidens were

called on to dance for his entertainment. In a very short
time El Morzillo, the conquistador's lame black horse,
was known as Tziminchac, the Mayan god of thunder
and lightning.

It is not known how long El Morzillo lived in this high
position. Perhaps he managed to eat the flower garlands
from around his neck and some of the tropical fruits
placed before him; maybe he even sniffed at an occasional roasted chicken. His lame foot should not have
been incurable, although his diet certainly was not what
El Morzillo might have expected.

No doubt the black horse missed his vigorous Spanish
master and pined for the sound of Spanish music and
voices. Eventually he died, as all horses must. The
Mayans carved a stone statue of him showing him seated
on his haunches—they were not engineers enough to
show him standing on all four feet—and they continued
to worship him as the god of thunder and lightning.

A hundred years passed. Details were forgotten but the
fame of El Morzillo lived on in the records of the conquest of Mexico. Finally, another Spanish expedition
followed Cortés's footsteps into Yucatan and Guatemala. In the expedition were two Franciscan priests,
Father Bartolome Fuensalada and Father Juan de Orbita—both very energetic in their efforts to convert the
native people and to destroy all traces of their "heathen"
worship.

Imagine the two priests' surprise when they entered
the largest temple in the island city of Tayasal and
found an enormous stone statue of a horse seated on its

haunches staring at them. It was, of course, El Morzillo in his role of Tziminchac, the god of thunder and lightning.

Father Orbita acted in prompt and characteristic fashion. As his fellow priest later described it, "the spirit of our Lord descended on him and, carried away with a fervent and courageous zeal in the glory of God, he seized a stone and, clambering to the top of the heathen idol, battered it to pieces, scattering the fragments over the floor of the shrine."

So perished the statue of Tziminchac the god of thunder and lightning, formerly El Morzillo the black warhorse of Cortés the conqueror of Mexico.

The ancient city of Tayasal has since fallen into ruin and in its place is a new town called Remedios. Boatmen of Remedios, who sail on Lake Peten, say that on clear moonless nights a person can still see Tziminchac deep down in the waters of the lake. There he receives the worship of the Mayas while he patiently waits for Cortés to come and reclaim El Morzillo, his faithful black warhorse.

Justin Morgan } *THE SINGING MASTER'S HORSE*

IN TALKING about Justin Morgan, one must be careful to indicate whether he means Justin Morgan the horse or Justin Morgan the man. Justin Morgan the horse was named for Justin Morgan the man. But if it were not for Justin Morgan the horse, Justin Morgan the man would have been forgotten long ago.

Justin Morgan the man was born in 1747 in West Springfield, a village in the Colony of Massachusetts. He grew up during stirring times in New England. Those were the days when the American colonists were beginning to talk about unfair oppression from England, of taxation without representation, and of seeking independence. Thomas Paine, Samuel Adams, John Hancock, Benjamin Franklin, and George Washington were growing up, too, and taking their places as leaders.

However, not everyone was active in politics or concerned about independence. Justin Morgan was in his

49

thirties when the Revolutionary War crackled and
flamed around him. He was a mild man, too busy making
a living for himself and his family to worry about the
tax on tea. He did not have time to think much about
what was being said and done in the Virginia House of
Burgesses or the Continental Congress. Further, Justin
Morgan was a sick man—he had tuberculosis (it was
called consumption in his day) and he could not do hard
physical work. For this reason, also, he could not take
an active part in the Revolutionary War.

But Justin Morgan was not a lazy man; he taught
school, served as town clerk, helped other New Eng-
landers learn penmanship, and conducted singing
classes. Singing was his favorite occupation; he loved
music and he wrote several hymns.

Justin Morgan the man also loved fine horses. He
could not afford to have many, but he owned several
good horses during his lifetime and served as trainer
and breeder for others.

War, independence, and the beginning of a new nation did not seem to effect him greatly, but in 1788 he
moved from his Massachusetts birthplace to a more
frontier-type home in Randolph, Vermont. Life was
hard and the singing master had to travel from small
town to village, to hamlet, organizing choirs and giving
lessons in order to make a living. When he died in
1798, Justin Morgan the man left a bridle, a saddle, a
whip, some clothes, a Bible, and two books—an estate
worth exactly $160.13.

But he did also leave Figure, the little horse he
brought to Vermont from West Springfield—the horse
that later also became known by the name Justin
Morgan.

Justin Morgan

Justin Morgan the horse was foaled not long after the
Revolutionary War. The records of his early years are
not clear—he may have been foaled in 1789 or perhaps
not until 1793; nobody cared until so many years had
passed that details could not be verified. By then Justin
Morgan the man was dead and that source of exact information was lost.

Tradition and fairly dependable accounts indicate
that Justin Morgan the horse was sired by True Briton,
a Thoroughbred stallion stolen by colonial patriots from
his owner, British Colonel James Delancey, during the
war. After the theft, True Briton's identity was disguised in one new name after another, until he was
finally best known as Beautiful Bay. The precise name
of the colt's mother is not known, though she was
called the "Wildair Mare" and was native to the Hart-
ford-Springfield area of the Connecticut Valley. It is
thought that she may have belonged to Justin Morgan
the man and had claim to Arab blood through her own
sire, Diamond. Thus, Justin Morgan the horse was a
combination of Thoroughbred and Arab, plus unknown
stock. He was a mixture, a mongrel, and the founder
of a new line of fine horses.

So much for family records.

Justin Morgan the horse was a jaunty, gentle, willing
little fellow, quite worthy of being called "the greatest
little horse in the world." That title was voted to him
by the Vermont Legislature in 1939, on the presumed
150th anniversary of his birth.

He was a small horse, standing only about fourteen
hands high and weighing some 950 pounds. Some ponies

are almost that large. But Justin Morgan the horse had a great heart, strong muscles, speed, and pulling power. These qualities were born into a dark bay body, held up by sturdy black legs, and decorated by a heavy, straight black mane and tail. There was not a white hair on him; his head was good, his forehead broad, his ears small and set far apart. His eyes were dark and prominent and showed a spirited but pleasant expression. He was a fast walker, could walk backward as well as forward, and he trotted smoothly without lifting his hoofs far off the ground.

When it came to working, Justin Morgan the horse could out-plow and out-pull them all. When the work day was over, he could race or pull a heavy log farther and better than any other horse in competition. His rivals were all bigger, but none of them could pull as much as he. Once, when hitched to a 1200-pound pine log that no other horse could move, Justin Morgan pulled the log, plus three grown men sitting on it.

Because his singing master owner, Justin Morgan the man, was not able to do much hard physical labor, the little horse was leased—for $15 a year—to a farmer named Robert Evans. In less than six months Evans and the sturdy little horse had cleared fifteen acres of heavy timbered land and had hauled the logs off to the sawmill. Farmer Evans was a hard worker and he worked Justin Morgan the horse hard as well, but he always fed him well and took good care of him. Farmer Evans continued as one of the horse's owners after Justin Morgan the singing master died.

On weekends and holidays Justin Morgan the horse was also popular as a parade mount. He stepped well and looked good; moreover, he was gentle and obedient

so that even poor riders felt at ease on him. No doubt
he took part in Fourth of July parades and other patri-
otic processions. In his own way he had a part in the
early days of the new nation. The United States of
America recovered from the Revolution and moved into
the War of 1812 during the little horse's lifetime.

Justin Morgan the man reared a family, and Justin
Morgan the horse had many descendants. He is credited
with being the first horse to found a new line in America—a line known today as the Morgan Horse. Every
true Morgan Horse is a direct descendant of Justin Morgan, and fortunately the little stallion was able to pass
on to his colts the qualities that made him so unusual.
Of his six or more sons who stood at stud, three—Bul-
rush, Sherman, and Woodbury—established distinct
"families" within the Morgan line.

Justin Morgan the horse had a full and busy life. He
passed through the hands of several owners, among
them Colonel John Goss, his brother David, and other
members of the Goss family. Each of them worked him
hard, but cared for him and treated him kindly.

As the years passed, Justin Morgan retained his
jaunty spirit. Not until he was past twenty did he begin
to show signs of age. His last job was pulling freight in
a six-horse team between the towns of Windsor and
Chelsea through mud, sleet, and icy weather. He was
able to do it, but not as easily as he once could. Night
found him tired and no longer ready for afterhours pulling contests.

Some horses enjoy old age in peaceful retirement.
Justin Morgan the horse certainly earned this but he
did not get it. Life in Vermont was hard for people and
for horses. During the winter of 1821 he ran loose in an

open lot with other horses. As was the custom of the time, there was no stable to protect them from the icy cold. One of the horses kicked old Justin Morgan in the flank and the ugly wound went untended. Veterinarians were unheard of in a place where doctors for human beings were scarce. And, when spring came, all that remained of the little old horse was a pile of bones in a fence corner.

But Justin Morgan the horse lives on in the hundreds of Morgan Horses that are descended from him. Although they were first native only to New England, the Morgans have since spread across the entire country and even overseas. There are now more Morgan breeders in Texas and California than there are in the Eastern states. Morgans now serve as cow ponies and general saddle horses, as well as trotters and harness racers.

If the men who owned Justin Morgan the horse seem harsh and unfeeling in retrospect, they were only acting according to the custom of their time. While they admired and appreciated the little horse's strength and good qualities, they had work to do and he was there to help them do it. As the years passed and his descendants continued to show his excellent characteristics, more and more honors were paid to his memory.

A number of historians have tried to gather the records of his life but exact details are scarce. The True Briton-Wildair ancestry is the one most often given for him, but others have been suggested. He has the distinction of being the first of his line and his descendants are more important than his ancestors.

The Morgan Horse Club, with headquarters in New

York City, is an organization of breeders interested in maintaining the Morgan line. *The Morgan Horse Register,* first published in 1894, keeps a record of all the horses that can claim direct descent from the first Justin Morgan.

The University of Vermont now maintains the Morgan Horse Farm started in the early 1900's by the United States Department of Agriculture at Middlebury, Vermont. On the farm a life-sized bronze statue of Justin Morgan the horse, by the sculptor Frederick G. Roth, stands looking over the countryside where the real horse once worked. On the base of the statue are these words:

1921

Given by

The Morgan Horse Club

to the

U.S. Department of Agriculture

in memory of

Justin Morgan

who died in

1821

This is not the great little horse's only monument. On the Brush Hill Farm at West Springfield, Massachusetts, there is a tablet marking his birthplace that reads:

From this farm came the stallion

Justin Morgan

progenitor of that useful breed known as

Morgan Horses.

Thus it appears that, if Justin Morgan the horse had never lived nor bequeathed his splendid characteristics to his many fine descendants, Justin Morgan the man would have lived, taught singing, died and been completely forgotten.

Marengo { *THE EMPEROR'S HORSE*

THROUGH THE YEARS it has become customary to expect heroes and leaders to ride white horses. Certainly, as we have seen in these stories, not all heroes and leaders have done so; they chose good horses regardless of their colors. But in popular opinion, leaders and white horses go together. Just notice the paintings of kings, nobles, and important military officers from the Middle Ages to the present. In many cases the artist has posed his subject on a white horse.

When possible, no doubt, some leaders did ride white horses. During the centuries of mounted warfare, a white horse was easy to see and soldiers were able to follow their leader through the dust and confusion of hand-to-hand, horse-to-horse battle. If the leader became separated from his men and was in danger of being captured by the enemy, it was easier for a rescuing force to locate him if he was high astride a white horse. Further, before a battle started, a good leader always rode up and down the battle lines, encouraging his men to fight bravely. The sight of their leader on his dashing white stud must have given the soldiers additional courage and inspiration.

In more recent times, after armies began to use gunpowder and fight with muskets and cannon fire, the leader on a white horse became a good target for the enemy to shoot at. But in spite of this, white horses were still favored by some leaders. Nowadays, even though generals and other military leaders ride in jeeps and command cars rather than on horseback, the white horse is still considered a favored steed for the military and for the "good guys" in Western movies.

Napoleon Bonaparte, who became the French emperor soon after the French Revolution, was true to the tradition of a general on a white horse and, in most of his military portraits, he is shown either riding or standing beside a white horse.

Napoleon was a medium-sized man but his legs were rather short. He was not a good rider at best, and during the roar and stress of battle he needed a steady horse that he could depend on. All Napoleon's white horses were especially trained to stand steady. White or light gray Arabians or Barbs for Napoleon's use came from the Imperial Horse Farm located at St. Cloud and, in fact, Napoleon owned sixty or more white horses. Their training was supervised by Armand Caulaincourt, Master of the Horse, and by Jardin, the head groom.

Among Napoleon's favorite horses were Marengo, Ali, Jaffa, Austerlitz, and Marie. But, of all the horses in his stables, Napoleon was fondest of the white stallion Marengo. The horse was named in honor of the Battle

Napoleon Bonaparte on Marengo

of Marengo in which the French cavalry won a victory over the Austrians. Napoleon rode him in many battles and also during his disastrous retreat from Moscow.

Marengo's training was strict and severe, like that given to all Napoleon's horses. He learned not to rear or shy when guns were fired close to him. Even cannon fire did not disturb him; he had been taught that the loud noise could not harm him.

He learned not to shy at things that usually frighten horses. Dogs and pigs were driven through his legs, first when he was trotting around the training ring and then out on the open road; regiments of soldiers marched by; wagons came close; sheep herds scattered around him, but Marengo learned to move ahead at a steady, even-gaited pace.

The beautiful white stallion and the short, stocky emperor made an impressive appearance together. It is no wonder that Napoleon chose to ride Marengo whenever he wanted to look his best on horseback.

With so many horses to choose from, Napoleon did not always ride his favorite. This probably was a good thing because, as a rider, Napoleon was hard on horses. He always went at a gallop; before one battle, while he was dashing about giving orders and getting his army ready, five horses sank dead from exhaustion under him. Napoleon was in many battles during the years that he tried to conquer all of Europe and during that time he had nineteen horses shot and killed under him. The Master of the Horse always rode just behind the emperor during combat, so that he could give Napoleon his own mount if Napoleon's horse was felled by a bullet.

When Napoleon was defeated and exiled to Elba,

Marengo was one of the horses he took with him. It was Marengo that he rode during the "Glorious hundred days" in which he tried to regain his empire, and it was Marengo he rode for eight hours during his final defeat at the Battle of Waterloo.

Through those long hours at Waterloo, when victory or defeat hung in the balance, the white horse carried his master faithfully. In that battle Marengo took his seventh wound, this one in the near haunch. It did not disable him, but Napoleon sent him behind the lines to be cared for and was remounted on another white horse, Marie.

Some accounts say that after the battle, when the weary, defeated former emperor climbed into his carriage to make his escape, he was almost captured by the victorious British forces. Abandoning his slow moving carriage, Napoleon trusted Marengo's fleet hoofs to save him. But Napoleon's day was over. This time, when he was sent to exile on the island of St. Helena, he was not allowed to take his faithful white warhorse with him.

After Napoleon's downfall, Marengo and another of the emperor's white horses named Jaffa were purchased by a Frenchman and sent to an English estate at Glastonbury in Kent. There Marengo spent a peaceful old age, living to be 36 years old and dying in September of 1829. He survived his imperial master by eight years.

Marengo's bones were purchased by the United Service Institution and his skeleton was mounted and put on display at Whitehall in London. It was one of the society's most prized relics.

Beyond this, one of the horse's hoofs was preserved

and made into a silver-mounted snuff box. For many years it was military tradition to hand the box around after dinner at the King's Guards mess at St. James Palace in London. As each Guard raised the lid to take a pinch of snuff, he could read the inscription on the box's silver lid: "Hoof of Marengo, barb charger of Napoleon, ridden by him at Marengo, Austerlitz, Jena, Wagram, Russian Campaign, and Waterloo."

Perhaps those were more battles than the horse Marengo saw in his lifetime, but they were all famous battles in which his master, Napoleon Bonaparte, emperor of the French, took part.

Copenhagen { *THE DUKE'S HORSE*

IF EVER A HORSE had a distinguished pedigree, that horse was Copenhagen, the handsome chestnut charger that the Iron Duke of Wellington rode during his campaigns against Napoleon.

Copenhagen was spirited and given to kicking, much like Eclipse his grandfather. The stallion Eclipse, to whom most Thoroughbred racers trace their ancestry, was at first so mean and unmanageable that he had to be worked hard for a year before he was controllable enough to race. Once ready for the track, he was so fast that after two years of constant winning, no horse could be found to run against him.

The mare Lady Catherine, a daughter of the great Eclipse, was Copenhagen's dam; his sire was John Bull, a son of the Rutland Arabian. Lady Catherine was owned by Field Marshal Lord Grosvenor of the British army. He took her with him to Denmark where the English forces were besieging the Danish allies of Napoleon in the city of Copenhagen. When the field marshal learned that his mare was expecting a foal, he sent her back to England away from danger. The Danish city surrendered after a long siege at about the same time that Lady Catherine's foal was born. Appropriately the new foal was named Copenhagen in honor of the English victory.

Copenhagen was five years old, a lively and sometimes hard-to-manage young horse, when the Duke of Wellington bought him for 400 guineas. That was a good price to pay—about two thousand dollars—but the Iron Duke loved fine horses and he admired the fiery chestnut.

The Duke of Wellington was proud of his horse's lineage. If anyone hinted that perhaps Copenhagen's grandmothers were not as distinguished as his grandsires, the Duke snorted indignantly.

"Copenhagen is much more thoroughly bred than most of the men I know," the Iron Duke stoutly maintained. Nobody ever disagreed with him to his face—they knew better.

All through the long, hard Peninsular Campaign, when the British forces fought doggedly across Spain for six years to drive Napoleon's marshals back into France, Copenhagen and the Duke of Wellington were always out in front. Once they galloped to rally a sagging line of English infantrymen when advancing French soldiers were only twenty yards away.

For a time, after the battles in Spain, it seemed as though Napoleon was defeated. He abdicated as emperor and was exiled to the island of Elba. But soon he was back in France for the "hundred days" in which he tried to reestablish himself as master of Europe.

The Battle of Waterloo, June 18, 1815, marked Napoleon's final downfall. In that battle the Duke of

The Duke of Wellington on Copenhagen

Wellington commanded the English forces—allied with troops from the Netherlands, Hanover, and Brunswick —against Napoleon. All day the battle raged, until the arrival of a Prussian army late in the day turned the tide against the French emperor.

Iron Duke that he was, Wellington climbed into the saddle early the day of the battle; by afternoon he was tired, but Copenhagen was still fresh and active. When the Prussians arrived, the Duke and his chestnut warhorse led an infantry charge that smashed Napoleon's famous Old Guard, and "Waterloo" became a word synonymous with defeat, though for the English it was a great victory. On both sides, however, the losses were heavy and 45,000 men lay dead or wounded on the battlefield.

At ten o'clock that night, after eighteen hours in the saddle, a weary Duke of Wellington dismounted in order to have a conference with the Prussian commander. The Iron Duke was bone tired, but not his horse. The chestnut still had energy enough to lash out hard with a final kick; there was so much power in his hoofs that, if they had struck the Duke, they could have injured him severely. But fortunately they missed and who could blame him? All day bullets and cannon balls had roared and whistled around him, so wasn't he entitled to one last kick in celebration?

After Waterloo, no honor was too great for the British to give to the Duke of Wellington, the man who had finally defeated Napoleon. And no honor was too great for the horse that had served him faithfully through so many battles. In gratitude, the British government gave the Iron Duke a 7,000-acre estate called Strathfieldsaye in Hampshire. Copenhagen was sent to the estate and spent the rest of his life there in comfortable retirement.

One of the greatest compliments the Duke of Wellington could pay his many friends was to allow them to ride his famous warhorse. Several times the Duke's eldest son, the Marquis of Douro, secretly put a saddle on the horse and pretended that he, too, was riding the warhorse into battle.

As Copenhagen grew older he lost some of his fire and was easier to manage. Sometimes the Duke even allowed the ladies who visited at Strathfieldsaye to ride the chestnut steed. One of them later said "He was a most unpleasant horse to ride," but perhaps she felt that way because of a tumble she took from his back when a stirrup broke during a jump.

That evening the Duke soothed her ruffled feelings by making a toast in her honor.

"Here's to the heroine of the day," he said gallantly, lifting his glass to her. "She got kicked off and didn't mind."

Copenhagen never forgot the sound of a bugle or failed to react to the sight of troops. He always snorted and neighed with pleasure and dashed to join them if he could.

Once when he did this, his rider heard a veteran of the Peninsular Campaign warn his comrades.

"Take care of that 'ere horse," the old soldier exclaimed. "He kicks out. We knew him in Spain!"

The demands of a busy political life often took the Duke to London, but whenever he left Strathfieldsaye the last thing he did was to walk out to the paddock to give Copenhagen a farewell pat. Usually the Duke carried along a piece of chocolate to feed him because the old charger had a taste for sweets and was especially fond of candy.

The women of the Wellington family were also proud of the famous old warhorse. Wellington's wife wore a bracelet made of hair from Copenhagen's mane and tail, as did several of her friends. Her daughter-in-law not only had a bracelet but also a breast pin made from the horse's hair.

Waterloo was the Duke's last battle, but a long career in politics lay ahead of him. Even after he became England's prime minister, he still found time for his horses and he always gave the grooms special instructions about their care. When the gallant old warhorse died in 1836, the Duke made a special trip from London and went immediately to the stables to see that Copenhagen received proper burial.

"There may have been many faster horses," the Duke said in tribute to his faithful old friend, "and no doubt there were many handsomer, but for bottom and endurance I never saw his fellow."

The old horse was buried with military honors on the Duke's estate. His grave was dug at the base of a great oak tree so that its wide spreading branches could shade his resting place. On the marble tombstone that marks the spot are these words:

Here lies Copenhagen
The charger ridden by the Duke of Wellington
the entire day
of the Battle of Waterloo
Born 1808, died 1836.
God's humbler instrument, though meaner clay,
Should share the glory of that glorious day.

Old Whitey *{ THE PRESIDENT'S HORSE }*

"OLD WHITEY" was what the soldiers called General Zachary Taylor's horse but the "Old" was just a term of affection. The horse was comparatively young. "Old Zach" and "Old Rough and Ready" were what the men called General Taylor, though in his case the term fitted. The general was a veteran Indian fighter, past sixty years of age when he led an American army through Texas and across the Rio Grande to fight a war against Mexico.

Old Whitey was not a dashing warhorse but he was dependable and steady, just like the general who rode him. He did not have a distinguished pedigree and exactly where the general got him is not clearly recorded. It is thought that early in the Mexican War, when the general needed a new mount, Old Zach's soldiers captured the white horse from a Mexican officer. General Taylor liked the horse's sturdy looks and, from then on, they fought the war together.

Battles and dangers were nothing new to Zachary Taylor, although he did not appear very warlike. Even though he had been an army man for forty years, he looked more like a farmer than like a general. He disliked uniforms and usually wore any kind of a coat or hat that suited the weather; the color and style did not matter as long as they were comfortable. A steady, dependable and unpretentious horse like Old Whitey suited Old Zach just fine.

Old Whitey was calm and unexcitable. In their letters to people back home soldiers and young officers often described how General Taylor sat on Old Whitey and watched the fighting from a hilltop, paying no attention to the bullets whizzing around them. Old Whitey would snatch a mouthful of grass whenever he had a chance and munch away on it, as unconcerned about all the noise and bullets as his master seemed to be.

There is no record that Old Whitey was ever hit by a bullet although his coat of white hair made him a good target. No bullets ever wounded the general, either, although sometimes they went through his coat. Cannon balls fell close by but they never hit Old Whitey or his master.

Old Whitey's feet got tired on the long marches across the dry desert country of northern Mexico, and the stony ground around Monterrey wore down his hoofs so badly that he was lame for a time. But whenever the fighting was fiercest, the men could look up to the highest piece of ground in the battle zone and see Old Whitey with Old Zach in the saddle, one leg swung over the pommel in a comfortable and unmilitary way, watching and giving orders.

Old Whitey and General Taylor were in four big battles together as "Old Rough and Ready" led his army southward into Mexico. Their last one, at Buena Vista,

was the fiercest. In it the Mexicans, led by General
Santa Anna, far outnumbered Taylor's forces. In full
view on the top of a plateau, the old general sat calmly
on his white horse. Soon an enemy battery began firing
its cannons in that direction.

"General, sir," the staff officers pleaded, "please move
back out of range."

General Taylor gave Old Whitey a nudge in the ribs
with the heel of his worn old army boot. The horse
moved forward, not backward as the other officers advised.

"We'll just ride up a little nearer," the general said,
"and then the balls will go over us."

The battle ended with Santa Anna's army in retreat,
and the war shifted away from General Taylor. The old
veteran was granted a well earned leave and sailed for
home aboard the *U.S.S. Monmouth,* taking his white
horse with him.

———

Home for General Taylor was at Cypress Grove, a plantation in Louisiana, overlooking the Mississippi River.
But before the two veterans reached there they landed
at New Orleans where all the people turned out to give
them a hero's welcome. Old Whitey carried his master
as easily in the triumphal parade as he had carried him
in battle. But onlookers noticed how the white horse
pricked up his ears, arched his neck, and even pranced
a little as though keeping time to the music of the military bands.

From the landing place on the river bank, the victory
parade marched through gaily decorated New Orleans
streets and under triumphal arches to Jackson Square;

guns boomed military salutes and the people cheered.
There was a religious service in the old cathedral facing the Square and, while Old Whitey waited outside,
souvenir hunters pulled a good many hairs from his
mane and tail.

But once home at the general's plantation Old Whitey
grew more hairs while he ate the lush green grass and
enjoyed the shade under the big oak trees. The house
was small, but it had a big porch covered with climbing
roses and honeysuckle vines. Old Zach rested, too, but
not for long. His military victories had made him famous, and his lack of political entanglements led the
Whig Party to choose him as their presidential candi-
date. In the fall of 1847 he was elected president of the
United States and next spring Old Whitey went along
with his master to Washington.

Grass growing on the White House lawn must have
tasted as good to Old Whitey as the grass of the
Louisiana plantation. He was allowed to graze at will,
and often he helped to welcome distinguished visitors.
His greetings were informal—a whinny, perhaps, and a
sniff, with a look of appreciation if the visitor was
thoughtful enough to bring an apple or a piece of sugar
to feed him.

One politician, who perhaps hoped to gain special
favor from President Taylor, presented Old Whitey with
a silver curry comb. But it was not used very often—the
horse's hair was thick and shaggy and usually there
were tangles in his mane and tail.

Of all the official activities, Old Whitey seemed to
enjoy the Sunday afternoon band concerts on the White
House lawn most. They may have reminded him of his
army days and he often grazed close by to listen while

the band was playing. Once he even tried to join a parade of out-of-town firemen when they marched to the White House to visit with the president.

In July of Old Whitey's second summer at the White House, there were gloomy expressions and worried looks on the faces of people who came and went. Old Zach was ill. Crowds gathered in the street to wait for news from his sickroom. Then the big bell in a nearby church steeple rang solemnly and soon all the church bells in Washington joined in. President Taylor, "Old Rough and Ready," was dead.

White House grooms brushed Old Whitey's shaggy coat and combed the tangles from his mane and tail. They put a saddle on him and fixed a pair of his master's boots in the stirrups, upside down. That was cavalry custom, to show that the boots were empty and the rider dead.

Old Whitey walked slowly after the flag-draped hearse containing his dead master's body in the presidential funeral procession. The newspaper reporters made special mention of him.

"All eyes were on the far-famed warhorse, with holsters and inverted spurs on the saddle," one reporter wrote. "Old Whitey pawed the ground and tossed his head at every boom of the cannon," another newsman added, "advancing as it seemed with a military air." "Poor fellow, he stepped proudly," a third writer noted.

———

A new president moved into the White House and Old Whitey went home with his master's family. Richard Taylor, Old Zach's son, owned a sugar plantation called

Fashion in Louisiana and Zach's daughters inherited Cypress Grove. The white horse spent time on both estates and life for him was easy. There was plenty of time to eat grass from the wide pasture lands or doze in the shade of the big oak and magnolia trees. Sometimes Richard Taylor or his wife rode the old veteran and the horse was a favorite with the general's grandchildren. Strangers even pulled an occasional hair from his mane or tail to keep as a souvenir, but that did not bother the horse very much.

More than a dozen years passed by. Life was pleasant and peaceful on the plantations, but great events were taking place in Washington and all over the country. The North and the South separated and went to war with each other. Richard Taylor became a colonel in the Confederate army and went off to fight the Yankees. Old Whitey was almost forgotten in the pasture.

A Union army marched into Louisiana and captured New Orleans. Yankee raiders rode through the country areas, collecting food supplies and horses needed by the army. One group rode up to the Fashion plantation and the officer in charge ordered any horses remaining brought out.

Perhaps Old Whitey remembered his own army days when he heard the officer's sharp commands; the sounds of boots and saddles creaking and sabers rattling were familiar. Perhaps he even came to the pasture fence to whinny a greeting.

One of the men tied a rope around his neck and started to lead him away.

Mrs. Richard Taylor hurried to his rescue.

"Stop! Stop!" she cried, rushing to where the officer in charge was sitting on his horse. "You can't take Old

Whitey. He's too old. He belonged to General Taylor in the Mexican War. The General rode him when he was president."

The Yankee officer shook his head.

"Sorry, ma'am," he said. "We need all the horses we can get. Our colonel is old, too, and he needs a steady horse. He also was in the Mexican War, so the two should get on just fine together."

So Old Whitey was led away with the rest of the plantation horses, back to the sound of bugles and the roar of battle. The colonel of the 14th Iowa Infantry rode him until a Confederate bullet knocked him out of the saddle during a battle at a place called Pleasant Hill. That was the last fight for the colonel, but not for Old Whitey.

A Captain Warren C. Jones took command of the Iowa regiment and rode Old Whitey for the remaining months of the Civil War. When the war ended, the old horse was sent to the dead colonel's farm where he pulled a plow in Iowa corn fields for two years. Then his last wartime companion, Captain Jones, bought him and made sure the old warhorse had an easy time for the rest of his days.

———

Not many horses have served in two wars or fought under as many flags as Old Whitey. During his long lifetime the white horse had carried men fighting under the red, white and green banner of Mexico, the Lone Star of Texas, the Stars and Bars of the Confederacy, as well as the Stars and Stripes of the United States.

When he died, the veteran Old Whitey surely had earned the military honors that attended his burial.

Traveller | *THE CONFEDERATE GENERAL'S HORSE*

IT WAS SOMETHING like a case of love at first sight in the spring of 1861 when General Robert E. Lee saw the gray colt. The Civil War had just begun and General Lee was busy directing Confederate operations in western Virginia when a young soldier named J. W. Johnson rode past his headquarters on the fine gray horse.

In spite of all the problems he had in organizing and training his Army of Northern Virginia, General Lee found time to ask about the horse. He sent an orderly to summon the young owner.

"My father raised that colt and gave him to me," the young man told the general proudly. "He's already won two prizes at the Greenbriar County Fair. I call him Jeff Davis but I'm thinking of changing his name to Greenbriar."

The general nodded understandingly. He loved horses

Robert E. Lee and Traveller

and was always glad to find others who appreciated a horse's good qualities.

"Will you sell him?" was the general's next question.

Young Johnson was somewhat embarrassed by the general's attention. He shook his head.

"Well, you see, sir," he answered slowly, "I can't. He's already promised to Captain Broun. I think he's buying him for his brother."

"I understand." But the general's voice sounded disappointed. "I'll have a talk with Captain Broun."

The Brouns did buy the gray horse and General Lee did talk with Captain Broun; and later he also talked with his brother. He watched the two young officers as they used the gray horse that summer and, although the horse remained their property, he often spoke to them about it.

"How is my colt?" he would say. "Take care of him because I'll be needing him some day."

Duty called General Lee back to Richmond and then to South Carolina. Captain Broun was also assigned to South Carolina where he rode the gray horse at the head of his company.

The next time the general spoke of the horse, Captain Broun saluted and held out the reins to his commanding officer.

"I know how much you admire him, sir," he said. "My brother and I want to present him to you."

"I can't accept him as a gift," the general answered, "but if you care to sell him, I'll be glad to try him out."

For several days the general rode the gray horse—Greenbriar was now the horse's name—and a price was agreed upon. Major Broun asked only the $175 he had paid young Johnson for the horse, but General Lee increased the price to $200 because of the wartime inflation.

"He certainly is a fine traveller—a fine Traveller," the general repeated happily when the gray horse was finally his own property. And Traveller was what he called the horse from that time on. Through the war and for the rest of Lee's life, the gray general and the gray horse were constant companions.

Any horse belonging to General Lee—and he owned several—had a good master who saw to it that his animals received the best of care. He and Traveller went through many battles together, but in spite of all the worries and problems Lee had to face as the tide of war turned against the Confederacy, he always made sure that Traveller was as well fed and as well groomed as possible.

Many little details, that showed Lee's thoughtfulness, were noticed and recorded by the men who served with him. He would take time to see that the horse's bridle was properly adjusted and the saddle blanket folded carefully. Whenever possible during a battle, he dismounted so that his horse could rest without the weight of a rider on his back.

Once, when a young courier brought a message during the Battle of the Wilderness and then sat on his weary, panting horse while awaiting an answer, General Lee took time to rebuke him.

"Young man, you should have some feeling for your horse," the general said sharply. "Dismount and rest him."

With that, the general reached into the saddlebag on Traveller's back, took out half a buttered biscuit, and fed it to the courier's mount.

Not everyone found Traveller as pleasing to ride as the general did. The horse had a smooth canter and a fast, springy walk, but he went at a high, choppy trot that took a good horseman like General Lee to ride comfortably.

As the war progressed, the two became inseparable symbols to the men in the Confederate army. Whenever the general rode along the lines or paid visits to their camps, the men cheered him; there was always a friendly feeling between the private soldiers and the commanding general and his horse. Traveller heard the cheers and tossed his gray head in response, and that made the men cheer even louder.

Battles are hard on the nerves of men and of horses, and Traveller sometimes reacted to the dangers of warfare. During the second Battle of Bull Run, when General Lee had dismounted and was waiting for reports, there was a sudden shout of warning.

"Yankee cavalry coming!"

The commotion startled Traveller, and General Lee reached for the dragging reins. He tripped and fell forward, catching himself on his hands. He was up in an instant and no enemy cavalry appeared. But when the general tried to mount again, both hands hurt him so much he could not hold the reins. The doctor reported bad sprains in both wrists and a broken bone in one hand. It was two weeks before the general could climb into Traveller's saddle again—a horseman needs good wrists and hands in order to use the reins efficiently.

There is no telling how many times Traveller's swift feet saved his master from capture, for General Lee did not hesitate to ride close to enemy lines while making his inspections. In the wooded hills of Virginia and on shady country roads, there was no way of knowing when raiders might appear or where enemy pickets might be hiding.

At least once Traveller actually saved his master's life in battle. The general was riding with a column of reenforcements at Spotsylvania when a Yankee artillery battery opened fire at long range. As shells began bursting around them the excited Traveller began to dance wildly. The general sought to control him, but each time a shell passed near, the gray horse reared up on his hind legs and pawed the air with his front hoofs.

"Steady, Traveller, steady," the general said.

A shell burst close by and Traveller reared again. As he did, another cannon ball whizzed under him, close to the saddle girth on his belly. If all four of Traveller's feet had been on the ground at that moment, the ball would have struck his master squarely.

The men who saw the near-miss were startled.

"Go back, general," they yelled at him. "For God's sake, go back!"

Reluctantly, General Lee reined Traveller and rode slowly out of range. There was no haste or alarm in his action; but a commanding general cannot risk his life recklessly—too much depends on his guidance and decisions.

Lee was always careful to avoid any appearance of panic. A few days after the above incident, when he and his staff were riding close behind the Confederate front line, a Yankee shell burst nearby, sending fragments ricocheting in all directions. Excited by the whine of the shells, Traveller and the other horses began to move faster; soon they were going at a gallop. General Lee pulled on the reins and signaled his staff officers to do the same.

"I did not want the men to think we were disturbed by the shelling," the general remarked later. "How could I order them to fight, if they thought I was nervous under fire?"

The fortunes of war turned against the Confederacy. The Union forces grew stronger while the Confederacy wore out. At last Lee realized his men could fight no longer. On an April morning in 1865, he mounted Traveller and rode to Appomattox where he met General Grant, the Union commander, and arranged for the Confederate surrender. Traveller munched grass outside the meeting place while the two generals talked. When General Lee came out, he stood for a moment waiting while the orderly adjusted Traveller's bridle. Then the general smoothed the horse's forelock, patted the gray neck and, with a sigh, mounted and rode away to tell his men that the war was over.

At camp near the Confederate headquarters, the men clustered around Lee on his gray horse, waiting to hear what he had to say.

"We have fought the war together, and I have done the best I could for you," the general said, his voice low but steady.

He could say little more—after four years of fighting, this was the end. The men crowded closer around him, patting Traveller's neck or stroking his flanks. It was a time of deep feeling for everyone. As the general rode through the army for the last time, the men cheered and Traveller tossed his gray head in answer, as he always did. The men cheered louder. The war was over.

Traveller carried General Lee home to Richmond, and later after a long rest, the two traveled together along the quiet Virginia roads to Lexington where Robert E. Lee was to be president of Washington College.

Life for the two of them was different from what it had been during the war but their companionship was closer than ever. Lee found both relaxation and exercise in long solitary rides on Traveller's back. Often with his daughters and friends he enjoyed pleasant horseback outings in the country.

The gray horse spent most of the time between rides grazing peacefully on the lawn in front of Lee's home on the college campus. He learned to keep a wary eye on strangers who might come too close and try to snatch some hairs from his tail as souvenirs. Hair snatchers made him nervous. It was sometimes hard to forget the noise and alarms of battle.

"Be patient with Traveller," Lee would say to the blacksmith when the horse danced skittishly and made shoeing him difficult. "Shells bursting around him during the war made him nervous."

When duties called Lee away from his Lexington home, he always mentioned Traveller in his letters. "How is Traveller?" he would ask. "Tell him I miss him and have, ever since we parted." And another time, "I hope Traveller is well and wants for nothing."

An artist friend spoke of painting Traveller's portrait and General Lee wrote his approval in a long, descriptive letter.

"If I were an artist like you," his began, "I would draw a true picture of Traveller; representing his fine proportions, muscular figure, deep chest, short back, strong haunches, flat legs, small head, broad forehead, delicate ears, quick eye, small feet and black mane and tail.

"Such a picture would inspire a poet," the general continued, "whose genius could then depict his worth and describe his endurance of toil, hunger, thirst, heat and cold, and the dangers and sufferings through which he passed. He could dilate upon his sagacity and affection, and his invariable response to every wish of his rider. He might even imagine his thoughts through the long night marches and days of battle through which he passed. But I am no artist, and can therefore only say he is a Confederate gray."

The general then went on to detail the battles and dangers the two had experienced together, and to describe the saddles and other equipment that admirers had presented to the famous gray horse. It was a letter that showed, between the lines, the deep affection a man can have for his horse.

As a colt, Traveller was dark iron-gray in color. But as the years passed, his coat grew lighter until six years after the war he was almost milk-white. The strain of war told on him, no doubt, but a horse can rest and graze and forget. The strain was harder on his master and forgetting was not so easy.

General Lee served as president of Washington College until his death in 1870. He rode Traveller often during those years, until rheumatism and heart trouble kept him out of the saddle for the last few months of his life.

The gray horse followed directly behind the hearse in his master's funeral procession. There were black crepe ribbons of mourning on his saddle and bridle, and two of Lee's former soldiers led him. But it was not a military funeral—Lee had struggled hard to put aside the hatreds of war and to stress the importance of peace.

Traveller lived for about two years after his master's death, well cared for and loved by the Lee family. One day while out in his pasture he stepped on a rusty nail; lockjaw set in and in spite of all his human friends tried to do, they were not able to save his life. He was buried in property owned by the college which was by then called Washington and Lee, in honor of his master.

In 1907 Traveller's bones were dug up and mounted. His skeleton stands in the museum at Washington and Lee University and his master lies buried in the chapel.

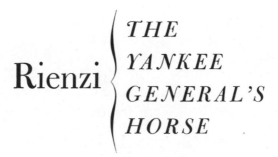

Rienzi { THE YANKEE GENERAL'S HORSE

WHEN Captain Archibald P. Campbell rode away as an officer of the 2nd Michigan Cavalry to fight in the Civil War, the people of his home town of Port Huron gave him a beautiful black Morgan horse. The people were proud of their state's cavalry unit and they wanted its officers to look as fine as possible.

Captain Campbell appreciated the gift and admired the horse, but he was not a very good rider. He preferred a gentler horse, one that he felt safe on, and he seldom rode the spirited black Morgan. Nonetheless, when the 2nd Michigan Cavalry was sent to fight the Confederate forces in Mississippi, the black horse was transported along with the other regimental horses. John Ashley, the regimental farrier, cared for him and took pride in keeping the horse groomed and curried to perfection. The Morgan's coat shone and his three white feet were never muddy or dusty.

87

Philip Sheridan and Rienzi

Such a fine looking horse could not pass unnoticed. Even Colonel Philip Sheridan, the regimental commander, admired him. The colonel rode him several times to try his gaits and liked what he found. The Morgan was fast; at his natural walking gait he could easily cover five miles an hour while his gallop was as smooth as riding the wind.

"That's a mighty fine horse, Captain," the colonel remarked one day when the Michigan officer visited his headquarters.

"Yes, sir," Captain Campbell agreed. "He's pure Morgan stock from the Black Hawk line."

"Must be about three years old," Phil Sheridan continued.

"That's right, sir," the captain answered. "He was foaled in 1858 near Grand Rapids, Michigan. He's a fine horse, but he has too much spirit for me. I'm not the rider you are, and never will be."

Colonel Phil Sheridan was a scrappy, short-legged Irishman. His friends called him "Little Phil," and being a short man, he liked big horses. The Morgan stood sixteen hands high—that was another reason the colonel liked him.

Captain Campbell admired his commanding officer. The two men worked well together and in a battle at Booneville the Michigan regiment enjoyed a welcome victory over a much larger force of Confederate soldiers. After the battle the regiment was stationed at Rienzi, Mississippi, and it was there and after that battle that Captain Campbell decided to give his elegant black horse to Colonel Sheridan.

"He will do you more good, Phil, than he will me," the captain said.

"I can't refuse a good horse," the colonel replied. "I'll call him Rienzi."

From that time on Rienzi was Phil Sheridan's favorite horse. In his memoirs, after he had become a famous general, Sheridan wrote his personal praise of his almost equally famous horse.

"I rode him almost continuously," Little Phil recalled, "in every campaign and battle in which I took part, without once finding him overcome with fatigue. On many occasions his strength was severely tested by long marches and short rations."

Remembering Captain Campbell's fears that the horse might be mean and dangerous, Sheridan went on: "I never observed in him any vicious habit."

The only indication of nerves that Sheridan noticed was Rienzi's habit of switching his tail when all the rest of his body was quiet. "But only a novice would be deceived by this," the officer added. "His intelligence, along with his fine thoroughbred appearance, were obvious to anyone who knew horses."

Rienzi's master was promoted from Colonel to Brigadier General and then to Major General. The black horse carried him faithfully, though not without being wounded several times in action.

Rienzi became famous in his own right because he carried General Sheridan on a most important ride to rally a retreating Union army. Together, they turned near-disaster into victory and added one more defeat to the crumbling Confederate cause.

Rienzi's famous gallop took place on a beautiful fall morning in October, 1864. General Sheridan's army had been fighting a successful campaign in the Shenandoah Valley and the secretary of war called him to Washington for a conference. The general did not like the idea of leaving his army, even for a short time, but orders were orders. Leaving the army camped at Cedar Creek, he and his staff rode to Winchester, left their horses and went on to Washington by train. After the conference, they returned to Winchester and spent the night there.

Early next morning the general awoke to the sound of cannon fire. Rienzi heard the same ominous sound as he munched his morning hay with the other horses and raised his head to listen. Soon orderlies came to saddle the horses; Rienzi switched his tail and stamped his white front feet nervously. By half past eight in the morning General Sheridan was in the saddle and Rienzi was leading the staff down the turnpike that led from Winchester to Cedar Creek. The sound of cannons had grown into a steady roar.

Rienzi's hoofs drummed on the road. As horse and rider topped a rise they saw a jumble of men and wagons moving toward them. General Sheridan asked a few questions and learned that his army was retreating under an unexpected Confederate attack!

Phil Sheridan was not a fighting Irishman for nothing; he could not believe in defeat. Rienzi was a powerful horse; he obeyed the urgings of his master's voice and spurs. Down the road they galloped, followed by the general's twenty-man escort. The battle line was miles away but man and horse knew they had to get there.

There was something electric about Phil Sheridan. As he rode, he rallied his defeated men.

"Face the other way, boys!" he shouted. "We're going back. Face the other way!"

There was something electric, too, about the clatter of Rienzi's hoofs on the turnpike. The black horse galloped strongly. The miles rolled under his hoofs. Sometimes the general and his horse had to leave the highway and detour around the mass of wagons and men.

"Come back to the front with me, boys!" the general called.

Amazingly, the defeated men responded. They cheered, and they turned around. Rienzi galloped on and the numbers of men following him increased with every step.

The distance from Winchester to the battle front was something like twenty miles; Rienzi covered it in record time. He galloped through the crowds of retreating men, tossing his head, switching his tail, adding his wordless encouragement to Sheridan's shouts.

"About face, boys! We are going back. We're going to lick them!"

There was no rest for the black horse or his rider when they did reach the battle zone. Up and down the lines of his battered army General Sheridan rode. Rienzi carried him bravely and the ranks took courage. By midafternoon the Union army was attacking and the Confederates were in full retreat. Rienzi and Sheridan covered at least seventy-five miles that day—both horse and man were tireless.

Such things did not happen often. There were not many generals like Sheridan and not many horses like Rienzi. The people of the North were thrilled when they learned of the exploit. President Lincoln telegraphed his congratulations, as did many other United States officials.

Everyone, and especially the people of the general's home state of Ohio, wanted to hear more about Sheridan's ride. A poet and an actor of the time worked together to produce a poem that became one of the best known of that day. The poet, Thomas Buchanan Read, and the actor, James E. Murdoch, presented it first at the Cincinnati Opera House and soon everybody in the North was quoting it. Rienzi got his share of the glory and became almost as famous as his master.

In a meter much like the rhythm of galloping hoofs, the poem's last stanza reads:

> Hurrah! hurrah for Sheridan!
> Hurrah! hurrah for horse and man!
> And when their statues are placed on high,
> Under the dome of the Union sky,
> The American soldier's Temple of Fame,
> There, with the glorious general's name,
> Be it said, in letters both bold and bright:
> "Here is the steed that saved the day
> By carrying Sheridan into the fight,
> From Winchester—twenty miles away."

But the war between the states was not over. Sheridan and Rienzi could not stop and take bows. They went on fighting. At the Battle of Five Forks a few months later, General Sheridan led his men in a charge against the enemy and actually jumped Rienzi over the Confederate breastworks to help capture 150 men.

Finally, the South could fight no longer and the war

came to an end. It was Sheridan, mounted on Rienzi, who met the Confederate officers coming to report that General Lee was ready to surrender.

Rienzi lived to be nineteen years old—not a great age for a horse even though Sheridan said about him:

"He lived to a ripe old age, and died in 1878, attended to the last with care and surrounded with every comfort due the faithful service he had rendered."

Because he was one of the most famous horses of the Civil War, Rienzi was mounted by a taxidermist and placed on display in the Governors' Island Museum in New York Harbor, along with other relics and mementos of the Civil War. The stuffed Rienzi stood in the Museum for many years and then he was moved to the Smithsonian Museum in Washington, D.C., where he may still be seen by visitors today.

Comanche { THE CAPTAIN'S HORSE

"IF YOU COULD ONLY TALK!"

Dozens of people said that to Comanche during the fifteen years he lived as the sole survivor of General Custer's final battle with Sioux warriors at the Little Big Horn in Montana.

If he could have spoken, the dun horse might have provided answers to some puzzling questions. Certainly, he could have given an eyewitness account of that fatal afternoon, June 25, 1876, when Yellow-haired Custer and 265 troopers of the U.S. 7th Cavalry were killed to the last man.

As sole survivor, Comanche lived in honored retirement, the "second commanding officer" of the 7th Cavalry. By order of the first commanding officer, Colonel Samuel Sturgis, no one was to ride him and he was to do no work. He was fed, well cared for, and his sole duties were to take part in regimental ceremonies and parades, when he was draped in mourning and led by a mounted cavalryman at the head of Troop I.

Comanche

If Comanche could have told his life story, leading up to that day at Little Big Horn, it would have begun with his birth on the plains of Texas-Oklahoma. As a colt, he ran beside his mother with a herd of mixed mustangs—American-bred and Spanish horses. The army was using this stock to develop a hardy breed of horses for the exacting demands of cavalry service in the West.

For his first few years the colt had no name. He had to wait a while for that. His coat was light tan with some yellow and there was a dark streak down his back—a "claybank" or "coyote dun" was the way he was later described.

Nameless and free, he galloped over the plains for about four years before he and other young horses of the herd were rounded up and driven to a big corral. The best of them were selected by a horse trader and driven as a smaller herd northeast across Missouri to a farm near St. Louis.

There the dun horse's training began. The cowboys were not at all gentle in their breaking tactics—a horse soon learned to accept bit and saddle their way or he was considered an outlaw. The dun horse was not an outlaw; he had spirit but not rebellion in his healthy young body.

His stay on the farm was short. The U.S. Cavalry needed horses for its campaigns against the western Indians and the Army quartermaster came to St. Louis on a horse-buying mission. Soon the dun horse and many others were loaded into freight cars and shipped to the cavalry corral at Fort Leavenworth, Kansas.

Army veterinarians looked at his teeth and his hoofs

and pronounced him sound. He was shod and the letters
"U. S." were branded on his left shoulder. The dun horse
and his fellows were now officially government property.

One morning a young yellow-haired cavalryman—he
was First Lieutenant Tom Custer, brother of General
George A. Custer of the 7th U.S. Cavalry—arrived at
Fort Leavenworth. The 7th needed some good remount
horses and Lieutenant Custer was to select them. The
dun was among the forty-one chosen and soon he
traveled again, this time to a cavalry camp near Ellis,
Kansas, where the troopers were stationed to protect the
settlers from Indian raids.

———

"I'll try that one," the red-haired captain said, with
just a trace of Ireland in his accent.

"Yes, sir," the orderly answered. "You mean that claybank dun with the stripe down his back?"

Captain Myles Keogh nodded. An Irish-born soldier
of fortune, he needed a second horse for his duties with
Troop I of the 7th. He found the dun horse satisfactory
—not so much in looks, perhaps, but steady and dependable. These were qualities the Irish cavalryman
respected.

"I'll buy him," Captain Keogh said, after a trial ride
to put the half-broken dun through his paces. "The
quartermaster can take the $90 he costs out of my pay."

"Yes, sir," the orderly replied. And the dun horse had
a new master.

Captain Keogh had two horses. His first horse was a
Thoroughbred with the good Irish name of Paddy. The
other was the claybank dun. The captain rode Paddy on

long marches and changed to the dun when the cavalry went into action. This practice gave him a fresh horse when the fighting began.

The dun saw his first action three months after Captain Keogh bought him. The captain's cavalry unit had moved southwest across the Kansas plains to Fort Dodge and from there south to the Cimarron where the Comanche Indians were on the warpath.

Once engaged, the troopers charged and the Comanches pulled back, shooting a cloud of arrows as they galloped away. Captain Keogh felt his dun horse stumble. He lifted the reins, the horse regained its stride and they galloped on. The Indians disappeared in a cloud of dust and the cavalrymen reformed ranks and returned to camp.

"He's a good horse," the captain said, dismounting and handing the reins to his orderly. "He stumbled once but kept right on going."

"No wonder," the orderly answered. "Look, sir, there's the stub of an arrow sticking out of his right quarter. I'd best take him to the farrier for treatment."

"Humm, wounded in his first action and all he did was stumble." The Irish captain was impressed. "I'll go along with you and see that he gets good care."

The farrier, whose duty was to shoe the cavalry horses, doctor them, and look after their wounds, went promptly to work. Soon he had extracted a short fragment of arrow, tipped with a flint point, from close under the hide of the horse's right hip. The dun horse winced and squealed as it came out.

"Steady, there," the farrier said as he cleaned and treated the wound.

Captain Keogh patted the horse's neck in sympathy.

"Look at that, sir," the farrier said when the task was finished. He handed a flint tipped fragment of wood to the officer. "It's a Comanche arrow if I ever saw one."

"Comanche—so it is," Captain Keogh said, examining the sharp stone point. "Hit by a Comanche arrow and he kept right on going. Comanche—that's a good name for him. I've been wondering what to call him."

So the dun horse had a name. He was Comanche for the rest of his life.

———

Captain Keogh owned Comanche for eight years. They were years of action with the cavalry. For two years they patrolled the Kansas plains and Comanche got a second wound. This was in his right leg and he was lame for several weeks.

Later the cavalry was transferred to Kentucky to deal with moonshiners and other outlaws there. Comanche was wounded for a third time in the right shoulder, but it was a slight nick and he recovered quickly.

From Kentucky, Captain Keogh and Comanche were sent to Dakota Territory where their troop was assigned to protect the survey team that was marking the boundary line between the United States and Canada. They covered more than 1,500 miles through summer heat and winter cold. Then in the spring of 1875 they were sent to Fort Lincoln to rejoin the main body of the 7th Cavalry.

There, there were ordinary patrols and routine duties, but every day reports came that the Sioux Indians, under the leadership of Sitting Bull, were growing more and more hostile. The Indians objected to the way white settlers were usurping their lands and killing off the buffalo herds. A year passed, then one fine June morning the cavalry rode out in a long column, followed by supply wagons and all the equipment needed for a hard campaign.

The officers' wives waved good-by, trying not to show their tears, as the cavalry band played "The Girl I Left Behind Me." It was a lively tune and perhaps Comanche tossed his head and stepped in time to the music. Captain Keogh was riding Paddy, while an orderly led the dun horse to keep him fresh for action.

Action came on Sunday afternoon, June 25, 1876. General Custer divided his force and led half of them in an attack on an Indian village. He did not know that more than 2,500 warriors were waiting out of sight behind a hill.

What happened after that is history. Every man in Custer's unit was killed. The fight was fast and furious. Little knots of troopers gathered to make a stand against the fierce Sioux warriors. One by one they fell. Riderless horses galloped wildly about while others lay wounded or dead. Indian boys and old men rounded up the horses that were not too badly hurt; they cut the throats of the others. Squaws swarmed across the battlefield taking whatever they wanted from the dead troopers' bodies.

Night came; the battlefield was silent and deserted. It was two days before other army units were able to reach the hill to see what had happened to Custer and his men.

They found only one creature alive and moving on that fateful field. It was the dun horse, Comanche. His reins were dragging, his saddle girth loose and the saddle dangling under his belly. Dried blood covered his flanks and a deep wound in his neck was still bleeding.

It was a time of great confusion. Nobody could believe the disaster that had happened. An entire cavalry unit wiped out—not a single man left alive! Bodies had to be identified and buried. Because of the confusion at least five different soldiers claimed to have found Comanche, the sole survivor.

How did he happen to survive?

Why hadn't the Indians taken him along with the other horses?

What had he done during the two days and nights after the battle?

When had Captain Keogh fallen?

When? Why? How?

These questions could never be answered. Comanche could not talk.

By easy marches and with as tender care as possible, the wounded horse was led across country to the junction of the Little Bighorn and Big Horn Rivers. There he was taken aboard the steamer *Far West* and bedded down in a stall near the vessel's stern wheel. On the ship with him were wounded cavalrymen, casualties from units that had also fought against Sitting Bull's warriors.

The steamer moved downstream making a fifty-four hour voyage to the town of Bismarck. Comanche, by this time too weak to stand, was placed on a big piece of canvas and dragged to a low wagon which took him to Fort Lincoln and Troop I stables. Army veterinarians rigged a belly sling in his stall so he could stand without putting weight on his shaky legs. Almost a year passed before his wounds were healed and the dun horse was well again.

From that time on Comanche was an honored, retired veteran. He was a symbol of pride and triumph over defeat. When people saw him, they remembered General Custer and his men at the Little Big Horn. The 7th Cavalry observed June 25th of each year as a day of mourning; a ceremonial parade was held and riderless Comanche led Troop I. The crepe on his saddle and the empty boots in his stirrups told silently of men who had died.

When he was not taking part in parades and ceremonies, Comanche had free run of the cavalry compound. The door of his stall was never closed; officers fed him sugar; enlisted men bought buckets of beer for him on pay days. On sunny summer afternoons he munched grass near the bandstand and seemed to enjoy the band concerts.

Comanche traveled with the 7th when it was transferred from Fort Totten to Fort Meade, and finally to Fort Riley. During most of the years of his honored retirement, Gustav Korn, blacksmith for Troop I, was detailed as his special attendant. Korn was one of the men who claimed to have found the wounded Comanche on the battlefield.

Trooper Korn seemed to have a real affection for the dun horse. But after fourteen years an Indian bullet ended that association, as other bullets had ended the life of Comanche's first friend, Captain Myles Keogh. Gustav Korn was one of the men killed when the 7th Cavalry clashed with Indians who were gathered for the Ghost Dance at Wounded Knee in the Dakotas. The action there was a massacre of Indians rather than a battle, but the cavalry did not emerge unscathed. And when Gustav Korn died, Comanche lost another good friend.

Perhaps the dun horse missed his long-time friend. Perhaps he was just getting old. But during the next and last year of his life Comanche seemed to lose much of his old spirit. He did not hang around the mess hall hoping for handouts and he seldom wandered up on Sundays to listen to the band.

Other men of the 7th took care of him, but the years had taken their toll. The old veteran, the 7th's "second commanding officer," died of an attack of colic on November 6, 1891, and his passing was duly noted in the regimental records.

Officers of the 7th took up a collection and persuaded a professor at the University of Kansas, who knew how to do such things, to preserve and mount Comanche's hide as a last tribute.

The job was done, to everyone's satisfaction. Because the cavalry was not equipped to care for stuffed horses, Comanche was left with the University of Kansas and was part of the school's display at the Chicago World's Fair in 1893. Thousands of people stared at the old veteran and newspapers published many stories about him.

For years after that, Comanche stood in the University's museum. He attracted much attention and souvenir hunters delighted in pulling hairs from his tail. That tail was renewed seven different times before he was finally placed in an airtight glass case to protect his old hide from the effects of time, changes in temperature, and the pluckings of souvenir collectors.

In 1947 a small war raged around Comanche. General Jonathan Wainwright, an ex-cavalryman and the Army's Chief of Staff, wanted Comanche returned to Fort Riley to be a part of the permanent display there. But Fort Riley was no longer the horse-cavalry post that Comanche had known. The modern cavalry was mechanized and traveled on wheels!

The Chancellor of the University of Kansas, in a clearly stated formal document, politely but firmly refused the army's request. Comanche belonged to the University and there he would stay. He is still there and, although he has never spoken a word, many people have worked hard to piece together his life's story.

Charlie { BUFFALO BILL'S HORSE

WILLIAM F. CODY, better known as Buffalo Bill, had many horses during his long and active life as scout, Indian fighter, buffalo killer, actor, and star of his own "Wild West" show. Horses were important to him. In his early scouting days, his life often depended on the speed and endurance of his horse. As a buffalo hunter, his reputation for killing the big animals depended on the skill and sure-footedness of his steed. Later, as a showman, his fame and fortune were closely linked to the spectacular appearance and training of his horses.

He remembered many of his horses and spoke about them with feeling and pride. He always expected the most from them and he did not spare them or himself to get it. The thousands of people who watched him perform or read about his exploits in the dime novels that featured him as hero, thought of him in connection with horses. Even Mark Twain wrote a sentimental short story called "A Horse's Tale" about an imaginary horse, Soldier Boy, who had belonged to Buffalo Bill, and who

106

later was stolen and then died in a Spanish bull ring. It was Mark Twain, too, who suggested that Buffalo Bill take his show abroad so Europeans could see what the real American West was like.

———

Buffalo Bill, himself, might have had some difficulty in picking a single favorite horse, but no doubt one known as Old Charlie would have been high on his list of candidates. He served the great scout and showman for many years, was horse "Star" of the "Wild West" show as long as he lived and became one of the most highly publicized horses of his day.

Charlie, a half-blood Kentucky horse, was a five-year-old when Buffalo Bill bought him in Nebraska about 1873. The two worked together for fifteen years. He was a dark horse, probably a bay or chestnut, with a white blaze on his forehead and short white socks on his hind feet. His mane and tail were long and flowing. He was a good looking horse but, because of his mixed ancestry, might not have won many ribbons in a horse show.

In their early days together, Buffalo Bill worked Charlie hard. One time on a hunt for wild horses, the two of them chased a herd across the prairie for fifteen miles before running them down. Afterwards, when he bragged about Charlie's speed and endurance, a nearby listener scoffed.

"Fifteen miles is nothing," the hearer snorted. "How's Charlie for real distance?"

"I'll bet you $500 that he can cover a hundred miles in ten hours," Buffalo Bill answered.

"Done," said the doubter. "Put up your money and get started."

Buffalo Bill on Charlie

Buffalo Bill won the bet. Charlie did even better than his master said he could by cutting fifteen minutes from the time and covering the hundred miles in nine hours and forty-five minutes.

"Charlie was an animal of almost human intelligence, extraordinary speed, endurance, and fidelity," Buffalo Bill later said of him.

When Cody shifted from the frontier to the stage, Charlie waited his turn. Cody acted for a few years in melodramatic stage productions like "Scouts of the Prairie," "Life on the Border," "Knight of the Plains," and "Buffalo Bill at Bay, or The Pearl of the Prairie." Finally, from these and other shows like them grew the great idea—The Wild West, Rocky Mountain, and Prairie Exhibition, which later became better and more simply known as Buffalo Bill's Wild West Show.

Every performance opened with a grand entry of all the performers with Buffalo Bill on Charlie in the lead. There were trick riding acts and roping exhibitions, buffalo hunts and stampedes, Indian war dances, a thrilling race plus a spectacular battle when Indians staged a simulated attack on the Deadwood Stage Buffalo Bill and other marksmen, including Annie Oakley, known then as "Little Sure Shot," demonstrated expert shooting at fast moving targets. Buffalo Bill rode Charlie at a gallop while firing his rifle and breaking dozens of glass balls that were tossed into the air. After the last spectacle, which was often the reenactment of a hand-to-hand fight between Buffalo Bill and an Indian chief named Yellow Hand, the showman would remount Charlie and the two would canter to the center of the arena where they acknowledged the thunderous applause of the crowd with bows in all directions. Then they would ride off, the gate would close behind them, and the show was over. It was quite a show and Charlie played a large part.

The Wild West Show played for audiences in the United States for four years and then, in the spring of 1887, Buffalo Bill took his show abroad. It was to play in England as a feature of the American Exposition during the Diamond Jubilee of England's Queen Victoria.

A steamship, the *State of Nebraska*, was chartered to take the show across the ocean. There were 83 performers and stars in the upper cabins and 38 workers in steerage, plus 97 Indians, many of whom were terrified at the idea of crossing such a great body of water. In addition to Charlie, there were 179 other horses, 18 buffalo, 10 mules, 10 elk, 5 wild Texas steers, 4 donkeys, and 2 deer. The voyage took fourteen days and many of the performers were seasick for the first days out; and one can be sure the animals were relieved when they felt firm ground beneath their feet again.

Charlie received his share of attention at the show grounds in London. Former Prime Minister Gladstone visited him; the Prince of Wales, who later became King Edward VII, examined him carefully; the Russian Grand Duke Michael, who had come to London to find a wife among the English nobility, seemed much more interested in riding Charlie in several of the staged buffalo hunts than he was in finding a bride.

Queen Victoria herself, who seldom went to the theater, came with her family to see the show and she was so fascinated that she stayed for the entire performance instead of leaving after an hour as she had originally planned. Again the Prince of Wales visited

Charlie, patted him, and asked Buffalo Bill about the horse's history.

"Old Charlie seemed to like the attentions of royalty," Buffalo Bill said later, "but he was very democratic just the same."

The attention from princes and grand dukes did not go to Charlie's head for he welcomed commoners as well. He was on friendly terms with the press and received favorable notices in all the London newspapers.

"I saw Buffalo Bill's horse, Charlie, 20 years old (a tame old gee-gee who licked my hand)," one reporter wrote in describing his visit to the show. "Mr. Cody has ridden him upwards of 14 years in all his campaigns and Western exploits."

Perhaps Charlie got his idea for hand kissing by watching the royal family and their friends in action. The Wild West Show performers had a good opportunity to do this because the Queen enjoyed the show so much that she invited them to give a command performance at Windsor Castle, especially for her family and many representatives of European royalty who were their guests. Along with Buffalo Bill, Annie Oakley, and the other performers, Charlie and his four-footed companions rubbed shoulders with the royalty there and thus got a chance to observe their hand-kissing activities first hand.

The London shows were followed by tours to other English cities where the audiences were equally enthusiastic. After almost a year in England, the show sailed for home on May 6, 1888, aboard the S.S. *Persian Monarch*. Everything went well until May 14, when Charlie's groom reported that the old horse was sick.

In spite of all efforts to save him, Charlie died three days later. Everyone on board was saddened by the loss of an old friend.

At first, Buffalo Bill thought of taking Charlie's body back to the United States and burying him on land. But the ship was still several days out from New York and the weather was rather warm. Finally, he agreed to burial at sea.

Charlie's body was brought on deck, wrapped in canvas and covered by an American flag. The entire company assembled and the 34-piece cowboy band struck up a sad tune. Buffalo Bill stood beside the body of his horse and made a farewell speech. Later, in a book called *Last of the Great Scouts,* his sister Helen Cody Wetmore reported what he said. Perhaps Buffalo Bill did make such a speech, for he was a great showman, an actor, and a man who loved horses. Perhaps, knowing him as she did, his sister wrote what she felt he would have wanted to say; people were more sentimental in those days. At any rate, while the horse's body slid down the skids and sank into the Atlantic Ocean, Buffalo Bill is alleged to have made this speech:

"Old fellow, your journeys are over," he said. "Here in the ocean you must rest. Would that I could take you back and lay you down beneath the billows of that prairie you and I have loved so well and roamed so freely; but it cannot be. How often at break of day, the glorious sun rising on the horizon has found us far from human habitation. Yet, obedient to my call, gladly you bore your burden on, little heeding what the day might bring, so that you and I but shared its sorrows and pleasures alike.

"You have never failed me," Buffalo Bill went on.

"Ah, Charlie, old fellow, I have had many friends, but few of whom I could say that. Rest entombed in the deep bosom of the ocean. I'll never forget you. I loved you as you loved me, my dear old Charlie. Men tell me you have no soul; but if there be a heaven, and scouts can enter there, I'll wait at the gate for you, old friend."

The sentiments were not so flowery on the tombstone of Buckskin Joe, another of Buffalo Bill's horses. Buckskin Joe was a big yellow army horse that Cody rode on many of his early scouting and hunting expeditions. When Buckskin Joe began to go blind and was too old to work, he was bought from the army by a friend of Cody's and sent to finish his life on Buffalo Bill's TE ranch in Wyoming. The stone marking Buckskin Joe's grave on the ranch read:

Old Buckskin Joe
The Horse that on Several Occasions
Saved the Life of Buffalo Bill
By Carrying Him Safely out of Range
of Indian Battles. Died of old age, 1882.

In his later years, as his own shoulder-length hair, mustache and goatee turned from brown to gray and then to white, Buffalo Bill usually rode white horses. He and his horse made a striking appearance as the old showman, dressed in fringed and beaded buckskin and flourishing a wide-brimmed white Stetson hat, rode to the center of the arena. When Cody and his show toured Europe in 1889, Rosa Bonheur, the famous French painter of horses, did a life-sized portrait of

Buffalo Bill riding a beautiful white horse. White horses, along with popping glass ball targets and the applause of admiring crowds came to be the trademark of Buffalo Bill, image of the American Wild West all over the world.

But it was non-white horses like Old Charlie and Buckskin Joe, and Indian ponies like Tall Bull and Brigham, as well as the many others that he rode, that helped make Buffalo Bill eternally famous. After his death in 1917, Buffalo Bill was buried on Lookout Mountain near Denver, Colorado. His memorial, located on a mesa overlooking the town of Cody, Wyoming, is a 12-foot-high bronze statue showing him on horseback as he was in his earlier scouting days. A horse named Smoky from the TE ranch was model for the bronze horse and in Smoky's statue are honored Old Charlie and all of the other horses that Buffalo Bill knew and loved.

Revelation { *THE HORSE SHOW WOMAN'S HORSE*

SOME HORSES are warhorses, some are race horses, and some are work horses. Some carry their masters to high adventures or on long journeys to distant places. Some race for honor and prizes. Some pull wagons or plows or drag heavy loads to earn their food and keep. Revelation did none of these things, but he worked, too, as a show horse. His owner was a woman who knew, loved, and showed fine horses.

A bright bay with white markings, Revelation was foaled in 1906 on a farm near Marion, Ohio. He was Standardbred with some racing blood from his sire, a stallion known as The Tramp.

For his first three years the bay colt lived on the Ohio farm. The farmer broke him to harness and the farmer's son drove him back and forth to school, hitched to the farm buggy.

The colt was a fine looking youngster and a buyer for a large firm of Chicago horse dealers paid the farmer

$125 for him. After a train ride to Chicago, the young horse was taken to the dealers' stables where he was groomed for showing and his tail was docked. Docking was a customary practice for harness horses. It was done by amputating several vertebrae at the end of the horse's tail and setting the tendons so that the horse always carried his short tail high. Docking in this manner effectively ruled out any chance for the reins to become caught under the tail, but it also prevented the horse from switching his tail to keep flies away.

The bay colt was still trembling with fright and pain when he was led out to be shown to a prospective buyer. Fortunately, the buyer was sympathetic and loved animals. Fortunately, also, she was a good judge of horses and could see possibilities in the green, frightened colt.

"You poor thing," she said, rubbing the colt's nose. "Have they been hurting you?"

The prospective buyer was a young woman from Kansas City named Loula Long. Her father, R. A. Long, had made a fortune in the lumber business and was also a breeder of fine horses. During the first three decades of the twentieth century, horses from his Longview Farm won ribbons in shows all over the United States, in Canada, and in England.

The bay colt, which had been bought for $125 in Marion, Ohio, was sold to the Longs for $1,500 and shipped to their farm near Kansas City. He was never sold again.

The Longs made a practice of giving their harness horses names ending in the letters "ion." Their first was Sensation, in 1909. By the time the bay colt was purchased there had been a number of "ion" horses before him. He received his name when a friend, who saw him in harness for the first time, said, "That horse is a revelation to me."

"You have named him," Loula Long said happily. "His name will be Revelation."

And so the bay colt was named.

Revelation made his debut at the Denver, Colorado, horse show in January of 1910. He had been given some months of training but this was his first appearance in a real horse show. There were crowds of spectators, the band was playing and people were cheering—there were many strange sights, sounds, smells, and sensations. The bay horse quivered with excitement, squealed, and gave the dashboard behind him a hard kick.

"Steady, Revie," Loula Long said. Then she lifted the reins, spoke a word of command, and Revelation was off on a 15-year career. He trotted into the ring pulling a shiny four-wheeled phaeton driven by his mistress, with a top-hatted footman riding on a rumble seat in the rear.

Around the show ring they went. Revelation seemed to sense he was competing with other horses for he carried his ears pricked forward, his neck arched, and stepped high and proudly. The judges studied the good and bad points of all the horses in the competition. Finally, when they reached a decision, the drivers were told to line up.

Revelation stood steady, quiet but quivering with excitement, and one of the judges placed a blue ribbon on his noseband. Two days later the bay horse won another blue ribbon in the Denver show. This made the first and second of more than sixty such top awards Revelation won during his career.

Even a natural show horse like Revelation cannot win all the time. His first loss came in 1914, but it was not really the bay horse's fault. The Longs entered their horses in the Canadian spring shows, first in Toronto, and then in Montreal and Ottawa.

In the Toronto show Revelation won the harness class, receiving the red ribbon that is the symbol of first place in Canada. With his team mate Realization, he also won first place in the pair class and was named champion horse when the Toronto show ended.

His victories continued in Montreal, but at Ottawa something seemed to be wrong. His step was not as high, his neck was not as proudly arched—Revelation was just not himself and as a result the championship went to another horse and he received only a reserve (second place) ribbon.

Loula Long was disappointed and Revelation seemed to share her disappointment. Even when she patted him and tried to explain that he could not always win, the bay horse seemed dejected and listless.

The Longs then went on to New York leaving their horses to be sent home to Missouri. Scarcely were the Longs settled in their hotel when a telegram arrived from Revelation's trainer.

"Revelation has pneumonia in both lungs," the telegram stated. "Little hope for recovery."

"Do everything possible to save him," the Longs wired back. "Report his condition every two hours."

The next three telegrams from Canada were gloomy ones.

"No change in condition," each one stated.

The fourth telegram was different.

"Slight change for the better," it reported.

At the Ottawa stables all hands were working hard to save the bay horse. The veterinarian was there and so was the trainer. The stable boys would not let Revelation lie down. Sick as he was, with both lungs affected, breathing was hard for him and lying down would only make it harder. Up and down the stable they led him, moving slowly and remembering his weakness, but keeping him on his feet. Hours passed and the men drank many cups of coffee, sharing some of them with the sick horse. He needed all the stimulant he could get to keep on fighting for his life.

In New York Loula Long hoped and prayed.

Revelation seemed to know that his people loved him. He seemed to know they wanted him to live. He fought, too, and together they won the battle.

A fifth telegram was delivered to the New York hotel. "Definite change for the better," was the report it carried.

After that, the reports were all cheerful. Revelation was getting well. He was sufficiently recovered to take part in the show at Dayton, Ohio, a few months later and with three other "ion" horses, Realization, Consternation, and Hesitation, won a blue ribbon in the heavy harness team competition.

Years passed, the blue ribbons accumulated, and Revelation was a known favorite at the shows. But age tells on horses as on people. It was time for the Denver horse show again; the year was 1925. Revelation and his owner, who in the meantime had become Mrs. Robert Pryor Combs, received the blue ribbon in the gig class and then, when the other contestants left the ring, the bay horse was told to remain. He may have wondered why, but he stood quiet and watched the others as they disappeared through the gate.

A judge approached—the same judge who fifteen years before had attached the first blue ribbon to Revelation's noseband. Then one of the show officials made a speech, announcing Revelation's retirement from the show ring.

"It is with a feeling of mingled joy and sorrow that we pause for a moment to pay tribute to the world's best-known and most popular harness horse," the speaker said. He then told of the bay horse's many victories.

"The name of Revelation stands for honesty and sincerity and intensity of purpose," the speaker went on. "Those who know him best love him most. He is easily the most picturesque and best-loved show horse in all the world. Tonight he stands before us for the last time, full of years and of honor. When those gates close behind him for the last time, his show ring career will have ended, and the tanbark will know him no more. At the end of this week, he will be returned home to dream away his declining years beneath the azure skies of Missouri in the pastures of the Longview Farm."

People were cheering and Loula Long Combs was crying. Revelation pricked up his ears and pranced nervously as attendants placed a great horseshoe of red roses around his shoulders. Then he was off for a last proud circuit of the ring, and his career as a show horse was over.

Retirement was pleasant. Revelation had a comfortable stall, and to keep him from being lonely a little, also retired, mare named Baby List shared the paddock with him. The two horses became devoted friends. Ten happy, quiet years passed and Revelation enjoyed his well earned rest.

Revelation had one glorious return to the show ring. In 1935, Mrs. Combs entered him in a special event, the Gay Nineties Class at the Royal American Horse Show at Kansas City. It was a great honor. Grooms worked hard to make Revelation's coat sleek and shiny. He was given short drives to limber up his stiff old joints, and he seemed to know that an important event was happening. Before the show began he was taken to Kansas City by truck—the driver being careful to go slow and easily so as not to jolt the old veteran riding in the horse van.

For the Gay Nineties Class the drivers wore special costumes. Loula Long Combs wore a big hat with lots of feathers and a long dress in 1890 style. Revelation was hitched to a shiny basket phaeton and the footman in the rumble seat was a 76-year-old man who had worked many years with the Longs' "ion" horses.

The band played and people cheered. Revelation stepped with some of his former style and he seemed to feel the old thrill as the judge once more pinned a blue ribbon on his cheek strap. It was a great night for the 29-year-old horse, a time of proud memories for Loula Long Combs and for Longview Farm.

Revelation died early one morning, about a month after the Kansas City show. Perhaps the thrills and excitement were more than his old heart could stand. Perhaps he knew that a great career had finally ended.

He was buried in an honored place in front of the harness-horse stable at Longview Farm and a sculptor designed a special monument to mark the site of his grave.

Exterminator $\left\{\begin{array}{l} THE \\ PONY'S \\ HORSE \end{array}\right.$

AS A GENERAL RULE, race horses and show dogs belong to everybody in general and nobody in particular. They have owners, of course, and are well cared for. As the "royalty" or "stars" of the worlds in which they live, they are admired from afar. Seldom is there one special person close enough to them to become a part of their life story.

In the case of race horses, there is the owner who takes great pride in backing a winner. But rarely, if ever, does the horse's owner take personal care of him, ride him, or have much of a hand in his training. The trainer is closer to the horse than the owner is, but even the trainer is further away than the groom or stable boy who actually takes care of the animal. The horse probably recognizes and is friendly toward all three, but there is not a very close bond between them. Sometimes a horse "belongs" to another animal—that was the case with Exterminator. He "belonged" to a pony and the pony belonged to him.

123

Exterminator, who was foaled in 1915, came from a well-known family in the horse world. His sire, McGee, and his dam, Fair Empress, were both Thoroughbreds. This pedigree made him eligible to run in the Kentucky Derby, a race exclusively for three-year-old Thoroughbreds. His first owner nominated him for the derby, even though he had run in only four races by the time he was three years old.

Exterminator is a high sounding name. His owner's wife thought of it when her husband announced that he had bought a chestnut Thoroughbred yearling.

"I think this colt can kill off all the competition," he said.

"Then let's call him Exterminator," his wife exclaimed.

For the next two years, few people called the horse by his official name. From the day he was born in 1915, Exterminator was far from handsome. Most new-born foals are long-legged and awkward looking, but the son of McGee and Fair Empress was longer-legged and bonier looking than usual. He developed into a gangling scarecrow of a colt, all bones, and badly put together. And, before long, that was what he was called—Bones. As a yearling he was all leg bones and ribs, backbone, neck—and muscles! In spite of Exterminator's high sounding name, the nickname Bones, and later Old Bones, stayed with him all his life.

During the next year Exterminator ran in four races and won two of them; then he went lame. That was his record when he was sold and moved to a new stable. He was not bought as a racer; instead, he was bought to be used in training another horse.

Exterminator's new owner was Willis Sharpe Kilmer,

a wealthy man who had a fine stable of Thoroughbreds. The brightest star in the Kilmer stable was another three-year-old named Sun Briar. It was Mr. Kilmer's ambition to have Sun Briar win the Kentucky Derby. Sun Briar looked like a winner, but looks are not everything, especially on the race track.

Sun Briar's trainer was Henry McDaniel, a man employed by owner Kilmer to see that the horse was in the best possible shape for the Derby. Trainer McDaniel decided that Sun Briar needed to have another horse work out with him, to run with him in training sessions and give him stiff competition—to almost but not quite defeat him whenever they practiced. Sun Briar seemed to run better when he could hear another horse close behind him.

Trainer McDaniel paid a great deal more for Exterminator—$11,000 in cash and two fillies in trade—than his employer had wanted him to and Mr. Kilmer was not at all pleased with the new horse. But when McDaniel assured him that Exterminator could give Sun Briar the stiff training competition he needed, the owner was satisfied. More than anything he wanted Sun Briar to wear the Kilmer colors to victory in the Kentucky Derby.

The days passed. Sometimes Sun Briar ran well and looked fine in the practice sessions. Sometimes he acted nervous, temperamental, sluggish. Sun Briar was a handsome horse compared to bony, awkward looking Exterminator, but a horse race is not a beauty contest.

The Kentucky Derby is run at Churchill Downs, a track in Louisville, Kentucky. The Derby is just one of many races at the famous track, but for racing fans everywhere it is THE race for three-year-old Thoroughbreds.

Kentucky has a great deal of rain in the spring which contributes to Kentucky's renown as the Blue Grass State. The spring of 1918 was a very wet one and heavy rain fell for two days before the Derby was scheduled. The practice track was a mass of sticky mud.

The mud did not bother work horse Exterminator. He ran happily through it, splashing mud in all directions. But Sun Briar, the star, was not so adventurous. He ran sluggishly, sulkily, and when he returned to his stall he refused to eat the hay that was waiting for him.

Reluctantly, Trainer McDaniel had to report to Mr. Kilmer and advise him against putting Sun Briar into the race. It was a big disappointment to the owner. There went his dream of seeing the brown and green Kilmer colors carried to victory on Sun Briar.

"Why not enter Exterminator?" Trainer McDaniel suggested. "He may not have Sun Briar's looks, but he does have speed and endurance."

At first Mr. Kilmer snorted angrily at the idea. Put his colors on an ugly horse like the bony chestnut! Run a work horse that nobody ever heard of in place of Sun Briar who was well-liked and famous. But at last he consented.

Derby Day was cloudy. The rain had stopped but the track was still very muddy. The other nine horses danced and pranced on their way to the starting post, but Exterminator walked calmly, unconcerned; he seemed half asleep—until the race started. Then, from the shout of "They're off!" until the time he crossed the finish line a length ahead of the horse closest behind him, Exterminator showed how fast and how well he could run.

Nobody had expected the big-boned, long-legged chestnut horse to win the Kentucky Derby. Certainly, his owner, Mr. Kilmer, had not, but nonetheless he was a proud and happy man when Exterminator carried the Kilmer colors to victory. Even Trainer McDaniel, who had much more faith in the big horse, had scarcely dared hope for victory. Only the big horse himself, when he was led up to the winner's box and a huge horseshoe of red roses placed around his neck, seemed to project a calm "I knew I could do it" attitude.

From that time on, for six years, Exterminator raced and carried the Kilmer stable's colors. Crowds at the race tracks learned to know him and they liked him. His big, bony frame, his calmness before a race when most other horses were nervous and excited, his dependably good performance, and his modest acknowledgment of victory made him a favorite. Newspaper reporters made up nicknames for him; they called him the Galloping Hatrack, "a skin full of bones," or most often just Old Bones, but they never wrote a bad thing about him.

Of course Exterminator did not win every time he raced. In his years on the track he was entered in a hundred races and he won fifty of them. He came in second seventeen times and third seventeen times—an unusually good record for any race horse. Through the years, he won $252,996 for his owner.

Because he was so fast, Exterminator had to carry heavier weights than the horses who raced against him.

As the years passed and his victories piled up, the weights he carried were increased until Old Bones, the Galloping Hatrack, was carrying a heavier handicap of weights than any other horse of his day. The weights were responsible for some of his defeats but they did not keep him from winning.

Exterminator ran his hundredth and last race in 1924. He was nine years old, much older than most of the horses running against him. He started well, but something went wrong with one of his legs and, although he gamely finished the race, he came in third. The veterinarian who examined him had a gloomy report—Old Bones would recover and be able to walk, but he could never race again. Sadly, Mr. Kilmer retired the big veteran to his horse farm in Virginia.

———

Life can be hard for a retired race horse. What does he do with his days when he still feels fit and wants to go on racing? Exterminator fretted and fumed, he pawed the floor of his stall and kicked the walls. He was not at all his calm, good-tempered self. He snorted and raged in boredom and exasperation.

Finally one of the grooms had an idea.

"Old Bones is lonesome," he said. "He needs some kind of a friend to keep him company. He's so big, a dog wouldn't do, but how about a pony?"

That was what they tried. They found a little old pony, gentle and affectionate, and put him in the paddock with Exterminator. The big horse walked over and sniffed at him; the pony raised its nose and sniffed back. Old Bones walked away and then stopped and looked over his shoulder.

"Well, are you coming with me?" he seemed to say. The pony followed him. Exterminator had found a friend.

"Just look at them together," the groom said happily. "Beside Old Bones, that pony's no bigger than a peanut."

And Peanuts was what they called the pony.

It was a wonderful friendship for three years, and then old Peanuts became ill. Poor Exterminator knew something was wrong; he guarded his sick friend faithfully. And when Peanuts died, Exterminator fought to keep the men from removing the pony's body from the stall they shared. He was still fighting the men as they finally managed to lead him away and he would not be calmed or comforted.

As quickly as possible, a second pony was found. Fortunately, lonesome Old Bones accepted it for a friend and the pony accepted him. Peanuts II was much younger than the first Peanuts had been. The two friends raced and played together, but they made a funny looking pair—the big-boned chestnut horse and the small chestnut pony. Peanuts II was so small he could actually run under Exterminator's belly.

People did not forget Exterminator, the Galloping Hatrack, who had won so many races. The racing fans had loved him, and many admirers came to visit him during his retirement. He was even invited to appear as guest of honor at the Pimlico track where he had won the Pimlico Cup during his racing days. Peanuts II went along and the crowd cheered them both—the retired old veteran and his frisky little friend.

Exterminator lived a long and happy life in retirement, from 1924 when he was retired at the age of nine, until he died of old age in 1945. He was buried on another Kilmer farm at Binghamton, New York, and his friend Peanuts II is buried beside him.

Exterminator, the gallant bag of Old Bones, may never have had one special human closely associated with him. But he did have two close companions that he gave his full affection to and from whom he received the same in return. Both of them were ponies named Peanuts.

Man o' War { *THE MOSTEST HORSE*

MAN O' WAR had something special that made him great, that made him beloved and remembered well above and beyond most other horses. His fame has lived on and, indeed, has become a legend.

There were many similarities between the two great contemporaries, Man o' War and Exterminator, but there were also many differences. They never met on the track and, for that matter, did not compete in many of the same races. Man o' War, although Kentucky-bred, did not run in the Kentucky Derby. Exterminator won the Derby and ran second in the Belmont Stakes in 1918, the year Man o' War was an untried yearling. Two years later, Man o' War won the Belmont and the Preakness, the two other races which, along with the Kentucky Derby, give the so-called "Triple Crown" to horses that win all three. Neither Exterminator nor Man o' War won that crown, but together they met the requirements.

Both horses were chestnut Thoroughbreds, but "Old Bones" was unpretentious, calm, and awkward looking,

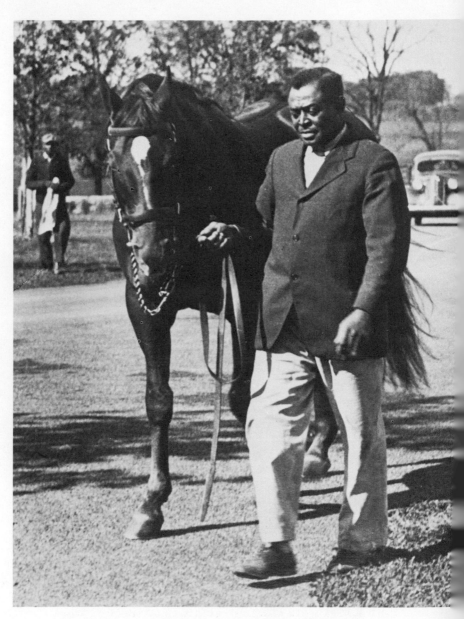

Will Harbut with Man o' War

while "Big Red" was handsome, spirited, and magnificently put together. Exterminator came to the starting post quietly. Man o' War pranced, danced, and fretted so that he sometimes got off to a slow start. In winning, Exterminator did not try to get very far out in front. Man o' War, on the other hand, always wanted to run faster than his jockey would let him, and once he finished a hundred lengths ahead of the horse he was racing against.

Both horses were greatly admired by racing fans and well cared for by owners. Each found his one closest friend after the great years of his career had ended. Man o' War's best friend was a Black groom named Will Harbut.

In his brilliant two-year career on the tracks, Man o' War ran in 21 races and won 20 times; in the remaining one he came in second. He won a total of $249,465 for his owner; Exterminator ran in 100 races during his eight-year track career and won $252,990. Both horses were retired with honors. Exterminator the gelding went to pasture, Man o' War the stallion went to stud, and both of them lived to the ripe old horse age of 30 years.

So much for statistical comparisons.

———

Man o' War came of a distinguished Thoroughbred lineage. His sire was Fair Play and his dam was Mahubah, whose Arab name meant "good greetings; good fortune." He was foaled on March 29, 1917. Both his parents were owned by August Belmont, a distinguished sportsman whose Nursery Stables near Lexington, Kentucky, produced many fine horses. Shortly after the foal's birth, the United States entered World War I, so

he was given an appropriately timely name—Man o'
War.

The next year the chestnut colt, already big for his
age, long-legged, lively, and as yet unbroken, was sold
at auction to Samuel D. Riddle, a wealthy sportsman
from Philadelphia, for the modest sum of $5,000. The
colt's new home was Glen Riddle, a 1,500-acre estate
on the Eastern Shore of Maryland. Because of his size
and the bright color of his coat, he soon had a new
nickname—"Big Red."

Man o' War did not take kindly to training. From
the very beginning to the end of his life, he hated the
process of saddling and bridling. He had a habit of
swelling up and holding his breath while the saddle
was adjusted. Then, when the cinch was buckled, he
would exhale which made the girth hang loose. His
handlers learned to lead him around for a time before
finally tightening the saddle girth. But when the time
came to run, Man o' War loved it.

In order to tame the fiery yearling, his trainer used a
steady older horse named Major Treat as a calming influence. Major Treat was a 10-year-old hunter; he was
wise, sedate, and friendly. The red colt liked him and
they became good companions; they had adjoining
stalls, shared the same pasture, and most of the time
when Man o' War went to the races, Major Treat went
with him. During his training period, Man o' War
worked out with another colt named Golden Broom,
owned by a neighbor. When he was through running
against Golden Broom, Man o' War expected to find
Major Treat waiting, and he seemed disappointed and
unhappy if his friend was not there to greet him.

Just before the 1919 spring racing season began, Big

Red came down with the flu. That delayed his entrance
into the world of racing. But by June he was ready and
on June 6, 1919, he ran his maiden race at Belmont
Park, New York, defeating six other two-year-olds. He
won that race at a canter and then won five more races;
as the sports writers described them, he "won easily,
with the second and third horses driving."

Man o' War's seventh race, at Saratoga on August 13,
was the only one that kept him from having a perfect
record as all-time winner; he lost by a close margin to
a colt named Upset. Why did he lose? Some say he
got off to a bad start. Others say he was boxed in by
Upset and his former training partner Golden Broom.
He got out of the box, but the race was over before he
could make up for the distance he lost in going around
them. Ten days later he redeemed himself by easily
defeating Upset and eight other contenders. Never
again did Man o' War see another horse cross the finish
line ahead of him.

Man o' War ran ten races as a two-year-old, and the
racing fans soon learned to know him and to admire
him tremendously. He was beautiful to look at, running or motionless. His chestnut coat had red fire in it.
His eyes were bright and lively, his nose was slender
with delicately flaring nostrils; the white blaze on his
forehead was almost kite shaped with a thin white tail
half way down the length of his face. Many sports
writers named him "Horse of the Year" for 1919, choosing him above the three-year-old Canadian-owned horse
Sir Barton, who won the triple crown that year.

When the 1920 racing season opened, owner Riddle
did not enter Man o' War in the Kentucky Derby. The
race was run early that year and Mr. Riddle did not

feel that his big chestnut three-year-old was quite
ready for the mile and a quarter contest. Instead, he entered Big Red in the Preakness Stakes at Pimlico on
May 18. The race was a mile and an eighth and Man o'
War won easily, as always, with the second and third
horses driving.

From Pimlico in Maryland, Man o' War with Major
Treat and their human attendants went to Belmont
Park in New York, but few owners there cared to enter
their horses in races against him. To give him a greater
handicap, more weight was added to the load he must
carry, but still he won. In the Withers Stakes at Belmont, his second race that year, only two horses were
entered to run against him; in the Belmont Stakes, his
third race, and later in the Stuyvesant Handicap on
the Jamaica, New York, track, only single horses were
entered against him. In the Stuyvesant Handicap and
twice afterwards, the betting odds against the big chestnut stallion were 100 to 1.

His fame brought hundreds of racing fans to the
racetrack paddock to admire him. Famous sportsmen
wanted to see him closer; photographers wanted to take
his picture; sports writers wanted to get all the information they could, direct "from the horse's mouth" if
possible.

The only horse to give Man o' War any real competition was John P. Grier, a chestnut colt owned by
Harry Payne Whitney. The two were entered in the
Dwyer Stakes at Aqueduct, New York, and the handi-
cappers decreed that Big Red must carry a weight of
126 pounds against 108 pounds carried by his rival.

It was a close race all the way as the two horses ran
nose to nose, breaking three world's records in the

process. Once John P. Grier pulled a little ahead of his
rival, but then Man o' War put on a great burst of
speed and forged ahead to win by a length and a half.
Some people said John P. Grier was never quite the
same after that race, but he had the distinction of being
the only horse ever to make Big Red exert himself to
the fullest.

For his seventh race in 1920, Man o' War met two of
his old rivals in a three-horse match for the Travers
Stakes at Saratoga. They were Upset, the only horse to
beat him in that seventh race the year before, and
John P. Grier. This time Big Red took the lead and held
it, and the sports writers reported, as usual, that he won
easily with Upset second and John P. Grier third, both
of them driving.

Man o' War's eleventh race that year, the last of his
career, was against the previous year's triple crown
winner Sir Barton at Kenilworth Park in Canada. Big
Red took the lead early and finished seven lengths
ahead.

After that, there were no more worlds to conquer.
Man o' War was too good and nobody wanted to race
against him. But there were fabulous prospects to
tempt his owner. Mr. Riddle turned down an offer to
sell Big Red for a million dollars, along with offers to
star him in the movies, to exhibit him at the Chicago
World's Fair, to take him abroad, even to race him in
a $50,000 match against Exterminator. Man o' War was
retired to stud, in the hope that he would pass along his
great speed and magnificent talents to many descendants.

Major Treat went with him, and so did his early
training partner the stallion Golden Broom. They went

first to Hinata Farm near Lexington, Kentucky, and later to Faraway Farm, a nearby property being developed by Mr. Riddle. Big Red spent the rest of his life there, siring 386 foals in the course of 22 years. Many of his descendants were winners, the most famous of them, War Admiral, was the 1937 triple crown winner.

The people who had cheered for him, admired him, and loved him, did not forget him. They cherished his memory and many came to see him; over the years more than two million fans visited Faraway Farm to admire the great Man o' War. As the years passed, many of Man o' War's sons retired and returned to the farm as stud horses; indeed, their sire outlived most of them. Eventually Major Treat died, as did many of Big Red's rivals and contemporaries, but the great one lived on.

Man o' War had been retired for ten years when his best friend and greatest admirer entered his life. This friend was Will Harbut, the Negro groom who became almost as famous as the great horse he cared for so devotedly.

Will Harbut was plump and quiet, with a white-toothed smile that gleamed against the dark skin of his face. Although technically uneducated, Will Harbut had a way with horses, a boundless admiration for Man o' War, and an unusual talent when it came to showing off the great horse to the hundreds who came to see him.

It was Will Harbut who fed Man o' War, curried him, and petted and pampered him. It was also Will Harbut who opened the stable gates at Faraway Farm every morning at nine o'clock and closed them again promptly at four o'clock in the afternoon. He would lead the visitors from horse to horse, reciting their lineage and their accomplishments.

He always saved the best until last. And, when he finally presented the idol of his life, Will Harbut would say, in a speech that seldom varied:

"An' here, ladies and gen'men, is Man o' War hisself. Come here, Red. He weigh thirteen hunnert and seventy-fi' pounds. I say, come here, you Old Red."

And Red would come, majestically walking to the door of his stall and posing for them proudly. Sometimes he would give Will a playful nudge with his nose, just for the sake of friendship.

"Stan' still, Red," Will would say, and Red would stand. Then the devoted groom would go on to tell of all the races Big Red had won and list his triumphs in great detail. The details varied but the conclusion was always the same.

"Yas, sah," Will Harbut would declare, "Man o' War broke all de records and he broke down all de horses. He's got everything a horse ought to have and he's got it where a horse ought to have it. He is de mostest horse!"

The years passed but Man o' War was not forgotten. Honors accumulated around him. He was made an honorary citizen of Lexington, Kentucky, and during World War II the First Cavalry Division made him their honorary colonel, even though the U.S. Cavalrymen no longer rode horses into combat. Artists painted his portrait, a sculptor made a life-sized statue of him, photographers took countless pictures of him, horse lovers continued to admire him.

On Big Red's twenty-first birthday owner Riddle gave

a party in his honor and the event was broadcast from
coast to coast by radio. Admirers sent birthday cakes
made of oats with carrots for candles. Will Harbut
beamed proudly when the Governor of Kentucky made
a speech and said, "Man o' War is now old enough to
vote."

There were birthday observances every year after
that, but when Big Red was 29, his friend Will Harbut
could not attend the party. Early in March of 1947 the
faithful Black groom suffered a heart attack that paralyzed his right side and took away his speech. He
lingered through the summer and died on October 3,
without ever making his famous introduction speech
again. His obituary, appearing in the official publica-
tion of the Thoroughbred industry said of Will Harbut:
"Among his survivors are his wife, six sons, three daughters, and Man o' War."

Big Red did not survive Old Will for very long. He
had suffered recurrent attacks of colic, and a final one
brought him death on Saturday, November 1, 1947.

His body was embalmed and placed in a huge oak
box lined with black and gold silk, the Riddle colors.
This stood in state in the hallway of the stable until
Tuesday afternoon when Big Red was buried in a
specially prepared grave in the paddock at Faraway
Farm. Operating tracks all over the United States observed a moment of silence in his honor.

A life-size bronze statue of him stands on a granite
slab over his grave, marking the last resting place of
Man o' War who, according to his friend Will Harbut,
was "the mostest horse" that ever lived.

Fritz { *THE WESTERN ACTOR'S HORSE*

"HE'S THE GREATEST all-around horse that ever lived." That was the way actor William S. Hart described Fritz, his pinto pony. Fritz worked in many motion pictures with Hart and was the first horse to gain stardom in Western movies.

Of course, there had been performing horses long before the movies began. As early as Roman times horses had been taught to do tricks. Horses performed in circuses and at county fairs, and sometimes the tricks they did—even to answering questions, spelling, and doing arithmetic—were quite amazing. But horses as co-stars with actors were products of the movies.

Westerns were among the earliest movies to be popular and no Western was complete without cowboys and horses. Besides being the first great Western star (Hart made his first movie in 1914), William S. Hart was the first to give his horse leading roles in his pictures. He thought of Fritz as a friend and fellow actor; he even seemed to feel that Fritz understood what was said to him and could answer in horse fashion.

William S. Hart and Fritz

William S. Hart wrote and directed most of his own pictures. A sincere, serious man who had spent his boyhood in the West, Hart tried to show the Old West as it really was. In their pictures, Fritz was a Western man's pony, a real partner and companion to his rider. The pinto wore a regular stock saddle and blanket, but there were silver conchos on his bridle and a heart-shaped decoration just under each eye.

The white-faced pinto was not a "trick" horse as some of the later horse stars were, but Fritz had his full share of action. William S. Hart did not use a double in his dangerous movie scenes, such as jumping off cliffs or diving into ice-filled rivers. He and Fritz took all the risks together.

In one picture Hart even rode Fritz through a big glass window.

"The little fellow got only a slight cut on his nose and I wasn't hurt at all," Hart said proudly.

It was whispered that the window was made of clear candy instead of glass, but Hart would not resort to tricks like that. The glass in the window he and Fritz jumped through was real.

In another picture Fritz ended a galloping scene by a spectacular leap across an overturned wagon. Once, while they were filming a picture in Mexico, the sturdy pony and his rider were almost drowned when the script had them swim through a swift underground river.

During World War I many Hollywood stars toured the United States selling bonds in the war loan drives. William S. Hart went on several tours and helped raise thousands of dollars for the war effort. Fritz took part in a drive, too, to collect money for the Red Star Animal Relief Society that helped animal victims of the war.

Actor Hart led the pinto pony through downtown Los Angeles and twenty girls dressed in Western outfits walked through the crowds with baskets to collect donations. Whenever their baskets were full, the girls would empty them into panniers fastened to Fritz's saddle.

"I doubt if there was ever such a tribute paid to a horse," Hart said later. "Traffic was blocked everywhere we went. Passage through the streets was next to impossible."

It took officials of the Red Star Animal Relief Society several days to count all the money—pennies, nickels, dimes, quarters, dollar bills, fives, tens, and twenties—that Fritz collected for them.

When William S. Hart began using Fritz in his pictures, the horse belonged to the motion picture company and not to the actor. The more he worked with the little pinto—Fritz weighed only a thousand pounds which is rather small for a horse—the more Hart liked him and wanted, to own him. At contract renewal time the actor had some disagreement with the film company he worked for and another company offered him a much larger salary.

"Stay with us for just one more picture," Hart's old director said, "and you can have Fritz."

Hart agreed to stay. The picture took five weeks to make and the actor figured the pinto cost him $42,500 in lost salary. "But he was worth it," Hart said years later, "and the old snoozer is worth it still."

Because Hart felt that one of his directors was unfriendly toward his pinto partner, the actor put Fritz out to pasture and ran an advertisement in a movie trade paper announcing that the horse had resigned from pictures. Hart made fifteen pictures without the pinto but, when the actor became his own director, Fritz returned to the screen.

While he was in temporary retirement, Fritz made a friend—a mare named Cactus Kate. She was owned by a cowboy and was also a movie horse but was used only in bucking scenes as she had the reputation of being a real outlaw. Because Fritz was so fond of the mare, Hart bought her and told his ranch foreman to ride her if he could. When the mare was saddled and Hart rode Fritz beside her, Cactus Kate made no attempt to buck or act up. From that time on she was gentle, steady, and dependable, and she was Fritz's constant companion.

Fritz also had another friend, a big pack mule named Lisabeth. The three—Fritz, Cactus Kate, and Lisabeth— were inseparable, and when he returned to the screen Fritz refused to work unless his friends were on the set to watch. The loyalty was shared by his friends and once, when only Fritz and Cactus Kate were taken to the studio, Lisabeth the mule broke out of her corral and galloped miles through Hollywood traffic to join them.

Like the good actor that he was, Fritz was inclined to be temperamental. Between pictures, he objected to confinement in a stall or stable. He wanted to be outdoors and in action. To show how he felt, he always bucked hard the first time he was ridden after being confined. Once when Hart tried to exercise him in a vacant lot in New York City, he gave the actor a real shaking-up, and another time a kick from one of his flying hoofs put a spectator on crutches for three months.

In addition to acting as the hero's horse in many of Hart's pictures, Fritz was the featured player in several. "Pinto Ben" was one of Hart's screen tributes to his horse and "The Narrow Trail" was another. The actor did not spare himself or his horse in his efforts for realism. In almost every one of his pictures Fritz had to take at least one hard fall. He was trained to do this when his rider pulled hard on the bit and shifted his weight so that the horse was thrown off balance. In falling, the horse always landed on his left shoulder.

The actor liked his pinto so much he worried that the horse might be seriously injured in one of those falls. Hart knew that a good horseman on a well-trained horse could accomplish the dangerous rides and stunts shown in motion pictures, but he also knew accidents were bound to happen. As the actor figured, there was about thirty per cent skill involved; the other seventy per cent was just plain luck. Hart reasoned that, if the rider worried about himself or the safety of his horse, he was apt to be too tense and careful, and that that was worse than being reckless.

"I am positive that a horse senses instantly the slightest uncertainty in the hand that guides him," Hart once said. "When that happens, it is bad, very bad, for both horse and rider."

Fritz was still strong and active, but for how many more falls would his luck hold? William S. Hart decided to stage one last spectacular scene for his pinto partner, something that would make his final exit seem real to the thousands of movie fans who admired him.

In this picture Hart was to ride Fritz at a gallop along the edge of a canyon with a sharp drop and a steep slope below. The enemies chasing him were supposed to shoot the hero's horse and both horse and rider were to fall over the edge and roll down the steep slope into the canyon. Hart knew he could take the fall and roll, but he did not want his pinto friend to be hurt.

He told the studio prop men to build a dummy horse, exactly the size and color of Fritz. The dummy's legs were jointed and on springs, its mane and tail were real horse hair; it cost $2,000 and it was Fritz's exact image. When everything was ready, the cameras rolled, Hart galloped his pinto along the canyon edge and made him fall on level ground. The cameras stopped while Hart mounted the dummy horse that was held erect at the edge of the canyon by strong steel wires. When the actor was in the saddle, the wires were released and the cameras started taking pictures again. Man and dummy horse fell over the edge and tumbled to the bottom of the canyon in a shower of dust and pebbles. The scene was so real that the actor had to explain how it was done to a board of censors before the picture could be shown. He was afraid that the Humane Society might object to having such rough treatment given to a living animal.

William S. Hart retired from the movies in 1926. He went to live on his Horseshoe Ranch near Newhall, California, taking Fritz, Cactus Kate, Lisabeth the mule, and his other animal pets with him.

When Fritz died of old age, he was buried on the ranch under a large oak tree. Hart saw to it that a monument made of cobblestones and a bronze plaque were erected to mark the pinto's grave. And when Hart himself died, he left a will giving $50,000 to the Society for the Prevention of Cruelty to Animals. Later, his ranch became a public park and a museum of the Old West that he and his pinto pony had brought to life in their pictures.

Tony { *THE MOVIE HERO'S HORSE*

THE SHOW MUST GO ON, as actors say, and when William S. Hart and Fritz retired, their places on the screen were soon taken by Tom Mix and his handsome sorrel horse Tony. The West of the movies was never the same again. Tom and Tony made it adventurous, glamorous, and romantic in ways that it had never been before.

As a young man Tom Mix did many things. He worked on a ranch, was a soldier in the Spanish-American War, a rodeo performer, a sheriff, and a Texas Ranger, before he became a movie star. Other glamorous details added by the studio publicity people over the years are harder to prove.

During his rodeo days and in his early pictures Tom Mix used a range-trained pony named Old Blue. But Old Blue was growing old and Tom knew that soon the horse should be retired and put out to pasture.

What horse could take Old Blue's place? Tom Mix looked at many horses before he found the one he wanted. Then he saw a two-year-old sorrel with white-

Tom Mix with Tony

stockinged feet and a long white blaze on his face. Tom knew this was the horse he had been looking for! He paid the owner $600 and gave the horse a name that went nicely with his own. "Tom Mix and Tony" shared the lights on signs above movie theaters in many countries during their twenty years of partnership on the screen.

Tony became a "thinking" horse because of the many tricks that Tom taught him. Often little "bits of business," as they are called in movie-talk, were written into the scripts just so that Tony could show off. Tony could carry messages and gallop for help when Tom was in trouble. Tony knew how to untie knots with his teeth, and sometimes set his master free when the villains had tied him up. When there were bad men or wild animals to fight, Tony used his hoofs and teeth while Tom used his fists. There were more fist fights than there were gun battles in the Western pictures Tom Mix and Tony made.

Mix was proud of his athletic ability. He thought nothing of jumping off a ten-foot wall and landing squarely in Tony's saddle, just as the horse galloped by. They never used doubles. Tom and Tony did their own stunts and the movie fans loved them for it.

Realizing that kids often got bored with "love stuff" in the movies, Tom Mix had very few romantic scenes in his pictures. There were always beautiful girls to be rescued, of course, and lots of villains to fight. Most of the time Tom and the girl got married at the end of the picture and Tony always attended the wedding, his white-blazed face usually appearing between Tom's and the girl's so there could not be much kissing. Sometimes, after all the adventure, Tom and the girl rode off together; sometimes just Tom and Tony rode off, leaving the girl behind.

With all the trick riding and stunts they did, accidents were bound to happen. In filming a picture called "Eyes of the Forest," Tom and Tony were to gallop along a narrow trail under a cliff just before the villain was to set off a dynamite charge. But something went wrong. The dynamite exploded just as they passed the place where it was hidden; both Tom and Tony were knocked unconscious and nearly buried in dirt. Tony recovered first and staggered to his feet, bleeding from a wound in his side. Tom was hurt, too, but refused to let a doctor examine him until after a veterinarian had cared for Tony's wound. Fortunately, neither of them was seriously hurt and after a few days' rest, both actors were able to finish the picture.

"Just Tony" was a picture Tom Mix made as a tribute to his sorrel partner, and Tony was the real star in that. Unfortunately, many of Tom Mix's best films were lost in a studio fire, otherwise the cowboy star and his sorrel horse might still be riding the late-late TV range.

———

Picture after picture—all full of the excitement and adventure shared by Tom and Tony—flashed across the screens in theaters all over the United States. Tom Mix and Tony were the idols of thousands of young Americans who looked forward all week to Saturday afternoons at the movies. Tom Mix got hundreds of letters from his fans every week and Tony got almost as many. When they were not filming pictures, Tom and Tony traveled from coast to coast making personal appearances.

Tom liked fancy cowboy clothes. At first he wore bright colors, but later he specialized in white suits, wide-brimmed white hats, and shiny black high-heeled boots. He had a horsehair belt with a diamond-studded buckle, and he even had a pair of diamond-studded spurs. He built a mansion in Beverly Hills with the initials "TM" on the big wrought iron gates.

Tony, on his part, had silver-mounted saddles, fancy bridles, and bright plaid saddle blankets. His stable at Tom's Beverly Hills mansion was elaborate, too, but Tony really had simple tastes. He was satisfied with good hay and oats to eat, or for a special treat he liked an apple best, or perhaps a carrot or banana.

On one of their tours, Tom and Tony visited President Warren G. Harding in Washington. Another time, when they were to appear at the Paramount Theater in New York, the studio publicity man arranged for Tony to visit a beauty parlor to have his hoofs polished and a permanent wave put in his mane and tail.

Tom and Tony went abroad where great crowds cheered them, for their pictures were as popular in Europe as they were at home. In England, the Prince of Wales, who was an enthusiastic horseman, paid a visit to Tony in his stall.

When they returned to Hollywood after the European tour, both Tom and Tony were invited to make footprints in the cement sidewalk outside Grauman's Chinese Theater, along with the other great movie stars.

Besides being in the movies, Tom Mix and Tony were also stars for three summers with the Sells-Floto Circus. When the circus moved from city to city Tom and Tony each had his own private railroad car to travel in. They both enjoyed performing for live audiences and hearing

the crowds applaud when they made their grand entry
and presented their stunts and tricks in the center ring.

It was a strenuous life. After twenty years with Tom,
Tony began to show signs of age. One of his forelegs
was not as strong as it should have been. Tom used Bus-
ter, a horse made up to look much like Tony, in some of
the most dangerous scenes just to spare his long-time
partner. Tony was jealous; he would snort and stamp
his feet angrily when he saw Tom riding his substitute.

In their last picture together, Tony stumbled and fell
when he was to leap across a stream. Neither Tom nor
Tony was hurt, but when the veterinarian examined
Tony's leg, he said that the horse's jumping days were
over. Tom explained the situation, man-to-man, to his
four-legged pal. He told Tony that he was to be retired to pasture for the rest of his life and that no one
would ever ride him again. Tony seemed to understand.

For the next six years Tom rode a horse called Tony,
Jr., that looked much like his old friend. Tom and Tony,
Jr., made a few pictures and they also traveled for two
summers with the Tom Mix Wild Animal Circus, but
things were not the same. Tom Mix was killed in an
automobile roll-over near Florence, Arizona, in 1940.
Tony lived four years longer and was 34 years old when
he died in 1944.

Today, on the 20th Century Fox lot in Hollywood, a
big sound stage bears a bronze plaque, dedicating it to
the memory of Tom Mix and Tony.

Gato and Mancha { THE SCHOOL TEACHER'S HORSES

HORSES HAVE TRAVELED thousands of miles for their owners and riders, but perhaps the record for the longest single trip is held by two horses from Argentina named Gato and Mancha. They traveled nearly ten thousand miles, from Buenos Aires to Washington, D.C., taking two and a half years to make the journey.

Argentina is a country famous for its horses. Its great stretches of pampas are like the wide prairies of the western United States. Its gauchos are magnificent riders, much like the cowboys of the American West. Their native horses, called Criollos or Crillos (creoles) are similar to the North American mustangs. Gato and Mancha were Criollos.

Criollos and mustangs are "native" in the sense that they are wild horses, escapees from horse herds and ranches established by the Spaniards who settled in North, Central, and South America. The horses that escaped, or were turned loose from time to time, found

the great plains of the North American West and the
wide pampas of Argentina fine places to live, to breed,
and to establish themselves as wild, free creatures of
the open country.

As generations passed, the mustangs and the criollos
developed definite and distinct characteristics. They
were hardy, sturdy animals, able to take care of themselves in the wild. They learned to live off the land, to
endure long, cold winters, hot dry summers, and to protect themselves against enemies. They could run long
and hard when they had to, or they could stand their
ground and fight. Because their diets were often scanty,
they were small horses, seldom more than 14½ hands
high. But they were tough, strong, and independent.

In Argentina, as in the American West, it was customary for the gauchos to capture wild horses, break
and train them for the saddle. During the long years
over which the South American countries were gaining
their freedom from Spain and Portugal, the revolutionary leaders and their armies rode criollos. Amazing and
hard-to-believe tales were told of the little horses'
courage and endurance.

As peace and independence came to the various
countries, horsemen wanted to improve their stock—
they wanted size and beauty as well as strength and
endurance. Horses were imported from Europe—
Arabians, Barbs, Thoroughbreds—and the criollo, like
the mustang, became scarce and wary.

———

Gato and Mancha belonged to a wild herd that ranged
over land claimed by an Indian chief in Patagonia.
Thirty members of the herd were rounded up and sold

by the chief to a horse dealer from Buenos Aires. That horse dealer happened to be the friend of a school teacher named A. F. Tschiffely.

School teaching was all right—Tschiffely had taught in England before moving to Argentina where he continued to teach for nine more years—but it was rather dull. The school teacher wanted variety; he was young and fit, and he wanted to do something different. He had heard many stories about the great feats of endurance of criollo horses but he did not quite believe them. Horsemen's tales around the campfire are one thing, real riding is something different.

The more he thought, the more he wondered, and an idea began to grow in Tschiffely's mind. Could a criollo horse carry him the length of two great continents, over mountains, through jungles, swamps, and deserts? He decided to find out.

From his horse-dealer friend he bought two of the Patagonian criollos. One of them was a pinto, reddish with large white splotches, a white face and white stockings. The pinto was named Manchado (meaning stained) but the name was soon shortened to Mancha. The other criollo was coffee-colored, a dark buckskin, and his name Gatadeo (meaning cat-colored) was soon shortened to Gato, or Cat.

Both horses were wild so Tschiffely had the task of breaking and training them to the saddle. It was no simple job, and he was tossed clear over a fence by one of them before he finally taught them to accept first a saddle, then a bridle, and finally a rider. The watching gauchos laughed and enjoyed the show. "He has bought his league of land" they shouted when the school teacher was bucked off and sent sprawling.

There were other problems to be solved and questions that could be answered only by experience. In planning his trip, Tschiffely soon discovered that there was no road leading north through South America. Some countries had a few good roads but mainly there were only trails and in some places there were no roads at all. How could he be sure of finding food and water for his horses and himself? To what mountain altitudes could horses from the plains of Argentina climb safely? Could they endure the cold of the mountains and the heat of the tropics? Could they swim the rivers when there were no bridges to take them across?

Tschiffely decided to make the trip alone. He rode one horse and used the other to carry his pack, and he traveled light. He took along only a few clothes and planned to buy others as he needed them. He had his camera and supplies, some medicine, one pot for coffee and another for meat and beans, a couple of books, and a .45 pistol. On April 23, 1925, he climbed into the saddle and the two-continent journey began.

One man and two horses become very well acquainted when they travel hundreds of miles and spend many months together. At first Tschiffely had to lead the pack horse. "But later," he said, "when we became friends, halter and ropes were discarded and we all stuck together." The school teacher always spoke of himself and his horses as "we"—this was Argentine custom. One man riding a horse is "I," but when a man is accompanied by two or more horses, the group becomes "we."

Early in their journey the mountains of Northern Argentina and Bolivia towered above them. Up and up they climbed, into altitudes where mountain sickness can be dangerous to both men and horses. Tschiffely dismounted and went up any steep slope on foot. In this way he knew when breathing became difficult and when he had to stop and rest. On horseback, he might not have realized how hard it was for Gato and Mancha to breathe in that thin mountain air.

Finding food for his horses was a real problem in the back country of Boliva and Peru. Horse feed was scarce, expensive, and a great temptation to thieves who would steal hay and grain right out from under a horse's nose. To prevent theft, Tschiffely never gave Gato or Mancha a full share of food at night; instead, he would get up and go out to the corral every two hours to feed them, taking care to scatter the fodder well over the ground so that it would be harder for thieves to pick up.

After crossing the high mountains, Tschiffely gave his horses three weeks of rest in Lima, the capital of Peru. This also gave them time to become accustomed to the hot lowland climate near the equator after the thin cold air of the mountains. Gato and Mancha were stabled in horse comfort at the Lima race track while schoolmaster Tschiffely enjoyed the luxury of a hotel.

From Lima on the seacoast, Gato, Mancha and their master turned northward across the hot Peruvian desert. It was a choice between inland desert or swampy seacoast, and Tschiffely thought the desert would be less hazardous than the swamps. Because of the intense heat, they traveled at night, plodding through heavy sand between water holes. Water would only be added weight to carry so they traveled without it.

"I crossed the desert safely with my horses," Tschiffely wrote later, "but I would not try it again for all the money in the world." The man seemed to feel the heat and dryness more than the horses; only rarely did Gato and Mancha seem to be suffering from thirst.

———

In Ecuador a 16-year-old Indian boy named Victor joined the party. He was an uninvited guest, a ragged orphan who tagged along because he liked the horses. Tschiffely watched Victor walk barefoot for several days over rough, stony trails. He then bought a little black Indian pony named Chico for him and Victor became an official member of the party. Mancha was Victor's favorite, but he loved all three of the horses. He helped care for them and acted as watchdog to see that no one stole their food or made off with the expedition's scanty equipment.

There were more mountains to be crossed in Ecuador, up steep trails worn by the hoofs of pack mules. After that, there were swamps where Gato, Mancha, and Chico sank to their bellies in mud. Because there were no trails in this area, Tschiffely led his party down the Guayaquil-to-Quito railroad track, and once, when a locomotive appeared from around a bend, the whole party had to squeeze into a narrow open space beside the track. It was a tight squeeze but the locomotive roared past them leaving them safe in a cloud of smoke and cinders.

In Quito, the capital of Ecuador, Gato, Mancha, and Chico enjoyed another three weeks of rest, munching alfalfa in the green fields on the edge of the city. Then the expedition was off again, traveling steadily north-ward.

When they reached the Magdalena River in Colombia they were in a hot country of trackless jungle and hostile Indians. The Magdalena is like the Mississippi—a great river with stern-wheel steamboats carrying cargoes up and down it. Gato, Mancha, and Chico were loaded into a barge pushed ahead of the steamboat, and for three days and nights they rode in cramped, stuffy quarters, surrounded by bags of coffee and other cargo. Tschiffely threw buckets of water over them to cool them and covered the barge roof with thick grass to soften the sun's heat. He thought the horses probably suffered more during that barge ride than at any other time on the trip. Although they didn't like them, as the trip progressed they had to take another boat ride from Colombia to Panama, and a third later to avoid a revolution taking place in Nicaragua.

Panama, it seemed, was unlucky. Victor contracted typhoid fever and had to be left in a hospital. Mancha cut his hind leg on a wire and was lame for a time. Chico, the Indian pony, remained in Panama, too.

From Salvador, Gato, Mancha, and Tschiffely crossed into Mexico and again bad luck found them. This time Gato went lame when a nail in his shoe caused an abscess. No sooner had this healed than he was kicked by a mule and cut badly on the knee. Another abscess formed, and after a month of doctoring, Tschiffely decided the only way to save Gato's life was to ship him by train to Mexico City in the hope that veterinarians there could cure him.

———

Mancha and his master plodded on alone, through swamps and across rivers that had no bridges. It was wild country and the Mexican government gave Tschiffely an escort of soldiers. Fortunately, Mancha was a good swimmer and he swam the bridgeless rivers with soldiers who could not swim hanging onto his tail.

When they approached Mexico City, a party of horsemen rode out to greet them; one of the men was riding Gato, now healed and healthy again. It was a happy reunion; Gato and Mancha greeted each other with friendly nickers and nuzzlings, and Tschiffely tickled the brown horse's nose and rubbed his forehead joyfully. And later, invited to appear in the bull ring there, they received great applause.

The three travellers then went on, crossing the border between Mexico and the United States at Laredo. The Texans welcomed them, as did the Oklahomans. But Tschiffely soon decided the United States had too many paved roads and too many automobiles—even in 1927—to make travel by horseback safe or comfortable. He said automobile drivers seemed to take delight in honking their horns, driving too close to the horses, shouting, and even throwing things at them.

Paved roads were much harder for the horses to travel on than mountain paths or jungle trails. Mancha, especially, often slipped on the pavement. To prevent this, when he was on the downgrade over the Blue Ridge Mountains, the spotted horse was shod with rubber padding. But Mancha had other troubles; once he was struck from behind and knocked down by an automobile. Tschiffely decided the driver's action was deliberate because the man honked, waved, and drove on without stopping.

With such difficulties to contend with, two horses were more than one Argentine school teacher could manage. As a result, Gato was left on a farm outside St. Louis, and Mancha and Tschiffely went on alone to Washington. Even there, their troubles continued. They got lost and Mancha was tied to a lamp post while his master went into a drug store to telephone for help. When the school teacher returned, a Washington policeman was waiting to give him a parking ticket, but when Tschiffely explained their difficulties, the policeman patted Mancha and sent them on their way.

Washington was the end of Mancha's long journey. Tschiffely had originally intended to ride on to New York, but he decided there were just too many automobiles to compete with. Gato and Mancha were shipped by train to New York where in October, 1927— two years, seven months and twenty days after their incredible journey began—they were the center of attraction for ten days at the International Horse Show in Madison Square Garden.

———

Gato and Mancha returned to their native Argentina by boat, a trip that was much faster and more comfortable than the long journey they had made north on foot. It was nearly three years from the time they left Buenos Aires until they returned. Both horses by then were judged to be about eighteen or nineteen years old, so they still had some years of rest and honor ahead of them.

At first Tschiffely thought Gato and Mancha should be placed on display in a public park in Buenos Aires, but later he changed his mind. They deserved a greater reward than becoming spectacles for people to stare at. So Gato and Mancha were taken to a great estancia, or ranch, and given their freedom to roam the pampas as their ancestors had, and to live the wild, free life they had known before being rounded up and tamed.

As for the man who rode them so far, he settled down and wrote a book about his experiences. It was called *Tschiffely's Ride*. He also wrote a long article for the *National Geographic Magazine*. In them both, he praised the horses extravagantly and readily admitted what he had once doubted years before in Argentina—that criollos could do everything the legends said they could.

As Tschiffely wrote his book he could see, in his mind's eye, the two criollos galloping across the vast rolling Argentine pampas.

He ended his book with the words:

"Good luck to you, old pals, Gato and Mancha!"

His wish came true and the two criollos enjoyed a long life and peaceful retirement. Gato lived until 1944 and Mancha survived until 1947. A taxidermist mounted them in lifelike poses and they are still on exhibit at the Colonial Museum at Lujan, near Buenos Aires.

Sources

The stories of these famous horses and their people have been gathered from many different places. For readers who might wonder where the stories came from, the following sources are listed.

Homer, the great Greek poet who wrote the *Iliad,* was the first to tell the story of Bellerophon and his winged horse Pegasus. According to Homer, one of the warriors who fought at Troy claimed to be Bellerophon's grandson. To this first account many other storytellers added details and today the tale, in a number of versions, can be found in most books of Greek mythology.

Another Greek writer named Plutarch in a book called *Lives of the Noble Grecians and Romans* told the story of Alexander the Great and his black horse Bucephalus. Alexander loved horses and no doubt he studied the books *On Horsemanship* and *The Cavalry Commander* by the Greek writer Xenophon.

Suetonius, a Roman writer, told about Emperor Caligula and his horse Incitatus in a book called *The Lives of the Twelve Caesars.*

The story of Sharatz and Prince Marko comes from *Hero Tales and Legends of the Serbians,* collected and retold in English by V. M. Petrovic.

The Persian poet Firdousī described the adventures

of the hero Rustum and his rose-colored horse Raksh in the epic *Shah-Nama,* or *The Book of Kings.*

Another long poem, this one from Spain, tells of the deeds of El Cid Campeador and his horse Babieca. It is not known exactly who wrote the *Poema del Cid*— only a part of the rich literature telling of the Spanish warrior's adventures.

Spanish writers whose names are well known have given us the story of Cortés and Morzillo. Captain Cortés, himself, told about his black horse in letters written from Mexico to King Charles I of Spain. Years later, one of Cortés' soldiers named Bernal Diaz told a great deal about all the conquistadors' horses in his book *The True History of the Conquest of New Spain.* The later story of Morzillo as Tziminchac, the Mayan god of thunder and lightning, is described by the American historian William H. Prescott in *The Conquest of Mexico,* and by R. B. Cunninghame Graham, a South American writer, in a book *Horses of the Conquest.*

There are many accounts of Justin Morgan the man and Justin Morgan the horse. Among these are *Cavalcade of American Horses* by Pers Crowell, *The Horse in America* by Robert West Howard, *Morgan Horses* by Peggy Jett Pittenger, and *The Morgan Horse* by Jeanne Mellin.

Biographies of Napoleon, the Duke of Wellington, General Lee and General Sheridan give some information about their famous horses, but the best account this author found was an article "War-horses of Famous Generals," by James Grant Wilson, published in the *Century Magazine* in 1913. There is a great deal about General Lee and Traveller in the four-volume work

Robert E. Lee by Douglas Southall Freeman and in Lee's own writings *Recollections and Letters of Robert E. Lee.* General Sheridan also wrote about his horse Rienzi in his *Personal Memoirs.*

The story of Old Whitey, President Zachary Taylor's horse, comes from several places. Among them are: *Zachary Taylor, Soldier in the White House* by Holman Hamilton, *Zach Taylor's Little Army* by Edward J. Nichols, and *The War With Mexico* by Donald B. Chidsey.

The best accounts of Comanche can be read in a book by Anthony A. Amaral called *Comanche, the Horse that Survived the Custer Massacre,* and a harder-to-find book by Edward S. Luce called *Keogh, Comanche and Custer.*

There are many accounts of Buffalo Bill, but among the ones that tell the most about his horses are *Buffalo Bill and the Wild West* by Harry Blackwell Sell and Victor Weybright, his life story as *Last of the Great Scouts* written by his sister Helen Cody Wetmore, and a pamphlet, *Buffalo Bill and His Horses,* by Agnes Wright Spring.

Mrs. Loula Long Combs told about her favorite show horse in her autobiography, *My Revelation,* in which she included quotations from many newspapers. The judge's speech when Revelation retired was first published in the *Breeder's Gazette,* April 23, 1925.

The story of Exterminator comes from many accounts of Kentucky Derby winners. One of the best of these is *Twenty Gallant Horses* by C. W. Anderson.

Man o' War's great exploits are told in many publications that deal with horse racing. They are summarized in the *New York Times,* November 5, 1947, *Time Maga-*

zine, November 10, 1947, and the *Reader's Digest,* February, 1948. His full biography is *Man o' War* by Page Cooper and Roger L. Treat.

William S. Hart told a great deal about the pinto pony Fritz in his autobiography *My Life East and West,* and a book about the movies called *The Western* by George N. Fenin and William K. Everson fills in some later details. *The Western* also tells about Tom Mix and Tony. The movie star's wife Olive Stokes Mix added more details in her biography of him called *The Fabulous Tom Mix,* as did another relative, Paul E. Mix, in *The Life and Legend of Tom Mix.*

A. F. Tschiffely told about the long journey he made with Gato and Mancha, first in an article "Buenos Aires to Washington by Horse" published in the *National Geographic Magazine* in February, 1929, and later in his book *Tschiffely's Ride.*